THE LAST EMPRESS

THE LAST EMPRESS

Anchee Min

BLOOMSBURY

AUTHOR'S NOTE

All of the characters in this book are based on real people.
I tried my best to keep the events the way they were in history.
I translated or transcribed the decrees, edicts and newspaper
articles from the original documents. Whenever there were
differences in interpretation, I based my judgment on my
research and overall perspective.

First published in Great Britain 2007
This paperback edition published 2008

Bloomsbury Publishing Plc,
36 Soho Square,
London W1D 3QY

www.bloomsbury.com

A CIP catalogue record for this book
is available from the British Library

Paperback ISBN 978 0 7475 9316 4
10 9 8 7 6 5 4 3 2

Export paperback ISBN 978 0 7475 9385 0
10 9 8 7 6 5 4 3 2

Typeset by Hewer Text UK Ltd, Edinburgh
Printed in Great Britain by Clays Ltd, St Ives plc

Bloomsbury Publishing, London, New York and Berlin

All papers used by Bloomsbury Publishing are natural,
recyclable products made from wood grown in well-managed
forests. The manufacturing processes conform to the
environmental regulations of the country of origin.

Thank you

Anton Mueller
for a masterly job of editing

Sandra Dijkstra
for always being there for me

My intercourse with Tzu Hsi started in 1902 and continued until her death. I had kept an unusually close record of my secret association with the Empress and others possessing notes and messages written to me by Her Majesty, but had the misfortune to lose all these manuscripts and papers.

— Sir Edmund Backhouse, coauthor of
China Under the Empress Dowager (1910) and
Annals and Memoirs of the Court of Peking (1914)

In 1974, somewhat to Oxford's embarrassment and to the private dismay of China scholars everywhere, Backhouse was revealed to be a counterfeiter . . . The con man had been exposed, but his counterfeit material was still bedrock scholarship.

— Sterling Seagrave, *Dragon Lady: The Life
and Legend of the Last Empress of China* (1992)

One of the ancient sages of China foretold that 'China will be destroyed by a woman.' The prophecy is approaching fulfillment.

— Dr. George Ernest Morrison,
London *Times* China correspondent, 1892–1912

[Tzu Hsi] has shown herself to be benevolent and economical. Her private character has been spotless.

— Charles Denby,
American envoy to China, 1898

She was a mastermind of pure evil and intrigue.

— Chinese textbook (in print 1949–1991)

THE BEGINNING

I N 1852, a beautiful seventeen-year-old girl from an important but impoverished family of the Yehonala clan arrived in Peking as a minor concubine to the young Emperor, Hsien Feng. Tzu Hsi, known as Orchid as a girl, was one among hundreds of concubines whose sole purpose was to bear the Emperor a son.

It was not a good time to enter the Forbidden City, a vast complex of palaces and gardens run by thousands of eunuchs and encircled by a wall in the center of Peking. The Ch'ing Dynasty was losing its vitality and the court had become an insular, xenophobic place. A few decades earlier, China had lost the first Opium War, and it had done little since to strengthen its defenses or improve its diplomatic ties to other nations.

Within the walls of the Forbidden City the consequences of a misstep were often deadly. As one of hundreds of women vying for the attention of the Emperor, Orchid discovered that she must take matters into her own hands. After training herself in the art of pleasing a man, she risked everything by bribing her way into the royal bedchamber and seducing the monarch. Hsien Feng was a troubled man, but for a time their love was passionate and genuine, and soon she had the great fortune to bear him his only son and heir. Elevated to the rank of Empress, Orchid still had to struggle to maintain her position as the Emperor took new lovers. The right to raise her own child, who was under the control of Empress Nuharoo, the Emperor's senior wife, was constantly at issue.

The invasion by Britain, France, and Russia in 1860, and the subsequent occupation of Peking, forced the Chinese court into exile in the distant hunting reserve of Jehol, beyond the Great Wall. There the humiliating news of the harsh terms for peace contributed to the decline of the Emperor's health. With the death of Hsien Feng came a palace coup, which Orchid helped to foil with the help of her brother-in-law Prince Kung and General Yung Lu. The handsome Yung Lu reignited romantic feelings in the still young Orchid, but in her new position of power there was little opportunity for a personal life. As coregent with Empress Nuharoo until her son's maturity, Empress Orchid was at the beginning of a long and tumultuous reign that would last into the next century.

THE
LAST
EMPRESS

1

MOTHER'S EYES WERE closed when she died. But a moment later they cracked open and remained open.

'Your Majesty, please hold the eyelids and try your best to close them,' Doctor Sun Pao-tien instructed.

My hands trembled as I tried.

Rong, my sister, said that Mother meant to close her eyes. She had waited for me for too long. Mother did not want to interrupt my audience.

'Try not to trouble people' was Mother's philosophy. She would have been disappointed to know that she needed help to close her eyes. I wished that I could disregard Nuharoo's order and bring my son to bid a final goodbye. 'It shouldn't matter that Tung Chih is the Emperor of China,' I would have argued. 'He is my mother's grandson first.'

I turned to my brother, Kuei Hsiang, and asked if Mother had left any words for me.

'Yes.' Kuei Hsiang nodded, stepping back to stand on the other side of Mother's bed. ' "All is well." '

My tears came.

'What kind of burial ceremony do you have in mind for Mother?' Rong asked.

'I can't think right now,' I replied. 'We will discuss it later.'

'No, Orchid,' Rong protested. 'It will be impossible to reach you once you leave here. I would like to know your intentions. Mother deserves the same honor as Grand Empress Lady Jin.'

'I wish that I could simply say yes, but I can't. Rong, we are watched by millions. We must set an example.'

'Orchid,' Rong burst out, 'you are the ruler of China!'

'Rong, please. I believe Mother would understand.'

'No, she wouldn't, because I can't. You are a terrible daughter, selfish and heartless!'

'Excuse me,' Doctor Sun Pao-tien interrupted. 'Your Majesty, may I have you concentrate on your fingers? Your mother's eyes will remain forever open if you stop pressing.'

'Yes, Doctor.'

'Harder, and steady,' the doctor instructed. 'Now hold it. You are almost there. Don't move.'

My sister helped to hold my arms.

Mother's face in repose was deep and distant.

'It's Orchid, Mother,' I whispered, weeping.

I couldn't believe she was dead. My fingers caressed her smooth and still-warm skin. I had missed touching her. Ever since I had entered the Forbidden City, Mother was forced to get down on her knees to greet me when she visited. She insisted on following the etiquette. 'It is the respect you deserve as the Empress of China,' she said.

We rarely had privacy. Eunuchs and ladies in waiting surrounded me constantly. I doubted Mother could hear me from where she had to sit, ten feet away from me. It didn't seem to bother her, though. She pretended that she could hear. She would answer questions I hadn't asked.

'Gently, release the eyelids,' Doctor Sun Pao-tien said.

Mother's eyes remained closed. Her wrinkles seemed to have disappeared, and her expression was restful.

I am the mountain behind you. Mother's voice came to my mind:

> *Like a singing river*
> *You break out to flow freely.*
> *Happily I watch you,*
> *The memory of us*
> *Full and sweet.*

I had to be strong for my son. Although Tung Chih, who was seven, had been Emperor for two years, since ascending the throne in 1861, his regime had been chaotic. Foreign powers continued to gain leverage in China, especially in the coastal ports; at home, peasant rebels called Taipings had spread through the interior and overrun province after province. I had struggled to find a way to raise Tung Chih properly. Yet he seemed to be so terribly shattered by his father's early death. I could only wish to raise him the way my parents had raised me.

'I am a lucky woman,' Mother used to say. I believed her when she said that she had no regrets in life. She had achieved a dream: two daughters married into royal families and a son who was a high-ranking Imperial minister. 'We were practically beggars back in 1852,' Mother often reminded her children. 'I will never forget that afternoon at the Grand Canal when the footmen deserted your father's coffin.'

The heat of that day and the smell of rot that came from my father's corpse stayed with me as well. The expression on Mother's face when she was forced to sell her last

3

possession, a jade hairpin that was a wedding gift from our father, was the saddest I had ever seen.

As Emperor Hsien Feng's senior wife, Empress Nuharoo attended my mother's funeral. It was considered a great honor for my family. As a devout Buddhist, Nuharoo disregarded tradition in accepting my invitation.

Dressed in white silk like a tall ice-tree, Nuharoo was the picture of grace. I walked behind her, careful not to step on the long train of her robe. Chanting Tibetan lamas and Taoist and Buddhist priests followed us. Making our way through the Forbidden City, we stopped to perform one ritual after another, passing through gate after gate and hall after hall.

Standing next to Nuharoo, I marveled that we had finally found some measure of harmony. The differences between us had been clear from the moment we entered the Forbidden City as young girls. She – elegant, confident, of the royal bloodline – was chosen as the Emperor's senior wife, the Empress; I – from a good family and no more, from the country and unsure – was a concubine of the fourth rank. Our differences became conflicts as I found a way into Hsien Feng's heart and bore my son, his only male child and heir. My elevation in rank had only made matters worse. But in the chaos of the foreigners' invasion, our husband's death during our exile at the ancient hunting retreat of Jehol, and the crisis of the coup, we had been forced to find ways to work together.

All these years later, my relationship with Nuharoo was best expressed in the saying 'The water in the well does not disturb the water in the river.' To survive, it had been necessary for us to watch out for each other. At times this seemed impossible, especially regarding Tung Chih. Nu-

4

haroo's status as senior wife gave her authority over his upbringing and education, something that rankled me. Our fight over how to raise Tung Chih had stopped after he ascended the throne, but my bitterness over how ill prepared the boy had been continued to poison our relationship.

Nuharoo pursued contentment in Buddhism while my own discontentment followed me like a shadow. My spirit kept escaping my will. I read the book Nuharoo had sent me, *The Proper Conduct of an Imperial Widow*, but it did little to bring me peace. After all, I was from Wuhu, 'the lake of luxurious weeds.' I couldn't be who I was not, although I spent my life trying.

'Learn to be the soft kind of wood, Orchid,' Mother taught me when I was a young girl. 'The soft blocks are carved into statues of Buddha and goddesses. The hard ones are made into coffin boards.'

I had a drawing table in my room, with ink, freshly mixed paint, brushes and rice paper. After each day's audience I came here to work.

My paintings were for my son – they were given as gifts in his name. They served as his ambassadors and spoke for him whenever a situation became too humiliating. China was forced to beg for extensions on payments of so-called war compensation, imposed on us by foreign powers.

The paintings also helped to ease the resentment toward my son over land taxes. The governors of several states had been sending messages that their people were poor and couldn't afford to pay.

'The Imperial tael storehouse has long been empty,' I cried in decrees issued in my son's name. 'The taxes we have collected have gone to the foreign powers so that their fleets will not set anchor in our waters.'

My brother-in-law Prince Kung complained that his new Board of Foreign Affairs had run out of space in which to store the debt seekers' dunning letters. 'The foreign fleets have repeatedly threatened to re-enter our waters,' he warned.

It was my eunuch An-te-hai's idea to use my paintings as gifts, to buy time, money and understanding.

An-te-hai had served me since my first day in the Forbidden City, when, as a boy of just thirteen, he'd surreptitiously offered me a drink of water for my parched throat. It was a brave act, and he had my loyalty and trust ever since.

His idea for the paintings was brilliant, and I couldn't paint fast enough.

I sent one as a birthday gift to General Tseng Kuo-fan, the biggest warlord in China, who dominated the country's military. I wanted the general to know that I appreciated him, although I recently demoted him in my son's name, under pressure from the court's pro-Manchu conservatives, who called themselves Ironhats. The Ironhats could not stand the fact that the Han Chinese, through hard work, were gaining power. I wanted General Tseng to know that I meant him no harm and that I was aware that I had wronged him. 'My son Tung Chih could not rule without you' was the message my painting sent.

I often wondered what kept General Tseng Kuo-fan from rebelling. A coup wouldn't be hard – he had the money and the army. I used to think that it was just a matter of time. 'Enough is enough,' I could imagine Tseng saying one day, and my son would be out of luck.

I signed my name in fine calligraphy. Above it I put my signature stamp in red ink. I had stone stamps of different sizes and shapes. Besides the stamp, which was given to me by my husband, the rest described my titles: 'Empress of China,' 'Empress of Holy Kindness,' 'Empress of the Western Palace.' 'Empress Tzu Hsi' was the one I used most often. These stamps were important to collectors. To make the artwork easier to sell later, I would leave out the name in my dedication, unless otherwise requested.

Yesterday An-te-hai reported that my paintings had risen in value. The news brought me little joy. I would much rather spend time with Tung Chih than feel forced to paint.

Anyone who examined my paintings could see their flaws. My brushstrokes showed that I lacked practice, if not talent. My handling of ink revealed that I was merely a beginner. The nature of rice-paper painting allowed no mistakes, which meant that I could be spending hours on a piece, work late into the night, and one lousy stroke would ruin the entire thing. After months of working on my own, I hired an artist-tutor whose job was to cover my flaws.

Landscapes and flowers were my subjects. I also painted birds, usually in pairs. I would place them in the center of the frame. They would perch on the same or separate branches, as if having a chat. In vertical compositions, one bird would sit on the top branch and look down, and the other would be on the bottom branch looking up.

I spent the most time on feathers. Pink, orange and lime green were my favorite feather colors. The tone was always warm and cheerful. An-te-hai suggested that I paint peonies, lotus blossoms and chrysanthemums. He said that I was good at painting these, but I knew he meant they were easier to sell.

A tip I learned from my artist-tutor was that the stamps could be used to cover flaws. Since I had flaws everywhere, I applied a number of stamps to each painting. When I was dissatisfied and wanted to start over again An-te-hai reminded me that quantity should be my objective. He helped to make the stampings look interesting. When I felt there was nothing I could do to save a work, my tutor would take over.

My tutor worked mostly on backgrounds. She would add leaves and branches to cover my bad parts and would add accents to my birds and flowers. One would think that her fine strokes would make mine an embarrassment, but she applied her skill only to 'harmonize the music.' Her artistry saved my worst paintings. It was amusing to watch her painstakingly try to match my amateur strokes.

My mind often wandered to my son while I was painting. At night it became difficult to concentrate. I would imagine Tung Chih's face as he lay in bed and wonder what he was dreaming. When my desire to be with him became desperate, I would put down my brush and run to Tung Chih's palace, four courtyards from my own. Too impatient to wait for An-te-hai to light the lanterns, I would rush through the darkness, bumping and bruising myself on walls and arches until I arrived at my child's bedside. There beside my sleeping son, I would check his breathing and stroke his head with my ink-stained hand. When the servant lit the candles I would take one and hold it close to my son's face. My eyes would trace his lovely forehead, eyelids, nose and lips. I would bend over and kiss him. My eyes would grow moist as I saw his father's likeness. I would remember when Emperor Hsien Feng and I were in love. My favorite moment was still the time when I sweetly tortured him by demanding that he memorize my name. I wouldn't leave Tung Chih until An-te-hai found me, his long procession of eunuchs trailing behind him, each carrying a giant red lantern.

'My tutor can paint for me,' I would say to An-te-hai. 'Nobody will know that I didn't apply the stamps myself.'

'But *you* would know, my lady,' the eunuch would reply quietly, and he would escort me back to my palace.

2

INSTEAD OF READING a book to Tung Chih in the cool shade of my courtyard, I signed an edict issuing death sentences to two important men. It was August 31, 1863. I dreaded the moment because I couldn't escape the thought of what my signature would bring to their families.

The first person was Ho Kui-ching, the governor of Chekiang province. Ho had been a longtime friend of my husband's. I first met him as a young man when he won the top rank at the national civil service examination. I attended the ceremony with my husband, who honored him with the title of *Jin-shih*, Man of Supreme Achievement.

In my memory, Ho was a humble man. He had deep-set eyes and protruding teeth. My husband was impressed with his broad knowledge of philosophy and history, and he appointed Ho first as mayor of the important southern city of Hangchow, and a few years later as governor of Chekiang. By the time he was fifty, he was the senior governor in charge of all the provinces of central China. Ho was granted military powers as well. He was the commander in chief of the Imperial forces in southern China.

Ho's file showed that he had been charged with neglecting his duties, resulting in the loss of several provinces

10

during the ongoing Taiping uprisings. He had ordered his men to open fire on locals while making his own escape. I resisted his request to reconsider his case. He seemed to feel neither remorse nor guilt over the death and suffering of the thousands of families he had abandoned.

Ho and his friends in the court denied the fact that my husband had personally ordered Ho's beheading before his death. The strong opposition I later encountered made me realize my vulnerability. I took Ho's request as a direct challenge to my son as ruler of China. Prince Kung was one of the few who stood by me, although he kept reminding me that I didn't have the support of the court's majority.

I did not expect that my disagreement with the court would turn into a crisis for the survival of my son and myself. I was aware that Ho's behavior mirrored that of the governors of many other provinces. I would be inviting endless trouble if I failed to proceed with the prosecution.

Within weeks, I received a petition requesting that I reconsider the case. Signed by seventeen high-ranking ministers, governors and generals, the petition claimed Ho's innocence and asked His Young Majesty Tung Chih to dismiss the charges.

I asked Prince Kung to help me investigate each petitioner's background. The information Kung soon brought me showed that without exception the petitioners had been either personally promoted or recommended to their posts by Governor Ho.

The argument ran back and forth as Tung Chih and I sat through the audiences. My son was tired, and he squirmed and fidgeted on his large throne. I sat behind him, slightly to the left, and had to keep reminding him to sit up straight. In order for Tung Chih to make eye contact with the more than one hundred ministers on the floor before him, his throne had been placed on a platform. He could see everyone, and he, in turn, could be seen by all. The Son of Heaven was not an easy image for his subjects to look upon. I tried to rush the audiences so my son would be able to go out and play. They were torture for a seven-year-old child, even if he was the Son of Heaven.

The collective voice asserted that Ho's dereliction was not what it seemed – the governor was not responsible. The minister of revenue in Jiangsu province spoke as a witness: 'I asked Governor Ho to come to help guard my state. Instead of being called a deserter, he should be regarded as a hero.'

Tung Chih looked confused and pleaded to leave.

I excused my son and carried on myself. I remained firm, especially after learning that Ho had attempted to destroy evidence and harass witnesses.

Prince Kung quit the proceedings after days of dreadful argument, excusing himself by saying that he preferred to leave the matter in my hands. I continued to fight the court, who now demanded 'a more credible investigator.'

I felt as if I were playing a game whose rules I failed to understand. And there was no time to learn them. In my son's name I summoned General Tseng Kuo-fan, who had been Governor Ho's temporary replacement. I let him know that I was desperately looking for people who would tell nothing but the truth. I asked him to be in charge of the new investigation.

I explained to Tung Chih that his father and I had always had great faith in General Tseng's integrity. In an effort to keep my son interested, I told him the story of Tseng's first meeting with Emperor Hsien Feng and how the hero-warlord was terrified when the Emperor asked him to explain why he was nicknamed 'Head-Chopper Tseng.'

Tung Chih was entertained by tales of Tseng's exploits and asked whether the general was a Manchu. 'No, he is Han Chinese.' I took the opportunity to drive my point home. 'You will see how the court discriminates against the Han.'

'As long as he can fight and win for me,' my son responded, 'I don't care what race he is.'

I was proud of him and said, 'That is why you are the Emperor.'

The court accepted my appointment of Tseng Kuo-fan, which made me think that someone must believe that Tseng was corrupt. I made it a condition that Tseng's findings would be part of the public record.

Within a month, Tseng delivered his findings before the assembled court, which pleased me greatly:

Although there were no paper documents left for my investigators to obtain, since the governor's mansion was burned down by the Taipings, the fact remains that Governor Ho Kui-ching failed in his duty to guard his provinces. Beheading would not be an inappropriate treatment, as it is the law of the Imperial government. Whether it was true or not that he was persuaded by his subordinates to desert is, in my opinion, rather irrelevant.

The hall was silent after Tseng Kuo-fan's statement was announced. And I knew I had won.

I resented the fact that it was I who had to give the final word for the execution. I may not have been as devout a Buddhist as Nuharoo, but I believed in the Buddha's teaching that 'to kill is to decrease one's virtue.' Such an awesome act would throw off one's inner balance and diminish one's longevity. Unfortunately, I was unable to avoid carrying out the sentence.

The second man to be prosecuted was General Sheng Pao, who was not only my friend but had also made significant contributions to the dynasty. I lost sleep over his case, although I never doubted my actions.

The trees outside my windows tossed violently in a sudden storm, like bare arms crying for help. Rain-soaked and wind-battered branches broke and fell on the yellow roof tiles of my palace. The large magnolia tree in the yard had started budding early this year, and the storm would surely ruin its blooming.

It was midnight and Sheng Pao was on my mind as I stared at the raindrops streaming down the windowpanes. There was no way to prepare myself. My thoughts couldn't silence an inner voice: *Orchid, without Sheng Pao you would not have lived.*

Sheng Pao was a fearless Manchu Bannerman, a fearless soldier, who grew up in poverty and was a self-made man. He had been the commander in chief of the northern Imperial forces for many years and had great influence in the court. He was feared by his enemies, so much so that his name alone could make any Taiping rebel shudder. The general loved his soldiers and hated war, for he knew the cost. Choosing to negotiate with rebel leaders, he had been able to take back many provinces without the use of force.

Sheng Pao had sided with me in my action against the former grand councilor Su Shun back in 1861. The coup that had occurred after my husband's death was a defining moment for me, and Sheng Pao had been the only military man to come to my aid.

The problems with Sheng Pao began after our return from Jehol, the Imperial hunting ground, to Peking with the body of my husband, Emperor Hsien Feng. As a reward for his service, I had promoted the general, securing for him unrivaled power and wealth. Before long, however, complaints of Sheng Pao's abuses were sent from all parts of the country. The letters were first delivered to the Board of War. No one dared to challenge Sheng Pao himself.

Prince Kung ignored the complaints and hoped that Sheng Pao would control himself. It was wishful thinking. It was even suggested that I turn a blind eye as well because Sheng Pao was too important.

I tried my best to be patient, but it reached a point where my son's authority as ruler was being questioned. I went to Prince Kung and asked him to sue Sheng Pao for justice.

Prince Kung's investigators discovered that the general had inflated casualty figures in order to receive additional compensation. He also claimed false victories to secure promotions for his officers. Sheng Pao demanded that the court grant all his requests. Raising local taxes for his personal use had become common practice for him. It was known that he indulged in excessive drinking and prostitution.

Other governors had started to follow Sheng Pao's example. Some of them stopped paying Imperial taxes. The soldiers were drilled to be loyal to the governors instead of to Emperor Tung Chih. A mocking slogan was becoming popular on the streets of Peking: 'It is not Tung Chih but Sheng Pao who is the Emperor of China.'

The extravagance of Sheng Pao's wedding became the latest news. And the fact that his bride was the former wife of a known Taiping rebel leader.

*   *   *

15

Shortly after sunrise, the sun broke through the clouds, but the rain hadn't stopped. A mist rose in the yard, climbing the trees like white smoke.

I was sitting in my chair, already dressed, when my eunuch An-te-hai entered, and with excitement in his voice he announced, 'My lady, Yung Lu is here.'

My breath halted at the sight of him.

Looking tall and strong in his Bannerman's uniform, Yung Lu entered the chamber.

I tried to get up to greet him but my legs felt weak, so I remained seated.

An-te-hai came between us with a yellow velvet mat. Taking his time, he put the mat down a few feet away from my chair. This was part of the ritual required for anyone meeting the Imperial widow in the second year after her mourning period. The etiquette felt ridiculous, because Yung Lu and I had seen each other many times at audiences, although we were forced to act like strangers. The purpose of the ritual was to remind us of the distance between Imperial men and women.

By now my eunuchs, servants and ladies in waiting stood against the walls with their hands folded. They stared at An-te-hai as he put on his show. Over the years, he had become a master of illusion. With Yung Lu and me as his actors, he staged a clever drama of distraction.

Yung Lu threw himself on the mat and knocked his forehead lightly on the ground and wished me good health.

I uttered, 'Rise.'

As Yung Lu stood, An-te-hai slowly pulled away the mat, attracting all the attention to himself while Yung Lu and I exchanged glances.

Tea was served while we sat like two vases. We began to talk about the aftermath of the prosecution of Governor Ho and exchanged opinions on the pending Sheng Pao case. Yung Lu assured me that my decisions had been sound.

My mind leapt as I sat beside my love. I could not forget what had happened four years before, when the two of us shared our only private moment, inside the tomb of Hsien Feng. I longed to know if Yung Lu remembered the event as I did. I could find no evidence as I looked at him. A few days earlier, when he took a seat at an audience and looked straight in my direction, I questioned whether our shared passion had ever taken place. As Emperor Hsien Feng's widow, I would have no future with any man. Yet my heart refused to stay in its tomb.

Yung Lu's position as the commander of the Bannermen constantly took him away from the capital. With or without his troops he moved where he was needed, making sure China's armies were fulfilling their duty to the empire. As a man of action, it was a life that suited him; he was a soldier who preferred the company of other soldiers over the ministers at court.

Yung Lu's frequent absences made my longing easier to bear. Only with his return would I realize the depth of my feeling. Suddenly he would be in my presence, reporting on some urgent matter or offering counsel at a critical moment. He might stay in the capital for weeks or months, and during those times would dutifully attend court. Only during these periods could I say that I looked forward to the daily audience.

Outside the audiences, Yung Lu avoided me. It was his way of protecting me from rumor and gossip. Whenever I expressed a desire to see him privately, he would decline. I kept sending An-te-hai anyway. I wanted Yung Lu to know that the eunuch was available to lead him through the back door of the audience hall to my chamber.

Although Yung Lu had reassured me of the rightness of my decision regarding Sheng Pao, I still worried. True, the evidence against him was damning, but the general had many allies in court, among them Prince Kung, who I'd noticed was keeping his distance. When Sheng Pao was finally escorted to Peking, my brother-in-law suddenly reappeared in my presence, insisting that Sheng Pao be sent into exile instead of being executed. I reminded Kung again that the original order for Sheng Pao's execution had been issued by Emperor Hsien Feng. Prince Kung didn't budge. He saw my insistence as a kind of declaration of war.

I felt vulnerable and scared when petitions for Sheng Pao's release arrived from the far corners of China. Once again Yung Lu came to my defense and steadied my hand. He gave me courage and the composure to think. Very few knew that Yung Lu had his own reasons to see Sheng Pao to his end: Yung Lu took offense when Sheng Pao slaughtered wounded soldiers. To Yung Lu, it was a matter of principle.

My strategy was simple: I assured Sheng Pao's subordinates that I would not behead Sheng Pao if a majority of them believed that he deserved to live. I also changed the rules so that those in Sheng Pao's clan would not be punished along with their leader. Relieved, the people could now vote with their hearts, and they wished Sheng Pao dead.

Sheng Pao was sent to the Board of Punishment, where he was put to a quick end. A sense of sadness and failure washed over me. For days I had the same dream: My father was standing on a stool at the end of a dark hall surrounded by steep walls. In his gray cotton pajamas he tried to

18

hammer a nail into the wall. He was terribly thin, his skin clinging to his bones. The stool he stood on was shaky and one of its legs was missing. I called to him and he turned, stiff-necked. His left arm reached toward me and he opened his palm. In it was a fistful of rusty nails.

I dared not have the dream interpreted, because in Chinese mythology rusty nails represented remorse and regret.

I couldn't have done what I did without the support of Yung Lu. My feelings for him would deepen over time, but our physical love would remain a thing of dreams. Every day I felt the absence of a man in my life. I worried more, however, about my son. Almost ten years before, I had lost a husband, but my son had lost his father. It was doubly tragic to my mind. It meant that Tung Chih would have to assume the full responsibilities of his position and so miss out on childhood. The joys of carefree days were not to be. Already, young as he was, I could detect a restlessness about him that occasionally broke out in hot flashes of temper.

Tung Chih needed a male hand to guide him. That was the second part of the tragedy. He was not only being hurried to assume a difficult role before his time, he also had no one on whom to model his character and behavior. In a court riven by political tension there were few father figures who did not also bring with them some hidden agenda.

Yung Lu and Prince Kung were the two men I had hoped would fulfill the role. But the conflict over Sheng Pao had made that difficult. Yung Lu had enjoyed great popularity until he took my side. Now his influence was in question. And I would soon begin to sense how deeply resentful Prince Kung was at my outmaneuvering him to claim the life of his old ally.

3

IF I HAD EXPECTED to fight Governor Ho Kui-ching and General Sheng Pao, I never expected to have to fight my brother-in-law Prince Kung. Our histories had been so intertwined for so long that an unraveling of our relationship was not something I was prepared for. Since the crisis that followed my husband's death in Jehol, we had been important, even essential, allies. Kung had remained behind in Peking as the court fled the approaching foreign armies and had the humiliating task of negotiating with the occupying invaders. When Grand Councilor Su Shun attempted to seize power in the exiled court beyond the Great Wall, Kung was still in Peking and free to organize a countercoup. More than any other man, he had saved Nuharoo, myself, and young Tung Chih.

And we were friends – or at least I felt affection for him and believed I understood what motivated him. He had genuine talent and was, I'd always thought, more capable than his brother, who ended up on the throne. More reserved and more disciplined than Hsien Feng, Prince Kung could seem cold, but at least he didn't let bitterness infect him. For this he had my respect, and that of much of the court. I had always felt that he acted for the good of China and not for his own selfish purposes.

But these were difficult times. Conflict swirled around us, coming from within as well as without, and the tensions led to a poisonous atmosphere that pitted faction against faction in the court.

It started slowly, but it became clear that Kung was frequently going around us when conducting court business. This was just what had happened in Jehol, the manipulative Su Shun insisting that Nuharoo and I need not trouble ourselves with the work of the court, which would be better left to men. In so many ways, Prince Kung made it clear to Nuharoo and me that he wanted us to be sisters-in-law, not political partners.

'It's true that as females we might lack knowledge of the foreign powers,' I argued, 'but that doesn't mean our rights should be cast aside.'

Without bothering to confront us, Prince Kung simply continued to go around us.

I tried to get Nuharoo to protest with me, but she didn't share my concern. She suggested that I forgive Prince Kung and move on. 'Preserving harmony is our family duty,' she said, smiling.

Without the daily reports being supplied to me, I had no idea what was going on. I felt blind and deaf when asked to make decisions during audiences. Prince Kung led the foreigners to believe that Nuharoo and I were mere figureheads. Instead of properly addressing Tung Chih in their proposals, the foreign powers addressed Prince Kung.

Tung Chih was nearly twelve when the Kung situation became intolerable. He would assume his full role as Emperor in a matter of a few years – that is, if there was still a role left for him to fulfill. In audiences he was unaware of the conflict going on just below the surface, but he could sense my own discomfort. The greater strain between us only made him more eager to avoid his duties. While Tung Chih sat tapping his foot or staring off into space until the audiences ended, I could only look out at the assembled ministers, nobles and subjects and feel that I was failing my son.

I realized that unless I convinced Nuharoo that she had much to lose, she would not offer her support. My son would be Emperor in name only while his uncle would wield the actual power. The reason that Governor Ho's and General Sheng Pao's executions encountered resistance was because the men were Prince Kung's friends. At my insistence the executions were eventually carried out, but now I realized how dear my 'bloody debt' was to be.

Unprepared and often speechless, Nuharoo and I allowed Prince Kung to conduct the audiences as if we did not exist. The disrespect was so obvious that the court soon felt free to openly ignore us. Yung Lu feared that the army would follow suit.

I knew that I had to stand up for myself and Tung Chih, and it had to be soon. When a low-ranking officer from a northern town sent a letter complaining about Prince Kung, I sensed the moment had arrived.

Within two hours I had composed an edict that presented the case against Prince Kung. I wrote it carefully and stuck to the facts, avoiding any unnecessary slights to the character of my brother-in-law. Then I did the most difficult thing: I summoned my son and attempted to explain what we were about to do. Tung Chih's face went blank and his eyes widened. He looked so young to me, so unprotected, even in his glorious silk robes emblazoned with the Imperial symbol. I hadn't meant to frighten him,

22

and sorrow filled my heart. Still, I needed him to understand.

Then, in the name of my son, I sent for Prince Kung.

A stunned silence settled over the audience as Tung Chih read the edict I had written and placed in his hands. It seemed to take the court by surprise, for no one challenged its claims. The night before, I had managed to persuade Nuharoo to be on my side, although she was absent at the announcement. In the edict I listed the numerous laws Kung had violated. My argument was strong and my evidence solid. My brother-in-law had no choice but to acknowledge that he had committed the wrongdoings.

I humbled Prince Kung by stripping him of all his posts and titles.

That same evening I asked Yung Lu to speak privately with him. Yung Lu made Kung understand that to unite with me was his sole option. 'As soon as you make a public apology,' Yung Lu promised on my behalf, 'Her Majesty will grant back all your posts and titles.'

My action was praised by Prince Kung's enemies as 'letting go of a dangerous beast.' They begged me not to reinstate him. These men had no idea what I wanted from Prince Kung. They couldn't imagine that punishing him was the only way for the two of us to get back together. To be treated as an equal was all I was asking.

To put an end to the rumor that Prince Kung and I were enemies, I issued another edict, granting Kung permission to do something he had long dreamed of: opening an elite academy, the Royal School of Science and Mathematics.

Tung Chih complained about a stomachache and was excused from attending the morning audience. I sent An-te-hai to check on him in the afternoon. My son would turn thirteen this year, and he had been Emperor for seven years. I understood why he hated his duties and would run away whenever possible, but still, I was disappointed.

I couldn't escape my thoughts of Tung Chih as I sat on the throne and listened to Yung Lu reading from Tseng Kuo-fan's letter about the replacements for Governor Ho and Sheng Pao, which still had not been finalized. I had to force myself to concentrate.

I kept my eyes on the door and hoped to hear the announcement that my son was coming. Finally he arrived. The audience of fifty men got down on their knees and greeted him. Tung Chih went to sit on the throne and didn't bother to nod.

My handsome boy had shaved for the first time. He had shot up in height lately. His moonlit eyes and gentle voice reminded me of his father's. In front of the court he appeared confident. But I knew that his restlessness had only continued to grow.

I left Tung Chih alone most of the time because I was ordered to. Nuharoo had made it clear that it was her duty to speak for the Emperor's needs. 'Tung Chih must be given a chance to mature on his own terms.'

The court had a hard time controlling Tung Chih's wildness. Eventually Prince Kung's son, Tsai-chen, was brought in to be Tung Chih's study mate. Although I was given no say in the decision, I was impressed by Tsai-chen's good manners and was relieved to see that the two boys became friends right away.

Tsai-chen was two years older than Tung Chih, and his experience in the outside world fascinated the young Emperor, who was forbidden to step outside the Imperial gates and who would do anything to get a story out of Tsai-chen. The boys also shared an interest in Chinese opera.

Unlike Tung Chih, Tsai-chen was a robust, well-built boy. Horseback riding was his passion. I hoped that under his friend's influence my son would pick up the Bannerman tradition, the ancient practices of the Manchu warriors who had conquered Han China two centuries before. Our family paintings depicted the Manchu emperors taking part in events through the year: martial arts, horseracing, autumn hunting. For six generations the Manchu emperors carried on the tradition, until my husband Hsien Feng. It would be a dream come true for me to see Tung Chih mount his horse one day.

'I depart for Wuchang this evening.' Yung Lu stood in front of me.

'What for?' I asked, upset by the suddenness of the news.

'Warlords in Jiang-hsi province have demanded the right to command private armies.'

'Don't they already do so?'

'Yes, but they want the formal sanction of the court,' Yung Lu replied. 'And of course they not only look to avoid taxes, they expect additional funding from the court.'

'It is a buried issue.' I turned my head away. 'Emperor Hsien Feng rejected the proposal long ago.'

'The warlords mean to challenge Emperor Tung Chih, Your Majesty.'

'What do you mean?'

'A rebellion is in the making.'

I looked at Yung Lu and understood.

'Can you leave the matter to Tseng Kuo-fan?' I felt uneasy about letting Yung Lu go to the frontier.

'The warlords will consider the consequences more seriously if they know they are dealing directly with you.'

'Is this Tseng Kuo-fan's idea?'

'Yes. The general suggested that you take advantage of your recent victories in court.'

'Tseng Kuo-fan wants me to bear more blood,' I said. 'Yung Lu, General Tseng would pass his "Head-Chopper" name to me, if that is what you mean by my recent victories. The thought does not appeal to me.' I paused and emotion filled my throat. 'I want to be liked. Not feared.'

Yung Lu shook his head. 'I agree with Tseng. You are the only person the warlords fear today.'

'But you know how I feel.'

'Yes, I do. But think of Tung Chih, Your Majesty.'

I looked at him and nodded.

'Let me go and straighten out the matter for Tung Chih,' he said.

'It is not safe for you to go.' I became nervous and began to speak fast. 'I need your protection here.'

Yung Lu explained that he had already made the arrangements and that I would be safe.

I couldn't bring myself to say goodbye.

Without looking at me, he asked for forgiveness and was gone.

4

IT WAS THE spring of 1868 and rain soaked the soil. Blue winter tulips in my garden began to rot. I was thirty-four years old. My nights were filled with the sound of crickets. The smell of incense fluttered over from the Palace Temple, where the senior concubines lived. It was strange that I still didn't know all of them. Visits were purely ceremonial inside the Forbidden City. The ladies spent their days carving gourds, raising silkworms and doing embroidery. Images of children appeared in their needlework, and I continued to receive clothing made for my son by these women.

My husband's younger wives, Lady Mei and Lady Hui, were said to have met with a secret curse. They spoke the words of the dead, and they insisted that their heads had been soaked in the rain throughout the season. To prove their point, they took down their headpieces and showed the eunuchs where water had seeped through to the roots of their hair. Lady Mei was said to be fascinated by images of death. She ordered new bed sheets of white silk and spent her days washing them herself. 'I want to be wrapped in these sheets when I die,' she said in an operatic voice. She drilled her eunuchs in the practice of wrapping her in the sheets.

I dined alone after the day's audience. I no longer paid attention to the parade of elaborate dishes and ate from the four bowls An-te-hai placed in front of me. They were usually simple greens, bean sprouts, soy chicken and steamed fish. I often took a walk after dinner, but today I went straight to bed. I told An-te-hai to wake me in an hour because I had important work to do.

The moonlight was bright, and I could see the calligraphy of an eleventh-century poem on the wall:

> How many flurries or squalls can spring stand
> Before it will have to return to its fount?
> One is afraid
> Spring flowers fade too soon.
> They have dropped
> Petals
> Impossible to count.
> Fragrant grass stretches
> As far as the horizon.
> Silent spring leaves only fluff behind.
> Spider webs catch but
> Spring itself would not stay.

An image of Yung Lu entered my mind, and I wondered where he was and whether he was safe.

'My lady,' came An-te-hai's whisper, 'the theater is crowded before the show is even created.' Lighting a candle, my eunuch drew near. 'Your Majesty's private life has been the talk of teahouses throughout Peking.'

I didn't want to let it bother me. 'Go away, An-te-hai.'

'The rumors expose Yung Lu, my lady.'

My heart shuddered, but I couldn't say that I hadn't anticipated this.

'My spies say it is your son who stirs up the rumors.'

'Nonsense.'

The eunuch backed himself toward the door. 'Good night, my lady.'

'Wait.' I sat up. 'Are you telling me that my son is the source?'

'It's just a rumor, my lady. Good night.'

'Does Prince Kung have a role in it?'

'I don't know. I don't think Prince Kung is behind the rumor, yet he hasn't discouraged it either.'

A sudden weakness ran through me.

'An-te-hai, stay awhile, would you?'

'Yes, my lady. I'll stay until you are asleep.'

'My son hates me, An-te-hai.'

'It is not you he hates. It is me. More than once His Young Majesty swore that he would order my death.'

'It doesn't mean anything, An-te-hai. Tung Chih is a child.'

'I've told myself that too, my lady. But when I look at him, I know he is serious. I am afraid of him.'

'Me too, and I am his mother.'

'Tung Chih is no longer a boy, my lady. He has already done manly things.'

'Manly things? What do you mean?'

'I can't say another word, my lady.'

'Please, An-te-hai, continue.'

'I haven't the facts yet.'

'Tell me whatever you know.'

The eunuch insisted that he be allowed to remain silent until he obtained more information. Without wasting a moment, he left.

*   *   *

All night long I thought about my son. I wondered whether it was Prince Kung who was manipulating Tung Chih in order to get back at me. The word was that after Kung apologized for his behavior, he ended his friendship with Yung Lu. They had split over the case of General Sheng Pao.

I knew Tung Chih was still bewildered and angry over my treatment of his uncle. Prince Kung was the closest thing to a father he had, and he resented that he had been the one to read the condemning edict before his uncle and the entire court. He might have only barely grasped the import of the words he read, but he could not have missed the look of humiliation in his uncle's eyes as they turned away from him. I knew my son blamed me for this and so much else.

Tung Chih was spending more and more time with Kung's son, Tsai-chen. I rejoiced that together they could escape from the pressures of the court in each other's company, however briefly. In my mind I joined them on their rides through the palace gardens and in the royal parks beyond. My spirits lifted when they returned, their faces flushed with color. I sensed a greater independence in my son. But I had begun to wonder whether it was true independence or simply his avoidance of me, his mother, whom he associated with the tiresome attendance at audiences, the person who told him to do things he didn't wish to do.

I didn't know how to quell his anger except to leave him alone and hope that it would pass. Increasingly we saw each other only at audiences, which just deepened my loneliness and made my nights longer. More and more my thoughts returned to the old concubines and widows of the Palace Temple, to wonder if their fate was not more tolerable than my own.

*   *   *

In order to protect me, Yung Lu had removed himself to a distant corner of the empire. I had been the subject of scorn and misunderstanding since the day I gave birth to Tung Chih, so I was used to it. I didn't expect the rumors and nightmares to stop until Tung Chih had gone through the ceremony of officially mounting the throne.

My only true wish was to establish a life of my own, a possibility I feared was slipping away. For the sake of my son's future, I could not remove myself from my duties as a regent. But to stay was to be embroiled in conflicts whose resolutions I could not grasp. I wondered what life was like for Yung Lu on the frontier. I had willed myself to stop fantasizing about us as lovers, but my senses continued to betray me. His absence made the audiences unbearable.

Knowing that I would never be in Yung Lu's arms, I was envious of those whose lips pronounced his name. He was the nation's most desirable bachelor, and his every move was observed. I imagined his doorsill being worn down by matchmakers.

To avoid frustration I kept busy and cultivated friendships. I reached out to support General Tseng Kuo-fan in his strategy to thwart the Taiping peasant rebels. In my son's name I congratulated his every victory.

Yesterday I'd granted an audience to a new man of talent, Tseng Kuo-fan's disciple and partner, Li Hung-chang. Li was a tall and handsome Chinese. I had never heard Tseng Kuo-fan praise anyone the way he did Li Hung-chang, calling him 'Invincible Li.' The moment I detected Li's accent, I asked if he was from Anhwei, my own province. To my delight, he was. Speaking the provincial dialect, he told me he was from Hefei, a short distance from Wuhu, my hometown. In our conversation I learned that he was a self-made man like his mentor, Tseng.

I invited Li Hung-chang to attend a Chinese opera at my theater. My true purpose was to find out more about him. Li was a scholar by background, a soldier-turned-general by trade. A smart businessman, he was already among the richest in the country. He let me know that his new field was diplomacy.

I asked Li what he had done before coming to the Forbidden City. He replied that he was in the middle of building a railway that would someday stretch across China. I promised that I would attend the inauguration of his railroad; in exchange, I asked if he could extend the track all the way to the Forbidden City. He became excited and promised that he would build me a station.

My making friends outside the royal circle disturbed Prince Kung. The gap between us began to widen again. We both knew that our dispute was not about recruiting talented allies – for he desired them as much as I – but about power itself.

I didn't mean to be anyone's rival, certainly not Prince Kung's. As confused and frustrated as I was, I realized that our differences were fundamental and impossible to resolve. I understood Kung's concerns, but I couldn't let him run the country his way.

Prince Kung was no longer the open-minded and big-hearted man that I had first come to know. In the past, he had appointed people for positions based on merit and been among the strongest advocates for embracing the many peoples of China. He promoted not only the Han Chinese but also foreign employees, such as the English-man Robert Hart, who for years had been in charge of our customs service. But when the Han Chinese filled the majority of the seats at the court, Prince Kung became uneasy and his views changed. My connections with such men as Tseng Kuo-fan and Li Hung-chang only made matters worse.

Prince Kung and I also had differences regarding Tung Chih. I didn't know how Prince Kung raised his children, but I realized – all too well – that Tung Chih was still an immature boy. On the one hand, I wished Prince Kung would be firm so that Tung Chih could benefit from having a father figure. On the other hand, I wanted the prince to stop ridiculing my son in front of the court. 'Tung Chih might be weak in character,' I said to my brother-in-law, 'but he was born to be the Emperor of China.'

Prince Kung officially proposed to have the court limit my power. 'Crossing the male-female line' was the name of my crime. I was able to quash the move, but it became increasingly difficult to offer posts to non-Manchus. Prince Kung's anti-Han attitude began to have a negative impact.

The Han Chinese ministers understood my hardship and did their best to help, including swallowing insults from their Manchu colleagues. The disrespect I witnessed on a daily basis devastated me.

When Prince Kung insisted in an audience that I hire back the Manchu officers who had failed in their duties, I walked out. 'The Manchus are like defective firecrackers that won't pop!' was what people remembered my saying. And now that phrase was being used against my son.

The consequences were mine to bear: I lost my son's affection. 'You've made Uncle Prince Kung a victim!' my son yelled.

I prayed to Heaven to make me strong, for I believed in what I was doing. Let Prince Kung be shaken by the fact that he was not able to stop me. I told myself that I had nothing to fear. I had been running the nation without him and would move forward as I must.

5

M Y SON'S ERA was described as 'the Glorious Tung Chih
Renaissance,' although Tung Chih had done nothing
to deserve the praise. General Tseng Kuo-fan was the man
who brought the glory. He had been battling the Taiping
forces since 1864. By 1868 he had succeeded in wiping out
most of the rebels. Since Tseng was my choice, the inner
court nicknamed me 'the Old Buddha' for being wise.

Grateful to General Tseng, I rewarded him with a
promotion. To my surprise, he turned it down.

'It is not that I wouldn't be honored,' Tseng explained in
his letter to me. 'I am more than honored. What I don't
want is to be seen by my peers as a symbol of power. I fear
that my rise in rank would feed the greed for power in the
government. I would like to make every general around me
feel comfortable and equal. I want my soldiers to know that
I am one of them, fighting for a cause, not for power or
prestige.'

In my reply I wrote: 'As coregents, all Nuharoo and I
desire to see is order and peace, and this goal simply cannot
be achieved without your being in charge. Until you accept
the promotion, we won't be able to rest our conscience.'

Tseng Kuo-fan reluctantly complied.

As the senior governor in charge of the provinces of Jiangsu, Jiang-hsi, and Anhwei, Tseng Kuo-fan became the first Han Chinese whose rank was equal to that of Yung Lu and Prince Kung.

Tseng worked tirelessly yet continued to be what others would describe as overcautious. He kept his distance from the throne. His suspicion was a classic one. In countless instances over China's long history, even as a powerful general was honored, plans were made for his murder. This was especially so when the ruler feared that the general had surpassed him in power.

Tung Chih was becoming susceptible to his uncle Prince Kung's negative attitude toward the Han. I begged them both to see things differently and to help me regain the trust of Tseng Kuo-fan. My thinking was that if Tseng were to provide stability, my son would be the one to benefit.

In Tung Chih's name I let Tseng Kuo-fan know that I would protect him. When Tseng revealed his doubts, I tried to reassure him – I promised that I wouldn't retire until my son showed sufficient maturity to assume the throne.

I convinced Tseng that it would be safe for him to act as he saw fit. With my encouragement, the general began to plan battles broader and more ambitious in scope. Gathering his forces from the north, he moved steadily south until he established headquarters near Anking, a strategically important city in Anhwei. Tseng Kuo-fan then ordered his brother, Tseng Kuo-quan, to station his army outside the Taiping capital at Nanking.

An-te-hai created a map to help me visualize Tseng's movements. The map looked like a fine painting. An-te-hai put little colored flags over its surface. I saw Tseng dispatch the Manchu general Chou Tsung-tang to the south to encircle the city of Hangchow, in Chekiang province.

General Peng Yu-lin was assigned to block the Yangtze River shoreline. Li Hung-chang, Tseng Kuo-fan's most trusted man, was given the job of blocking the enemy's escape route near Soochow.

The flags on the map changed daily. Before New Year's Day of 1869, Tseng launched a grand attack, wrapping up the Taipings like a spring roll. To further secure his position, he pulled in forces from north of the Yangtze. For the final enclosure, he worked with Yung Lu, whose soldiers came from behind to cut the Taipings' supply line.

'The encirclement is as tight as a sealed bag,' An-te-hai said, sticking out his chest and striking a Tseng-like pose. 'Nanking is crumbling!'

I moved the little flags around like chess pieces on a board. It became a pleasure. By Tseng Kuo-fan's moves, I could trace how his mind worked and thrilled at his brilliance.

For days I sat by the map, ate my meals there and kept up with all the battle news. From a recent report I learned that the Taipings had pulled out their last forces from Hang-chow. Strategically, this was a fatal mistake. Li Hung-chang soon rounded up the remnants of the army at Soochow. Li's counterpart General Chou Tsung-tang moved in and took Hangchow. The rebels lost their base. With all the Imperial forces in place, Tseng Kuo-fan charged.

Tung Chih cheered and Nuharoo and I wept when the report of the final victory reached the Forbidden City. We climbed into our palanquins and went to the Heavenly Altar to comfort Hsien Feng's spirit.

Once again in Tung Chih's name I issued a decree honoring Tseng Kuo-fan and his fellow generals. A few days later I received a detailed report from Tseng confirming the victory. Then Yung Lu returned to the capital. In

37

our usual quiet manner we shared our excitement. As my ladies in waiting and An-te-hai looked on, Yung Lu informed me of his own role in the battles and praised General Tseng's leadership. Expressing concern, he told me that Tseng had recently lost most of his sight following a serious eye infection. Delays in treatment had worsened the condition.

I summoned Tseng Kuo-fan for a private audience as soon as he had returned to Peking.

In his flowing silk robe and peacock tail hat the Chinese general threw himself at my feet. His forehead remained down to express his gratitude. As he waited for me to utter 'rise,' I myself rose and bowed in his direction. I ignored etiquette; it seemed the proper thing to do.

'Let me take a good look at you, Tseng Kuo-fan,' I said with tears in my eyes. 'I am so glad you returned safely.'

He rose and went to sit on the chair An-te-hai provided.

I was surprised to see that he was no longer the vital man I remembered from only a few years before. His magnificent robe could not hide his frailty. His skin was leather dry and his bushy eyebrows looked like snowballs. He was about sixty years old, but a slight hunch in his back made him look a decade older.

After tea was served I suggested that he follow me to the drawing room, where he could sit more comfortably. He wouldn't move until I told him that I was tired of sitting on a chair whose deeply carved wood hurt my back. I smiled and said that the ornate furniture in the audience hall was good only for show.

'You see, Tseng Kuo-fan, I can barely hear you.' I pointed at the distance between us. 'It is not easy for either of us. On the one hand, it is considered rude if you raise your voice. On the other hand, I can't bear to not hear you.'

Tseng nodded and moved to sit near me, on my lower left. He did not know that I had fought for this meeting. The Manchu clansmen and Prince Kung had ignored my request to honor Tseng with the private audience. I pleaded that if it hadn't been for Tseng Kuo-fan, the Manchu Dynasty would have come to an end.

Nuharoo had refused to take my side when I went to her for support. Like the rest, she took Tseng Kuo-fan for granted. Eventually I persuaded her to back the invitation, but a few hours before the meeting was to take place, she again changed her mind.

I was beside myself with anger.

Nuharoo yielded, but sighed and said, 'If only you had one drop of royal blood in you.'

True, I had not a drop. But that was precisely what drew me to Tseng Kuo-fan. By treating him with respect, I was respecting myself.

My negotiations with the Imperial clan had ended in compromise: I was to meet Tseng for fifteen minutes.

'I heard that you have lost your sight. Is that true?' I asked while watching the clock ticking on the wall. 'May I know which eye is bad?'

'Both eyes are bad,' Tseng replied. 'My right eye has gone blind almost completely. But my left can still detect light. On a good day I can see blurred figures.'

'Have you recovered from your other maladies?'

'Yes, I can say that I have.'

'You appear to kneel and rise freely. Is your frame still sound?'

'It is not what it used to be.'

The thought of ending the meeting made my voice break. 'Tseng Kuo-fan, you have worked hard for the throne.'

'It has been my pleasure to serve you, Your Majesty.'

I wished that I could invite him to see me again, but I was afraid that I would not be able to keep my word.

We sat and remained quiet.

As etiquette required, Tseng kept his head lowered, his eyes resting on a spot on the floor. The steel clasp of his riding cloak made a clinking noise every time he changed position. He seemed to search for my exact location. I was sure he could not see me even with his eyes wide open. Reaching for his teacup, his hands groped the air. When An-te-hai brought in sweet sesame buns, his elbow almost upset the tray.

'Tseng Kuo-fan, do you remember the first time we met?' I tried to cheer us up.

'Yes, of course.' The man nodded. 'It was fourteen years ago . . . at the audience with His Majesty Emperor Hsien Feng.'

I raised my voice a bit so I was sure he could hear me. 'You were strong with a stout chest. Your gathered eyebrows made me think that you were mad.'

'Was I?' He smiled. 'I was impatient back then. I wanted to live up to His Majesty's expectations.'

'You did. You have achieved more than anyone could have expected. My husband would be proud. I have already visited his altar to report the news you brought him.'

Tseng lowered his head and began to weep. Glancing up after a time, he peered in my direction, struggling to see. The light in the sitting room was too dim, however, and he again lowered his gaze.

An-te-hai came in to remind us that our time was up.

Tseng collected himself to bid me goodbye.

'Finish your tea,' I said softly.

As he drank, I looked at the silver mountains and ocean waves embroidered on his cloak.

'Would it be all right if I asked my doctor to visit you?' I asked.

'It would be very kind of Your Majesty.'

'Promise me that you will take care of yourself, Tseng Kuo-fan. I am counting on seeing you again. Soon, I hope.'

'Yes, Your Majesty, Tseng Kuo-fan will do his best.'

I never got to see him again. Tseng Kuo-fan died less than four years later, in 1873.

Looking back, I felt good about honoring the man personally. Tseng opened my eyes to the wider world outside the Forbidden City. He not only made me understand how the Western nations took advantage of their Industrial Revolution and prospered, but also demonstrated that China stood a chance to accomplish great things. Tseng Kuo-fan's last advice to the throne was to build a strong navy. His historic achievement, the triumph over the Taiping rebels, gave me the confidence to pursue such a dream.

6

S INCE HIS INFANCY, Tung Chih had been taught to think that I was his subordinate more than his mother. And now that he was thirteen, I had to be careful what I said to him. Like handling a kite in a capricious wind, I held on to a thin thread. I learned to silence myself whenever tense breezes blew.

One morning soon after my final meeting with General Tseng, An-te-hai requested a moment with me. The eunuch had something important to tell me, and he asked for my forgiveness before opening his mouth.

I said 'rise' several times, but An-te-hai remained on his knees. When I ordered him to come closer, he shuffled toward me on his knees and settled in a spot where I could hear his whisper.

'His Young Majesty has been infected with a terrible disease,' An-te-hai said gravely.

I stood up. 'What are you talking about?'

'My lady, you've got to be strong . . .' He pulled at my sleeve until I sat back down.

'What is it?' I bounced back up.

'It is . . . well, he got it from the local brothels.'

For a moment I couldn't register the meaning of his words.

'I was informed about Tung Chih's nightly absences,' An-te-hai continued, 'so I followed him. I am sorry I couldn't bring the information to you sooner.'

'Tung Chih is the master of thousands of concubines,' I snapped. 'He didn't need to . . .' I stopped, realizing I was being foolish. 'How long has he been visiting the brothels?' I asked, composing myself.

'A few months.' An-te-hai reached out to hold my elbow.

'Which ones?' I asked, shaking.

'Different ones. His Young Majesty was afraid of being recognized, so he avoided those the royals frequent.'

'You mean Tung Chih went to those used by commoners?'

'Yes.'

I couldn't still my imagination.

'Don't let despair take hold of you, my lady!' An-te-hai cried.

'Summon Tung Chih!' I pushed the eunuch away.

'My lady.' An-te-hai threw himself before me. 'There is need to discuss a strategy.'

'There is nothing to discuss.' I raised my hand and pointed to the door. 'I shall confront my son with the truth. It's my duty.'

'My lady!' An-te-hai knocked his forehead on the ground. 'A blacksmith wouldn't hit an iron bar when it is cold. Please, my lady, think again.'

'An-te-hai, if you are afraid of my son, are you not also afraid of me?'

I should have listened to An-te-hai and waited. If I had controlled my emotions, as I had been careful to do in my court, An-te-hai wouldn't have ended up paying for it. I would not have lost both my son and An-te-hai.

Standing in front of me, Tung Chih looked as if he had come out of a pool of water. Sweat glistened on his forehead. Holding a handkerchief, he kept wiping his face and neck. His complexion was blotchy and pimples marked his jaw line. I had thought that his skin condition was due to his age, that his body elements were out of balance. When I asked about the brothels, he denied all. It wasn't until I called in An-te-hai that Tung Chih admitted what he had done.

I asked if he had seen Doctor Sun Pao-tien. Tung Chih replied that there was no need because he didn't feel sick.

'Summon Sun Pao-tien,' I ordered.

My son stared at An-te-hai with narrowing eyes.

It was a mess after Doctor Sun Pao-tien arrived. The more Tung Chih tried to lie, the more the doctor suspected. It would be days before Sun Pao-tien would announce his findings, which I knew would break me.

I sent An-te-hai to search Tung Chih's palace. I canceled the day's audience and looked through my son's belongings. Besides opium, I found books of an illicit nature.

I summoned Tsai-chen, Prince Kung's fifteen-year-old son, Tung Chih's closest companion. I pressured and cajoled Tsai-chen until he confessed that it was he who loaned the books and he who had taken Tung Chih to the brothels. Showing no guilt, Tsai-chen described brothels as 'opera houses' and whores as 'actresses.'

'Summon Prince Kung!' I called.

Prince Kung was shocked no less than I, which made me realize that the situation was worse than I had imagined.

When I forbade Tsai-chen from ever visiting again, Tung Chih was even more upset.

'I'll see you off,' my son said to his friend.

'Tsai-chen will leave with his father!' I told my son. Then I told An-te-hai to block the door so Tung Chih couldn't get out.

'You bunch of dead bodies!' Tung Chih shouted, kicking An-te-hai and the other eunuchs. 'Molds! Poisonous snakes!'

As I waited for the results from Doctor Sun Pao-tien, I visited Nuharoo to inform her of what had happened. Without mentioning Tung Chih's outrageous behavior, she worried about the possibility of venereal disease but even more about the Emperor's reputation – and hers, since as the senior mother she was responsible for the important decisions in Tung Chih's personal life. Nuharoo suggested that we begin the selection of an Imperial consort right away, 'so that Tung Chih can start his life as a grown man.'

An-te-hai was silent on our way back to my palace. The look in his eyes was that of a beaten dog.

At first Tung Chih showed no interest in the consort selection. Nuharoo was determined to carry on anyway. When I called Tung Chih to arrange a date to inspect the maidens, he instead wanted to discuss An-te-hai's 'misconduct' and the proper punishment.

I ignored my son and said, 'What's going on between us should not interfere with your duties.' I threw a court report at him. 'This arrived this morning. I want you to take a look.'

'Foreign missionaries have made converts,' Tung Chih said as he riffled through the document. 'Yes, I am aware of that. They have attracted layabouts and bandits by offering free food and shelter, and they have helped the criminals. The issue is not religion, as they claim.'

45

'You have done nothing about it.'

'No, I haven't.'

'Why not?' I tried to keep my voice calm but wasn't able to. 'Was whoring all over the city more important?'

'Mother, every treaty protects Christians. What can I do? Father was the one who signed it! You are trying to say that I am bringing down the dynasty, but I am not. Foreigners were having their way in China before I was born. Look at this: "Missionaries demand rent for the last three hundred years on long-standing Chinese temples which they declare are former church properties." Does that make sense to you?'

I was speechless.

'I'd like to believe that the missionaries are good men and women,' my son continued, 'that only their code of morals is defective. I agree with Uncle Prince Kung that Christianity lays too much stress on charity and too little on justice. Anyway, it's not my problem, and you shouldn't try to make it mine.'

'Foreigners have no right to bring their laws to China. And that is your problem to fix, son.'

'The business of running the nation makes me sick, period. Sorry, Mother, I have to go.'

'I am not done yet. Tung Chih, you don't know enough to know what to do yet.'

'How could I not know enough? You have made the court's papers my textbooks. I have been considered weak as far back as I can remember. You are the wise one, the all-knowing Old Buddha. I don't send spies to invade your rooms and empty out your closets. But that doesn't mean I'm stupid and know nothing. I love you, Mother, but –' He stopped and then broke down sobbing.

*   *   *

46

In the darkest moments of my life, I would go to An-te-hai and ask him to comfort me. I was beyond shame.

It would be unimaginable for any woman to stand the thought that her body was being touched by a eunuch, a creature from the underworld. But I felt as low as the eunuch.

That night, An-te-hai's voice soothed me. It helped me escape reality. I was taken to distant continents to experience exotic voyages. Excitement would fill An-te-hai's expression as he blew out the candles and came to lie by my side on the bed.

'I have found my hero,' An-te-hai whispered. 'Like me, he was an unfortunate one. Born in 1371 and castrated at the age of ten. Luckily, the master he served was a prince who was good to him. In return he rendered outstanding service and helped the prince become the Emperor of the Ming Dynasty . . .'

The sound of a night owl quieted, and the moonlit clouds stood still outside the window.

'His name was Cheng Ho, the greatest explorer in the world. You can find his name in every book of navigation, but none reveals his identity as a eunuch. No one knew that his profound suffering was what made him extraordinary. The ability to endure hardship that only I, a fellow eunuch, can understand.'

'How do you know Cheng Ho was a eunuch?' I asked.

'I discovered it by accident, in the Imperial Registration Record of Eunuchs, a book nobody else would care to read.'

In Cheng Ho An-te-hai recognized an achievable dream. 'As the admiral of the Treasure Fleet Cheng Ho headed seven naval expeditions to ports all over Southeast Asia and the Indian Ocean.' An-te-hai spoke in a voice of passion. 'My hero traveled as far as the Red Sea and East Africa, exploring more than thirty nations in seven voyages. Castration made him a broken man, but it never stayed his ambition.'

In the darkness An-te-hai walked to the window in his white silk robe. Facing the bright moon, he announced, 'I shall from now on have a birth date.'

'Haven't you one already?'

'That was a made-up one, because no one, including myself, knew when I was born. My new birthday will be July 11. It will be in memory and celebration of Cheng Ho's first naval expedition, which set off on July 11, 1405.'

In my dream that night, An-te-hai became Cheng Ho. He was dressed in a magnificent Ming court robe and was out on the open sea, heading toward the distant horizon.

'. . . He flaunted the might of two generations of Chinese emperors.' An-te-hai's voice woke me. Yet he was in deep sleep.

I sat up and lit a candle. I looked at the sleeping eunuch and suddenly felt crushed as my thoughts fled back to Tung Chih. I had an urge to go to my son and hold him close.

'My lady.' An-te-hai spoke with his eyes shut. 'Did you know Cheng Ho's fleet included more than sixty large ships? A crew nearly thirty thousand strong! They had one ship to carry horses, and another one carried only drinking water!'

7

Nuharoo summoned me on the eighth anniversary of our husband's death. After our greeting, she announced that she had decided to change the names of all the palaces in the Forbidden City. She began with her own palace. Instead of the Palace of Peace and Longevity, its new name would be the Palace of Meditation and Transformation. Nuharoo said that her *feng shui* master advised that the names of palaces occupied by females should be changed once every ten years in order to confuse the ghosts who came to haunt their old palaces.

I didn't like the idea, but Nuharoo was not the type of person to compromise. The problem was that if we changed the name of a palace, the names that went along with it also had to be changed – the palace's gates, its gardens, its walkways, its servants' quarters. Nevertheless, she forged ahead. Nuharoo's gate was now the Gate of Reflection instead of the Gate of Restful Wind. Her garden was now called the Spring Awakening instead of the Magnificent Wilderness. Her main walkway used to be the Corridor of Moonlight and now was the Corridor of a Clear Mind.

To my mind, the new names were not as tasteful as the old ones. The old name for Nuharoo's pond, Spring Ripple,

49

was better than its new name, the Zen Drops. I also liked Palace of Gathering Essence better than Palace of the Great Void.

For months Nuharoo spent her time working on the names. More than one hundred title boards and nameplates were taken down and new ones created and installed. Sawdust filled the air as the carpenters sanded the boards. Paint and ink were everywhere as Nuharoo ordered the calligraphers, whose style she found deficient, to redo their work.

I asked Nuharoo if the court had approved her new names. She shook her head. 'It would take too long to explain the importance to the court, and they wouldn't like it because of the expense. It's better that I don't bother them at all.'

She started to call the palaces by their new names on her own. It caused great confusion. None of the Imperial departments, which would take orders only from the court, were notified. The gardeners had great difficulty figuring out where they were supposed to work. The palanquin bearers went to the wrong places to pick up and drop off their passengers, and the supply department made a mess sending items to incorrect addresses.

Nuharoo said that she had invented an excellent new name for my palace. 'How do you like "the Palace of the Absence of Confusion"?'

The name had always been the Palace of Long Springs. 'What do you expect me to say?'

'Say you love it, Lady Yehonala!' She called me by my formal title. 'It's my best work. You have to love it! My wish is that the new names will inspire you to retire from the world to pursue calmer pleasures.'

'I'd be more than happy to retire tomorrow if I could forget about the threat of being overthrown.'

'I am not asking you to quit the audiences,' Nuharoo said, patting both of her cheeks with her silk handkerchief. 'Men can be wicked and their behavior should be monitored.'

It amazed me that she didn't really mean it when she had told me to leave the business of governing to men. What struck me was how she achieved power by appearing to want nothing to do with it.

I was glad that most of the palaces that underwent name changes were the inner quarters occupied by concubines. Since there was no official record of the changes, everyone except Nuharoo continued to call the buildings by their old names. To avoid offending her, the word 'old' was tacked on to all the names. For example, my palace was referred to as the Old Palace of Long Springs.

Eventually Nuharoo grew tired of the game. She admitted that the new names were confusing. Her house eunuchs got so mixed up that they lost their way while trying to carry out her orders. She meant to send her lotus-seed cake to me, but it ended up on the gatekeeper's table.

'The eunuchs are too stupid,' Nuharoo concluded. So everything was changed back to the way it had been, and the new names were soon forgotten.

An-te-hai sent Li Lien-ying, who was now his most trusted disciple, to give me a head massage. With a good rubbing I felt the tension in my body dissolve like clay in water. I looked at myself in the mirror and saw that wrinkles had crept onto my smooth forehead. My eyes had bags beneath them. While my features retained their beauty, their youthful glow had disappeared.

I did not tell An-te-hai about my conversation with Tung Chih, yet he sensed it. He sent Li Lien-ying to guard me at night and moved his sleeping mat out of my room. Years later, I would find out that my eunuch had been threatened by my son. An-te-hai was to either stay away or be removed – meaning murdered. As if to make sure that no eunuch developed a close relationship with me, An-te-hai rotated my room attendants. It took me a while to realize his intention.

Among all my attendants, I adored Li Lien-ying, who had served me since he was a young boy. He was sweet-tempered and as capable as An-te-hai, though I couldn't talk with him as I had with An-te-hai. As masters of serving another, Li Lien-ying was a craftsman, but An-te-hai was an artist. For example, An-te-hai had been devising a way to get Yung Lu into my inner garden for some time. He had arranged for bridge and roof repairs around my palace, so outside workers would have to be brought in, and with them Imperial Guards. An-te-hai believed that this would give Yung Lu a chance to supervise. The plan hadn't worked, but An-te-hai had continued his effort.

Li Lien-ying was a much more popular eunuch than An-te-hai. He had a talent for making friends, a skill An-te-hai lacked. Servants never knew when An-te-hai would show up to inspect their work. And if he was dissatisfied, he would make a scene, try to 'educate' them.

A rumor began to circulate among the servants that An-te-hai would soon be replaced as chief eunuch by Li Lien-ying. An-te-hai became furiously jealous and suspected that Li had stolen my affection. One day An-te-hai found an excuse to interrogate Li. When Li protested, An-te-hai charged him with being disrespectful and ordered him whipped.

To show fairness, I had An-te-hai whipped and withheld his food for three days and confined him to the eunuchs' quarters. A week later I went to see him. He was sitting in his small yard examining his bruises. When I asked what he had done during his confinement, he showed me something he had built from scraps of wood and bits of rag.

I was in awe of what I saw. 'A little dragon boat!' It was a miniature ship, modeled after one of Cheng Ho's fleet. It was no bigger than An-te-hai's arm but was intricately detailed, with sails, rigging, and tiny cargo crates.

'Someday I'd like to travel south to see Cheng Ho's burial site in Nanking,' An-te-hai said. 'I will make an offering and ask his spirit to accept me as a distant disciple.'

The late summer of 1869 was hot and humid. I had to change my inner shirt twice a day. If I didn't, sweat would make the dye run on my court robe. Since the Forbidden City had few trees, there was no escape from the heat. The sun baked the stone paths. Every time eunuchs poured water on the ground, we could hear a hissing sound and see white steam.

The court tried to cut audiences short. Blocks of ice were brought in, and carpenters devised makeshift box chairs to hold the blocks. The summoned, who wore heavy court robes, would sit right on top of the ice. By noon, puddles of water would spread out from beneath the boxes. It looked as if the ministers had urinated.

Nuharoo wore a moss-colored dress when she entered the Hall of Spiritual Nurturing during a break in the audience. The eunuchs began to work the wooden fans to draw wind. Nuharoo frowned because the fans made a terrible noise, like the slamming of windows and doors.

She sat down elegantly on a chair opposite me. We glanced at each other's dresses, makeup and hair while exchanging greetings. I hated wearing makeup in the summer and applied it only lightly. I sipped tea and made an effort to appear interested. By now I knew Nuharoo well enough to predict that any proposal of hers would have nothing to do with the nation's urgencies. I had made many attempts in the past to brief her on court business. She would either change the subject or simply ignore me.

'Since you have to go back to the audience, I shall be brief.' Smiling, Nuharoo took a sip of her tea. 'I have been thinking how the dead like to hear the living cry on the day their spirits return home. How do we know that our husband does not desire the same?'

I did not know what to make of her words, so I muttered something about how the pile of court documents on my table was growing higher and higher.

'Why can't we create a picture of Heaven to welcome the spirits?' Nuharoo said. 'We could dress the maids up in the costumes of moon goddesses and scatter them around in decorated boats on Kun Ming Lake. Eunuchs could hide in the hills and behind pavilions and play flutes and string instruments. Wouldn't Hsien Feng like that?'

'I am afraid it would be expensive,' I said flatly.

'I knew you would say that!' She pouted. 'Prince Kung must be responsible for putting you in such an unpleasant mood. Anyway, I have already ordered the party. Whether or not the court has the taels, the minister of revenue is responsible for paying for the Emperor's memorial. This is a small gesture.'

Between audiences, I took time to take care of things that Prince Kung thought were unimportant. For example, an article came to my attention. It was published in *The Court's Updates,* a newspaper read by many government officials. It reprinted the essay of the top winner of that year's civil service examination, called 'The Ruler Who Surpasses China's First Emperor.'

The author flattered my son beyond belief. The choice of title was alarming. It told me that something unhealthy was developing in the heart of our government.

I asked for the list of examination winners from the judges. When it was delivered, I circled the author's name with a red brush pen. I removed him from first place and sent the list back.

It wasn't that I didn't enjoy flattery. Then again, I could distinguish between puffery and praise that was earned. But people tended to accept newspaper articles at face value. What I was afraid of was that if I failed to stop the tendency toward flattery, my son's regime would end up losing its valuable critics.

'I have not heard the whistling of the pigeons. What has become of them?' I asked An-te-hai.

'The pigeons are gone,' the eunuch replied. Although his movements were still stylish and his gestures elegant, An-te-hai looked nervous and his large eyes had lost their brightness. 'They must have decided to find a more genial home.'

'Was it because you neglected them?'

An-te-hai was silent. Then he bowed. 'I let them go, my lady.'

'Why?'

'Because the cages don't suit them.'

'Their cages are grand! The royal pigeon house is as big as a temple! How much bigger would the pigeons want? If you think they need more space, ask the carpenters to enlarge the cages. You can make them two stories high if you want. Make twenty cages, forty cages, a hundred cages!'

'It is not the size, my lady, nor the number of cages.'

'What is it, then?'

'It's the cage itself.'

'It never bothered you before.'

'It does now.'

'Nonsense.'

The eunuch lowered his head. After a while he uttered, 'It is painful to be locked up.'

'Pigeons are animals, An-te-hai! Your imagination has become addled.'

'Perhaps. But it is the same imagination that finds fault with the assumption of happiness and glory in your life, my lady. The good thing is that pigeons are unlike parrots. Pigeons can fly away, while parrots are chained. Parrots are forced to serve, to please by mimicking human words. My lady, we have also lost our parrot.'

'Which one?'

'Confucius.'

'How?'

'The bird refused to say what he was taught. It had been speaking its own language and therefore was punished. The eunuch training him did his best. He tried tricks that had worked in the past, including starvation. But Confucius was stubborn and didn't say another word. He died yesterday.'

'Poor Confucius.' I remembered the beautiful and clever bird, which was my husband's gift to me. 'What can I say? Confucius was right when he said that men are born evil.'

'The pigeons are lucky,' An-te-hai said, looking at the sky. 'High up they went and disappeared in the clouds. I am not sorry for helping them escape, my lady. I am actually happy for what I did.'

'What about the reed pipes you tied on the pigeons' feet? Did you let them take the music with them? They would be fed under any roof if they brought music.'

'I removed the pipes, my lady.'

'All of them?'

'Yes, all of them.'

'Why would you do such a thing?'

'Aren't they Imperial birds, my lady? Aren't they entitled to freedom?'

I was preoccupied with Tung Chih. Every minute I wanted to know where he was, what he was doing, and whether Doctor Sun Pao-tien was succeeding with his treatment. I ordered Tung Chih's menu sent to me, because I didn't trust that he was being fed properly. I sent eunuchs to follow his friend Tsai-chen to ensure that the two boys remained apart.

I was restless and felt caught in a mysterious force telling me that my son was in danger. Both Tung Chih and Doctor Sun Pao-tien avoided me. Tung Chih even went to work on the court papers so I would have to leave him alone. But my worry didn't go away. It turned into fear. In my nightmares, Tung Chih called for my help and I couldn't reach him.

In an effort to distract myself, I ordered a performance of a pon-pon opera and invited my inner court to join me. Everyone was shocked because pon-pon opera was considered entertainment for the poor. I had seen such operas performed in villages when I was a young girl. After my father was demoted from his post, my mother had ordered a performance to lighten his mood. I remembered how much I had enjoyed it. After I came to Peking, I longed to see one again, but I was told that such a low form was forbidden in the palace.

The troupe was small, just two women and three men, and had old costumes and pitiful props. They had trouble getting past the gate because the guards didn't believe that I had summoned them. Even Li Lien-ying could not convince the guards, and the troupe was released only when An-te-hai showed up.

Before the opera, I greeted the master performer in private. He was a bone-thin, half-blind man with rheumy eyes. I assumed that the robe he wore was his best, but it was covered with patches. I thanked him for coming and told my kitchen to feed the actors before they went onstage.

The set was simple. A plain red curtain was their background. The master sat on a stool. He tuned his erhu, a two-stringed instrument, and began to play. He produced a sound that reminded me of fabric being torn. The music was like a cry of grief, yet it was strangely soothing to my ears.

When the opera had begun, I looked around and noticed that I was the only one left in the audience besides An-te-hai and Li Lien-ying. Everybody else had quietly left. The melody was not quite what I had remembered. The tone sounded like wind riding high in the sky. The universe seemed filled with the fabric-tearing noise. I imagined that this was how spirits being chased would sound. My mind's eye could see stony fields and fir forests gradually being covered by sand.

The music finally faded. The master performer lowered his head to his chest as if falling asleep. The stage was silent. I envisioned the Gate of Heaven opening and closing in darkness.

Two women and a man entered the scene. They were wearing big blue blouses. They each had a bamboo stick and a Chinese chime made of copper. They circled the master performer and beat their chime to the rhythm of his erhu.

As if suddenly awoken, the man started to sing. His neck stuck up like a turkey's and his pitched voice became ear-piercing, like cicadas rattling on the hottest summer day:

> There is an old lobster
> Who lives in a hole beneath a giant rock.
> It comes out to look at the world
> And it goes back.
> I lift the rock to say hello.
> Ever since I have seen it
> The lobster stays in its hole.
>
> Day after day,
> Year after year,
> Quietly
> Wrapped by darkness and water,
> A confident creature
> The lobster must be.
>
> It hears the earth's sound
> And witnesses its changes.
> The mold on its back is growing
> Into beautiful green.

Beating their chimes in rhythm, the three others joined the singing:

O lobster,
Know you I do not.
Where do you come from?
Where is your family?
What made you migrate and hide in this hole?

I wish my son had stayed for the entire performance.

8

I HAD BEGUN to read *The Romance of the Three Kingdoms,* a Chinese emperor's history of the period following the Han Dynasty, encompassing four hundred years. The six volumes were as thick and heavy as large bricks. The book was a mere chronicle of victories, one following another seemingly without end. I had hoped to get to know the characters' interests, not just their military ventures. I wanted to know why these men fought, how each hero was raised and what role his mother played.

After reading the first volume, I came to the conclusion that the book was not going to provide what I was interested in. I could list the names of all the characters, but I still didn't understand the men. The verses and poems about famous battles were exquisite, but I couldn't grasp the reasons they were fought. It didn't make sense to me that men would fight for the sake of fighting. In the end, I comforted myself by thinking that I would be safe – and accomplish great things – as long as I could distinguish the good men from the bad. During what would be my fifty years behind the throne, I would learn that this was not the case. Often the worst plans were presented by my best men, and with the best of intentions.

I learned to trust my instincts more than my judgment. My lack of perspective and experience had made me cautious and alert. On occasion my insecurities would cause me to doubt my instincts, which resulted in decisions that I would come to regret. For example, I expressed reservations when Prince Kung proposed that we hire an English tutor to teach Tung Chih about world affairs. The court was against the idea as well. I agreed with the grand councilors that Tung Chih was at an impressionable age and could easily be manipulated and influenced.

'His Young Majesty is yet to understand what China has suffered,' one councilor argued. 'The notion that England is responsible for the decline of our dynasty has not taken deep enough root in Tung Chih's mind.' Others agreed: 'To allow Tung Chih to be educated by the English means betrayal to our ancestors.'

The memories of how my husband died were still fresh. The smell of the burning of our home – the Grand Round Garden, Yuan Ming Yuan – had not dissipated. I couldn't imagine my son speaking English and befriending his father's enemies.

After several sleepless nights, I made up my mind. I dismissed Prince Kung's proposal and told him that 'His Young Majesty Emperor Tung Chih should understand who he is before anything else.'

I would spend the rest of my life regretting the decision.

If Tung Chih had learned to communicate with the British, or traveled or studied abroad, he could have been a different emperor. He would have been inspired by their example and witnessed their leadership. He might have developed a forward-looking future for China, or at least been interested in trying.

*   *   *

It was a cloudless afternoon when Nuharoo announced that all was ready for the final selection of Tung Chih's bride. I went along because I felt I had to. In order to ensure Nuharoo's continuing support at court, I needed to maintain harmony between us. I felt unready to see Tung Chih married; I could not get used to the idea that he was a grown man. Wasn't it just yesterday that he was a baby lying in my arms? Never before had I felt so acutely the pain of being robbed of time with my child.

Because of Nuharoo's restrictions and my own court schedule I had hardly been a presence during Tung Chih's childhood. Although I had kept on my doorframe the marks measuring my son's height over the years, I knew few of his favorite things or his thoughts, only that he resented my expectations for him. He couldn't stand when I questioned him, and even my morning greetings made him frown. He told everyone that Nuharoo was much easier to please. The fact that she and I competed for his affection made matters worse. It was understandable that he had little respect for me; I was desperate for his love. Yet the more I begged, the less he wished to be with me.

Now, all of a sudden, he was an adult. My time to be close to him was up.

With a smile on his face, Tung Chih entered the Grand Hall dressed in gold. Unlike his father, he would participate in the selection. Thousands of fine maidens from all over China were led through the gates of the Forbidden City to pass before the eyes of the Emperor.

'Tung Chih has never been willing to rise early, but today he was up before the eunuchs,' Nuharoo told me.

I wasn't sure if I should take this as good news. His visits to the brothels haunted me. With Doctor Sun Pao-tien's help, Tung Chih seemed to have brought the disease under control. But no one was sure that he was completely cured.

Tung Chih would be given the liberty to do whatever he liked with his private life now that he had officially ascended to the throne. For him, marriage equaled freedom.

'Tung Chih's mischief is due to his boredom,' Nuharoo said. 'Otherwise, how can you explain his academic achievement?'

I wondered whether Tung Chih's tutors had been telling the truth about his academic progress. Nuharoo would immediately fire a tutor if he dared to report any failure. I had tested the tutors on Tung Chih's real abilities by suggesting that he take the national civil service examination. When the grand tutors became nervous and avoided all further discussion of the subject, I knew the truth.

'Tung Chih needs to be given responsibility in order to mature,' Prince Kung advised.

I felt that that was the only conceivable alternative. Yet I had my concerns. Tung Chih's taking up the throne would mean my giving up power. Although I had long looked forward to my retirement, I suspected that it would not be Tung Chih but the court and Prince Kung who would take over what I now held.

Nuharoo was eager to have me retire too. She said that she longed for my companionship: 'We will have so much to share, especially when the grandchildren arrive.' Would she feel safer after I stepped down? Or had she other intentions? Tung Chih's being in control would mean that Nuharoo would have more influence over his decisions. Hadn't I learned that she was never what she appeared to be?

I decided to comply with the court's proposal, not because I believed that Tung Chih was ready, but because it was time for him to take charge of his life. As Sun Tzu's *Art of War* put it, 'One will never know how to fight a war unless one fights a war.'

On August 25, 1872, the selection of Imperial consorts was completed. Tung Chih was barely seventeen years old.

Nuharoo and I celebrated our 'ease into retirement.' We would be called the Grand Dowager Empresses, although she was only thirty-seven and I almost thirty-eight.

The new Empress-select was a cat-eyed eighteen-year-old beauty named Alute. She was the daughter of a Mongol official of the old stamp. Alute's father was related to a prince who was my husband's distant cousin.

Tung Chih was lucky to have such a girl. The court would not have approved of his choice just because she was beautiful. The reason the court consented to Alute was that the marriage would serve to heal the discord between the Manchu throne and her powerful Mongol clan.

'Although Alute is a Mongolian, she was never allowed to play under the sun or ride horses,' Nuharoo said proudly, since Alute was her choice. 'That is why her skin is so fair and her features delicate.'

I was not overly impressed by Alute. She was shy to the point of being mute. When we were given time to spend together, conversation faltered. She would agree with whatever I said, so I had little sense of who she really was. Nuharoo said that I was being picky. 'As long as our daughter-in-law does what we say, what's the point of learning her thoughts?'

My preference was a seventeen-year-old bright-eyed girl named Foo-cha. While less exotic-looking than Alute, Foo-cha was also highly qualified. She had an oval face, quarter-moon-shaped eyes, and sun-bronzed skin. She was the daughter of a provincial governor and had been privately educated in literature and poetry, which was unusual. Foo-cha was sweet but spirited. When Nuharoo and I asked what she would do if her husband spent too much time dallying with her and ignored his official business, Foo-cha replied, 'I don't know.'

'She should have answered that she would persuade her husband to perform his duty, not his pleasure.' Nuharoo picked up her pen and crossed off Foo-cha's name.

'But isn't honesty what we are looking for?' I argued, knowing that Nuharoo could not be swayed to change her mind.

Tung Chih seemed interested in Foo-cha, but he fell helplessly in love with Alute.

I didn't insist that Tung Chih make Foo-cha his Empress. Foo-cha would become Tung Chih's second wife.

The Imperial wedding was set for October 16. The preparations, especially the purchase of all the ceremonial goods and materials, began under Nuharoo's supervision. As a way of placating me, Nuharoo allowed me to decide on the theme of the wedding and suggested that An-te-hai be in charge of the shopping.

When I told my eunuch of Nuharoo's decision, he was excited. But I warned him, 'It will be an exhausting journey over a great distance in a short period of time.'

'Don't worry, my lady. I will take the Grand Canal.'

I was intrigued by An-te-hai's idea. The Grand Canal was the ancient, eight-hundred-mile-long engineering marvel that linked Tungchow, near the capital, with Hangchow in the south.

'How far will you travel by the canal?' I asked.

'To its end, Hangchow,' An-te-hai replied. 'It will be a dream come true! The amount I am being asked to purchase will require a fleet of ships, perhaps as grand as Cheng Ho's! The chief eunuch of the celestial Ch'ing Dynasty will get to be the Grand Navigator! Oh, I can't even begin to imagine the trip! I'll stop at Nanking to shop for the best silk. I will pay my respects at Cheng Ho's burial site. My lady, you have just made me the happiest man on earth!'

I had no idea that my favorite would never return.

The events surrounding An-te-hai's death would remain a mystery. But clearly it was my enemies' revenge. My only comfort was that for one moment An-te-hai had been completely happy. I didn't realize how much I loved and needed him until he was gone. Many years later I would conclude that maybe it was not all bad for him. Although he had my blessing and great wealth, he was sick of living in a eunuch's body.

9

In the mornings I found myself looking forward to the sound of An-te-hai's footsteps in the courtyard, and then his delightful face appearing in my mirror. In the evenings I expected his shadow on my mosquito net and his voice humming the tunes of my favorite opera.

No one told me how my favorite died. The report, dated two weeks before I received it, was sent by Governor Ting of Shantung province and stated that An-te-hai was arrested and prosecuted for violating provincial law. In the report Ting asked for permission to discipline the eunuch, but did not mention the measures he would take.

I requested that An-te-hai be sent back to Peking for me to discipline. But Governor Ting claimed that my messenger didn't reach him in time.

There was no doubt in my mind that Governor Ting knew An-te-hai's background. Ting must have had powerful backing or he wouldn't have had the courage to challenge me.

As it turned out, all evidence pointed to three people: Prince Kung, Nuharoo and Tung Chih.

The day An-te-hai died, I gave up on Tung Chih, for I realized the depth of my son's disaffection toward me.

*   *   *

I was expected to forget An-te-hai. 'After all, he was only a eunuch,' everyone said. If I were a dog, I would have barked at Prince Kung, who sent me invitations to banquets held by foreign embassies; at Nuharoo, who pleaded with me to join her at operas; and at my son, who sent me a basket of fruit picked with his own hands in the Imperial fruit garden.

My heart was shattered, and the pieces were pickled in sadness. When I lay in bed, the darkness was impossible to penetrate. I would picture white pigeons circling my roof and An-te-hai's voice gently calling me.

During my own investigation, I tried to find evidence that would exonerate Tung Chih. When I could not deny the facts, I only hoped that my son had been manipulated by others and so was not truly culpable.

'I want to know exactly where, when and how my favorite died,' I told Li Lien-ying, now An-te-hai's successor. 'I want to know An-te-hai's side of the story and his last wishes.'

No one was willing to come forward. 'No one in the palace or the court will speak for An-te-hai, and no one is willing to serve as his witness,' Li Lien-ying reported.

I sent for Yung Lu, who came as fast as he could from the northern provinces. When he entered the hall of my palace, I ran to him and almost fell on my knees.

He helped me to a chair and waited until I stopped weeping. He gently asked if I was sure that An-te-hai was blameless. I asked Yung Lu what he meant. He replied that during the voyage south An-te-hai's behavior was, if not criminal, certainly out of the ordinary.

'Why are you siding with my enemies?'

'I judge only based on facts, Your Majesty.' Yung Lu stood firm. 'If you want me to find out the truth, you have to be willing to accept it.'

I took a deep breath and said, 'I am listening.'

'Forgive me, Your Majesty, but An-te-hai might not have been the person you thought you knew.'

'You have no right to . . .' Again I began to cry. 'You didn't know An-te-hai, Yung Lu! He might have been a eunuch, but he was a true man at heart. I have never known a person who loved life more than An-te-hai did. If you had known his stories, his dreams, his poems, his love of opera, his suffering, you would have understood the man.'

Yung Lu looked skeptical.

'An-te-hai was an expert in court etiquette and dynastic laws,' I continued. 'He would never have violated them. He knew the consequences. Are you telling me that he asked to die?'

'Look at the facts, please, and then ask how they tell otherwise,' Yung Lu said quietly. 'An-te-hai did something he shouldn't have. I am sure you're right that he knew the consequences. In fact, he must have contemplated the result of his action before committing himself to it. This makes the case complicated. You can't deny that An-te-hai offered his enemy a chance to eliminate him.' Yung Lu looked intensely at me. 'Why did he make himself a target?'

I felt lost and shook my head.

Yung Lu requested permission to assemble a team of professional investigators. Within a month, a detailed report was presented to me. Besides Governor Ting, the witnesses included An-te-hai's fellow eunuchs, boatmen, shop owners, dressmakers, local artists and prostitutes.

The weather had been favorable when An-te-hai sailed down the Grand Canal. The eunuch accomplished his mission at the factories in Nanking, where the silks and brocades were woven for the upcoming Imperial wedding.

An-te-hai also inspected the progress of the gowns Nuharoo and I had ordered, as well as those for Tung Chih and his new wives and concubines. An-te-hai then visited the grave of his hero, the Ming navigator Cheng Ho. I could only imagine his excitement.

I vividly remembered the moment An-te-hai came to bid me farewell. He was dressed in a splendid floor-length green satin robe with a pattern of ocean waves. He looked handsome and full of energy. I had great hope that this might be a new beginning for him.

Only a few months before, An-te-hai had gotten married. It was the talk of Peking. For the eunuch population, An-te-hai set an example of hope that they, too, might be redeemed from their status. Mentally, marriage might somehow reinstate their manhood and bring them peace. But things had not gone well.

An-te-hai moved away from the eunuchs' quarters to live with his four wives and concubines. Both he and I hoped that his new companions would lift his spirits. He could have had maidens from good families, since he was offering a fortune in dowries, but he purchased women from brothels. I suppose he thought they would share an understanding of suffering and might better accept, or at least be sympathetic to, what he couldn't provide as a husband. An-te-hai purposely avoided picking the pretty women. He looked especially for those who had survived the abuse of men. Wife number one was a twenty-six-year-old who was very ill and had been left to die in her brothel.

It was difficult to compliment An-te-hai's ladies when he brought them to me. They looked like sisters, and their facial expressions were dull. They snatched cookies from the tray and loudly slurped their tea.

A month or so after An-te-hai's wedding, he moved back to the Forbidden City. The chief eunuch made no mention of his life at home. But everyone except me seemed to know exactly what had happened. From Li Lien-ying I learned that An-te-hai's wives had failed to meet his expectations. The women were rude, loud and unreasonably demanding. They took pleasure in ridiculing his shortcomings. One of them ran away to have an affair with a previous client. When An-te-hai found out, he went after the wife and beat her almost to death.

On the day An-te-hai departed on his buying trip, his recent troubles seemed a distant memory. But still I worried for him. The journey was long, the undertaking huge.

'Be happy for me, my lady,' he reassured me. 'I feel like a fish going back to its home spring.'

'It's a three-month trip. Maybe you can start looking again for a wife,' I teased.

'A decent one this time. I'll take your advice and bring back a girl from a good family.'

We parted at the port on the Grand Canal where a procession of junks waited. An-te-hai stood on one of the two large dragon barges, decorated with a flying dragon and phoenix. I was sure with such a presentation local authorities would be awestruck. They would be eager to answer An-te-hai's requests or offer their protection.

'Come back for your birthday, An-te-hai.' I waved as he boarded.

My favorite one smiled. A brilliant smile. The last one.

My enemies described An-te-hai's procession as an 'extravaganza.' The eunuch was said to be drunk all the time. 'He hired musicians and he dressed in dragon robes like an

72

emperor,' Governor Ting's report read. 'Dancing to the sound of pipes and cymbals, An-te-hai received the congratulations of his retinue. His behavior was illegal and marked by folly.'

The court echoed, 'The law says that the punishment for any eunuch who travels outside Peking is death.' They had forgotten that this was not An-te-hai's first trip. Over a decade earlier, as a sixteen-year-old, An-te-hai traveled alone from Jehol to Peking on a secret mission to reach Prince Kung. He was not punished but honored for heroism.

No one seemed to hear my argument. An-te-hai had behaved foolishly, had even broken the law. But the punishment did not fit the crime, especially since it had been carried out against my express wishes. It was clear that the court was trying to justify Governor Ting's crime. What enraged me was how well constructed the plot was. I was provided with just enough specific information to hint at its outlines, but still I was helpless.

An-te-hai was beheaded on September 25, 1872. He was thirty years old. There was no way that I could have prevented the murder, because my enemies meant it to be a prelude to my own death.

I could have ordered Governor Ting's punishment. I could have removed him from his post or ordered his beheading. But I knew that it would be a mistake – I would fall right into my enemies' trap. If An-te-hai were beside me, he would have advised, 'My lady, what you are up against is not only the governorship and the court, but also the nation and the culture.'

I wanted to confront Prince Kung. I couldn't prove his involvement, but I knew he supported An-te-hai's murder. My relationship with Prince Kung was beyond saving. By getting rid of An-te-hai, he let me know that he was capable of complete domination.

Nuharoo didn't want to discuss the death of my eunuch. When I went to her palace, her attendants pretended not to hear me at the gate. It only confirmed to me that Nuharoo was guilty. I could accept her dislike of An-te-hai, but I could not forgive her for taking part in murdering him.

Tung Chih didn't bother to hide his pleasure that An-te-hai was gone. He seemed confused by my sadness and concluded that An-te-hai was exactly who he thought he was – my secret lover. Tung Chih clumsily kicked over the altar I had placed in a room set aside to mourn An-te-hai.

It was through the confession of a local musician whom An-te-hai had hired during his trip that the deeper and darker reasons behind his death began to reveal themselves.

'One night An-te-hai asked us to play our instruments louder,' the musician's account read.

It was already past midnight. I was afraid of attracting the local authorities' attention, so I begged him to let us stop. But the chief eunuch insisted that we carry on, and we obeyed. Our barges were brightly lit, and the junks were decorated with colorful lanterns. It was like a festival. We often traveled on the water after dark, and villagers would follow us for miles on the shore. Some of the locals were invited on board to join the party. We drank until dawn. As I had predicted, the authorities interfered. At first An-te-hai succeeded in getting them to back off. He pointed up at the yellow flag flying from our barge, which had a blackbird on it, and told the officer to count its legs. The bird had three legs. 'You don't offend this bird, because it represents the Emperor,' An-te-hai said to him.

An-te-hai liked my music and we became friends. He told me how miserable he had been. I was shocked when he said that he was looking for a way to end his life. I thought he was drunk, so I didn't take his words seriously. How can anyone believe that the most powerful eunuch of our time was suffering? But before long I believed him, because I noticed that he deliberately invited trouble. It got me scared. It was lucky that I quit the day before Governor Ting showed up. I still don't understand why An-te-hai would throw away his good life.

Maybe An-te-hai meant to take his own life; maybe he decided that enough was enough. I should have known that he was braver than anyone else. His life was like grand opera, and he was Cheng Ho's reincarnation.

It was after midnight and every sound in the Forbidden City courtyard had faded. I lit An-te-hai's favorite jasmine-scented candles and read him a poem I composed.

How fair the lakes and hills of the south,
With plains extending like a golden strand.
How oft, wine cup in hand, have you been here
To make us linger, drunk though we appear.

By Lily Pond new-lit lamps are bright,
You play the Water Melody at night.
When I come back, the wind goes down, the bright moon
*   paves*
With emerald grass the river waves.

10

FOLLOWING TUNG CHIH's wedding, Nuharoo and I ordered the astrologers to choose an auspicious date for the Emperor's assumption of power. The stars pointed to February 23, 1873. Although Tung Chih had already taken up his duties, mounting the throne was not considered official until elaborate, lengthy ceremonies were completed. They could take months: all the senior clansmen had to be present, and all would have to visit ancestral temples and perform the proper altar rituals. Tung Chih had to ask the spirits for their permission, and for their blessing and protection.

Not long after his investiture, the Tsungli Yamen, the Board of Foreign Affairs, received a note from the ambassadors of several foreign nations asking for an audience. The board had gotten such requests before, but it had always offered Tung Chih's youth as a reason to deny them. Now Tung Chih consented to the request. With Prince Kung's help, he rehearsed the etiquette thoroughly.

On June 29, 1873, my son received the ambassadors of Japan, Great Britain, France, Russia, the United States and the Netherlands. The guests gathered at nine in the morning and were led to the Pavilion of Violet Light, a large raised building where Tung Chih sat upon his throne.

I was nervous because it was my son's first appearance before the world. I had no idea how he would be challenged, and hoped that he would make a strong impression. I told him that China couldn't afford another misunderstanding.

I would not attend the event, but I did what a mother could: I made sure that my son had a good breakfast and took care of the details of his dress – checking the buttons on his dragon robe, the jewels on his hat, the laces on his ornaments. After what he had done to An-te-hai, I had sworn to withhold all affection from Tung Chih, but I was unable to stick to my words. I could not unlove my son.

A few days later, Prince Kung sent me a copy of a foreign publication called *The Peking Gazette*. It let me know that Tung Chih had done well: 'The ministers have admitted that divine virtue certainly emanated from the Emperor, hence the fear and trembling they felt even when they did not look upon His Majesty.'

I can now retire was the thought that came to mind. I would leave the business of the court to others, giving me time for private pleasures of which I'd only been able to dream. Gardening and opera were two interests that I planned to pursue. In particular, I had become curious about cultivating vegetables. My desire to grow tomatoes and cabbages had brought a sour face to the Imperial minister of gardens, but I would try again. Opera had always been my special delight, and perhaps I would take voice lessons so that I could sing my favorite songs. And of course I dreamed of grandchildren: on a special visit to Alute and Foo-cha, I promised my daughters-in-law promotions in rank if they succeeded. I had missed raising Tung Chih as a baby and wanted a new opportunity.

When I sat down to do paintings for my son, I found myself trying out different subjects. Besides flowers and birds, I painted fish in a pond, squirrels playing in trees, deer standing in broad fields. Some of my best pictures I selected to be embroidered. 'For my grandchildren,' I said to the royal tailors.

My son wanted to begin restoring my former garden home, Yuan Ming Yuan, which had been burned down by the foreigners nine years before. If I hadn't been concerned about the cost, I would have been thrilled. 'Yuan Ming Yuan was the symbol of China's pride and might,' my son insisted. 'Mother, it will be my gift for your fortieth birthday.'

I told him that I could not afford to accept such a gift, but he said that he would manage the cost.

'Where will the funds come from?' I asked.

'Uncle Prince Kung has already contributed twenty thousand taels,' my son replied excitedly. 'Friends, relatives, ministers and other officials are expected to follow. Mother, for once just try to enjoy life.'

It had been nine years since I last visited Yuan Ming Yuan. The place had been further wrecked by wind, weather, scavengers and thieves. Man-tall weeds covered the entire area. As I stood by the broken stone pillars, I could hear the creaking sound of carriage wheels and the footfalls of eunuchs and remembered the day we barely escaped the advancing foreign armies.

I had never told Tung Chih that Yuan Ming Yuan was the place where he was conceived. In that one moment I had it all – Emperor Hsien Feng's only desire was to please me. Brief as it was, it had been real, and it had come at the time of my greatest despair. I had spent everything I had to bribe Chief Eunuch Shim to get a single night with His Majesty. When Hsien Feng ridiculed me, I risked my life to speak to him openly and honestly. It had been my boldness that had gained his respect, and then his adoration. I remembered Hsien Feng's voice gently calling me 'my Orchid.' I remembered his tireless desire for me in bed, everywhere, and mine for him. The happiness we both felt. The tears that came in the middle of our lovemaking. His eunuchs were terrified that His Majesty would disappear during the night, while my eunuchs waited by the gate to receive him. As the 'lady of the night' I was supposed to be prepared like a plate of food offered to His Majesty, but His Majesty offered himself to me. He was thrilled by his own love.

Later, when Hsien Feng took up with other ladies, I experienced something close to death. It was impossible to go on living, yet I couldn't take my own life because Tung Chih was inside me.

The first place Tung Chih wanted to restore was the palace where I had spent most of my time living with Hsien Feng. I thanked Tung Chih and asked how he came to know that the palace was special to me. 'Mother,' he replied, smiling, 'when you are quiet about something, I know that is what you care about the most.'

I never doubted Tung Chih's motives. I didn't know that the true reason my son was so eager to rebuild Yuan Ming Yuan was to get me away from him so that he could continue his secret life, which would soon destroy him.

The royal counselors encouraged Tung Chih because they were eager for me to retire. They resented taking my orders and looked forward to governing without my interference. With their approval, Tung Chih ordered the restoration to begin even before the funding was in place. The project was plagued by trouble from the start. When the chief lumber supplier was caught embezzling, the funding stopped. It was the beginning of a never-ending nightmare.

A local official wrote an indignant letter to the court accusing Tung Chih of caving in to my greed. He described the restoration of Yuan Ming Yuan as a misuse of national funds. 'The dynasty before ours, the Ming, was one of China's longest, lasting sixteen rulers,' the official pointed out. 'But later Ming emperors wasted their energies on pleasure. By the end of the sixteenth century, the Ming Dynasty had lapsed into a coma, waiting to be pushed aside. The treasury was empty, taxes became impossible, and the traditional signs of misrule – flood, drought and famine – were everywhere. People transferred their loyalty to a new leader because the dynasty had forfeited the mandate of Heaven.'

The court didn't need a minor functionary to remind them that the country was still ravaged by the recent Taiping rebellion and that the Moslem uprisings in the west had not yet been suppressed. However, they rebuked the official for 'obstructing the Emperor's filial duty to his mother.' Tung Chih was determined to see his goal realized, but after a year and a great deal of expense, he was pressured by Prince Kung to abandon the project.

For years I would be blamed for whatever happened at Yuan Ming Yuan, but I was no longer in a position to advise Tung Chih – I was officially retired. What puzzled me was Prince Kung's change of mind. It was he who first supported the restoration by giving a donation to begin construction, but now he was among those who begged Tung Chih to call off the project.

Throwing a temper tantrum, Tung Chih accused his uncle of using disrespectful language and demoted him. It was Nuharoo who persuaded Tung Chih to reinstate his uncle's position a few weeks later.

I stayed away because I felt that Tung Chih needed to learn how to be an emperor. It had been too easy for him to order others around without ever suffering.

11

ON A WARM DAY in the summer of 1874, I watched my eunuch Li Lien-ying cutting gardenias in my garden. He removed and discarded flower buds and side shoots, then sliced the stems into three-inch pieces, carefully making the cut below a node. 'New roots will form at this point,' he explained as he inserted the cuttings into containers. 'By next spring the plants should be ready to go out in the garden.' A month later the cuttings failed to send out any new leaves.

To test if the roots were growing, Li Lien-ying gently pulled on a cutting. He felt no resistance, which indicated that roots were not forming. He told himself to be patient and wait for a few more days. 'I have been doing this for years,' he said to me. 'It is how I've patched up the old gardenia gardens.' But the cuttings began to wilt and eventually died. The eunuch believed that it was Heaven's sign that something terrible was going to happen.

'Nothing will happen,' the master gardener said to Li. 'It could be your mishandling. Maybe the water was contaminated by an animal's urine, or there were insects hidden in the moss. In any case, the plants died of too much stress.'

I couldn't help but think of my son. He had been like a houseplant, protected until now from the rigors and uncertainties of the garden.

Tung Chih caught a cold that didn't go away for months. He had developed a fever, and by autumn his body was very weak.

'Tung Chih needs to go outdoors and exercise,' Prince Kung urged.

My son's other uncles, Prince Ts'eng and Prince Ch'un, assumed that Tung Chih's nightly dissipations had begun taking a toll on his health. When Doctor Sun Pao-tien requested a meeting to discuss Tung Chih's real condition, he was rebuffed.

I couldn't bear the sight of Tung Chih in a sickbed. It reminded me of his father's dying days. I summoned Alute and Foo-cha and the other wives, and asked them, as they knelt before me, if they had any idea what was wrong with their husband.

Their revelation shocked me: Tung Chih had never quit going to the brothels. 'His Majesty prefers flowers in the wild,' Foo-cha complained.

Alute resented my questioning. I explained that I didn't mean to intrude or offend and that I was not interested in disrupting her privacy.

Eyebrows twisted into the shape of two flying swords, Alute said that as the Empress of China she had the right not to answer. 'It's between Tung Chih and me,' she insisted. Her white, porcelain-smooth skin turned pink.

I tried not to show my irritation. I told her that I only meant to help.

'I am not doubting your motives,' Alute said to me. 'It's just . . . I don't feel lesser in status.'

I was confused. 'What are you talking about? Who made you feel "lesser in status"?'

Alute nodded at the other wives. 'Everybody here is afraid of speaking her thoughts in front of you, but I am going to. Dowager Empress, Tung Chih is *your* responsibility, not ours.'

I was offended. 'Alute, you have no right to speak for the others.'

'I'll speak for myself, then. As His Majesty's mother, have you asked your son about what is wrong with him?'

'I wouldn't come to you for help if I could talk to him myself.'

'There must be a reason he abandoned the Forbidden City for a whorehouse.'

'You are angry, Alute. You really think it is my fault?'

'Yes, I do.'

'Facts, Alute.'

The girl bit her lip, then said, 'Emperor Tung Chih was fine with me until you told him to go to Foo-cha. You couldn't bear the idea that he would have a child with me and not with Foo-cha. That was how Tung Chih got sick of all of us, because he was sick of you!'

Alute may have had a point, but I rejected it because of her rudeness. 'Alute, how dare you! You have no right to disrespect me.'

'But the child in my belly does!'

I was dumbfounded. I asked Alute to repeat what she had said.

'I am pregnant,' she announced proudly.

'Oh, Alute!' I was thrilled. 'Why didn't you tell me? Congratulations! Rise! Rise! Well, I must go to share this wonderful news with Nuharoo! We are going to have a grandchild!'

'Not yet, Your Majesty.' Alute stopped me. 'Until Tung Chih returns to me, I am not sure I will have the strength to carry the pregnancy.'

'Tung Chih is . . .' I tried to find words to comfort her. 'It hurts when you know that he is with other ladies. Believe me, Alute, I know how that feels.'

'I hate what you are saying.' Alute began to cry.

'Well,' I said, feeling guilty, 'be glad that you have Tung Chih's child.'

'It's not up to you or me to decide whether the child will come into the world. My body and soul are in so much pain that I can feel it seeking revenge. I am afraid that something unexpected is going to happen.'

'It is Heaven's will that you have been given a child, Alute. The dragon seed will survive no matter what.'

Without asking permission, Alute walked to the window and stood with her back to me. Outside, the giant oak trees were bare.

'The oak nuts have been dropping everywhere,' Alute said, shaking her head. 'It's hard to walk without stepping on them. It is a bad omen. What am I going to do? I am not made to bear misery.'

'Alute,' I said gently, 'I am sure nothing is wrong. You are just tired, that's all.'

She ignored me, continuing to face the window. Her voice grew thin and distant. 'It gets louder. I hear the sound of nuts dropping and cracking on the ground day and night.'

I stared at the back of my daughter-in-law. Her silky black hair was elaborately braided and fastened onto a plate. Pink floral hairpins studded with diamonds glinted in the light. Suddenly I understood why she was Tung Chih's first choice: like him, she had her own mind.

*   *   *

85

It was on a morning in early winter that Doctor Sun Pao-tien broke the news that my son was not going to live.

I trembled in front of the doctor like a young tree in a storm. My mind's eye saw red lanterns floating down from the ceiling.

I tried to understand the doctor, but I couldn't. He was explaining Tung Chih's condition, but it sounded as if he were speaking a foreign language. Then I must have passed out. When I came to, Li Lien-ying was in front of me. He was following the doctor's instructions, pressing his thumb between my nose and the top of my upper lip. I tried to push him away, but I had no strength.

'Tung Chih has been visited by the heavenly flowers,' I finally heard him say.

'Tell Doctor Sun Pao-tien' – I drew in my breath and cried – 'if there is any mistake, I won't hesitate to punish him!'

After lunch the doctor came again. Getting down on his knees, he began his report. 'His Majesty's condition is complicated. I can't be sure which entered his body first, smallpox or venereal disease. At any rate, it's a deadly situation, beyond my power to cure or even control it.'

The doctor confessed that it had been a struggle for him to come forward with the truth. His medical team had been accused of bringing His Majesty bad luck. Everyone had been trying to keep Tung Chih's sickness a secret.

I asked the doctor to forgive me and promised that I would control my emotions.

An effort was made to stabilize Tung Chih's condition. In December of 1874, the spots on his body dried out and his fever abated. The palaces celebrated the signs of recovery. But it was premature. A few days later, Tung Chih's fever returned, and it persisted.

I can't recall how I passed my days. My mind was capable of only one thought: to save my son. I refused to believe that Tung Chih would die. Sun Pao-tien suggested that I seek out Western doctors for a second opinion. 'They have the tools to take His Majesty's body fluid and blood samples,' he whispered, knowing that he was not supposed to make the suggestion. 'However, I doubt their diagnosis will be different.'

The court rejected my request for Western doctors, fearing that foreigners would take advantage of Tung Chih's condition and see an opportunity to invade.

I lay beside my feverish son. I listened to the sound of his labored breathing. His cheeks burned. In his waking hours he quietly whimpered and moaned.

Tung Chih requested that Nuharoo and I resume the regency. I refused at first, because I knew I wouldn't be able to concentrate on court matters. But Tung Chih insisted. When I read his decree to the nation, I realized what my help would mean to him.

The ink handwriting on rice paper was my son's last calligraphy. Of all things, I was saddened by the fact that my grandchild would never see the way his father held the brush pen.

'I beg the two Empresses to have pity on my state and allow me to take care of myself,' Tung Chih's edict read. 'In looking after the affairs of state for a time, the Empresses will crown their great goodness toward me and I will show them everlasting gratitude.'

Every day after an audience, I went to sit with Tung Chih. I spoke with Doctor Sun Pao-tien and Tung Chih's attendants. I examined the growing pustules on my son's skin and wished that they were on my own body. I begged

87

for Heaven's mercy and prayed: 'Please do not be too cruel to a mother.'

I ordered that no one was to disturb Tung Chih's rest, but the doctor advised that I let my son see anyone he wished. 'His Majesty might never have the chance again.'

I complied. I sat by my son and made sure no one would exhaust him.

Alute refused to come when Tung Chih sent for her. She said that she would not enter the room unless I wasn't there.

I yielded.

It was two in the morning when my son opened his eyes. Although his cheeks were still hot, he was in good spirits. He asked me to sit by his side. I helped prop him up against the pillows. I begged him to let me feed him a little porridge. He shook his head.

'Let's have some fun together before I die.' He managed a bright smile.

I broke down and told him that I didn't know what fun he was talking about. As far as I was concerned, my happiness would end if he died.

Tung Chih held my hand and squeezed it. 'I miss the moon,' he said. 'Would you help me get out to the courtyard?'

I wrapped a blanket over his shoulders and helped him out of bed. Just getting dressed was an effort and he was soon out of breath.

With an arm on my shoulders, he stepped into the courtyard.

'What a beautiful night,' he sighed.

'It's too cold, Tung Chih!' I said. 'Let's go back in.'

'Stay for just a moment, Mother. I am enjoying myself.'

With a moonlit background the trees and bushes looked like black paper cutouts.

I looked at my son and wept. The moonlight bleached his face, making him look like a stone sculpture.

'Remember the time when you tried to teach me poetry, Mother? I was hopeless.'

'Yes, of course. It was too much for you. It would be too much for any child.'

'The truth is that I was not inspired. My teachers said I had to feel it first and then describe it.' Tung Chih laughed a weak laugh. 'I was writing but wasn't feeling anything. Believe it or not, since my days are numbered, I have been full of inspiration.'

'Stop it, Tung Chih.'

'Mother, I have a poem for you, right here.' He pointed at his head. 'May I recite?'

'I don't want to hear it.'

'Mother, you will like it. It is called "To a Love."'

'No, I won't listen.'

Softly, Tung Chih began:

Parting but to journey back in lingering dreams
Along the winding corridor of filigree and the curving
    balustrade,
In the courtyard only the spring moon is full of sympathy,
For we who parted shining still upon the fallen flowers.

12

O N THE MORNING of January 12, 1875, my son died.
The Hall of Spiritual Nurturing was filled with
freshly cut winter plum flowers, their waxy little petals
and bare stems standing elegantly in vases. The flowers
were Tung Chih's favorite. He had once dreamed of picking
them in the snow, something he was never allowed to do. I
was in my mourning gown, embroidered with the same
winter plum flowers, which I had stayed up stitching late
into the night. Tung Chih's face was turned toward the
south, and he was arrayed in robes patterned with the
symbols of longevity. He was nineteen years old and had
been Emperor since 1861. He had ruled for under two
years.

I sat by Tung Chih's casket while craftsmen finished the
ironwork. Painters leaned over the structure applying their
final touches. The casket was covered with carved and
painted golden dragons.

I smoothed my child's cold cheeks with my fingers.
Etiquette did not allow me to embrace or kiss him. Tung
Chih died with a string of fever blisters around his mouth.
During his last two weeks the blisters had popped every-
where, rotting his body from the inside. Sores had covered

his tongue and gums, so many that he could not swallow. There had not been an uninfected spot left on his skin. Pustules had grown between his fingers and toes, oozing pus. The black medicinal paste applied by Sun Pao-tien had made him look grotesque.

Every day for those last weeks I had cleaned my son, and every day I discovered a new outbreak of pox. The new sprouted on top of the old. His hands and feet looked like ginger roots.

When it became too much to bear, I ran out of the room and my knees hit the ground. I could not pick myself up. Li Lien-ying reminded me that I hadn't been eating.

In the afternoons Li Lien-ying would chase after me with a bowl of chicken soup in his hands. He bobbed and weaved with the bowl held high because I had already kicked several of his bowls.

My hands had developed blisters. I had been doing too much work, cutting up hens, ducks, fish and snakes and offering them at sacrificial altars. I looked up at the sky and cried, 'The hungry demons have been well fed. By now they are so full they should leave my son alone!'

Incense smoke made the Forbidden City look like it was on fire. My tears ran like a leaking fountain. Doctor Sun Pao-tien said it would be best if I no longer consulted him. I went to a lama, who advised that I concentrate on Tung Chih's next life. 'The eternal robe and coffin would be a proper start.' The lama implied that I had not offered the gods my total submission. Instead of helping my son, I was only deepening his trouble.

I thought about taking my own life to accompany my son. As I looked for a way, I realized that I was being followed. Eunuchs and maids hovered about me. Their usual placid expressions were anxious. They whispered behind my back. Whenever I got out of bed late at night, a chorus of coughing would erupt among the eunuchs.

My chef hid the kitchen knives and lye, my ladies in waiting removed all ropes. When I ordered Li Lien-ying to get opium, he brought back Doctor Sun Pao-tien. The Imperial Guards blocked me when I tried to exit the gate of the Forbidden City. When I threatened punishment, they said that Yung Lu had issued an order to keep me from harm.

My son had died in my arms as the sun was rising. The gardenia bushes in the courtyard were victims of a late killing frost, their leaves shriveled and black. Squirrels had stopped jumping from tree to tree. They sat on branches chewing nuts and making loud chattering noises. Feathers dropped from the sky when a flock of wild geese flew by overhead.

I remembered holding Tung Chih and feeling his heartbeat grow weak. I remembered falling asleep in a sitting position, so I didn't know exactly when his heart had stopped beating.

Nuharoo's chief eunuch brought the message that his lady was too grief-stricken to leave her palace.

The court had begun preparations for the memorial ceremony. Messengers were sent so the provincial governors could begin their journey to the capital.

After the doctor and his team withdrew, the Forbidden City became quiet. The sound of footsteps disappeared, as well as the bitter smell of Tung Chih's herbal medicines.

The eunuchs and maids wrapped all the living quarters with white silk cloth. The funeral dresses once worn for my husband were brought out, cleaned and pressed, made ready to be worn for his son.

Tung Chih was removed for the last time from his bed. I helped to change him. His eternal robe was made of golden thread. My boy looked like a sleeping doll with stiff limbs. I washed his face with cotton balls. I didn't like the way the royal makeup artist had done his face, layer upon layer of paint, with a wax coating to seal the makeup. My son looked unrecognizable; his skin had the shine of leather.

Finally I was left alone with Tung Chih. I touched his makeup. I washed off the layers of paint. His skin was once again itself, although scarred with the pox. I bent over and kissed his forehead, eyes, nose, cheeks and lips. I wiped cottonseed oil over his face, starting with his forehead. I tried to keep my hand from trembling by pressing against the arm of my chair. I painted his lips and cheeks with a touch of rouge to make him look the way I remembered him. I left the rest of his features untouched.

Tung Chih had a beautiful full forehead. His eyebrows had just grown into their permanent shape like two fine brushstrokes. When he was a young boy, the color of his eyebrows had been so light it looked as if he had no eyebrows at all. Nuharoo was never satisfied with the makeup Tung Chih usually wore for audiences. Especially his eyebrows. Many times he arrived late at court because Nuharoo insisted on doing his face all over again.

Tung Chih's bright eyes had been the joy of my life. Like mine, they were single-lidded and almond-shaped. In my mother's opinion, his best feature was his straight nose. It went well with his high cheekbones, which were characteristic of a Manchu. His lips were full and sensuous. In death, he was still handsome.

I followed the lama's advice and tried to treat my son's death as a natural event of life. But remorse had begun its tortuous path. My heart was soaked in its own poison.

Tung Chih's coffin was as big as his father's. It would be borne on the shoulders of 160 men. When Li Lien-ying told me that it was time to bid farewell, I stood only to fall back on my knees. Li held my arms and I rose like a hundred-year-old crone. We moved toward the coffin, where I would take a last look at my son.

Li Lien-ying asked if Tung Chih would like to take his favorite old toy, a paper model of Peking, with him. The inner circle of the city would stay with him; the outer city would be left for the paper-burning ceremony, to help send Tung Chih's spirit on its way.

'Yes,' I said.

By the coffin, the eunuch asked for my son's forgiveness for having to take the inner city apart so it would fit. 'Here is your Ladder Lane,' Li Lien-ying said. 'As Your Majesty can see, it looks like a ladder going upward onto the slope. Here comes Bag Lane and Grout Lane, the streets that we can enter but not go through. And now, on this side, the Soochow lanes. Your Majesty once asked me if the original streets were built by people from the south. They might not have been from Soochow but from Hangchow. Your Majesty didn't have time to bother with the details and small differences, but now time is on your side.'

For a moment my mind flew elsewhere, and Li Lien-ying became An-te-hai. What would An-te-hai say about all this? There had never been a memorial service for him. Few mentioned him after his execution. His wives and con- cubines divided his fortune and soon forgot him. None mourned him. I secretly hired a stone carver who built a tablet for An-te-hai's grave. Because of my status I was never able to visit the site and had no idea what his resting place looked like. It was Tung Chih's misfortune that he never became An-te-hai's friend.

Finishing his packing of the coffin, Li Lien-ying continued to speak to my dead son. 'I never had the chance to tell you what "Horse God's Lane" or "Horse God's Temple" meant. Your ancestors might ask you such questions, and it is important that you are prepared. The early Manchus were people who lived on horseback. Without the help of their horses, there would have been no conquering China. Manchus adore, admire and respect horses. Temples built in Peking honor legendary horses who died in important battles. Maybe in your next life Your Majesty will have the opportunity to visit the lanes and temples honoring horses.'

It was in death that Tung Chih would learn of the city he had lived in. With my eunuch's help I burned the rest of the city, the outer city, for my son's spirit to carry away. The names were copied from the originals: Sweet Water Well Lane, Bitter Water Well Lane, Three-eyed Well Lane, Four-eyed Well Lane, Sheep Mart, Pig Mart, Donkey Mart. The vegetable market stood beside the dynasty's arrow factory, and the military training ground, the Big Fence Place, was filled with paper horses and soldiers.

Also included in the sacrificial burning was the paper shopping area mimicking the Royal Well Lane, Peking's largest, which extended for miles. Li Lien-ying didn't forget the execution site, called the Livestock Market. All this, he believed, would be a necessity for Tung Chih as a ruler in his next life. I ordered that the famous Porcelain Kiln be included, which was the largest bookstore, built in an abandoned kiln. Since my son would have all the time to appreciate the details, we added Dog Tail Lane, Wood-chopper's Lane, and Open Curtain Lane.

It was cold and dark when I returned to my palace. Li Lien-ying tried to close the windows, but I stopped him. 'Leave them open. Tung Chih's spirit might visit.'

The giant pale moon hanging outside above the bare trees brought back memories. I recalled a moment in Jehol when Tung Chih begged me to let him bathe in the hot springs. I refused him because he had a cold. I remembered breathing the fresh air and wishing that I could raise Tung Chih there. We stood among the wild tall bamboo that evening. The leaves danced in the breeze. Thick ivy draped forty or fifty feet down from century-old oaks like Heaven's curtains. The stone-paved ground was bleached by moon-light, as white as it was tonight. The shadowy jasmines on each side of the path looked like frozen ocean waves.

I went to the library looking for material that would help me construct Tung Chih's obituary. A slim book, *Convalescent Home for the Winter Plum Flowers,* caught my eye. It's author was J. Z. Zhen of the early Ch'ing Dynasty. I found myself unable to put the book down once I started reading.

In southern China, especially in Soochow and Hang-chow, a floral winter plum tree has been popular. It has become a subject for famous painters. However, the tree's beauty lies in its sickness: abnormal shapes and bent branches with giant knots and exposed roots were preferred. Straight and healthy trees were considered plain and tasteless. Foliage was trimmed off and the tree reduced to bare trunks.

Once the tree growers understood what their custo-mers wanted, they began to shape the trees. In order to suppress normal growth, the trees were bound like a woman's feet. The branches were braced to form desired shapes. The trees grew sideways and downward. They were considered 'fabulous' and 'elegant' when released.

Winter plum flowers all over China are diseased now, because the growers had invited worms to create knots. The grotesquely shaped branches caused the tree to suffer a slow death, while merchants profited.

One man gathered his family fortune and went to the local nursery. He purchased three hundred pots of diseased winter plums. Turning his house into a convalescent home, the man began to care for the trees. He cut off the braces, destroyed the pots, and planted the trees in the ground. He left the trees alone to grow naturally and covered the soil with rich compost. Although the sickest winter plum didn't survive the disease, the population did.

Tung Chih was like those winter plum trees, I thought, closing the book. Since birth, he had been bent and twisted into a showpiece. I had dreamed of him swimming in the lake near my hometown of Wuhu. I even fancied him riding on the back of a water buffalo like the boys I knew when I was a girl. But Tung Chih was a winter plum that was bound and braced and skewed. His schooling included everything but common sense. He was taught pride but not understanding, revenge but not compassion, and universal wisdom but not truth. Endless ceremonies and audiences drove him to desperation. Tung Chih achieved the desired form, but at the cost of his life. He was deprived of an understanding of himself and the world, robbed of options and opportunities. How could he not have grown sideways?

Flirting with brothel girls might have been Tung Chih's attempt to find out who he was behind the mask of an emperor. Maybe he possessed a hunter's nature and had needed to pursue freedom and adventure. Three thousand concubines competing for his dragon seeds killed the hunter in him. Had I seen things from his point of view, I might have learned of his suffering. After his funeral I discovered more obscene materials in his bedroom. They were hidden inside his pillows, between his sheets, under his bed. The books had the lowest taste and quality. The private world of my son, the Emperor of China.

I remembered my husband once saying to me, 'You come to occupy my bed like an army.' He said it with disgust in his voice. I had participated in forcing the same displeasure on my son, which made his death a true revenge.

I sent Li Lien-ying to invite my daughter-in-law Alute for tea. To my shock, she sent back a message threatening to commit suicide.

I was confused and asked for an explanation.

'I will be entitled to the regency when I give birth to a son,' Alute declared in her return message. 'And I expect you to hand over power. However, I have been told that you will never step down because you live only for that power. I can see no other option but to remove myself from this indecent world. I have decided that my unborn child should go with me.'

I had never taken Alute seriously when she acted like this. I had let it pass when she hadn't bothered to be sweet or humble in front of me. She didn't like my wedding gift, a light green silk-embroidered summer dress. Openly she criticized my taste and insisted on redecorating her entire palace. When I invited her to my favorite opera, *The Peony Pavilion*, she kept her head turned away throughout the performance. She believed that as an Imperial widow I should be ashamed of myself for enjoying a silly romantic opera.

I was displeased, but I left her alone. I thought that if she was this way with me, she would be the same with her eunuchs, her maids and her fellow concubines, who would in turn do her great harm. The Forbidden City was a place where females ganged up on one another. It seemed that Alute took my silence as an invitation for more insults.

Would Alute be capable of ruling the country, assuming my grandchild would be a male and she took over the regency? She seemed to believe that she could handle a national crisis without any training or experience. As an outsider, she saw glamour and glory in my position. I, on the contrary, could see reflections of a double-edged sword. If Alute only demonstrated some aptitude and merit, I would gladly assist her.

Everything Alute did told me that she was spoiled and had no idea of the consequences of her actions. Instead of taking part in her husband's mourning, she spent her days with senior court members, my opponents.

If Alute left me with a choice, I would be able to show her the way. But she couldn't conceive that transferring power would involve contending political factions at court and in the government nationwide. She didn't believe there could be a struggle. Alute let me know that she didn't desire my help and that her distrust of me was solid and final.

How could an innocent girl who didn't know me hate me so much? I was more puzzled than upset. Although Alute was Nuharoo's pick, I didn't think Nuharoo was aware of the depth of Alute's hatred.

I feared this girl Alute, and I worried for my grandchild. The fact that Alute had considered taking her unborn's life scared me. What would she do to China if she were given total power?

I wrote back to Alute after she rebuffed my proposal for a sensible solution between us: 'The ministers, governors and commanders in chief of China would not be willing to serve unless their ruler proved to be worthy of their devotion and lives. It would not be as easy as attending a dinner party, doing embroidery or watching an opera.'

Alute answered me with her suicide.

She left the court an open letter, which she might not have written alone. The language was vague and her metaphor obscure.

'When a bird is dying, its song is sad,' Alute began. 'When a lady is dying, her words are kind. This is the condition in which I find myself today. Once went a girl to her death, and she could not walk erect. A bystander said to her, "Are you afraid?" She replied, "I am." "If you are afraid, why not turn back?" The girl replied, "My fear is a private weakness, but my death is a public duty."'

Did Alute believe that she had a duty to die? I saw it as nothing but a protest and a punishment against me. I had not only lost Tung Chih but his unborn child. No enemy could destroy me more.

Alute's maid said that her mistress was pleased with the decision to end her life. Alute treated the suicide as an event to celebrate. She awarded the servants with money and keepsakes for helping her. The servants were called to witness the suicide act. Alute declared that anyone who dared to disrupt her would be whipped to death. When the morning of the set date arrived, Alute dosed herself with opium and then dressed herself in an eternal robe. The servants were then dismissed. Alute shut herself in her bedroom, and by afternoon she was dead.

The opium Alute took was smuggled into the Forbidden City by her father, who had learned of his daughter's plan. Although he was against it, as a patrician loyalist who had been given a high royal title upon his daughter's marriage, he complied with her wish. He feared that her misbehavior would cost him his own good life. After he had supplied Alute with enough opium to kill her, he wrote to the court that he had nothing to do with his daughter's action.

I summoned the father and asked him if he had said anything to upset Alute. The man replied, 'I told her to stop grating on Your Majesty's nerves.'

I felt sorry for Alute, for she had received no support from her family. More than that, I resented her for killing my unborn grandchild. Then it dawned on me that I had never received confirmation of Alute's pregnancy from any doctor, nor had I seen her belly swell.

Doctor Sun Pao-tien came at my summons. He reported that an examination had never taken place, because Alute had never granted his entrance.

Was it possible that all was staged?

If the pregnancy was false, Alute's suicide would make more sense. She would have ended up being one of scores of Tung Chih's backyard ladies. She would not have been given the role of regent, since she was childless. By accompanying Tung Chih to his grave, she achieved virtue and would be honored. In the meantime, her letter placed the responsibility for her death squarely on me.

Beneath Alute's shy manners was a strong and willful mind, an unquiet character with a monstrous ambition.

My opponents made good use of Alute. It disgusted me to look at her father, who appeared to be harmless. I couldn't forgive a man who would encourage his daughter to kill herself. If this was how Alute was raised, it might be fortunate that she didn't have a child.

In Alute's imagination I had posed a great threat. She might have fantasized about her life as regent, and I was the only obstacle she needed to overcome. The way Alute worded her letter sounded confident. The fact that she had no doubt she was carrying a male child was in itself evidence of a mental disorder.

Grandchild or no grandchild, the possibility would continue to haunt me. What saddened me was that the death of her husband had aroused no sympathy in Alute. If she had truly loved Tung Chih, she wouldn't have murdered his child.

It hurt me to think of the possibility that my son was cheated out of his only love. The thought led me to other possibilities, such as the reasons behind Tung Chih's addiction to whores. Was it because he was denied affection? Tung Chih was no angel, but he was a child who had always been hungry for love.

I tried to stop my thoughts from dwelling on guilt. I told myself that Tung Chih and Alute were once true lovers and that should count and continue to count.

Before spring, an official accused me of 'precipitating the Emperor's relapse.' I paid no attention to this; the idea was ridiculous. What I didn't expect was that the story made its rounds and was picked up and published by a respected English journal. It made me the center of an international scandal – the prime suspect of Emperor Tung Chih's 'murder.'

'The loving Alute was visiting Tung Chih on his sickbed,' the article read. 'She complained about her mother-in-law's interfering and domineering ways, and she was happily looking forward to the day Tung Chih would be well again. It was at that moment the raging Dowager Empress Lady Yehonala entered. She rampaged through the room, seizing Alute by the hair and hitting her while Tung Chih suffered a terrible nervous crisis, which caused the fever to return and eventually to kill him.'

13

I DREAMED OF ice floating on a lake in the midst of its melting, thin and fragile. The ice didn't look like ice but pieces of rice paper. Tung Chih had no idea what southern China's winter looked or felt like. He was used to the solid ice of Peking winters. He was never allowed to skate on the frozen palace lake; instead he watched his cousins play all day long. The most Tung Chih was allowed was to tie straw strings around his shoes so that he could walk on the ice with the help of his eunuchs.

In my childhood memory, winter was always cold and damp. When the northwest wind blew strong against the windows and made the panes rattle as though someone were knocking, Mother would announce that the coldest part of winter had arrived. Because the temperature never really dropped below freezing in the south, few of the houses had heaters.

I remember Mother taking out all of our winter clothes from cases made of sandalwood. We put on thick cotton jackets, hats and scarves, and everyone smelled of sandalwood. When it was cold in the house, people went out into the street to warm themselves under the sun. Unfortunately, most southern winters were sunless. The air was damp and the color of the sky remained gray until the season passed.

Today I woke in a well-heated room. Li Lien-ying was so grateful when I didn't push away my breakfast that he was almost in tears. He served me a southern-style meal: hot porridge with preserved tofu, root vegetables and peanuts, with roasted seaweed and sesame seeds. He told me that I had been ill and had slept around the clock.

I looked up and my neck felt stiff and achy. I noticed that the red lanterns in the room had been changed to white. Thoughts of Tung Chih returned, and my heart suffered a stabbing pain. I pushed to get myself up. My eyes caught a pile of documents lying on the desk.

'What must I know?' I asked.

There was no response. Li Lien-ying looked at me as if he didn't understand. I realized that I was still used to An-te-hai's ways and that Li Lien-ying hadn't yet learned the role of being my eunuch secretary.

'You may brief me, starting with the weather.'

Li Lien-ying was indeed a quick learner. 'The icy wind has been blowing down sandstorms from the desert,' he began, helping me to dress. 'Last night the braziers were lit in the courtyards.'

'Go on.'

'Li Hung-chang moved his army from Chihli on your orders. He has secured the Forbidden City. Governors of the eighteen provinces have hurried to get here, some by carriage and some on horseback. They are entering the gates at this moment. Yung Lu has been notified of the situation and should be here within days.'

I was surprised. 'I did neither the ordering nor the summoning.'

'Empress Nuharoo did.'

'Why didn't she inform me about it?'

'Empress Nuharoo was here several times while you were sleeping,' Li Lien-ying explained. 'Her exact words were "Tung Chih has left no heir, and an emperor has to be chosen."'

'To the Hall of Spiritual Nurturing! Palanquin!' I ordered.

Nuharoo was relieved when she saw me enter the hall. 'Three candidates have been suggested.' She presented me with notes of the day's discussion. 'All members of the Imperial clan are present.'

Although my fatigue persisted, I tried to look as if I had never left the court. I examined the candidates. The first was a two-month-old named P'u-lun, grandson of Emperor Tao Kuang's eldest son – my husband's brother Prince Ts'eng. Since Tung Chih's 'Tsai' generation was followed by the 'P'u' generation, the infant was the only nominee who complied with Imperial family law, which stated that the successor to the throne could not be a member of the same generation as his predecessor.

I quickly dismissed P'u-lun. My reason was that my husband had told me that P'u-lun's grandfather Prince Ts'eng had been adopted from a junior branch of the Imperial family and so was not of the true bloodline. 'We know of no precedent for the grandson of an adopted son to mount the throne,' I said.

The truth behind my rejection was that I had some idea of the kind of man Prince Ts'eng was. While pleasure-seeking had been his hobby, he was a corrupt political radical. He had little respect for me until he learned about my son's death. He knew that I would have the power to choose an heir.

When an advocate of Prince Ts'eng's, a court official, produced a document from the Ming Dynasty's records proving the prince's legitimacy, I reminded the court, 'That particular Ming prince's reign ended in disaster, with the prince himself captured and murdered by the Mongols.'

The next male child in line was Prince Kung's eldest son, Tsai-chen, Tung Chih's former playmate. As hard as I tried, I could not forgive the fact that he had introduced Tung Chih to the brothels. I rejected Tsai-chen by saying, 'The law requires that the living father of an emperor retire into private life, and I don't think the court can function without Prince Kung.'

I wanted to yell at Nuharoo and the court: How could we entrust a playboy with the nation's responsibilities? I would have ordered Tsai-chen's beheading if he were not Prince Kung's son!

The last one in line was Tsai-t'ien, my three-year-old nephew, son of Prince Ch'un, my husband's youngest brother, who was also the husband of my sister, Rong. Although we would be violating the 'no-same-generation' rule if we selected Tsai-t'ien, we had no other option.

In the end, both Nuharoo and I gave our votes to Tsai-t'ien. We let it be known that we would adopt the child if the court were to accept our proposal. In fact, I had already been thinking about adopting Tsai-t'ien. The idea came when I learned that three of my sister's children had died 'accidentally' in their infancy. The deaths were regarded as the work of fate, but I was aware of Rong's mental condition. Prince Ch'un complained about his wife's ongoing deterioration, but no action was taken and Rong was given no treatment. I was concerned for Tsai-t'ien's survival the moment he was born. I had spoken to Rong about putting him up for adoption, but she insisted on caring for the baby herself.

Tsai-t'ien was underweight for his age and his movements appeared wooden. His nurses reported that he would cry through the night, while his mother continued to believe that feeding her child a full meal would kill him.

The child's father encouraged the adoption. 'I am willing to do everything to help my son escape his mother,' Prince Ch'un told me. 'Isn't it enough that three of my sons have died under your sister's care?' When I expressed concern about his own separation from Tsai-t'ien, he said he would be fine, since he had children with his other wives and concubines.

Next the court heard a report on the character and history of the nominee's father. I was not surprised that Prince Ch'un was found to be a man of 'double characters.' I had learned from my husband, Emperor Hsien Feng, that 'brother Ch'un would tremble in every limb and fall into a faint at his father's temper.' And yet he was also 'the big braggart' of the family. Prince Ch'un represented the hardliners of the Manchu clan. While claiming to have no interest in politics, he had been a longtime rival of his own brother Prince Kung.

'My husband can't help but be a man of honesty because his lies are too dumb,' my sister used to say. Prince Ch'un was tireless in telling the world about his philosophy of life. He constantly expressed his disgust of power and wealth. Displayed in his living room was a couplet of his own calligraphy warning his children of how wealth would corrupt, destroy and cause disaster. 'Without power means without danger,' the couplet read. 'And without wealth means without disaster.' Although Ch'un was a prince, he neither held significant titles nor performed court duties. Nevertheless, he had not been shy about demanding increases in his annual taels. He even criticized Prince Kung, complaining about his brother's compensation for hosting parties for foreign diplomats.

Despite all that, and with Yung Lu working in the background to persuade the clan members, the court gave its approval of Prince Ch'un. Tsai-t'ien was seriously considered and finally chosen. The last remaining obstacle was that Tsai-t'ien was Tung Chih's first cousin and by law could not officiate at Tung Chih's grave. In other words, Tung Chih could not adopt his cousin as a son and heir.

After days of debate, the court decided to have another open vote.

Outside the wind blew, and the lanterns in the hall flickered. The votes were counted: seven men voted for Prince Ts'eng's grandson P'u-lun, three voted for Prince Kung's son Tsai-chen, and fifteen voted for Prince Ch'un's son, my nephew Tsai-t'ien.

While Prince Ch'un told the court that it would be unnecessary to secure the approval of his wife regarding the official adoption of Tsai-t'ien, I made it clear that the decision would not become valid until the court received Rong's assent.

Knee-high weeds clogged the lawns and ivy covered the pathways. Inside my sister's grand mansion, diapers, food, dishes, bottles, toys and stained pillows were strewn about. Roaches darted across the floor and flies zipped through windows. Rong's eunuchs and maids whispered to Li Lien-ying that their mistress allowed no cleaning.

'Orchid!' Rong came to greet me. She looked as if she had just climbed out of bed. She wore floral-patterned, bright pink pajamas, and on her head was a woolen hat suitable for a snowstorm. Her breath gave off a rotten odor. I asked how she had been and why she wore the hat.

'Strange creatures have invaded my mind,' Rong said, guiding me through her cluttered hallway. 'I have been having headaches.'

We entered the living room and she collapsed into a large armchair. 'The creatures have been feeding on me.' Pulling over a silver tray filled with cookies, she began to eat. 'They love sweets, you see. They leave me alone every time I eat cookies. Tricky creatures, nasty.'

My sister was no longer slim and beautiful. Folks back in Wuhu used to say, 'When a woman is married and gives birth, she turns from a flower into a tree.' Rong was a bear. She was twice as big as her former self. I asked how she felt about her son being selected Emperor.

'I don't know.' She made loud chewing sounds. 'His father is a con man.'

I asked what she meant.

She wiped her mouth and fell back into the chair. Her belly stuck out like a pillow. 'I thank Heaven I am not pregnant.' She grinned. Bits of cookie clung to her mouth. 'But I told my husband otherwise.' She leaned over and whispered, 'He said that it was impossible, because we haven't done you-know-what for years. I told him this pregnancy was made by the demons.' She started to laugh. 'That scared a scorpion out of him!'

I didn't know what to say. Something was terribly wrong with my sister.

'Orchid, you are incredibly thin. You look awful. How much do you weigh?'

'A little over a hundred ten,' I replied.

'I've missed you since Mother's burial.' Instantly Rong broke into tears. 'You never care to see me unless there is business.'

'You know that is not true, Rong,' I said, feeling guilty. A eunuch came in with tea.

'Didn't I tell you that this house serves no tea?' Rong yelled at the eunuch.

'I thought the guest might like –'

'Get out,' Rong said.

The eunuch picked up the cups and gave Li Lien-ying a resentful look.

'Idiot pud-nut,' Rong said. 'Never learns.'

I looked at my sister and then said gently, 'I came to see Tsai-t'ien.'

'The little debt seeker is napping,' Rong responded.

We went to the child's room. Tsai-t'ien was sleeping under his covers, curled up like a kitten. He looked a lot like Tung Chih. I reached out to touch him.

'I don't want this child.' Rong's voice was strangely clear. 'He has given me nothing but trouble and I am sick of him. Truthfully, Orchid, he will be better off without me.'

'Stop it, Rong, please.'

'You don't understand. I am scared of myself too.'

'What is it?'

'I don't feel any love for this child – he is from the underground. He made his three brothers die so that he could have his turn to slide through my body and live. When I was pregnant I wanted him so badly, but after he came out, I knew I'd made a terrible mistake. I dream of my three dead children all the time.' Rong began to sob. 'Their ghosts have come to tell me to do something about their younger brother.'

'You will come around, Rong.'

'Orchid, I can't cope anymore. Take my son, will you? You will be doing me a great favor. But you must be extremely careful with his demon-possessed spirit. It will take away your peace. His trick is to cry around the clock. No one here gets any sleep! Orchid, take my trouble. Strangle this son of a demon if you have to!'

'Rong, I won't take him because you want to abandon him. Tsai-t'ien is your son, and he deserves your love. Let me tell you, Rong, the only thing I regret is that I wasn't able to love Tung Chih enough –'

'*Oh, Mulan, the heroine!?*' Rong cried.

Awakened by his mother, Tsai-t'ien opened his eyes. A moment later he broke into a muted cry.

As if disgusted, Rong turned away from him and returned to her chair.

I picked up Tsai-t'ien and held him. Gently I rubbed his back. He smelled of urine.

Rong came and grabbed her son from me. She threw him back onto the bed and said, 'See, you offer him a penny, he demands a dollar!'

'Rong, he is only three years old.'

'No, he is a three-hundred-year-old! A master of torture. He pretends to be crying but he is having fun.'

An overwhelming anger and sadness came over me. I felt that I couldn't stay in that room. I started walking toward the door.

Rong followed behind. 'Orchid, wait a minute.'

I stopped and looked back.

She gripped the boy's nose with her fingers.

Tsai-t'ien began to scream, struggling for air.

Rong pressed. 'Cry, cry, cry! What do you want?'

Tsai-t'ien tried to break away, but his mother wouldn't let go.

112

'Do you want me to kill you? So that you will shut up? Do you?' Rong put her hands around Tsai-t'ien's neck until he began to choke. She laughed hysterically.

'Rong!' I lost all my restraint and rushed toward her. My nails dug into her wrists.

My sister screamed.

'Let go of Tsai-t'ien!' I said.

Rong struggled but would not release the child.

'Listen, Rong.' I squeezed her wrists tighter. 'This is Empress Tzu Hsi speaking. I am going to call the guards and you'll be charged for murdering the Emperor of China.'

'Good joke, Orchid!' Rong spat.

'Last time, sister, let go of Tsai-t'ien or I'll order your arrest and beheading.'

I pushed Rong against the wall and pinned her chin with my right elbow. 'From this moment on, whether or not you agree to the adoption, Tsai-t'ien is my son.'

14

U NDER COVER OF darkness, a detachment of guards led by Yung Lu marched through the streets to the residence of Prince Ch'un and Rong. They gathered up the sleeping Tsai-t'ien and brought him back to the Forbidden City, where he was to spend the rest of his life. The soldiers' feet and their horses' hooves were bound in straw and sacking so that the news of the Emperor's successor would not spread through the city prematurely and provoke riots and disorder, which often accompanied a change of ruler.

It was dawn when Tsai-t'ien arrived at my palace. I had been waiting for him, dressed in my official robe. Barely awake, Tsai-t'ien was presented to me. In the Hall of Ancestors, led by the minister of court etiquette and with other ministers in attendance, we performed the adoption ceremony. I held Tsai-t'ien and got down on my knees. Together we bowed to the portraits on the wall. My adopted son was then dressed in a dragon robe made of silk. I took him to Tung Chih's coffin, where, with the help of the ministers, he completed the ceremony by kowtowing on his own.

I held Tsai-t'ien in my arms as he received his court. We were surrounded by the light of candles and lanterns. Memories of Tung Chih again came to haunt me.

On February 25, 1875, my nephew, now my son, assumed the Dragon Throne. He was proclaimed the Guang-hsu Emperor – the Emperor of Glorious Succession. His name was changed from Tsai-t'ien to Guang-hsu. Peasants in the countryside would start counting the years with this 'first year of the Guang-hsu Emperor.'

As we had done before, Nuharoo and I announced to the court and the nation that 'we look forward to handing over the affairs of the government as soon as the Emperor completes his education.' In our decree we also explained the reasons we had been compelled to select Tsai-t'ien for the throne, and why he should become the heir by adoption to his uncle the Emperor Hsien Feng instead of to his cousin Tung Chih. 'As soon as Guang-hsu produces a male child,' we declared, 'the child will be offered to his uncle Tung Chih as an heir by adoption to officiate at his grave.'

My opponents challenged the decree. 'We are deeply shocked at the blasphemous neglect of Emperor Tung Chih's ancestral rites,' they declared. In downtown meeting places and teahouses, vicious slanders and gossip spread. One lie suggested that Guang-hsu was my own son by Yung Lu. Another suggested that he was fathered by An-te-hai. A local judge named Wu K'o-tu dramatically caught the nation's attention: he poisoned himself in protest and called the succession 'improper and illegitimate.'

In the middle of this chaos, my brother sent me a message saying that I must grant him permission to see me. When Kuei Hsiang arrived dressed in a satin robe embroidered with colorful good-fortune symbols, he had his daughter with him.

'Your niece is four years old,' he began, 'and she hasn't been granted an Imperial name.'

I told him that I had a name picked out. And I apologized, telling him I had been grief-stricken and hadn't seen to many things. 'The name is Lan-yu, or simply Lan.' The name meant 'honorable abundance.'

Kuei Hsiang was thrilled.

I took a good look at my niece. She had a bulbous forehead and a small pointed chin. Her narrow face highlighted her protruding upper front teeth. She appeared unsure of herself, which was unsurprising given how she had been raised. My brother was what the Chinese would call 'a dragon at home but a worm outside.' A typical Manchu, he had little respect for women, regarding his wives and concubines as his property. He wasn't unkind, but he was prone to ridiculing others. I hadn't witnessed his treatment of his daughter, but her behavior offered more than I needed to know.

'My wife thinks our daughter is a beauty, but I told her that Lan is so plain that we will have to give a discount to her marriage suitor.' Impressed by his own sense of humor, he laughed.

I offered Lan a cupcake, and my niece thanked me in an almost inaudible voice. She chewed like a mouse and wiped her mouth after every bite. She fixed her eyes on the floor, and I wondered whether she had found something interesting to look at. Teasing, I asked her. 'Crumbs,' she replied.

I suggested that my brother take Lan to visit Princess Jung, my husband's daughter. The princess had suffered a great misfortune – her mother, Lady Yun, had committed suicide – but had grown into a thoughtful young woman.

'What do you want us to learn from the girl?' Kuei Hsiang asked.

'Ask Jung to tell the story of how she survived,' I replied. 'It will be the best lesson for Lan. And please, brother, don't belittle your daughter. I think Lan is beautiful.'

Hearing my words, Lan raised her eyes. When her father answered, 'Yes, Your Majesty,' she giggled.

'I know of Princess Jung,' Lan said in a small voice. 'She studied in Europe, is it not true?'

'She tried but was forced by the court to return home.' I sighed. 'However, it is her courage that I admire. She has a positive spirit and leads a productive life. You will meet her when she comes to help me in my work.'

'But Orchid,' my brother protested, 'I'd prefer your influence, not the influence of a disgraced concubine's daughter.'

'It is my influence, Kuei Hsiang,' I said. 'Jung lived with me, and she witnessed how many of my dreams went unrealized. The courage to keep dreams alive despite all is what matters.'

My brother looked confused.

Guang-hsu cried for hours on end, and I became frustrated. I sang nursery songs until I became sick of their tunes. I compared Guang-hsu's situation with how peasants grew rice. 'Roots of rice shoots must be broken in order to encourage splits,' the village saying went. I remembered working in rice fields to help break the roots. The tearing sound bothered me at first, for I didn't believe that the rice would survive. I left a small patch untouched, to see what would happen. The torn shoots came back healthier and stronger than those that went untorn.

Guang-hsu's attendants said, 'His Young Majesty continues to wet his bed every night and is afraid of darkness and people.' My adopted son also had a speech impediment, wore the expression of a prisoner and was sad all the time. After a few months, his weight began to drop.

I summoned Guang-hsu's former wet nurses. They told me that Guang-hsu had been a happy baby when he was born. It was his mother, my sister, who tried to 'fix his ill manner' by hitting him every time he tried to eat or laugh.

Nuharoo and I couldn't do enough to make the little boy happy. Guang-hsu quivered and screamed when repairmen pounded nails or sawed wood. The summer's rolling thunder became another problem. On hot days before the rain came, we would keep his door and window shut so the noise wouldn't bother him. Guang-hsu wouldn't venture out on his own. The kitchen was no longer allowed to chop vegetables; the chefs used scissors instead. The maids were instructed to be quiet when washing dishes. Li Lien-ying used a slingshot to scare away the woodpeckers.

To help the Emperor smooth the transition, I ordered one of his former wet nurses to come to the Forbidden City to live with us. I hoped that Guang-hsu would find comfort in her. But Nuharoo sent the wet nurse right back. 'Guang-hsu should forget all his former conditions,' she insisted. 'He ought to and will be treated as palace born.'

Tension began to build between Nuharoo and me, something that was all too familiar from when we raised Tung Chih. I feared that I would again be fighting another losing battle.

During an especially heated argument that nearly came to blows, Nuharoo ordered me to go, and I stormed out. She took over Guang-hsu's care, which for her meant leaving the young boy to her eunuchs. Nuharoo wasn't one to devote time and energy to a child. As it happened, her frustrated eunuchs did what Guang-hsu feared most:

they locked him inside a closet, then scared him by knocking loudly on the closet door.

When Li Lien-ying learned what had happened, and protested, Nuharoo's chief eunuch responded, 'His Young Majesty has fire in his chest. Give him a chance to sing and he will douse it.'

For the first time, and without getting permission from Nuharoo, I ordered her chief eunuch whipped. As for the rest of the servants, they got no food for two days. I knew it was not the servants' fault; they were merely doing what they were told. But the beating was necessary to warn Nuharoo that I had reached the limit of my patience.

Nuharoo told Li Lien-ying that in all our years together she had never seen me act with such wild rage. She called me a village shrew and then retreated. Deep down, she must have known that as much as I held myself responsible for Tung Chih's death, I held her responsible as well. Nuharoo's wisdom told her that it would be foolish to sprinkle salt over my wound.

I wanted to spend as much time with Guang-hsu as possible, but over the next couple of years I felt like an acrobat spinning plates on thin sticks, desperately trying to keep a dozen dishes in the air, knowing that whatever I did, some would come crashing down.

China's economy was collapsing under the weight of forced war compensations. The foreign powers threatened to invade because our payments were late, or so they said. My audiences were devoted to discussions of how best to play the foreigners against each other so we could gain time. News of peasant uprisings and calls for help from local officials arrived daily.

I did not even have time to bathe properly. My hair got so dirty that the roots hurt. I could not wait for elaborate meals to be prepared for me; I usually ate my food cold at my writing table. I kept my promise to always read my son a bedtime story, but I often fell asleep before the end. He would wake me up to finish, and I would kiss him good night and go back to work.

By the time Guang-hsu was seven years old, I had developed chronic insomnia, which was soon followed by a persistent pain in my abdomen. Doctor Sun Pao-tien told me that I suffered from a liver ailment. 'Your pulse is telling me that your fluids are not in proper balance. The risk to your system could be dire.'

One day I felt too exhausted to work. Nuharoo let me know that she would take over the audiences until I regained my strength.

This made me happy, because I was able to concentrate on what I most desired: raising Guang-hsu. Several times my tongue slipped and I called him Tung Chih. Each time, Guang-hsu would take out his handkerchief and wipe my tears with amazing patience and sympathy. His inborn tenderness touched me. Unlike Tung Chih, Guang-hsu was growing into a sweet and affectionate child. I wondered if it was because he was weak himself, and so understood what it was like to be in pain.

As time went on, Guang-hsu also began to reveal a strong sense of curiosity. Although he was never able to completely defeat his fears, his self-confidence became more robust. He had lovely manners and delighted visitors with his enthusiastic questions about the outside world. He loved to read, write and listen to stories.

For years the minister of Imperial etiquette had protested against my allowing Guang-hsu to sleep in my room. I insisted on keeping him with me until he was ready to face his enormous bedroom without fear. I was accused of coddling him, and worse, but I didn't care. 'To the court Guang-hsu was never a child to begin with,' I complained to Nuharoo.

Guang-hsu soon developed interests of his own. He fell in love with clocks and spent endless hours in the palace's Grand Clock Room, where clocks of all kinds were on display, gifts from foreign kings, queens and ambassadors. This pleased me, for in my early days in the palace I too was drawn to these new and intricate objects. I had soon lost interest in them, but Guang-hsu never tired of their sounds and tried to figure out what made the clocks 'sing.'

One afternoon Li Lien-ying came to me, a terrified look on his face. 'His Young Majesty has destroyed the grand clocks!'

'Which ones?' I asked.

'The Emperor Hsien Feng Clock and the Tung Chih Clock!'

I went to check and found that the clocks had been taken apart, the tiny pieces scattered over the table like chewed-up chicken bones.

'I trust that you have a plan to put the clocks back together,' I said to Guang-hsu.

'What if I can't?' Guang-hsu asked, holding a small screwdriver in his hand.

'I will give you credit for trying,' I encouraged.

'Would you be mad if your favorite bird clock no longer sings?'

'Well, I can't say I would be happy, but a clock expert must learn to put the broken parts together too.'

15

Y UNG LU STOOD before me in his purple satin court robe. My heart's ice began to melt in the spring sun. Like ghost lovers, our meeting places had been in our dreams. At dawn we would slip back into our human skin, but the dreams continued. In my costumes and makeup, I would imagine my head against his chest and my hands feeling his warmth. I walked the steps of a gracious empress, yet I felt the passion of a village girl.

I had no one to share my thoughts of Yung Lu after An-te-hai's death. When I turned forty, I accepted the fact that Yung Lu and I would not consummate our passion. We lived under the eyes of our nation. Newspapers and magazines made their living selling gossip about us.

There was nowhere Yung Lu and I could be with each other without exposing ourselves. The money offered for information about my private life tempted eunuchs, maids and the lowest-ranking servants to lurk, to pry, to tell tales.

Yet moments like this reminded me of how impossible it was to deny my love. My emotions found a home in Yung Lu's presence. The look in his eyes rescued me from fear and prevented me from falling into self-destructive thoughts. Whatever misery I was experiencing, he assured me that he was with me. At audiences and court I relied on his judgment and support. He was my harshest and most honest critic, guiding me to see all sides of whatever issue was before me. But once I had made a decision, he saw to it that my orders were carried out.

'What is it?' I asked.

'I . . .' His expression was of a reluctant executioner. He gathered his breath and pushed the words out of his chest. 'I . . . am going to get married.'

I resisted the feelings that assaulted me. Making a tremendous effort, I pressed back my tears.

'You don't need my permission,' I managed to say.

'That is not why I am here.' His voice was low but clear.

'Why *are* you here, then?' I turned to look at him, angry and terrified.

'I request your permission to move away,' he said quietly.

'What does that have to do with –' I stopped, because I understood.

'My family will go with me,' he added.

'Where are you going?' I heard myself ask.

'Sinkiang.' Sinkiang was in the far northwest, a Moslem state, a remote desert region, as far from the capital as could be.

I didn't mean to break down, but I began to lose control. 'Do you really think that I can survive without you?'

He stood in silence.

'You know who I am. You know what I am made of, and you know the reason I show up every morning for audiences.'

'Your Majesty, please . . .'

'I want . . . to be informed that you are safe so that I will be able to rest.'

'Nothing has changed.'

123

'But you are leaving!'

'I will write letters. I promise . . .'

'How? Sinkiang is impossible to reach.'

'It will not be easy, Your Majesty. But . . . it will be good for you if I leave,' he insisted.

'Convince me.'

He glanced around the room. Although the eunuchs and maids had made themselves unseen, they were not gone. We could hear their movements in the courtyard.

'Moslems have led uprisings, Your Majesty. The province is full of unrest. Our troops now have it under control, but just barely. In the most recent crisis, large groups of rebels have been gathering along the border of Gansu province.'

'Why do you have to go to the frontier yourself? Isn't the capital more important?'

He did not answer.

'Nuharoo and I can't do without you.'

'My men are already scheduled to depart, Your Majesty.'

'Self-imposed exile, that's what it is!'

He stared straight at me.

'You don't care that I have lost my son . . .' I shut my eyes, trying to press back the tears. My mind knew that he was doing the right thing.

'As I said, it will be good for the future,' he murmured.

'You will not have my permission.' I turned away from him.

I heard the sound of Yung Lu's knees hitting the floor. I wasn't able to look back at him.

'I'll get the court to support me, then.'

'What if I reject the court's decision?'

He got up and marched toward the door.

'Never mind, Yung Lu!' My tears ran down my cheeks. 'I . . . I will grant you permission.'

'Thank you, Your Majesty.'

I sat down on my chair. My handkerchief was brown and black with smeared makeup.

'Why does it have to be Sinkiang?' I asked. 'It is a harsh land of sickness and death. It is a place ruled by religious fanatics. Where will you get a doctor if you become ill? Where will you get help if you lose a battle to the Moslems? Where will you station your reserve troops? Who is in charge of your supply lines? How will you possibly keep me informed?'

She was a Manchu but had the Han name of Willow. She treated her eunuchs and maids as if they were her own family. That alone told me she was not of the royal bloodline. A royal would treat her eunuchs and maids as slaves. She was Yung Lu's young bride. Mrs. Yung Lu – my tongue was yet to get used to Willow – was in her late twenties. The age difference caused whispers; Yung Lu was old enough to be her father. But Willow kept smiling and her lips remained sealed. For her wedding she wore a light blue silk gown embroidered with water hibiscuses. Like her name, she had a slender figure and moved gracefully.

I was glad Nuharoo made an excuse not to attend the wedding. Her dominance would have distracted me from observing the celebration, especially the newlyweds.

When Yung Lu introduced his bride to me, she couldn't have been any sweeter. She took a bold look at me, which surprised me. It was as if she had been waiting for this moment all her life.

Many years later, after we became friends and after her husband's death, Willow would tell me that she knew the truth all along – Yung Lu had never hid it from her, which made her an extraordinary character in my eyes. She was the daughter of a warlord friend of Yung Lu's, the leader of a Mongol tribe. Yung Lu's exploits had repeatedly been the topic at the family's table when she was growing up. Whenever Yung Lu visited her father, young Willow would find reasons to linger. She was in love with him before she met him.

Willow would eventually tell me that I had been the subject of her study before she began her relationship with her husband. In fact, I was the only subject she was interested in during Yung Lu's visits. She asked many questions and was impressed with his answers. She said that it was their mutual interest in me that led to letter writing, friendship and the discovery of a deeper feeling for each other. She was the only person to whom he confided his secret.

It was only after Willow had turned away numerous matchmakers that Yung Lu woke to her love. Her devotion and openness touched him. He proposed and she accepted. He knew that he would not be able to maintain a healthy relationship with his wife if he continued to see me at audiences.

Willow didn't fool me with her pretended innocence. The moment we met, I felt as if someone had peeked through a window into my soul. There was a strange and mysterious understanding between us. Years later, Willow would recall my receiving her at the wedding celebration. She remembered me as being warm and sincere. She asked how I was able to keep my poise. I told her that I had practiced acting on the stage of life. 'And so have you,' I said to her.

Yung Lu could not put up a false front. He tried but could not give Willow what her heart desired. His guilt was apparent in every look. His avoidance of me and his awkward apologies made her feel worse.

I drank a good deal of wine during the celebration. I suppose I was trying to forget. I was dressed in a golden silk gown embroidered with phoenixes. My hair was fastened onto a thin board and piled into the shape of a cloud. Li Lien-ying had secured the cloud with dark blue jade hairpins. My phoenix earrings were light blue. I wanted to please Yung Lu, but I was unable to maintain my cheerfulness. The thought of being denied the chance to see him left me drunk and sobbing. I was so woozy and nauseated I had to run outside and vomit in the bushes.

It was in that shameful, desperate moment that Willow sat down next to me and quietly offered her sympathy. She never told me what I had said to her that night. I was sure that I was rude and nasty. Li Lien-ying told me afterward that Willow held my hand and would not let those who were curious get near me.

That was how I began my friendship with Yung Lu's Willow. She never once uttered a word about her husband's secret. Her compassion for my tragedy overcame her jealousy. The gesture of friendship she offered was to keep me informed of her husband's lasting love for me all the way to his end.

'It is impossible not to love you, Orchid – if I may call you by name,' said Willow, and I understood why Yung Lu loved her.

In turn, I wanted to do the same for Willow. When she came back to Peking to give birth to her daughter a year later, I received her. The harsh life of the desert had darkened her skin, and wrinkles had climbed onto her forehead. She continued to be cheerful, but she couldn't hide her anxiety: Something in the desert climate had caused Yung Lu to suffer from chronic bronchitis.

I sent bags of herbal medicine to Sinkiang, along with fine tea, dried meat and several kinds of preserved soybeans. I let Willow know that she could always depend on me.

16

W ENG TONG-HUR, known as Tutor Weng, a well-known
historian, critic, poet and calligrapher, was appointed
to oversee Guang-hsu's education. Nuharoo and I had
taken part in the selection and sat through the interviews.
I was especially careful this time, for I had learned a hard
lesson when selecting Tung Chih's tutors. I regretted that I
had neither checked up on nor attended my son's lessons.
When Tung Chih complained that his teachers were boring, I punished him. It never occurred to me that the tutors
could be at fault – they might know a great deal about their
subjects, but little of how to teach a child.

After Tung Chih died, I had spoken with several eunuchs
who had witnessed the Imperial tutors at work. I was told that
my son was made to memorize a text regardless of whether he
understood it. The tutors were in their sixties or seventies,
and were more interested in leaving behind a personal legacy
than helping Tung Chih learn. Although I was told their
spirits were high as the day began, they grew tired after lunch.
They would fall asleep in the middle of lessons.

While a tutor snoozed and snored, Tung Chih would
amuse himself by playing with the ornaments hanging from
the tutor's hat and clothes. He bragged to his eunuchs

129

afterward that he plucked the peacock feather from the tutor's hat.

'The feather stuck out about two feet from the back of the tutor's head,' the eunuch recalled. 'His Young Majesty liked the dot on the feather, which he called the eye. It amused him to see the way it moved whenever the tutor nodded. He would ask the same question repeatedly so the tutor would nod.'

'I'd like to make sure that this time,' I said to the court, 'Emperor Guang-hsu doesn't repeat Emperor Tung Chih's experience.'

Tutor Weng was no stranger to Nuharoo and me. He had been our teacher in history and literature in 1861, right after our husband died and we became the acting regents. At that time no male was allowed to spend time with us except Tutor Weng. He was charged with a mission of national importance: two young women with no formal education or experience were ruling China.

Tutor Weng had come at Prince Kung's recommendation. Back then the scholar was in his forties and was a towering figure. Within days Nuharoo and I were spellbound. His brilliance lay in his ability to inspire thinking, a rewarding experience for me. After eighteen years Tutor Weng had become an important advisor.

At the time of Tung Chih's death, Tutor Weng had been the head of China's top literary school, the Hanlin Academy. He had also been the chief judge of the national civil service examination. He was no longer a slender man – his waist was as thick as a bath bucket. He had white hair and a gray beard, but his energy was still unflagging. His voice sounded like a temple bell. He had a righteous air and spoke with a sense of urgency.

130

Tutor Weng's impeccable moral standards were another reason he was our choice. While most ministers vied with each other to be ever more elaborately gracious in their expression of admiration toward us, Tutor Weng never flattered. He was brutally honest.

Unfortunately, my craving to be liked by people I admired made me vulnerable to manipulation. My relationship with Tutor Weng was a good example.

'I am deeply honored by the challenge,' Tutor Weng said, bowing to Nuharoo and me. 'And I understand my responsibility.'

'His Young Majesty Guang-hsu is the only one left of the bloodline of the Ch'ing Dynasty,' Nuharoo said. 'Lady Yehonala and I believe that with you in charge of his education, we can count on China's future prosperity.'

Leaves were snowing down from the giant oak, walnut and mulberry trees. Squirrels ran around busily storing their winter food. The fall days had been warm this year. The trees began dropping their nuts and soon covered the ground. The eunuchs had to sweep the courtyards over and over because Nuharoo insisted that the palace gardens should not look like a natural forest with piled-up dead leaves. Afraid that she might be hit by dropping nuts, she always walked beneath her umbrella.

I loved my morning walks and loved kicking the fallen leaves. The sound of nuts popping off the trees reminded me of my childhood days in the countryside. It made my spirit come out of its dark shadow.

Tutor Weng began one lesson by asking Guang-hsu if he had read *The Romance of the Three Kingdoms*. My adopted son replied that it was his favorite. The tutor then asked if he enjoyed the characters and if he could name them.

'The Three Kingdoms' prime minister was Chu-ko Liang! Who lived sixteen hundred years ago!' Guang-hsu became excited. 'A powerful commander who was magical in predicting the enemy's next move!'

Dressed in his robe patterned with tall grass, Tutor Weng charmed his student by praising his knowledge. 'However,' the teacher said and pivoted his head, 'his predictions were not magical but the result of hard work.'

'Please explain!' Guang-hsu couldn't wait.

'Your Majesty, have you ever read a real letter composed by Chu-ko Liang?'

Guang-hsu shook his head.

'I would like to show you a letter. Are you interested?' The tutor bent over until his face was inches from his student's.

'I would be delighted!' cried Guang-hsu.

The title was 'On Departure.' It was a letter of advice from the ancient prime minister to his Emperor. Chu-ko Liang, who was very ill, was about to lead his army against the northern invaders. The departure was his final effort to rescue his failing kingdom.

'"Your father, my friend Emperor Liu, died in the middle of achieving his goal,"' Tutor Weng began to read. '"Although the Three Kingdoms has been established, the known truth is that our kingdom is the weakest. Your Majesty must realize that the reason you have been served well is because the ministers and generals lived to repay your father's kindness and trust." In other words, Guang-hsu, it is crucial that you rule with fairness and justice and know who your true friends are.'

Guang-hsu listened attentively as the venerable minister went on to recommend people whom he trusted – all the characters Guang-hsu knew well from the book he'd read.

Artfully, Tutor Weng presented the ancient situation to mirror the present. By placing Guang-hsu in the historical moment, he offered a valuable perspective.

Like Guang-hsu, this was the first time I truly comprehended the ancient classic. I realized that the elements Tutor Weng illustrated for my son were at the heart of Chinese morality.

Tutor Weng was near tears when he recited the last paragraph: ' "The late Emperor knew that I was a careful person, and it was why he gave me such a grand responsibility. I could not sleep at night, worrying that there might be things I could have done but hadn't." ' Tutor Weng put down his book and raised his chin toward the ceiling and began to recite from memory: ' "I am asking to be punished by death if I fail to defeat the northern enemy on this trip. I am leaving you with the dynasty's most intelligent and experienced officers." ' The tutor looked at Guang-hsu. 'Join me now, Your Majesty.'

Together, student and teacher read: ' "I hope you have the mercy to make use of them. As for myself, Your Majesty, I have been given trust and friendship by your father. To devote my life to his son, until the day I die, would be my pleasure and happiness.'

It started to happen in my sleep. I could hear the cracking of my thought-jammed skull. I could feel it while dressing or when I sat down to eat. Having 'dead thoughts,' or being 'sick of having the same thoughts,' was how I expressed the feeling. It was getting to me. The doctors said that it had to do with approaching old age.

When I was younger, I was used to my dark thoughts. They came and went like companions. I wasn't afraid of them. Often I let myself sink deep into the ocean bed of my mind and explore the murky terrain. Nuharoo said that she had the same experiences and the same sinking feelings. It was why she had turned to Buddhism. It was to save her from falling.

I called myself a Buddhist and even claimed to be able to see the Buddha beyond the wooden statue. In truth, however, I could not. 'It doesn't cost much to offer food and animals to every altar in the palace,' An-te-hai used to advise. 'My lady, worshiping many gods will ensure an abundance of luck.'

'Insincerity will be your true misfortune,' Nuharoo predicted. 'Lady Yehonala, you will never find peace of mind.'

I didn't doubt that she was right, so I tried to help myself. Yet often it wasn't Buddha's voice but An-te-hai's that I would hear. 'It is the dealing of the inner life cycle, my lady. It is death and birth. You are alive if you are aware of your dealings. But if you feel that you have given up, that is the beginning of the end.'

I had always been afraid of spiritual death, so I sought meaning in everyday existence. Tung Chih, Yung Lu and An-te-hai were my elements. Fighting hopelessness had been my existence. I found myself achieving balance and harmony along the way, though I never questioned how I achieved it or whether I was only fooling myself.

I hadn't opened any doors since becoming an empress. In a dream I opened a door. I was surprised to see that red and pink flowers covered my entire courtyard. A heavy rain had fallen. The flowers were whipped down, but they still appeared full of vitality. Their wet heads drank the water from puddles. One by one the flowers began to rise like court officials. Their fragrance was strong, a mixture of gardenias and rotten vegetables.

Li Lien-ying brought in a dream interpreter, who asked what else I had seen in my dream. I told him that I had seen windows.

'What is inside the windows?' the interpreter asked.

'Red- and pink-faced women,' I replied. 'They squeezed into the windows like a bunch of poison poppies competing for sunshine. Every one of them had an extraordinarily long and thin neck.'

The interpreter's hand moved quickly in the air as if taking notes on an invisible pad.

'Whose window was it?' The interpreter closed his eyes.

'I don't remember.'

'I am getting to the bottom of it. I am ready to unlock the meaning of your dream, but you must provide that last detail. Let me ask you again: whose window was it?'

'It is my husband's window, I think.'

'Where is it located?'

'At the Hall of Spiritual Nurturing.'

'That's it! And then you summoned a fruit picker.'

Shocked, I said that he was right.

'And with that fruit picker you took down the poppy heads one by one.'

'Yes, I did.'

'You then gathered those poppy heads in a basket, put them in a grinder and made soup.'

I admitted that it all happened as he described.

'The problem is the soup. You should not have drunk it.'

'But it was only a dream.'

'It interprets truth.'

'What truth?'

The man paused.

Quickly Li Lien-ying placed a bag of taels in his hand.

The interpreter resumed, asking whether it was safe to utter what he knew.

Li Lien-ying assured him. The man drew in a breath and said, exhaling, 'My lady, you have been poisoned by your own sickness.'

I asked what kind of sickness. The man was reluctant to answer, but said that it contained elements of jealousy, resentment and secret yearnings for intimacy.

It was then that I asked him to stop.

'What would you advise?' Li Lien-ying said, grabbing the man's sleeve.

The interpreter said that he knew of no effective treatment.

'We'll try anything,' Li Lien-ying begged.

'Wait until autumn is deep. Leave Her Majesty's door open from evening until dawn. The purpose is to invite crickets in. The crickets will do the labor of suffering for her – they will sing themselves to death.'

'How many crickets should I invite?' Li Lien-ying asked.

'As many as you can. There is a trick to luring them. You must place fresh grass and shelled soybeans in the room. Also lay wet bricks in each corner. The crickets will come to eat and then look for mating partners. They will sing throughout the night. Consider your treatment a success if you find dead crickets under your bed the following morning.'

By the time I got used to the singing of crickets and waking up to find their dead bodies in my shoes, my dreams began to change. They became less frightening, more about my being tired and trying to escape.

I was again able to appreciate the beauty of the turning seasons. Walking along the garden paths had never meant so much to me. I would watch a worm-damaged plant swing in the wind and marvel at its way of surviving. I would feel the force of life and experience rapture at the simple sight of insects sucking nectar from flower hearts. I would find myself breathing freely, and I would feel the spirit of Tung Chih and An-te-hai.

I still missed Yung Lu terribly, but had the strength to bear it.

17

I HAD BEEN sitting in front of the mirror since three in the morning. I opened my eyes and saw that the wide board that held my hair made my head look like a giant mushroom.

'How do you like it, my lady?' Li Lien-ying asked.

'It's fine. Let's finish as quickly as possible.' I rose so that he could get me into the heavily layered court robe.

I hardly paid attention to how I looked these days. My mind had been dealing with Russia to the north, British India to the west, French Indochina to the south, and Japan to the east.

A number of countries and territories – including Korea, the Ryukyu Islands, Annam and Burma – that had sent representatives and tribute to us during Tung Chih's reign, sent them less frequently, and soon not at all. The fact that China was unable to claim back its privileges showed that our standing was diminishing. With every defection, our outer defenses were further weakened.

I now wished that Tutor Weng would quit his pointless displays of sincerity and get on with preparing Guang-hsu for the business of rule. Lacking flexibility and cunning, Nuharoo and I were unable to adopt a line of conduct when problems threatened to overwhelm us. No one seemed to understand that our country had been heading downhill for centuries. China was like a diseased and dying person, only now the rot of the body had become visible.

Like a hungry tiger, Japan had been hiding in the bushes, waiting for the moment to attack. In the past we underestimated the degree of its hunger. We had been too kind to our small and resource-poor neighbor from ancient times. Had I known that Japan's Meiji Emperor had stirred up his nation to swoop down and rob us, I would have encouraged the court to concentrate solely on defense.

Ten years earlier, in 1868, while I was concentrating my energy on establishing elementary schools in the countryside, Japan's Emperor had set in motion a full-scale reform, transforming its feudal system into a powerful modern capitalistic society. China had no idea what it meant when Japan began pressing to expand in a bracelet extending from its main islands in the north to Formosa in the south. Formosa, which the Mandarins called Taiwan, had been an island state paying tribute to the Chinese throne for centuries. In 1871, when some sailors from the Ryukyu Islands were murdered there by what most likely were local bandits, the Japanese seized on the incident as an excuse to interfere.

The Imperial bureaucracy and our own naiveté led us to fall for Japan's conspiracy. At first we tried to clarify that we were not to blame. Our Board of Foreign Affairs offered a carelessly worded response to Japan's demand for reparations: 'We cannot be responsible for the actions of savages beyond the pale of civilization.' This was interpreted by the Japanese as an invitation to take over the island state.

Without warning, the Japanese army invaded, claiming revenge on behalf of the people of the Ryukyu Islands.

It was too late when our provincial governor there realized that he had not only let the Japanese supplant us in the Ryukyus, but also relinquished our authority over the 250-mile-long, vitally important island of Taiwan.

After days of discussion and delay, our court concluded that China could not take on the new military power of Japan. We ended up paying 500,000 taels to Japan as an indemnity, only to receive more bad news six years later, when Japan 'accepted' the Ryukyu Islands' official 'surrender.'

The British were also determined to extract all they could from any incident. In 1875 a British interpreter, A. R. Margary, was murdered in our southwestern Yunnan province. Margary was accompanying an expedition to reconnoiter trade routes from Burma into the mountains of Yunnan, Kweichow and Szechuan, provinces rich in minerals and ore. The foreigners paid no attention to warning signs of danger from Moslem rebels. The interpreter was ambushed and killed by either bandits or the rebels.

The British representative Sir Thomas Wade forced China's hand over a new treaty, to which I sent Li Hung-chang, then the viceroy of Chihli province, to negotiate. The Chefoo Convention was signed, by which several more ports were opened for trade with Western nations, including my hometown of Wuhu, on the Yangtze River.

With his hair smoothly braided in the back, the fifty-five-year-old Li Hung-chang came to beg for forgiveness. He was in his black court robe, embroidered with the brown and red symbols of bravery and luck. Although thin-framed, Li's posture was erect and his expression solemn.

He had a southerner's fair skin, and his small, single-lidded eyes glowed with intelligence. His nose looked long on his chiseled face, and his lips were hidden behind a neatly trimmed beard.

'The British are trying to send another expedition from India through Burma, to delineate the Burmese-Chinese frontier,' Li Hung-chang reported while on his knees.

'Are you implying that Burma has been annexed by Britain?'

'Precisely, Your Majesty.'

I believed that if I had the viceroy's devotion, I would have China's stability. Against the court's advice, I continued Li Hung-chang's appointment as China's most important provincial official. Li would hold the same post in Chihli for twenty-three years.

I purposely ignored the fact that Li was overdue for rotation to another part of the empire. It was my intention to allow him to increase his wealth, connections and power. I was behind Li's reorganization and modernization of the northern military forces, under the name of the 'New Army,' which wags called the Li family army. I was fully aware that the field commanders were directly beholden to Li Hung-chang rather than to the throne.

My trust of Li Hung-chang was based on my sense of him as a man of Confucian values. He trusted me because I had proven to him that I would never take his loyalty for granted. In my view, the only thing the throne could offer was the return of trust and loyalty. I believed that a rebel would be less likely to start an uprising if he was given a province to own. I not only gave Li free rein, but also made him want to serve me.

It was a good business for both of us. Li's profits were one of China's major sources of tax revenue. By 1875 our government was completely dependent on Li Hung-chang. For example, while Li's soldiers supervised the shipment of salt to Peking, which allowed him to oversee the salt monopoly, I received revenue from him to keep China running.

Li Hung-chang never asked the throne to fund his army. This didn't mean that he paid the soldiers from his own coffers. As a smart businessman, he used his own provincial treasury. I was sure that he spent a fortune bribing the Manchu princes who otherwise would have stood in his way. Li also provided so much employment for the nation that if he were to collapse, the country's economy would soon follow. Convinced that China should make wide-spread improvements, Li built weapons factories, ship-yards, coal plants and railways. With my approval and support he also funded China's first postal and telegraph services, its first schools of technology and schools for foreign-language interpreters.

I was unable to push through Li's proposal to establish China's first navy because most court members refused to adopt his sense of urgency. 'Too costly' was the official excuse. Li Hung-chang was accused of scaring the nation in order to get his personal armed force funded by the government.

Letters of complaint from conservatives, especially the Manchu Ironhats, kept coming in. Nothing Li Hung-chang did could please them. The Ironhats grumbled that he was taking their share of the profits, and they threatened revenge. If Li Hung-chang had not cloaked all his deals in secrecy and had his loyalists planted everywhere, he could easily have been assassinated. Still, he was blackmailed for taking kickbacks from commercial contracts and bribes from foreign traders. The conservatives warned me that it was only a matter of time before Li would stage a coup and put himself on the throne.

Li Hung-chang had his own way of fighting the court. He lived outside Peking and came to the capital only when seeking permission to expand his businesses. When he realized that he needed a political voice at court, he created partnerships with his powerful friends, Manchu and Han Chinese alike. Besides Prince Kung, Li had friendly governors in key provinces. His most important partnership was with the governor of Canton, Chang Chih-tung, who built China's largest modern iron foundry. Li made a deal with the Canton governor: instead of ordering the material for his railway from foreign companies, he got it from Canton. The two men were described as 'the Northern Li and the Southern Chang.'

I received both men in private audiences. Both deserved the honor, but I also realized the importance of staying involved. There had been enough incidents when I had ended up being the last to know.

Every governor was aware that my approval at the court carried weight, and winning me over had become a vital part of court politics. As a result, people wished to impress me, which led to flattery and dishonesty. Although outrageous lies would not pass my peasant's common sense, I couldn't avoid being fooled sometimes.

'People change,' I told my adopted son during an intermission at the court. 'Manchu royal decadence is a perfect living example.'

Guang-hsu was learning fast. One day he asked why Li Hung-chang bought me gifts, like the cases of French champagne that had recently been delivered.

'To secure his relationship with the throne,' I replied. 'He needs protection.'

'Are you pleased with the gifts?' Guang-hsu asked. 'What about the English toothbrush and toothpaste he sent? Wouldn't you have preferred an antique Han vase or some other beautiful object? Most ladies would.'

'I am more pleased with the toothbrush and paste,' I replied. 'And I especially liked Li's handwritten how-to manual. Now I get to protect my teeth from falling out and can also contemplate how to prevent the country from its own decay.'

I insisted that Guang-hsu attend my private audiences with Li Hung-chang and Chang Chih-tung. My son learned that it was I who had picked Chang to be the governor of Canton after he had won first place in the civil service examination as a young man.

Guang-hsu asked Chang, 'Did you study as hard as I do?'

The governor cleared his throat and looked to me for help.

'If you want to know the truth, Guang-hsu,' I said, smiling, 'you see, he had to compete with millions of students to win, while you –'

'While I won without sweat.' Guang-hsu understood. 'I can tell my tutor what grade I want and he'll give it to me.'

'Well, Your Majesty deserves the privilege.' The governor bowed.

'You know your good grades are not real,' I couldn't help but respond to my son.

'That's not totally correct, Mother,' Guang-hsu argued. 'I sweat differently. Other children can afford to play, because they don't have to bear the responsibility of a nation.'

'That's exactly right, Your Majesty.' Both governors nodded and smiled.

By the time Guang-hsu was nine, he demonstrated an admirable dedication to the role of Emperor. He even asked to be given less water to drink in the morning so that he wouldn't have to go to the chamber pot during an audience. He didn't want to miss anything.

His education included Western studies. For the first time in palace history, two tutors in their twenties were hired. They were from Peking's foreign-language school and were here to help teach the throne English.

I enjoyed listening to Guang-hsu practice his lessons. The young tutors tried to keep a straight face when he mispronounced words. Playfulness seemed to be the best encouragement. I remembered how Tung Chih's tutors took the fun out of learning by disciplining him too much. When Prince Kung had attempted to introduce Tung Chih to Western culture, one senior tutor had resigned in protest and another threatened suicide.

My dream for Tung Chih was being realized through Guang-hsu. Tutor Weng was introducing him to the idea of the universe, and Li Hung-chang and Chang Chih-tung were offering him their knowledge of the world, gained through experience.

Li Hung-chang also sent Guang-hsu Western books in translation, which Chang also relished, telling the young Emperor stories of his dealings with foreign merchants, diplomats, missionaries and sailors in Canton.

I disagreed with Tutor Weng's emphasis on classic Chinese literature. The classics dwelled too much on fiction and fatalism. 'Guang-hsu must learn the true makeup of his people,' I insisted.

I felt so blessed with Guang-hsu's progress that I invited peony and chrysanthemum growers to come to the palace to check the soil in my garden. I couldn't wait for the time I would be able to spend my days thinking of nothing but growing flowers.

When Guang-hsu repeatedly expressed his desire to devote his life to Nuharoo and me, I felt uneasy. Nuharoo believed that it had nothing to do with his early trauma. 'He was taught piety by his tutors, that is all,' she said.

My instinct told me that my sister had broken something inside the boy, something we were yet to discover. I suspected my own role in the matter. How much was Guang-hsu affected when he was wrenched from the family nest? However terrible it had been, it was his nest. The palace offered him a meaningful existence, but at the price of tremendous pressure. I never stopped questioning myself. Left alone, would Guang-hsu have fallen into reckless dissipation like the rest of the Manchu royals? What right did I have to determine the course of the boy's life?

Around the age of forty-five I had become uncertain of the life I had chosen for myself. When I first entered the Forbidden City, I never doubted my aspirations to live there. Now I felt even more strongly about what I had missed and what had been taken away from me – the freedom to wander, the right to love and, most of all, the right to be myself.

I would never forget Chinese New Year's celebrations in Wuhu. I had enjoyed the harvest, the fresh rice, salted and roasted soybeans and picked vegetables. All the girls gathered together with their treats and watched local opera performances. I missed visiting relatives and friends. Although I had every luxury and my duties were often rewarding, Imperial glory also meant loneliness and living in constant fear of rebellion and assassination.

Tung Chih's death had changed my perspective toward life. I didn't miss his being the Emperor, I missed holding his tiny feet in my palms when he was born, missed the first time he smiled his toothless smile. I missed taking him to gardens and watching him run free. His favorite thing to do was to fashion willow branches into play horsewhips. Nothing was about being Emperor, but being with each other.

Tung Chih's death had robbed me of happiness, and I was determined to prevent Guang-hsu from being robbed of the same. I avoided anything that would cause regret and remorse, or so I thought. I wasn't sure that I was escaping it.

I wanted to see Guang-hsu become the Emperor on his own terms, not mine. I wished to see him become a man before a ruler. I knew Chinese teachings wouldn't do much to help that, but I hoped that the Western studies might give him that chance.

My attendance at the audiences and Nuharoo's preoccupation with her religious ceremonies often left Guang-hsu at the mercy of the eunuchs after his schooling. I would later discover that several of Guang-hsu's attendants had been extraordinarily malicious. I expected that An-te-hai's death would agitate the eunuch population, causing insecurity and even rage. But I never expected this expression of revenge.

Behind my back, the eunuchs wrapped the nine-year-old Guang-hsu in a heavy blanket and rolled him in the snow. The blanket made him sweat profusely, but his uncovered limbs were exposed to the cold. When I became suspicious about his chronic coughing, the eunuchs withheld information until I investigated and found out the truth.

His health remained delicate, and the eunuchs continued to torment the boy over An-te-hai's murder. Not all the eunuchs intended to torture Guang-hsu, but their superstitions and antiquated traditions affected how they cared for him. For example, they sincerely believed that starvation and dehydration were acceptable methods of medical treatment.

What I couldn't forgive were those who failed to provide Guang-hsu with a chamber pot in time, and who laughed and humiliated him when he wet his pants. These fiends I punished severely.

Unfortunately, the most vicious acts were committed as if they were nothing out of the ordinary. Then it was I who was called abusive and cruel.

I could not forgive myself even after the eunuchs were punished. Guang-hsu's suffering pained me. I began to doubt my making him Emperor. The irony was that the Manchu princes constantly wished for fate to put their sons in Guang-hsu's shoes.

Future critics, historians and scholars would insist that Guang-hsu had led a normal life until I, his aunt, wrecked him. Guang-hsu's life in the Forbidden City was described as 'deprived.' He was constantly 'tormented by the evil murderess' and, it was said, he lived like 'a virtual prisoner until he died.'

Although it was true that I did not adopt Guang-hsu out of love, I grew to love him. I could not explain how it had happened, nor did I feel the need to. Salvation was what I found in the little boy. Anyone who was once a mother or who had the misfortune to lose a child would understand what happened between Guang-hsu and me.

I remembered that Guang-hsu was too young to detect my intentions as I taught by example that ruling our vast country was a balancing act. I hinted that placing trust in his ministers would not be good enough to secure his position as the one and only ruler of China. It was people like Li Hung-chang and Chang Chih-tung who could float or sink his 'boat.' I let Guang-hsu watch how I played both men against each other as I turned the court into a real-life stage.

During one October audience Li Hung-chang got carried away with his proposal to demolish the ancient Chinese school system and replace it with a Western model. As a counterweight to his enthusiasm, I used Chang Chih-tung. As a product of the traditional Chinese system, Chang preached the importance of 'educating the soul before its body.'

At this audience, as I had predicted to Guang-hsu, Li suddenly felt he was under attack. 'It is my way to lead him to reconsider his approach,' I explained to Guang-hsu later. 'My calling for Chang served to remind Li Hung-chang that he is not the only one the throne depends on.'

Such tactics of manipulation were not something I wished to teach my son, but they were necessary to his survival as Emperor. Guang-hsu had inherited Tung Chih's vulnerable empire, and I saw it as my duty to prepare him for the worst. As the saying went, 'The devil that can hurt you is the devil you don't know.' The damage would be even worse if the child were to be betrayed by his parent or guardian – a lesson I learned with Tung Chih's death.

18

THE TEMPERATURE SUDDENLY dropped and water in the giant jar in the courtyard outside the audience hall glazed over with ice. Inside, the wood-burning heaters glowed red in the four corners. Nuharoo and I were glad that we had had the windows repaired. The gaps had been sealed to stop the whistle of the northwest wind. The eunuchs also changed the draperies. The thin silk curtains were replaced by thick velvet.

As soon as Guang-hsu was able, I talked with Tutor Weng and made the audiences his classroom. It was not easy for my son. His tutor would help him digest what he saw and heard. Often the matters were too complicated for a child to grasp. To make it work, I took time preparing Guang-hsu for the upcoming discussion.

'Was it Russia's business to protect Sinkiang?' Guang-hsu asked about the situation back in 1871, when tsarist forces had moved into our far western wilderness of Sinkiang, a region called Ili, after its river.

'Russia went on behalf of our court, to prevent Ili from becoming an independent Moslem state,' I replied. 'We didn't invite the Russians, though.'

'You mean the Russians invited themselves in?'

'Yes.'

Guang-hsu tried to comprehend. 'But . . . weren't the Moslem uprisings swept away?' He pointed at the map and his finger traced the places. 'Why are the Russians still here? Why didn't they return to where they came from?'

'We don't know,' I said.

'Yung Lu is in Sinkiang, isn't he?' the child persisted.

I nodded.

'Has he done something to drive the Russians away?'

'Yes, he has asked our charitable Russian neighbors for the return of Ili.'

'And?'

'They refused.'

'Why?'

I told Guang-hsu that I wished I could explain. Unlike Tung Chih, at least Guang-hsu understood that China did not hold a strong hand at the bargaining table. Guang-hsu tried hard to fathom the decisions he was forced to make, but often it was impossible. The child couldn't perceive why China had to carry on long and exhaustive diplomatic negotiations with Russia only to have to yield in the end. He would never understand why a treaty in his name he had just signed, in February of 1881, imposed a payment of nine million rubles to Russia for China's own territories.

I began to see how Guang-hsu was reacting to the audiences. He was under constant pressure and suffered terribly. When he heard bad news, I could feel his nervousness and saw fear written on his face. I was guilty of joining the ministers who grumbled impatiently about when Guang-hsu would catch up by growing up.

Soon it was no longer simply a learning experience for Guang-hsu. Shocked on a daily basis, his mood and health were adversely affected. Yet my choice was either to shelter him or to let him live the truth. Either way it was cruel. When we summoned the minister of agriculture to give his prediction on the next year's crops, Guang-hsu broke down. He felt personally responsible when the minister forecasted drastic harvest shortfalls resulting from flood and drought.

Now an adolescent, Guang-hsu did show determination and self-discipline. I was relieved when he exhibited no desire to cavort with the eunuchs and no interest in slipping out of the palace to carouse. He seemed to prefer solitude. He would eat his meals alone and was uneasy around company. When dining with Nuharoo and me, he sat quietly and ate whatever was put on his plate. My sadness over the loss of Tung Chih affected him so profoundly that Guang-hsu made sure that his behavior would please me.

I wished that I could tell the difference between his seriousness in study and his encroaching melancholy. Even though my experience told me that daily audiences could be a tremendous strain, I didn't realize that to a child they could be poison.

Eager to bring him to maturity, I denied the possibility that I could be robbing him of his childhood. Guang-hsu's pleasant appearance fooled me. Only later would he confess that he feared that he wasn't living up to my expectations.

I didn't tell Guang-hsu that losing was simply a way of learning how to win. I was afraid of repeating my mistakes with Tung Chih. Spoiling and pampering were in part what had killed my son. Tung Chih rebelled because he knew that he didn't have to worry about losing my affection.

Guang-hsu followed strict protocol and etiquette. Tutor Weng took every measure to prevent him from the possibility of abusing his privileges. Thus Guang-hsu was turned into a palace hostage. Only later would I learn that each and every time the ministers addressed their problems to the child, he would consider them his own. He became ashamed of himself for his inability to solve the problems of the empire.

Around 1881 my health declined. I lost my normal cycle and again had trouble sleeping. I ignored my fatigue and sudden flushes of heat and hoped they would go away. By the time the country celebrated my forty-sixth birthday in November, I was seriously ill. It took me longer to rise and dress, and I had to drink ginseng tea to keep up my strength. Nevertheless, I continued to attend audiences and supervise Guang-hsu's study. I encouraged Tutor Weng to introduce the Emperor to people from outside the capital.

Guang-hsu granted the governors of twenty-three provinces private audiences. The senior governors that had been appointed by my husband, Emperor Hsien Feng, were especially grateful. I attended each audience and was glad to meet with my old friends. We often had to pause to dry our tears.

By the onset of winter I was completely exhausted. My chest was congested and sore, and I had terrible diarrhea. One morning I passed out during an audience.

Dressed in her golden court robe, Nuharoo visited me the next morning. It was the first time I saw her hair wrapped on a black board in the shape of a V, rich with jewelry and ornaments. I complimented her and asked if she would conduct the audiences. Nuharoo agreed, then added, 'But don't expect me to be a slave.'

*   *   *

I hadn't had the leisure of waking up to daylight for years. As winter became spring, my energy slowly returned. Spending the day in the sunshine, I worked in my gardens. I thought of Yung Lu and wondered how he was doing in the distant Moslem state. I had written to him but received no response.

Guang-hsu stopped by after audiences and brought me dinner. He had grown taller and was sweet and gentle. He kindly placed a piece of roasted chicken on my plate and asked if I was enjoying the new blooming camellias.

I asked Guang-hsu if he wondered about life outside the Forbidden City, and also if he missed his parents. 'Mother and Father are permitted to visit me at any time,' he replied. 'But they haven't come.'

'Maybe you should invite them.'

He looked at me for a moment and then shook his head. I couldn't tell if he had no desire to meet them or was afraid of offending me. My past comments about my sister must have influenced his attitude. Although I had never intentionally disparaged Rong, I hadn't had good things to say about her either.

I asked Guang-hsu if he remembered the death of his cousin Tung Chih, and how he felt about being chosen to succeed him.

'I don't remember much about Tung Chih,' Guang-hsu said. Regarding the night of his departure from home, he recalled being held in Yung Lu's arms.

'I remember his dark face and the decorative buttons on his uniform. The buttons were cold against my skin. I felt strange. I remember that it was pitch-dark.' He looked at me intently and added, 'I enjoyed riding with the Bannerman.'

'You are being kind, Guang-hsu,' I said, comforted but still feeling guilty. 'It must have been terrible to be pulled away from your warm bed and a deep sleep. I am sorry to have put you through it.'

'There was a purpose in my chaotic beginning,' the boy said in an old man's tone.

I sighed, again impressed by his sensitivity.

'Good living needs no reasoning, convincing or explaining, while bad requires plenty.' Guang-hsu smiled. 'Three of my brothers died by my mother's hand. I would have been next if you hadn't adopted me.'

He rose and offered me his right arm. We stepped into the garden. He came up to my eyebrows and looked thin in his yellow satin robe. His movements recalled his cousin's.

'I am sure my sister didn't mean harm,' I said.

'Mother is very ill. My father said that he's given up.'

'Prince Kung's wife told Nuharoo that your father has moved out and is living with his fifth concubine. Is it true?'

'I'm afraid so.'

'Will Rong be all right?'

'Mother fell from her bed and broke her hip last month. She blamed the doctors for her pain. I shouldn't have sent Doctor Sun Pao-tien.'

'Why not? What happened?'

'She hit him.' After a pause, Guang-hsu added, 'She hits everybody who tries to help her. Sometimes I wish she was dead.'

'I am sorry.'

Guang-hsu went quiet and wiped his eyes.

'I wasn't thinking of your welfare when I adopted you,' I confessed. 'The welfare of the dynasty was the only thing on my mind. Tung Chih had a tragic end. I still can't forgive myself. I let him down . . . and I am afraid to let you down, Guang-hsu.'

The young man dropped to his knees and kowtowed. 'Mother, I beg you to stop thinking about Tung Chih. I am here, alive, and I love you.'

19

IN APRIL, the news that Nuharoo had collapsed swept through the Forbidden City.

'Her Majesty has been feeling ill since last week,' Nuharoo's chief eunuch reported at court. His skinny neck protruded forward, making him look like an overripe squash hanging from a vine. 'She had no appetite. She went to bed before we had a chance to warm her sheets. The next day she insisted on getting up, but couldn't. I helped her dress and noticed that her clothes were damp with cold sweat. She put her weight on my shoulders while we did her hair and makeup. She made it to the Hall of Spiritual Nurturing in the palanquin, but she fell unconscious before the audience was called.'

'Why didn't you inform Doctor Sun Pao-tien earlier?' I asked.

'Her Majesty wouldn't let me,' the eunuch replied.

'It was four in the afternoon and I gave Her Majesty some medicine to dissipate her ailment,' Sun Pao-tien stepped up and reported.

'What is wrong with her?' I asked.

'We don't know for sure yet,' the doctor said. 'It could be her liver or the grippe.'

'Her Majesty insisted on keeping her condition a secret,' the chief eunuch said. 'After five days she dismissed the doctors. My lady had a seizure last night. She knotted up on the floor. Her eyes rolled back and foam came out of her mouth. Before the doctors arrived Her Majesty lost control of her body. I must complain that Doctor Sun Pao-tien was not helping.'

'The eunuchs kept rolling my patient up and down and around as if she were an acrobat,' the doctor protested.

'It was the only way we could keep her dry!' Nuharoo's eunuch shot back.

'My patient was having a seizure!' The gentle doctor lost his patience.

'We should have gone first to the priest at the temple.' The eunuch battered his head with his fists. 'His prayers are known for making the dying sit up and walk.'

I stopped the eunuch and asked Sun Pao-tien to continue.

'My colleague and I found out that Her Majesty's breathing has been constricted by phlegm. We have been trying to find a way to suck it out.'

'It was not working!' all the eunuchs cried in unison.

I asked why I hadn't been informed.

'My lady didn't want the court, and especially you, to be told. She believed that she would be fine in no time.'

'Have you any proof?'

'Here.' The eunuch fumbled in his pockets and produced a piece of wrinkled paper. 'My lady signed the instructions.' Tears and mucus had gathered at the tip of the eunuch's nose and dripped. 'She came back miraculously last time. So we thought she would get over this attack.'

'*Last time*? What do you mean? This has happened before?'

'Yes. The first time was when my lady was twenty-six years old, and then again when she was thirty-three. This time I am afraid she will not survive.'

When I rushed to Nuharoo's palace, sounds of crying filled the air. The courtyard was packed with people. Seeing me, the crowd made way. I arrived at Nuharoo's bedside and found her practically buried in fresh gardenias. Doctor Sun Pao-tien was at her side.

It shocked me how illness had changed her appearance. Her eyebrows were in the shape of a big knot and her mouth sagged to one side. Her breathing was labored and there was a gurgling noise in her throat.

'Take away the flowers,' I ordered.

None of the attendants moved.

'How can she breathe with the flowers weighing on her chest?'

The eunuchs threw themselves down. 'It is what Her Majesty wanted.'

'Nuharoo,' I whispered.

'She can't hear you,' said the doctor.

'How can this be? For years she was not ill for even a day!'

'Her duties at court have worn her out,' the doctor explained. 'She may not last the night.'

A few minutes later Nuharoo opened her eyes. 'You came in time, Yehonala,' she said. 'I get to say goodbye.'

'Nonsense, Nuharoo.' I bent down. When I touched her pale, thin shoulder, my tears came.

'Bury me with my gardenias,' she said. 'The court will want to bury me their way. You make sure that I don't get bullied in death.'

'Whatever you say, Nuharoo. But you are not going to die.'

'My way is the only way, Yehonala.'

'Oh, my dear Nuharoo, you promised that you wouldn't drive yourself so.'

'I didn't.' She closed her eyes. A eunuch wiped her face with a towel. 'I didn't quit because I didn't want to embarrass myself.'

'What is there to be embarrassed about?'

'I wanted to show . . . that I was as good as you.'

'But you are, Nuharoo.'

'That's a lousy lie, Yehonala. You are happy because I am going to be out of your way for good.'

'Please, Nuharoo . . .'

'You can order the eunuchs to get rid of their brooms now.'

'What are you talking about?'

'You can collect the fall leaves, pile them as high as you want in the courtyards. The hell with stains on the marble.'

I listened and wept.

'Buddha is on the other side waiting for me.'

'Nuharoo . . .'

She raised her hand. 'Stop, Yehonala. Death is ugly. I've got nothing left.'

I held her hand. It was cold, and her fingers felt like a bundle of chopsticks.

'There is honor, Nuharoo.'

'You would think I care.'

'You have saved up plenty of virtue, Nuharoo. Your next life will be a splendid one.'

'I have been living inside these walls . . .' Her voice drifted. 'Only the dusty winds of the desert penetrated . . .' She turned slowly to face the ceiling. 'Two and a half miles of walls and the two hundred and fifty acres enclosed have been my world and yours, Yehonala. I will not call you Orchid. I promised myself.'

'Of course not, Nuharoo.'

'No more rehearsing the protocols . . . the endless comedy of manners . . .' She paused to catch her breath. 'Only a practiced ear could detect the real meaning of a word wrapped in filigree . . . the idea hidden in amber.'

'Oh, yes, Empress Nuharoo.'

A half hour later, Nuharoo ordered that she be left alone with me.

When the room was cleared, I pulled over two thick pillows and sat her up. Her neck, her hair and her inner robe were sweat-soaked.

'Will you,' she began, 'forgive me?'

'For what?'

'For . . . for driving Hsien Feng out of your bed.'

I asked if she meant the concubines whom she had brought in to seduce Hsien Feng during my pregnancy.

She nodded.

I told her not to worry. 'It was only a matter of time until Hsien Feng abandoned me.'

'I will be punished in my next life if you don't forgive me, Lady Yehonala.'

'All right, Nuharoo, I forgive you.'

'Also, I plotted your miscarriage.' She wouldn't stop.

'I knew. You didn't succeed, though.'

A tear streamed down from the corner of her eye. 'You are kind, Yehonala.'

'No more, please, Nuharoo.'

'But there is more I'd like to confess.'

'I don't want to hear it.'

'I must, Yehonala.'

'Tomorrow, Nuharoo.'

'I might not . . . have the chance.'

'I promise to come tomorrow morning.'

She decided to go ahead anyway. 'I . . . gave permission for An-te-hai's murder.'

Her voice was almost inaudible, but it hit me.

'Tell me you hate me, Yehonala.'

I did, I hated her, but I couldn't say it.

Her lips trembled. 'I need to depart with a clear conscience.'

She squeezed my fingers. Her expression was sad and helpless. Her mouth opened and closed like a fish out of water.

'Offer your mercy, Yehonala.'

I was not sure I had the right to forgive. I took my hand out of hers. 'Get some rest, Nuharoo. I will see you tomorrow.'

Using all her might she yelled, 'My departure is irreversible!'

I pulled away and headed toward the door.

'You have wished my disappearance, Lady Yehonala, I know you have.'

I stopped and turned around. 'Yes, but I changed my mind. We haven't been the best partners, but I cannot imagine having no partner at all. I am used to you. You are the most wretched fucking demon I know!'

A faint smile crossed Nuharoo's face, and she murmured, 'I hate you, Yehonala.'

Nuharoo died the next morning. She was forty-four years old. Her last words to me were 'He didn't touch me.' I was stunned because I was sure she meant that Emperor Hsien Feng did not make love to her on their wedding night.

I followed Nuharoo's burial instructions and covered her

with gardenias. Her coffin was carried to the royal tomb site and she was laid next to our husband. Luckily, it was April, the season for gardenias. I had no trouble shipping tons of flowers from the south. The farewell ceremony was held in a sea of gardenias in the Hall of Buddha Worshiping, attended by thousands. Hundreds of wreaths in all shapes and sizes arrived from around the country. The eunuchs piled them up, filling the hall.

Nuharoo's passion for gardenias was new to me. The plant was not native to Peking; it was popular in southern China. From her eunuchs I learned that Nuharoo had never seen gardenias before her final illness. She had requested that gardenias be planted around her tomb, only to be told that they wouldn't survive the harsh northern weather. And the desert soil was unsuitable for them.

Nuharoo had surprised me with her feelings after all. I remembered how content she was when I first met her at sixteen. She believed that the world outside was a shabby thing compared to the 'Great Within.' I could only wonder how excited she would have been if she had traveled to the south and saw with her own eyes the green fertile plain – the land of gardenias.

Two thousand Buddhist monks attended the burial ceremony. They chanted around the clock. Guang-hsu and I stayed up late for the 'soul ceremony,' when Nuharoo's spirit was said to ascend to Heaven. Eunuchs placed the candles in folded-paper boats and floated them on Kun Ming Lake. Guang-hsu ran along the shore, following the drifting candles.

I sat on a flat boulder by the lake. Quietly I read a poem to wish Nuharoo a good journey to Heaven.

Gardenias fill the courtyard free from dust
By climbing the trumpet vine, its fragrance reinforced;
Softly they heighten the fresh green of spring,
Gently they trail their perfume, ring on ring.
A light mist hides the winding path from view,
From covered walks drips chill and verdant dew.
But who will celebrate the pool in song?
Lost in a dream, at peace, the poet sleeps long.

The foreign press described Nuharoo's death as 'mysterious' and 'suspicious' and speculated that I was the murderer. 'It is generally believed that Tzu Hsi brought about the death of her colleague,' a reputable English newspaper stated. 'She made up her mind to kill because she was discovered by Nuharoo in bed with a leading man of the opera.'

I was able to remain detached until Tung Chih was brought into the stories. 'She Did It Again: Yehonala Sacrificed Her Own Child on the Altar of Her Ambition!' shouted one headline in the British press, and the story was picked up by the Chinese papers. The article stated, 'When Emperor Tung Chih was critically ill, his mother, far from providing him with the proper medical care, allowed the disease to wreak havoc with his delicate constitution. Should we have any reason to doubt that she had not allowed the same to happen to her coregent?' Another paper echoed, 'Yehonala seemed intent on orchestrating the early death of her son and that of Nuharoo. Everyone at court knew that Tung Chih and Nuharoo would not live to see old age.'

I felt defenseless. To justify further foreign encroachments in China, I had to be made into a monster.

'It is inconceivable that Yehonala did not know of the shameful exploits of her son and Nuharoo,' one Chinese

164

translation read, 'and the fatal consequences of such adventures. It was within her power to forbid these revels, yet she did nothing to prevent them.'

Day after day, slanderers from around the world poured their venom: 'We see how complete was the Dowager Empress's estrangement from her son and how total her lust for power.' 'For the young girl from the poorest province in China, no price is too high to maintain her despotic grip on the Celestial Empire.'

I dreamed that Yung Lu would come back to defend me. I cried at Tung Chih's altar and walked back in the middle of the night through the Hall of Spiritual Nurturing like a ghost. During the day's audiences, I would break down and weep like a schoolgirl. Guang-hsu kept passing me handkerchiefs until he started to weep himself.

20

THE POWERFUL STRATEGIST and businessman Li Hung-chang told me that not only was China facing an unavoidable war, but we were already deeply into it. For a week the court had discussed nothing but France's ambitions in our southern border provinces, including Vietnam, which China had long ago ruled before the Vietnamese gained a quasi-independence in the tenth century.

Soon after my husband's death in 1862, France colonized southern Vietnam, or Cochin China. Like the British, the French were hungrily drawn to trade in our southwestern provinces and had set their sights on control of the navigable Red River in northern Vietnam. In 1874 France forced the King of Vietnam to accept a treaty giving it the privileges of overlordship that China had traditionally enjoyed. Much to France's irritation, the King continued to send tribute to my son in exchange for protection.

To help hold the Vietnamese territory in the south, I granted freedom to a former Taiping rebel leader and sent him to repel the French. The rebel had been born in the area and considered it his homeland. He fought valiantly and succeeded in keeping the French at bay. But when the

166

King died, the French negotiated another treaty with his successor, which stated, 'Vietnam recognizes and accepts the protectorate of France.'

In response to our court's ultimatum, the French launched a surprise military attack. Since we hadn't expected to go to war, our southwestern borders were neither strengthened nor prepared. By March of 1884 Li Hung-chang came to report that all of the major cities in Vietnam had fallen into French hands.

My court was divided over the crisis. Publicly, the dispute was over how best to deal with French aggression. Beneath the surface, however, was a widening gap between two political factions: the conservative Manchu Ironhats and the progressives, led by Prince Kung and Li Hung-chang.

I asked Guang-hsu, who had just turned fourteen, how he felt about the situation, and he replied, 'As yet I do not know.'

I wasn't sure whether or not my son meant to be humble. Months of sitting through court audiences seemed to have worn the boy down. He looked bored and listless. He had told me half jokingly that he would prefer a game of chess over attending an audience. When I told him that he must do what duty dictated, Guang-hsu responded, 'I'm trying to glue myself to the dragon chair.'

I tried to encourage him. 'You are saving the nation, Guang-hsu.'

'I haven't achieved anything. I just listen to the same arguments, day in and day out.'

It was then that I discovered that Guang-hsu had skipped his audiences during the entire time I was making preparations for Nuharoo's funeral. This upset me more than receiving the news of cities falling in Vietnam.

I didn't know what else I could do to inject a sense of urgency into the young Emperor. One day during lunch I illustrated our position on a napkin, drawing a triangle representing the divided court with the Emperor caught in the middle.

I tried not to push too hard. I remembered how Tung Chih ran away while appearing obedient. I remembered his resentment and the irritation that had come into his voice. I told myself to make life Guang-hsu's game instead of mine.

The first thing I did was waive Guang-hsu's duty to officiate at the Confucian rites. Although I agreed with the court that Tung Chih's spirit required the performance of time-honored prayers and rituals for the comfort and security of his departed soul, I believed that Guang-hsu needed a break.

I didn't want Guang-hsu to live in Tung Chih's shadow. However, the court regarded his ascent to the throne as nothing but that. Without Nuharoo's supervision I began to bend the rules. A few ministers questioned my actions, but most court members understood it when I said, 'Only when Guang-hsu has succeeded will Tung Chih's soul truly be at rest.'

'Uncle Prince Ts'eng threatened suicide when I agreed to allow foreigners to live and trade in China,' Guang-hsu reported. 'He has asked my father to join him in funding the Boxers.'

I was all too aware of the Boxers, a peasant movement with deep roots in traditional Chinese culture – or so their leaders claimed. Their numbers were growing rapidly.

'Unfortunately,' I informed my son, 'the Boxers' mission is to murder foreigners.'

'Are you on Prince Kung's side, then?' Guang-hsu asked.

I let out a sigh.

'My father is full of nonsense,' Guang-hsu went on. 'His poems and calligraphy are exhibited everywhere.'

'Prince Ch'un wants China to stay closed. What are your thoughts?'

'I agree with Uncle Kung,' Guang-hsu replied. Then, looking me straight in the eye, he said, 'I don't understand why you tell me to cease when I try to let the court know my opinion.'

'The Emperor's job is to unite the court,' I gently pointed out.

'Yes, Mother,' Guang-hsu said obediently.

'I heard that you want to inspect the new navy.'

Guang-hsu nodded. 'Yes, very much. Li Hung-chang is ready, but the court won't give me permission to receive him. My father thinks he is the real Emperor, though I wear the clothes.'

'What do you think of Prince I-kuang's handling of the Board of Foreign Affairs?'

'He seems to be more capable than the rest. But I don't really like him, or my other uncles.' Guang-hsu paused for a moment and then continued. 'To tell you the truth, Mother, I have been establishing contacts with people outside the court circle. Thinkers and reformers, people who know how to really help me.'

'Make sure you understand what reform means in practice.' I didn't want to admit that I had little idea myself.

'I do, Mother. I have been working up a reform plan.'

'What would be your first edict?'

'It would be to remove privileges from those who enjoy government salaries while contributing nothing.'

'Are you aware of the size of this group?'

'I know there are hundreds of royal pests who are paid for their princeships and governorships. My father, uncles, brothers and cousins are their patrons.'

'Your younger brother, Prince Ch'un Junior, has become the new star of the Ironhats,' I warned him. 'His gang vowed to destroy anyone who supports Prince Kung and Li Hung-chang.'

'I'll be issuing the edicts, not Prince Ch'un Junior.'

'Support Prince Kung and Li Hung-chang and maintain good relations with the conservative party,' I advised.

'I am prepared to abandon them,' Guang-hsu said in a calm voice. His determination pleased me, although I knew I couldn't afford to encourage him further.

'You should not abandon them, Guang-hsu.'

The Emperor pivoted his head toward me and stared.

'They are the heart of the Manchu ruling class,' I explained. 'You must not turn blood relatives into enemies.'

'Why?'

'They can use the family law to overthrow you.'

Guang-hsu seemed unsure. He got off his chair and paced the hall.

'Funding the Boxers is one of the Ironhats' strategies,' I said, taking a sip of tea. 'They are backed by our friend the Canton governor, Chang Chih-tung.'

'I know, I know, they are the influential leaders and are resentful if not hostile toward all foreigners.' Guang-hsu went back to his chair and sat down. He let out a heavy sigh.

I rose to add hot water to his teacup.

'Should I trust Li Hung-chang?' Guang-hsu asked. 'He seems to be the most successful dealmaker with the foreign powers.'

'Trust him,' I replied. 'However, keep in mind that your brother Ch'un cares about the Manchu Dynasty no less than Li Hung-chang.'

The spring air was gritty with sand blown by the strong desert wind. It wasn't until April that the wind softened to a breeze. Under the warm sun the eunuchs let go of their brown winter robes that made them look like bears. The Imperial backyard concubines slipped into their ankle-length chipaos, dresses of Manchu design that cleverly complimented the female figure.

I missed strolling the streets of Peking under the sunshine. It had been over a quarter of a century since I'd had the pleasure. Images of the city came to me only in my dreams. I missed looking into lanes and courtyards where fermiana trees were in bud and loquat trees bloomed in bunches. I missed the baskets of the peony sellers by the busy crossroads. I remembered the scent of their freshly cut flowers and the sweet smell of date trees.

Ball-like willow catkins chased each other inside the Forbidden City. They flew over the inner walls and through the windows and landed on my desk while I outlined what I had read in reports from overseas.

Guang-hsu sat beside me. 'Li Hung-chang says he has sent reinforcements to the trouble spot, but from others I hear different,' Guang-hsu said, cupping his hands together under his chin.

No one else was in the room. We could hear the echoes of our own voices. I reminded the Emperor of the possibility that people would say anything to discredit Li.

'It is difficult to know who's telling the truth,' Guang-hsu agreed.

I wished that there were others whom I could depend on for information. Li Hung-chang was the only one who had established his credibility beyond the shadow of a doubt. I liked him, although never his news. Whenever I heard my eunuch's voice announcing Li's arrival, my insides would stir. I had to make an effort to sit up straight so that I could hold the bad news in my stomach.

On August 22, 1885, the French opened fire without warning, yet they refused to call it a war. The message from Li Hung-chang read, 'Our junks and numerous ships were set ablaze and they sank within minutes.'

Guang-hsu's hands shook slightly as he turned the pages. 'Our supplies are strangled now that the French navy blockades the straits between Taiwan and Fukien. Where is Li Hung-chang's Northern Army?'

'You sent him to deal with Japan over the issue of Korea,' I reminded him. 'Li's army must remain in the north.'

With both hands Guang-hsu held his head.

'Have some tea, Guang-hsu' was all I could say.

Pressing his eyes with his fingers, he said, 'We can't afford not to deal with Japan.'

I agreed. 'To Japan, Korea is the point of access to Pechili Bay and then to Peking itself.'

Guang-hsu rose and went to read the court's memorandum. 'What else can the court advise me? "Exercise restraint . . . Do not arouse conflict with Japan while at war with the French . . ."'

'The court had hoped that Japan would be grateful after we let them have Taiwan.'

'Tutor Weng said that our kindness and sense of self-restraint should not be regarded as an invitation for invasion.'

'He's not wrong, but –'

'Mother,' Guang-hsu interrupted me, 'do you know that the week the Americans signed the treaty with Korea, Tutor Weng became constipated? He tried to punish himself by eating nothing but breadsticks.'

I sighed and tried to concentrate. 'America's involvement only complicates matters.'

Guang-hsu held himself with both of his arms and sat down again.

We stared at each other.

'Mother, is the United States implying that Korea is now an equal among nations and independent of China?'

I nodded.

'I don't feel well, Mother. My body wants to desert me.'

I wanted to say 'Shame and self-punishment don't inspire courage,' but instead I turned my head away and began to weep.

As Emperors, both of my sons had no way to escape. Guang-hsu had to continue to live Tung Chih's nightmare. I felt like the ghost who came to snatch a substitute so the dead son's soul could be given a new life. I felt that it was my hands that were pulling and tightening the rope around Guang-hsu's neck.

'Who else is on the way to invade us?' Guang-hsu asked in a panicked tone. 'I am sick of being told after the battle is lost and the treaty drafted!'

'It's not your fault that we lost Taiwan, Vietnam and Korea,' I managed to say. 'Since 1861 China has been like a mulberry tree nipped away at by worms. Your frustration is no different from my husband's.'

My words of understanding didn't comfort Guang-hsu. He began to lose his playfulness. In the months to come, the distress would claim him. Unlike Tung Chih, who chose to escape, Guang-hsu did nothing but endure the bad news.

Li Hung-chang negotiated with the French, and Prince Kung invited Robert Hart of our customs service to conduct diplomacy on our behalf. We were lucky, because in the end Hart proved to be a true friend of China.

Before the end of summer, we had unceremoniously ceded Vietnam to France. Li Hung-chang volunteered his disgrace in order for the throne to save face.

A painful moment came when Guang-hsu realized that after protracted war, long suffering, capricious decision-making and the tragic death of thousands, China had obtained only the abolition of the original indemnity to France.

In the meantime, Korea, financed by Japan, began Western-style reforms and proclaimed independence.

'Korea is the thumb of China's hand!' Guang-hsu shouted during an audience.

'Yes, Your Majesty,' the court echoed.

'We are weakened, but not shattered!' The Emperor waved his fist.

Everyone's attitude was 'Let the boy blow off steam.' In the end, Guang-hsu consented to the resolution of the Sino-French War in order to concentrate our defenses in the north, against Japan.

Often, by the time news reached the throne, the moment for action would have already passed. It was written clearly in the dynastic laws that authority was to be fully respected and etiquette strictly followed, but I was forced to adapt the laws to changing situations. Greater autonomy had brought efficiency and successful outcomes on a number of occasions. Many times the initiative was Li Hung-chang's, who was doing all he could to hold back the Japanese.

With the force Li Hung-chang sent into Korea went a man who would soon be playing an important role on China's political stage. His name was Yuan Shih-kai, a stocky twenty-three-year-old who was ambitious and courageous. When the pro-Japanese faction had attempted a coup in December 1884 at a ceremonial banquet in Seoul, Yuan, the chief of staff of the garrison, took the King of Korea hostage after a fierce struggle in the palace's very courtyard and silenced the Japanese and their Korean disciples.

Yuan Shih-kai's prompt and confident military action averted the fall of Korea to Japan. For this Guang-hsu rewarded him. Besides a rank-jumping promotion, Yuan was made the Chinese Resident in Seoul.

The treaty Li Hung-chang negotiated with Japan in 1885 stated that both countries would withdraw their troops from Korea. It stipulated that a third power would organize reforms in Korea, and that China and Japan could intervene with military assistance only after notifying each other. Five years later Korean envoys would come to Peking and kowtow like vassals before Guang-hsu. It brought my son great relief, although both he and I knew it was only a matter of time before we would lose control again.

In the meantime, I advised Guang-hsu to accept Li Hung-chang's proposal to upgrade Taiwan's status from that of a prefecture of Fujian to a full-fledged province. If it was inevitable that we would lose the island, at least the gesture might gain us honor. Guang-hsu's 1887 edict declared that Taiwan would be 'the twentieth province in the country, with its capital at Taipei,' and that Taiwan's modernization drive would 'include the building of the first railroad and the beginning of a postal service.' We fooled no one but ourselves.

21

IT SNOWED LAST NIGHT. Although it was not heavy, it continued until dawn. It had been a tough week. My head felt battered and swollen. Tutor Weng had given the Emperor and me an intensive introduction to Japan's transformation through political reform. Tutor Weng elaborated on the importance of freedom of expression.

'The general view regarding scholars as subversives must be changed.' The grand tutor's gray beard hung in front of his chest like a curtain, making him look like a kitchen god. 'We must follow the Japanese model.'

'First I'll ban the practice of prosecuting heretics.' Guang-hsu was excited.

'But how will you convince the court?' I asked him. 'We must keep in mind that the Manchu Dynasty was founded on military power. Our ancestors secured their position by purging and slaughtering all subversives.'

'Mother.' My son turned to me. 'You are the senior member of the royal clan and have earned great authority. The court can say no to me, but it will have difficulty saying no to you.'

I promised to help. In front of the court, I granted permission to Tutor Weng's proposal, which would introduce Japanese-style reforms. However, behind the Forbidden City gates I expressed my private concern to Tutor Weng. I told him that I lacked confidence in the intelligence of our scholars, especially the group who named themselves Ming-shih, 'men of wisdom.' By reputation they were inclined to petty chatter and self-indulgence. As a young girl back in Wuhu, I remembered such men as my father's friends. They spent their days reciting poetry, discussing philosophy, singing operas and drinking. They were known to frequent playhouses and 'flower boats' – floating brothels.

I was more concerned about Japan's growing aggression and encouraged the Emperor to work with Li Hung-chang in setting up an admiralty board to oversee naval affairs. I asked Guang-hsu to personally see to the Imperial funding of vessels and munitions of war.

My biggest challenge had been the outrage expressed by the Manchu royals over cuts in their annual taels. To quiet them, I appointed Prince Ch'un as the comptroller of the new board. The man was not the equal of his brother the brilliant Prince Kung, whom I would have preferred to work with. But Prince Kung had made a fatal mistake, which put him on the sidelines. Prince Ch'un was ineffective in all things, but he was the father of the Emperor and I had no other candidate. Aware of his shortcomings, I appointed Li Hung-chang and Tseng Chi-tse, son of Tseng Kuo-fan, as his advisors, knowing that they would more than fulfill their roles.

Future historians would describe Prince Ch'un's appointment as my revenge against Prince Kung and as another example of my thirst for power. The truth was that Kung was a victim of Manchu inner-court politics. His liberal views made him a target not only of the Ironhats but also of his own jealous brothers, including Prince Ch'un and Prince Ts'eng.

During the conflict with France, the Ironhats advocated that China go immediately to war. Prince Ch'un was encouraged to claim his authority in his son's government. By the time I became involved, Prince Kung's trouble with the court's majority was out of control. Believing that China should do everything to avoid a war, Kung worked independently with envoys whom he sent to Paris to negotiate. With Robert Hart's assessment of the situation, Prince Kung brought France to a compromise settlement, and Li Hung-chang was dispatched to formalize the agreement.

When Li's settlement turned Indochina into a joint protectorate of China and France, the nation's emotions were stirred. Prince Kung and Li Hung-chang were attacked as traitors. Letters denouncing the two piled up on my desk.

Although I supported Prince Kung, I couldn't ignore the growing dissension in the court. Emperor Guang-hsu was being pushed around by his hot-blooded brother and Ironhat leader Prince Ch'un Junior.

I realized that the only way to get Prince Kung out of trouble was to fire him for relatively benign reasons: arrogance, nepotism and inefficiency. I convinced my brother-in-law that an edict of dismissal would clear him of the charge of treason.

In anger and disappointment, Kung offered his resignation, and it was granted.

Li Hung-chang was left vulnerable. To save his own skin, he switched sides – a move I could not criticize and for which I could offer only sympathy. Then Prince Ch'un replaced Prince Kung as the chief minister.

The nation suffered the consequences of the departure of Prince Kung, a man I had depended on for security for so many years. With both Yung Lu and Prince Kung gone, I became nervous. China was now almost solely in the hands of the Manchu hardliners – a notoriously grasping, villainous and uneducated group that numbered in the thousands.

The Manchu ancestors had set up a system of rotating appointments every two or three years to prevent officials from establishing private interests. The rotation often meant that a new governor would fall into the grip of his clerks and underlings, who knew their area well. I was suspicious of the new governors who came to tell the Emperor of 'recent achievements.'

According to Li Hung-chang, thirty percent of the nation's annual revenue was siphoned off through extortion, fraud and corruption. Our government was bedeviled by the lack of competent and honest men. And, above all, by a shortage of funds and the means to generate them.

Guang-hsu had been talking about remitting land taxes. I pleaded with him to stay his hand. Past summers had brought ruin to half of China. In the poorest provinces families exchanged their children – parents could not bear to watch their own die and then be forced to eat them. In the meantime, our exports lagged perilously behind imports. Even the tea trade, which we had virtually monopolized in 1876, had been stolen by British-run India. We now supplied only a quarter of the world's consumption of tea.

My room was stuffed with papers. Brushes, paint, ink stones and signature stamps cluttered every surface. My walls were covered with paintings in progress. My subjects continued to be floral studies and landscapes, but my strokes revealed my increasing anxiety.

I sent my painting instructor away because I was driving her crazy. She could not understand why I couldn't paint the way I used to. She was terrified by my mad brush-strokes. Her eyebrows were like two peaks and her mouth gaped with silent shock as she fixed my strokes. She dotted the black ink everywhere until the painting dripped and my rose turned into a zebra.

Li Lien-ying told me that my paintings were not selling because the collectors believed that they were not mine.

'The new pieces lack elegance and calmness,' my eunuch said.

I told him that the beauty of the Imperial parks no longer inspired me. 'Hostile and inhuman, the pavilions stand there only to help rally oppression!'

'But my lady, we who inhabit the Forbidden City live like bats in caves. Darkness is our mean.'

I threw my brush across the room. 'I am sick of looking at the shady courtyards and the long, dark, narrow stone paths! The identical Forbidden City apartments whisper murder in my ears!'

'It's a sickness of the mind, my lady. I'll make arrangements to hang a large mirror by the entrance. It will help deflect the intruding evil spirits.'

The day Li Lien-ying hung the new mirror, I dreamed of journeying to a Buddhist temple high in the mountains. The upward path by a cliff was less than a foot wide. Hundreds of feet below was a mirror-like lake. It sat in a valley between two hills. In my dream the donkey I rode refused to move. Its legs were shaking.

I woke remembering a summer holiday, traveling on a river with my family. Our boat was infested with fleas. They didn't seem to bother anyone but me. In the evening, when I brushed the dirt off my sheet to get ready for sleep, the dirt jumped right back and covered the sheet again. It was then that I discovered that it was not dirt but fleas.

Drifting on the water, I could hear the boatmen sing songs to keep each other in rhythm. I remembered reaching out and dipping my hands in the dark green river. The sunset was red, then gray, and then instantly the sky was black. The water flowed through my fingers, warm and smooth.

Yung Lu had been visiting me in my dreams. He always stood on top of a fortress in the middle of a desert. Many years later, when I described to him what my mind's eye saw, he was surprised by its accuracy. His skin was weather-beaten and he wore a Bannerman's uniform. His posture was as erect as the stone guards made for tomb burial.

In the middle of the night I heard something hit my roof. A rotted branch had dropped from an old tree. I followed my astrologer's advice to avoid omens and moved from the Palace of Concentrated Beauty to the Palace of Peaceful Longevity, which was on the far east side of the Forbidden City. The new palace was quieter, and its greater distance from the audience hall encouraged Guang-hsu's independence, for now it was less convenient for him to consult me.

At the age of fifty-one, I realized how much I wanted Yung Lu back. Not only for personal reasons: his presence would calm Guang-hsu and the court. I needed him to perform the same function Prince Kung did for the young Emperor.

In a letter to Yung Lu, I reported Nuharoo's death, Guang-hsu's upcoming ceremony of mounting the throne and Prince Kung's resignation. I made no mention of how I had survived the seven long years without him. To ensure his return, I enclosed a copy of a petition signed by the ministers at the court demanding Li Hung-chang's beheading.

I had never expected that this would be the scene of our reunion: Yung Lu wolfing down dumplings in my dining room, his hunger giving me an opportunity to observe him. Wrinkles now crossed his face like valleys and rivers. The biggest change I noticed, though, was that he was no longer stiffly formal.

Time, distance and marriage seemed to have calmed him. I didn't experience the anxiety I had anticipated. I had visualized his return so many times – like variations of the same scene in an opera, he would enter again and again but in different settings and in different costumes, offering me different words.

'Willow asked me to apologize.' Yung Lu pushed away the empty dish and wiped his mouth. 'She is still unpack-ing.'

I did not think Yung Lu understood his wife's sacrifice. Or he pretended not to understand.

Yung Lu continued, 'Guang-hsu demands indepen-dence, and I wonder if you think him ready.'

'You are the throne's last standing advisor,' I said.

'If the court wants Li's beheading,' he said slowly, 'then Emperor Guang-hsu has a long way to go.'

I agreed. 'I hope I get to retire before I die.'

22

I NO LONGER celebrated the Chinese New Year after Tung Chih died. I found myself living more in the past than the present. I dreaded the moment when I would hear the sound of distant fireworks, because I couldn't help but keep count of Tung Chih's age, as if he had lived. He would be twenty-six. Ever so vivid, Tung Chih would appear in my mind's eye.

My son would look pale. His sad eyes would say, 'I didn't mean to abandon you, Mother,' his expression full of remorse.

I would freeze until Tung Chih's image evaporated, then get down on my knees, facing where he had stood, and weep.

Over the years certain images would grow and sharpen while others would alter or fade. I could clearly see Tung Chih running toward me holding his red-eyed rabbit. I could smell berries on his breath. However, I could no longer remember what he said to me.

An-te-hai often came to my mind as well. I missed his vibrancy, humor and enlightenment. I remembered his poems. I would see his image appear and disappear at the corner of a pavilion or behind a bush. He would smile and sometimes be holding a comb in his right hand. He would ask, 'What hairstyle has my lady in mind for today?' or 'Time for your longevity walk, my lady.'

The ghostly images of Emperor Hsien Feng and Nuharoo also visited me. My husband was always distant and cold, while Nuharoo, unlike the living, breathing person, was affectionate and even humorous. She would order me to create a ceramic opera troupe to bring to her altar.

I regularly inspected the tombs of my husband, Tung Chih and Nuharoo. I wanted to make sure the provincial governor did his job, that no robbers had raided the sites. I wanted to reassure myself that the surrounding sculptures, forests and gardens were well maintained.

Nuharoo's burial ceremony had been elaborate, just the way she'd requested. I followed her instructions: masses of gardenias piled high as snowdrifts, and I wore a black satin court robe embroidered with three hundred bats. I hated it because it made me look like a vulture.

I could have ignored her wishes, but I decided to honor them. It was her way of making sure that I didn't steal her last show. She wanted an open casket, a custom favored by nobles in the West, but rejected the idea at the last minute. She loved the idea that people would admire her eternal robe, a work of such craftsmanship it had taken thirty royal tailors several years to complete.

I remembered the day when Nuharoo and I first inspected the tomb, shortly after Hsien Feng died. She stood tall in her white ceremonial robe and expressed her dissatisfaction with the design of her coffin. The day was as cold as today. The desert wind never ceased. My earrings sang like wind chimes.

I also remembered that I walked alone into the tomb. Ante-hai, like a crazy matchmaker in a comic opera, was determined to see Yung Lu and me together. And his plan had worked. But reality had swept back and life had gone on.

More than half of the people who had made up my life were now dead. I had seen them off to their next lives in glorious fashion, all except for An-te-hai. His remains were nowhere to be found, so he went without a burial. Years later, and after many bribes, I would finally find him. My favorite was wrapped in dirty rags and shipped back to me. His head was loosely sewed back onto his neck. I knew he wanted to be buried 'in one piece' because he dreaded returning as a 'tailless dog.' When An-te-hai had become the highest-ranking eunuch, he had been able to buy back his penis from the butcher who castrated him. He spent a fortune for his 'dried-up root.'

I remember his eyes lit up when describing his next life, which he would live as a normal man. It touched me profoundly. He knew his place in life, and it was with his charm that he fought against misfortune. I admired his effort and wished that I had his courage. Until I lost him, I didn't realize how much I had loved him – his presence, his birds, his plants, and his wild imagination.

The night I mourned for An-te-hai I wore my pink dress, his favorite. I blew out the memorial candles and slipped into the heated bed. Closing my eyes, I summoned An-te-hai's spirit.

Li Lien-ying was in awe of An-te-hai's 'luck.' He watched me with tears in his eyes when I burned candles and incense on An-te-hai's birthdays. And on every birthday I would tell Li Lien-ying the same stories: 'When I first met An-te-hai, he was a shy fifteen-year-old boy with bright eyes and rouge lips . . .'

* * *

I spent New Year's Eve with the sick and old concubines of my father-in-law, Emperor Tao Kuang. I used to fear these ladies, but now I was among them. They refused doctors and medicine, for they believed that it would interrupt the Buddha's way. Every few months one of them would die, leaving behind a pile of embroidered handkerchiefs, pillowcases and ornamental gourds with images of playing children carved into them.

A week ago Princess Jung, Lady Yun's daughter, whom I had not seen for ages, visited me. Many years before, her mother had been put to death because she had tried to harm me when I was pregnant. I had taken in Princess Jung, treated her with kindness, and saw to it that she was raised properly. After completing her education, she married a Manchu prince and lived near Peking. During our visit we talked about her half-brother, Tung Chih, and inspected the items that would be displayed in the newly completed Tung Chih Memorial Hall, near the ancient city of Sian. Leaning over Jung's shoulder, I examined my son's towels, handkerchiefs, combs, necklaces, hats, shoes, kneeling mats, chairs, washbasins, vases, bowls, cups, spoons and chopsticks. By the time we finished, I was trembling so much that Jung had to hold me up.

Around the New Year of 1888 I received the terrible news that Prince Kung's son Tsai-chen had died. He was Tung Chih's playmate and best friend. He also died of a venereal disease.

Although Prince Kung blamed himself for his son's death, he never allowed himself to mourn. Right after Tung Chih's burial, Prince Kung had thrown Tsai-chen out and sworn he'd never speak to him again. When the news of his son's illness came, he was shocked. But when he entered his son's room and saw a silk robe embroidered with pink peonies hanging on the dresser, he turned around and left, and Tsai-chen died that night.

I invited Prince Kung for dinner and suggested that we drink and talk about the good times. We told stories about our dead sons, about the way they met and the way they played together.

Li Lien-ying had been standing over one of the royal tailors for the past three days, supervising the making of my dress for a clan gathering to discuss Guang-hsu's marriage.

I put on the dress and looked at myself in the mirror. My wrinkles were too numerous to hide, and my teeth were not as white as they used to be. Fortunately my hair remained lacquer black. Li Lien-ying was thrilled that I agreed to try a new hairdo. He said that I had put him out of practice for too long.

To sort my earrings, bracelets and necklaces, my eunuch got up before dawn. He laid out the combs, pins, strings, scented-oil bottles and hair boards. I heard him filling up the washbasin and thought that maybe I should stop talking about An-te-hai so much.

In Li Lien-ying's hands I became a work of art. My dress was 'moonlight on snow,' embroidered with a silver turnip pattern, and my new hairstyle was a 'piled-up jewelry cake.'

Rong came with her husband, Prince Ch'un. The family had grown to more than thirty people. I hadn't seen my sister for a long time and noticed changes in her. Her back was hunched and her belly stuck out. Wearing the Manchu four-inch platform shoes, she walked with a drunkard's steps. A large jade hair board was fastened on the back of her head. The centerpiece was a jade grasshopper. Her teeth protruded so badly they looked as if they were flying out of her mouth. Infected gums made her jaws puffy. One side of her face was visibly bigger than the other.

Rong started criticizing me the moment she arrived. She was loud and animated. Warned by Prince Ch'un of her deteriorating mental condition, I tried to ignore her.

The royal brothers sat down together. Prince Kung, Prince Ch'un and Prince Ts'eng showed little affection for one another. They sat in silence smoking pipes.

My brother, Kuei Hsiang, arrived drunk. His wife wore a hair board with ornaments piled up like a pagoda. Since she could hardly turn her head, she talked while her eyes rolled from side to side.

Emperor Guang-hsu, now seventeen, looked handsome and confident in a sunlight-colored silk robe. He had made it clear to the royal clan that he wouldn't take more than one Empress and two concubines. I gave him my support.

By now I was familiar with the unique ways of boys raised as the Son of Heaven. They lived inside their heads. For Tung Chih, living had meant escaping himself. For Guang-hsu it meant denying his own humanity, for he believed that it was pleasure that had destroyed Tung Chih.

The list of choices for the new Empress was long. The royal clan spent days in discussion. Finally my brother's twenty-year-old daughter, Lan, was nominated.

My room became dark after the sun set. The eunuchs came and added coal to the heaters. Guang-hsu and I sat facing each other. He let me know that he wasn't keen on getting married. I convinced him that in order to claim himself as an adult and officially mount the throne, he must first get married.

'I can't afford to waste time,' he complained. 'But wasting time is mostly what I do!'

'What do you think of your cousin Lan?' I asked.

'What about her?'

'She is plain,' I said, 'but character-wise, she is well versed in art, literature and music.'

'If she is your choice,' Guang-hsu said, 'she will be mine.'

'She is three years older than you and perhaps more mature. She might not strike your fancy, but you grew up together and you know each other. It is you, however, who must choose.'

'We get along.' Guang-hsu's face turned red. 'I have seen her paintings, although I don't really feel as if I know her.'

'She would like very much to be your Empress.'

'Has she really said that?' Guang-hsu asked.

I nodded.

'Well, that's nice . . .' He hesitated and rose from his chair. 'I suppose she is the right one, then. You like her, and that's what matters to me.'

'Do you mind Lan's lack of beauty?'

'Why should I mind?'

'Most men would.'

'I am not most men.'

'Well, both of you are not only my closest blood relations but also people I can truly trust. However, I would not be able to forgive myself if matching you two led to unhappiness.'

Guang-hsu went quiet. After a while he said, 'In my eyes Lan is beautiful and has always been kind.'

I began to relax and felt hopeful.

'Within the family,' Guang-hsu continued, 'Lan was the one who always protected me when others ridiculed me.'

'You are not doing this to please me, are you, Guang-hsu?'

'It would be dishonest to deny that I intend to please you,' he said. 'I don't think I am allowed to postpone my

189

marriage, since I have already postponed it twice. The world thinks that the reason I am not married is because you refuse to step down.'

I was moved by his concern for me. I said nothing, but my eyes grew tearful – I lost Tung Chih but gained Guang-hsu.

'Mother, let's just get it over with. If there is any chance that I shall fall in love, Lan would be the one.'

Now I felt nervous and asked Guang-hsu to give himself a few months to think about Lan before making a final decision.

We walked along the shore of Kun Ming Lake where the view was serene. Shrouded in mist, the hills looked like a giant watercolor painting, and the rippling lake reminded me of watered silk.

I sighed when Tung Chih came to mind. 'I wished that I had known how to please Alute.'

'Let me make you happy again, Mother,' Guang-hsu said softly.

The Big Dipper hung bright in the purple sky. That night Li Lien-ying applied green-tea-enriched dandelion cream on my skin and massaged my limbs. Something unsettling had descended over me, but I couldn't figure out what it was. In the future I would wish that I had continued my conversation with Guang-hsu.

I could only say that it was exactly what life was about: a mystery in which one can never know where one truly is.

23

GUANG-HSU CHOSE two sisters from the Tatala clan – which had close connections to the Yehonala clan – as his concubines. The girls were favorite students of Tutor Weng. Guang-hsu first heard his grand tutor praising them, and then was impressed when he met them. The girls' father was the secretary of the Imperial Board of Justice, a friend of Prince Kung's who was known for his liberal views.

I didn't quite know how to react when Guang-hsu presented the girls to me. The younger one, Zhen, or Pearl, was barely fourteen years old. She was beautiful and acted more like Guang-hsu's younger sister than his concubine. Pearl was curious, bright and vivacious. The elder girl, Chin, or Lustrous, was fifteen. She was rotund with a placid but stiff expression. Guang-hsu seemed happy with his selection and asked for my approval.

Although there were a number of girls who came highly recommended, and who in my opinion were much better qualified in terms of beauty and intelligence, I promised myself not to interfere with Guang-hsu's decisions. I was a little selfish and thought that the less attractive the girls, the safer it would be for my niece Lan. I would be doing Lan a disservice by surrounding her husband with beauties. Despite my prayers that Guang-hsu and Lan would eventually fall in love, I asked myself, what if they don't?

Pearl and Lustrous completed a harmonious package. When I lined them up with Lan, I thought the arrangement ideal: Pearl was young, Lustrous was passive, and Lan was given a chance to shine. My goal was to encourage Guang-hsu to have children with all of them.

The three girls came for tea in beautiful dresses. They reminded me of my youth. I intended to let them know of my regrettable relationship with Alute. The girls didn't expect my frankness and were stunned.

'I am sorry to put you through this,' I explained. 'If you don't already know the story, you will hear it sooner or later from palace rumors. It's better that I tell you my own version.'

I warned them to put aside their expectations of life inside the Forbidden City. 'Don't focus on how life should be but how life is.' I let Lan know that I was thrilled to share with her a passion for literature and opera, but I cautioned her that poetry and opera are diversions, not serious pursuits.

The girls didn't seem to understand, but each nodded obediently.

'Alute and Tung Chih fell in love the first time they met,' I went on. 'But Tung Chih abandoned her after a few months for other women.' I mentioned how I lost my husband to Chinese concubines. 'It takes character, an iron will and endurance to survive inside the Forbidden City.' To make my point clear, I emphasized that I would not tolerate another Alute.

While Lan, who already knew the story, listened, Lustrous and Pearl widened their eyes as I spoke of my late daughter-in-law Alute. I had to stop to wipe my tears, for the memory of Tung Chih was unbearable.

Pearl wept when I described Alute's sad end.

'I'd never do what Alute did even if I become disappointed with my life and wish to kill myself,' she cried. 'Alute was wrong to murder her baby!'

'Pearl,' Lustrous interrupted. 'Stop, please. Negative emotions will harm the Grand Empress's health.'

'Would you say that you have survived and prospered?' Lan asked me at our third tea party.

'Survived, maybe – definitely not prospered' was my reply.

'Everyone in the country believes that your life is a fairy tale,' Pearl said. 'It's not true?'

'To an extent I suppose it is true,' I agreed. 'I live in the Forbidden City, thousands cater to my needs, my wardrobe is beyond imagining, but –'

'You are worshiped by millions,' Lan interrupted.

'Are you not, Grand Empress?' the sisters followed.

I paused, debating whether I should reveal my true thoughts. 'I will say this: I have gained prestige but lost happiness.'

Despite her sister's elbow-pushing, Pearl voiced her disbelief and begged me to explain.

'My father was the governor of Wuhu when I was seven years old,' I began. 'I played with my village friends in the fields, hills and lakes. Our family was financially better off than most of the other townspeople, who relied entirely on the year's crops for survival. My biggest wish was to be able to afford a New Year's present for my best friend, a skinny, long-legged girl nicknamed Grasshopper. Grasshopper said that if I really meant to make her happy, all I had to do was allow her to clean my family's feces pit.'

'What?' the Imperial ladies cried. 'She wanted your shit?'

I nodded. 'To have a steady supply of feces to fertilize his land is every farmer's dream.' Sipping the finest tea, I described how Grasshopper and her family came to our house to collect this 'gift.' How each member carried wooden buckets and a bamboo pole. How they sang songs as they emptied the pit. How Grasshopper worked in the pit on her knees, scraping the sides.

The three delicate ladies were wide-eyed. Pearl looked so taken aback that she held a hand over her mouth, as if afraid of something she might say.

'I will never forget the smile on Grasshopper's face.' I drank up my tea. 'She made me know what happiness is. I have never known such simple contentment since entering the Forbidden City.'

'You sound like you haven't been lucky!' Pearl couldn't help saying.

'No,' I sighed.

Guang-hsu and Tutor Weng joined us for dinner. Pearl, in all her innocence and natural charm, begged Guang-hsu to share what he had learned that day. As a student of Tutor Weng herself, they teased each other. Guang-hsu seemed to enjoy Pearl's challenge, and their friendship flourished in front of my eyes.

'I am convinced that China's only hope of salvation is in learning and emulating the science and technology of the Western nations,' Guang-hsu said in a high-pitched voice, and Pearl nodded respectfully.

When Pearl asked the Emperor to explain how a clock worked, Guang-hsu sent his eunuch to bring a few items from his collection. Like a performer, he took a clock apart, pointing out its inner workings. She stared in awe of him, their two heads practically glued together as they continued exploring.

I could tell that Lan wished for the chance to talk with the Emperor about poetry and literature. Later, when I was alone with my niece, I asked of her feelings. We were sitting in front of her dressing mirror.

'Guang-hsu paid more attention to his concubines than to his Empress,' Lan complained.

I didn't want to be the one to have to tell her this, but believed she ought to prepare herself: 'This could be just a beginning, Lan.'

My niece raised her small eyes and glanced at herself in the mirror. She was judging herself critically. A moment later she lowered her head and began to weep. 'I am ugly.'

I put my hands on her shoulders.

'No!' She shook me off. 'Look at my teeth. They are crooked!'

'You are beautiful, Lan.' I gently stroked her arms. 'You remember Nuharoo, don't you? Who was the prettier, she or I? Everyone agreed that she was, including myself, because that was the truth. I was no rival of Nuharoo. But Emperor Hsien Feng abandoned her for me.'

My niece raised her tearful eyes.

'It's all in the effort,' I encouraged her.

'What does Guang-hsu see in Pearl?'

'Her vibrancy, perhaps . . .'

'No, it's her looks.'

'Lan, listen to me. Guang-hsu was raised with beauties in his backyard. To him they are nothing but walking ornaments. As you know, Tung Chih abandoned three thousand beauties from all over the country for brothel whores.'

'I don't know how to be vibrant!' Lan's tears streamed down her cheeks. 'The more I think about it, the more nervous I become. I can't even get Guang-hsu to look at me.'

As we bid each other goodnight, I told Lan that there was still time if she wanted to cancel the marriage.

'But I want to be the Empress of China,' Lan said, her tone surprisingly determined.

It was the first time I discovered her stubbornness.

'I want to be like you,' she added.

On February 26, 1889, Guang-hsu's wedding was celebrated by the nation. The Emperor was not yet eighteen. Like Nuharoo, Lan entered from the center gate, the Gate of Celestial Tranquility. Lustrous and Pearl entered from the side, the same gate I had entered thirty-seven years before.

A week later, on March 4, I retired from the regency. It was the second time I had done so. I was fifty-four years old. From then on I was officially called the Dowager Empress. I was happily able to return to the gardens of the Summer Palace, leaving the court's headaches to Guang-hsu and his father, Prince Ch'un.

The Manchu hardliners feared Guang-hsu's commitment to reform, which he demonstrated in his very first decree: 'I shall overturn the old order in the Middle Kingdom and sweep away reactionary forces who cannot bring themselves to acknowledge reality. And this means demotion, removal, exile and execution for the stone-minded.'

Although I offered no public support to Guang-hsu, my silence spoke for itself.

Despising Emperor Guang-hsu and doubting my resolve to withdraw from power, one of the hardliners' representatives, a provincial judge, submitted a petition insisting that I continue the regency. What amazed me was the number of signatures he collected. People must have thought that I hadn't meant what I said. I learned that the judge had assumed that I was waiting for just such a proposal.

Instead of rewarding the judge with a promotion, I canceled the court's plan to discuss the petition. I called it a waste of time and fired the provincial judge, making sure that it was a permanent dismissal. I explained to the nation, 'The regency was never my choice to begin with.'

My intention was to let people know that bad ideas grow like weeds in the court.

I marked my retirement by hosting a celebration during which I handed out awards to a great many people. I issued half a dozen edicts to thank everyone, living and dead, who had worked during the regency.

Among the important personages I honored was the Englishman Robert Hart, for his devotion and achievement as the inspector general of China's customs service. The edict was issued despite strong objections from the court's ministers. I granted Hart a most prestigious title, the ancestral rank of First Class of the First Order for Three Generations. It meant that the honor was retroactive, bestowed on his ancestors rather than on his descendants. It might seem whimsical from a foreigner's point of view, but for a Chinese, nothing could be more honorable.

I played mute and deaf when the Clan Council cried, 'A foreign devil now outranks most of us and our ancestors!'

I could not argue enough that Robert Hart represented the kind of revolutionary change China desperately needed. Yet the court collectively denied my request to meet with him in person. The minister of the Board of Etiquette threatened to resign as he laid out his records showing that in all of Chinese history a female of my status had never received a foreign male. Thirteen more years would pass before I finally got to meet with Robert Hart.

I never expected that the restoration of my retirement home would become a scandal. It began with a gesture of piety. When I decided to settle in the Summer Palace – originally called Ch'ing I Yuan, Garden of Clear Rippling Waters – it was Prince Ch'un who insisted that it be restored. As chief minister, he spoke on behalf of the Emperor. Ch'un meant to provide me with a comfortable home, which I gratefully accepted.

I did not want to embarrass Prince Ch'un by pointing out that he had resisted the same idea when it was proposed by Tung Chih after he mounted the throne back in 1873. At that time Ch'un claimed that there was a shortage of funds. How, I wondered, would he raise the funds now? I could only conclude that he wanted to keep me strolling in my gardens rather than meddling in state affairs.

I remained passive because it was time for Prince Ch'un to step into my shoes. As the minister of the Board of Admiralty, he had been a roaring tiger, tearing apart Li Hung-chang's effort to modernize China. What surprised me was his unlikely collaborator, Tutor Weng. Weng was a liberal and a strong advocate for reform who had supported Li's initiatives. But when he became Prince Ch'un's new minister of revenue, he discovered that he didn't like sharing power with Li. Prince Ch'un and Tutor Weng had already sent numerous memorandums denouncing Li and my approval of Li's projects. Both men were convinced that they could do a better job if they were given total control.

I had hinted to Li Hung-chang about what would be coming when I retired. It was frustrating to witness how Li was forced to endure humiliation, attacks on his character, even assassination attempts. The only thing I could do was show him how much I valued him. In a message delivered to Li by Yung Lu, his closest ally at court, I wrote, 'If it becomes too much, you have my permission to take a leave of absence for any reason.' I told him that I would grant any amount of compensation he might claim.

Li Hung-chang assured me that would be unnecessary and that my understanding of his sacrifices was all he needed to carry on. 'It is not at all a good time for experimenting or allowing the stubborn-minded Ironhats time for self-discovery,' I wrote him, 'but that is how things are for me here.'

I had lived with my husband in the Summer Palace. It was divided by lakes, called North Sea, South Sea and Middle Sea. Unlike Yuan Ming Yuan, which was a man-made wonder, the Summer Palace was designed to harmonize with nature's ways. The Garden of Clear Rippling Water, surrounding the palace itself, was only a small portion of the greater park area. Across its expanse, airy pavilions sat amid the lush green landscape, and the three large lakes glinted between shallow hills. My memories of the place were more than fond.

It was Guang-hsu who finally convinced me to allow the restoration to take place. He personally read his statement to the court urging the start of construction. 'It is the least China can bestow on its Grand Empress, who has suffered so much.' I could see that Guang-hsu was attempting to assert his independence, and I felt that I needed to support him.

When loyal ministers wrote to warn me of a 'father-and-son plot' that intended to isolate me politically, I wrote on the back of their letters, 'If there is a plot, it is one of my own design.' I was more concerned about where the money would come from. The first priority of the admiralty and revenue boards was to establish China's navy, and I wanted that priority honored.

In June, Guang-hsu published his decree regarding the restoration of my home: '. . . I then remembered that in the neighborhood of the Western Park there was a palace. Many of the buildings were in poor condition and required restoration to make them fit for Her Majesty the Grand Empress's use as a place of solace and delight.' He conferred a new name on the Garden of Clear Rippling Waters: it would now be known as the Garden for the Cultivation of Harmonious Old Age.

After demurring, I issued an official reply: 'I am aware that the Emperor's desire to restore the palace in the west springs from his laudable concern for my welfare, and for that reason I cannot bear to meet his well-meaning petition with a blunt refusal. Moreover, the costs of the construction have all been provided for out of the surplus funds accumulated as a result of rigid economies in the past. The funds under the control of the Board of Revenue will not be touched, and no harm will be done to the national finances.'

My statement was meant to mollify those who opposed the plan, but I ended up falling into a trap. Soon I would be locked in two battles, an experience I would barely survive.

The first battle would be started by Tutor Weng. When the scholar-reformer was given the highest power, he encouraged Guang-hsu's already great passion for reform. When he could have played a moderating role, Tutor Weng instead pushed him harder, setting the Emperor on a course that would ultimately prove disastrous both for our family and for China.

The second battle would be my fight against taking the responsibility for China's lost war with Japan. Years later, when all of the men ran away from blame, I would be the one to bear the disgrace. What could I do? I had been fully awake, yet I did not escape the nightmare.

'In the end,' one future historian would write, 'the Board of Revenue did remain inviolate, but important funds, estimated at thirty thousand taels, were defrauded from the Board of Admiralty for Grand Empress Tzu Hsi – the amount would have doubled the entire fleet, which would have enabled China to defeat its enemy.'

Unfortunately, I lived to read this criticism. It was when I was old and dying. I couldn't, didn't and wouldn't yell, 'Go and take a look at my home!' The money I was charged with stealing would have built it three times with pure gold.

24

O UR TROUBLES WITH Japan over Korea had been going on for a decade. When Queen Min of Korea called for help, I sent Li Hung-chang. The Queen was under the threat of Japanese-backed mobs. I took the matter personally. I knew that I would seek the same help if such a thing should ever happen to me.

It took two years for Li Hung-chang to work out an agreement with Japan's prime minister, Ito Hirobumi. Li convinced me that the agreement would prevent the escalation of the Korean situation into a full-scale Sino-Japanese military confrontation.

I frantically did what I could to get Li's draft agreement approved. The Manchu Clan Council hated the very existence of Li Hung-chang and did their best to block his effort. Prince Ch'un and Prince Ts'eng said that my living in the Forbidden City for so long had warped my sense of reality, and that my trust in Li Hung-chang was misplaced. My instinct told me, however, that I would end up with Queen Min's own troubles if I relied on the Manchu royals instead of Li Hung-chang.

As a result of my advocacy, the Li-Ito Convention was signed. China and Japan kept peace for a while. The

Manchus stopped their campaign for Li Hung-chang's beheading.

But in March of 1893 Li sought an emergency audience with me at the Summer Palace. I was up before dawn to greet him. Outside in the garden, the air was crisp and cold, but the camellias were blossoming. I served Li hot green tea, for he had been traveling all night.

'Your Majesty.' Li Hung-chang's voice was tense. 'How have you been?'

I sensed unease and asked him to come to the point.

He knocked his forehead on the ground before letting out his words. 'Queen Min has been deposed, Your Majesty.'

I was stunned. 'How . . . how could that happen?'

'I don't have all the information yet.' Li Hung-chang rose. 'I only know that the Queen's ministers were brutally murdered. As of this moment, Korea's radicals are staging a coup.'

'Does Japan have a role in it?'

'Yes, Your Majesty. Japan's secret agents infiltrated Queen Min's palace disguised as Korean security guards.'

Li Hung-chang convinced me that there was nothing I could do to help Queen Min. Even if we could mount a rescue mission, we didn't know where the Queen was being held or even if she was still alive. Japan was determined to swallow Korea. The conspiracy had been kept alive for over ten years. China had been taking turns with Japan in backing rival factions in Seoul.

'I am afraid that China alone can no longer stop Japan's military aggression,' Li said.

The next weeks were tense, my days harried, my nights sleepless. Exhausted, I tried to supplant the worries of the moment by returning to something even more potent, replaying my earliest memories of my hometown of Wuhu.

Staring at the golden dragon ceiling above my bed, I recalled the last time I was with my best friend Grasshopper. She was kicking the dirt with her feet, her legs as thin as bamboo stalks.

'I have never gone to Hefei,' she said. 'Have you, Orchid?'

'No,' I replied. 'My father told me that it's bigger than Wuhu.'

Grasshopper's eyes lit up. 'I might get lucky there.' She lifted her blouse to reveal her belly. 'I am sick of eating clay.'

Her belly was huge, like a bottom-up cooking pot.

'I haven't been able to shit,' she said.

I felt extremely guilty. As the daughter of the local governor, I had never known hunger.

'I am going to die, Orchid.' Grasshopper's tone was flat. 'I will be eaten by a tableful of people. Will you miss me?'

Before I could answer, she went on. 'My younger brother died last night. My parents sold him this morning. I wonder which family is eating him.'

Suddenly my knees gave way and I collapsed.

'I am leaving for Hefei, Orchid.'

The last thing I remembered was Grasshopper thanking me for the feces from my family's manure pit.

The giant trees surrounding my palace made a wave-like sound. I lay in the dark, still unable to sleep. Leaving the past, I stumbled again into the present and thought about Li Hung-chang, the man from Hefei. Hefei, in fact, was his nickname. He too, I assumed, knew the hunger of peasants, and this had much to do with our mutual understanding and ambition to bring change to the government. It had come to bind us. I both looked forward to and dreaded audiences with Li. I didn't know what additional bad news he had to bring me. The only sure thing was that it would come.

Li Hung-chang was a man of courtesy and elegance. He brought me gifts, exotic and practical; once he presented me with reading glasses. The gifts always came with a story, about the place of their making or the cultural influences behind their design. It was not hard to imagine why he enjoyed great popularity. Besides Prince Kung, Li was the only government official that foreigners trusted.

I still could not sleep. I had a feeling that Li Hung-chang was on his way again. I imagined his carriage rambling through the dark streets of Peking. The Forbidden City's gates opening for him, one after another. The guards' whispers. Li being escorted through the mile-long entrance, along hallways and garden corridors and into the inner court.

I heard the temple's bell strike four times. My mind was clear but I was tired, and my cheeks were burning hot, my limbs cold. I sat up and pulled on my clothes. I heard the sound of footsteps, recognized the shuffle of soft soles and knew it was my eunuch. In the shadow of the moon Li Lien-ying came in. He lifted my curtain, a candle in his right hand. 'My lady,' he called.

'Is it Li Hung-chang?' I asked.

Li knelt before me wearing his prized double-eyed peacock-feather hat and yellow silk field marshal's riding jacket. I was afraid of what he would say. It seemed only a short while since he had brought me the terrible news of Korea's Queen Min.

He stayed on his knees until I asked him to speak.

'China and Japan are at war' was what he told me.

Although not surprised, I was still shaken. For the past few days the throne had ordered troops, under the leadership of Yung Lu, moved north to help Korea contain its revolt. Guang-hsu's edict read, 'Japan has poured an army into Korea, trying to extinguish what they call a fire that they themselves have lit.'

I had little confidence in our military might. The court wasn't wrong in describing me as one who 'got bitten by a snake ten years ago and has since been afraid of straw ropes.'

I lost my husband and almost my own life during the 1860 Opium War. If England and its allies were superior then, I could only imagine them now, more than thirty years later. The possibility that I would not survive was real to me. Ever since his return from Sinkiang, Yung Lu had been working quietly with Li Hung-chang on strengthening our forces, but I knew they had far to go. My thoughts were with Yung Lu and his troops as they made their way north.

Li was in favor of allowing time for the joint efforts of England, Russia and Germany, who, under Li's repeated pleading for support, had agreed to persuade Japan to 'put out the war torch.'

'His Majesty Emperor Guang-hsu is convinced that he must act,' Li said. 'The Japanese fired two broadsides and a torpedo, sinking the troopship *Kowshing*, which was sailing out of Port Arthur with our soldiers on board. Those who did not drown were machine-gunned. I understand His Majesty's rage, but we can't afford to act on emotion.'

'What do you expect me to do, Li Hung-chang?'

'Please ask the Emperor to be patient, for I am waiting for England, Russia and Germany to respond. I am afraid any wrong move on our part will lose us international support.'

I called Li Lien-ying.

'Yes, my lady.'

'Carriage, to the Forbidden City!'

Li Hung-chang and I had no idea that Japan had obtained England's promise not to interfere and that Russia had followed suit. We blistered our lips trying to persuade the enraged Guang-hsu to allow more time before issuing a war decree.

As the weeks passed, Japan became more aggressive. China's waiting showed no promise of being rewarded. I was accused of allowing Li Hung-chang to squander the precious time needed to mount a successful defense. I continued to trust Li, but I also realized that I needed to pay attention to the pro-war faction – the War Party – now led by Emperor Guang-hsu himself.

Once again I moved back to my old palace in the Forbidden City. I needed to attend the audiences and be available to the Emperor. Although I praised the Ironhats for their patriotism, I was reluctant to commit my support, for I remembered that thirty years ago they were certain they could defeat England.

Those who were against war, the Peace Party, led by Li Hung-chang, worried that I would withdraw my support.

'Japan has been modeling itself after Western cultures and has become more civilized,' Li tried to convince the court. 'International laws should act as a brake to any intended violence.'

'It takes an idiot to believe that a wolf would give up preying on sheep!' Tutor Weng, now the war councilor, spoke amid great applause. 'China can and will defeat Japan by sheer force of numbers.'

It took me a while to figure out Tutor Weng's character. On the one hand, he encouraged Guang-hsu to model China after Japan, but on the other, he despised Japanese culture. He felt superior to the Japanese and believed that 'China should educate Japan, as she has throughout history.' He also believed that Japan 'owes China a debt for its language, art, religion and even fashion.' Tutor Weng was what Yung Lu would have described as 'good at commanding an army on paper.' What was worse, the scholar told the nation that China's reform program would be like 'sticking a bamboo in the sun – a shadow will be produced instantly.'

Although he had never run a government, Tutor Weng was confident in his own ability. His liberal views inspired so many people that he was regarded as a national hero. I had trouble communicating with him, for he advocated war but avoided facing the mountain of decisions required to prosecute it. He advised me to 'pay attention to the picture on an embroidery instead of the stitches.' Discussing strategy was his passion. He lectured the court during audiences and would go on for hours. In the end, he would smile and say, 'Let's leave the tactics to generals and officers.'

The generals and officers on the frontier were confused by Tutor Weng's instructions. ' "We are what we believe" is not the kind of advice we can tell our men to follow,' they complained. Yung Lu, in a personal letter to me from the front, was especially contemptuous of Weng. But my hands were tied.

'Understanding the moral behind the war will win us the war,' the grand tutor responded. 'There is no better instruction than Confucius's teaching: "The man of virtue will not seek to live at the expense of humanity." '

When I suggested that he at least listen to Li Hung-chang, Tutor Weng simply said, 'If we fail to react in a timely fashion, Japan will enter Peking and burn down the Forbidden City, the same way England burned down Yuan Ming Yuan.'

The Emperor's father, Prince Ch'un, echoed, 'There is no betrayal worse than forgetting what the foreigners have done to us.'

I left Tutor Weng alone but insisted that a new Board of Admiralty for war be set up under Prince Ch'un, Prince Ts'eng and Li Hung-chang. Six years earlier, Li had contracted with foreign firms to build fortified harbors, including major bases at Port Arthur in Manchuria and Weihaiwei on the Shantung Peninsula. Ships were purchased from England and Germany. By now we had twenty-five warships. No one seemed to want to hear it when Li said, 'The navy is far from ready for war. The naval academy has just finished drafting its curriculum and hiring its instructors. The first generation of student officers is only in training.'

'China is equipped!' Prince Ch'un convinced himself. 'All we need is to put our people on board.'

Li Hung-chang warned, 'Modern warships are useless in the wrong hands.'

I couldn't stop the court from shouting patriotic slogans in response to Li.

Emperor Guang-hsu said he was all set to go to war: 'I have waited long enough.'

I prayed that my son would do what his great ancestors had done, rise to the occasion and put his enemies to flight. Yet deep in my heart, fear sank in. For all Guang-hsu's admirable qualities, I knew he was incapable of playing a dominant role. He had been trying hard, but he lacked a dynamic strategy and the necessary ruthlessness. A secret I kept from the public was Guang-hsu's medical and emotional problems. I just couldn't see him controlling his ill-tempered half-brothers, the leaders of the Ironhats. And I couldn't see him winning over the Manchu Clan Council either. I wished that Guang-hsu would tell me I was wrong, that despite his shortcomings he would be lucky and win the day.

I resented myself for not ending Guang-hsu's dependence. He continued to seek my approval and support. I kept silent when the entire Clan Council suggested that I resume daily supervision of the nation. I meant to provoke my son. I wanted him to challenge me, and I wanted to see him explode in rage. I was giving him a chance to stand up and speak for himself. I told him that he could overrule the council if he felt he should take power into his own hands. That was the case with the dynasty's most successful emperors, such as Kang Hsi, Yung Cheng and his great-grandfather Chien Lung.

But it was not to be. Guang-hsu was too gentle, too timid. He would hesitate, fall into conflict with himself and in the end give up.

Maybe I already sensed Guang-hsu's tragedy. I had begun suffering his fear. I felt that I was failing him. I got angry when his half-brother and cousin, Prince Ch'un Junior and Prince Ts'eng Junior, took advantage of him. They spoke to Guang-hsu as if he were below them. Sick of hearing my own voice, I continued to tell my son to act like an emperor.

I must have confused Guang-hsu. In retrospect, I could see that the monarch was not acting himself. It was I who demanded that he be someone he was not. He wanted so much to make me happy.

*   *   *

I returned to the Summer Palace, tired of the endless bickering between the War Party and the Peace Party. The burden of arbitration was left solely to me, not because I had any special competence but because nobody else could do any better.

Behind my back and in the midst of the national crisis, Prince Ch'un requisitioned the funds Li Hung-chang had borrowed for the naval academy. Ch'un built motor launches for the amusement of the court at the lake palaces in Peking and on Kun Ming Lake, near where I lived.

Later on, Li Hung-chang would confess, 'The Emperor's father was in a position to demand money from me at any time. I let him have his way in exchange for not interfering with my business affairs.'

Other admiralty funds were used by Prince Ch'un and Prince Ts'eng to shower gifts on me, underwriting lavish and unnecessary projects in order to win my support. The repair of the Marble Barge was an example.

Enraged, I confronted Prince Ch'un: 'What pleasure would the costly damn barge bring me?'

'We thought Your Majesty would enjoy going out on the water without wetting her shoes,' my brother-in-law said. He further explained that the Marble Barge was originally built by Emperor Chien Lung for his mother, who was afraid of water.

'But I love the water!' I yelled. 'I would swim in the lake if I were only allowed to!'

Prince Ch'un promised to stop the project, but he lied. It was hard for him to quit – he had already dispersed most of the funds, and he needed an ongoing excuse to push Li for additional money.

Li Hung-chang parried with Prince Ch'un. Instead of going to foreign banks for loans, Li launched a 'Navy

211

Defense Fund Drive.' He made no effort to hide the fact that the money he raised would actually benefit 'the Dowager Empress's sixtieth birthday party.' Li meant to shoot down Prince Ch'un, but I was being used as collateral. Li Hung-chang must have believed that I deserved this treatment because I was responsible for teaming him up with Prince Ch'un in the first place.

Guang-hsu declared war on Japan, but he had little confidence in overseeing it. He relied on Tutor Weng, who knew wars only through books. I had yet to learn how conflicted Guang-hsu was as a man. Lan let me know that her husband was a romantic at heart, but was afraid of women.

'We have been married for five years.' Lan's lips trembled and she broke down. 'We slept together only once, and now he wants a separation.'

I promised to help. The result was that the couple agreed to continue to live together in the same compound. What saddened me was that Guang-hsu had built a wall around his apartment in order to block Lan's entrance.

When I talked with Guang-hsu, he explained that his neglect of Lan was out of self-defense. 'She told me that I owe her a child.'

He described Lan's midnight intrusions. 'She scared my eunuchs, who thought that her shadow was that of an assassin.'

When I tried to make Guang-hsu understand that Lan had her wifely rights, he said that he didn't think he was able to perform his duty as a husband.

'I haven't been cured yet,' he said, meaning his involuntary ejaculations. 'I don't think I ever will be.'

Guang-hsu had bravely mentioned his condition to me before, but I had hoped things would improve with greater experience in love.

I was unable to overcome the feeling that I had created a tragedy. It made me feel even worse to know that Lan believed I could force Guang-hsu to love her.

During the day, Guang-hsu and I conducted audiences dealing with the war against Japan; in the evening, we buried ourselves in documents and drafts of edicts. The only time we could relax a bit was during late-night breaks. I tried to talk casually about Lan, but Guang-hsu knew my intention.

'I am sure Lan doesn't deserve me,' Guang-hsu said. The regret in his eyes was sincere. He held himself responsible for not being able to produce an heir, and said that for some time he had been feeling weak and tired. 'I am not asking you to forgive me.' He made an effort to push back his tears. 'I let you down . . .' He began to weep. 'I am beyond shame as an Imperial man. Soon the world will know.'

'Your condition will remain a secret until we find a cure.' I tried to comfort him, but now I saw that beyond being despondent he might be truly ill.

'What about Lan?' Guang-hsu raised his tearful eyes. 'I am afraid there will come a day when she will publicly attack me.'

'Leave her to me.'

Lan refused to accept my explanation of Guang-hsu's medical condition. Stubbornly she believed that her husband meant to reject her. 'He is listless with me, but he is full of spirit when with his other concubines, especially Pearl.'

I made sure that Lan would not let her feelings of frustration run away with her. 'We are the ladies of masks,' I told her. 'Cloaking ourselves in divine glory and sacrifice is our destiny.'

I was grateful that Guang-hsu allowed me to bring in doctors to examine him, and he answered their most intimate questions. He had borne so much pain and humiliation. I admired him for being above himself in conquering his personal sufferings.

The diagnosis was delivered, and it broke my heart: Guang-hsu had a lung condition. He had contracted bronchitis, and was vulnerable to tuberculosis. The image of Tung Chih lying on his bed came back to me. I held Guang-hsu in my arms and wept.

25

THE CITY OF PEKING ran out of firewood during the New Year of 1894. The wood we did receive was green and damp and produced thick smoke. We coughed and hacked while conducting audiences. The minister of the Board of the Interior was summoned and questioned. He kept apologizing and promising that the next load would be smoke free. According to Yung Lu, the northern section of the railroad responsible for transporting the wood had been destroyed by desperate peasant rebels. The tracks were dislodged and the wooden ties were sold for burning. The troops Yung Lu sent could not fix the problem fast enough.

Early on the morning of New Year's Day, an urgent message woke me: Prince Ch'un had died. 'The Emperor's father had a stroke while inspecting naval installations,' the message read.

Doctor Sun Pao-tien said that exhaustion had claimed Prince Ch'un's life. The prince had been determined to show his readiness to launch a counterattack against Japan. He had denounced his brother Prince Kung and Viceroy Li Hung-chang. He bragged about his ability to get the job done, 'the way a Mongolian plays jump-rope without breaking a sweat.'

Prince Ch'un wouldn't consult with Kung or Li. He was not about to 'pick up a rock and smash his own toes with it' – he refused to 'insult' himself. I had seen the same self-defeating behavior in the rest of the Imperial family. Prince Ch'un might have covered his home with calligraphed maxims about pursuing the simple life, but power meant everything to him.

I remembered being concerned about the discoloration of Prince Ch'un's lips. He believed that his dizziness was just a part of his morning-after hangover. He continued to throw banquets, believing that small talk and private deals were the way to get things done.

Guang-hsu was grief-stricken. He was much closer to his father than his mother, of course. Kneeling between his uncles, he couldn't bring himself to finish the death announcement at the morning audience.

Later, at the reception before the burial, my sister made a show of demanding that her younger son, Prince Ch'un Junior, be given his father's position.

When I denied her request, Rong turned to Guang-hsu and said, 'Let's hear what the Emperor has to say.'

Guang-hsu stared blankly at his mother as if not understanding her.

'It's my birthright!' Prince Ch'un Junior claimed. He towered over Guang-hsu by half a head. As the leader of the new Manchu generation, the young Ch'un was a man of neither modesty nor patience. His eyes were bloodshot and his breath thick with alcohol. He reminded me of a bull in the mood for a fight.

'Discipline your younger son,' I said to my sister.

'Guang-hsu is nothing but an embroidered pillowcase stuffed with straw,' Rong said. 'Ch'un Junior should have been the one for the throne!'

I could hardly believe my sister. I turned to look at Guang-hsu, who was visibly distraught. Then I nodded at Li Lien-ying, who then yelled, 'Her Majesty's and His Majesty's palanquins!'

While riding back to the palace, I realized I had witnessed in our family the decay of the whole royal class. It didn't occur to young Prince Ch'un that he could fail just as his father did.

Rong and I had grown so far apart that even seeing each other became unbearable. It worried me that Prince Ch'un Junior could be next in line if something should happen to Guang-hsu. Ch'un Junior had the physical stature but little in the way of a mind. Although I had been encouraging the young Manchus to pursue the path of their ancestors and had been rewarding them with promotions, I was disappointed in my nephew. I insisted that he take an apprenticeship under either Prince Kung or Li Hung-chang. Since the boy refused to follow my instructions, his position in court remained insignificant.

For the next few weeks, while Guang-hsu conducted audiences, I sat in one royal temple or another receiving guests who came to mourn Prince Ch'un. Surrounded by beating drums, loud music and chanting lamas, I performed rituals and gave my approval to various requests regarding the prince's funeral: the number of banquets and guests, the style and scent of candles, the color of the dead's wrapping sheets and the carvings on the dead's decorative buttons. No one seemed to care about the ongoing war. The daily death toll from the frontier didn't seem to bother Ch'un Junior or his Ironhat friends. They drank to excess and fought over prostitutes.

217

I was feeling my age. My bleak view of the future made me sick to my stomach.

'That's because you are not drinking scorpion soup, my lady,' Li Lien-ying said.

I told him, 'You look like you have a smile mask sewn on your face.'

Li Lien-ying ignored me and continued with his advice. 'The theory behind the scorpion soup is that it takes poison to fight poison.'

On September 17, 1894, at the mouth of the Yalu River, the Japanese destroyed half of our navy in a single afternoon, and not a single ship of theirs was seriously damaged. The coast was now literally clear, and Japan could land men and arms and march on Peking.

On November 16, Li Hung-chang reported that the Manchu princes, whom he was forced to do business with, had profited from the war by supplying our troops with defective ammunition. Only one month into the fighting, Port Arthur had been captured. Rather than surrender, Li Hung-chang's field commanders led their soldiers to commit suicide.

Thanks to the dead Prince Ch'un, who had been fabricating field reports and then supplying only the good news to me, I had foolishly felt secure enough to begin preparing for my sixtieth birthday party. Thinking that it would be the moment to celebrate my retirement, I had planned to use the occasion to befriend the wives of foreign ambassadors. I hadn't been able to invite any of them until now, when I was considered officially retired. In the eyes of the court, China's pride would not be injured as much. The foreign embassies seemed to share the same ease. Being retired meant that I didn't have to be taken seriously.

Perhaps I had never been taken seriously, on or off the throne. What pride had China left to be injured? As long as I was free to help my son, I didn't care what people thought. If being retired meant having more opportunities to make friends who might be of service to the country, I would not only welcome it, I would enjoy it as well.

As it turned out, Japan's continued aggression forced me to cancel all my plans. This annoyed a great many nobles and functionaries who had been expecting lavish handouts.

I resumed my role as the Imperial arbitrator and was shocked to realize that I had become a target of the court – accused of bankrupting the country. I found out that during my short period of retirement, Tutor Weng mismanaged the already shaky royal treasury. When questioned about his responsibility, he claimed that all funds had been disbursed by the late Prince Ch'un for the restoration of the Summer Palace – my home.

I insisted the court open up all of Tutor Weng's books and records for examination, but no action followed. What I didn't realize was that Tutor Weng, who never personally profited a penny, had fattened so many pockets that he created an extensive network of supporters – a wealth greater than money could buy. Sparing Tutor Weng, the nation began to hold me responsible for its defeats. Rumors of my extravagant style of living, including my sexual appetites, soon spread.

I had trusted Tutor Weng with both of my sons. I would have shared the blame if Tutor Weng had admitted his part. After all, it was to me that the court and the Emperor came for the final word.

While the rumors continued, the conflict between Tutor Weng and me became public. I reminded myself not to lose perspective, but I was determined to pursue Weng's investigation.

Guang-hsu wasn't able to bring himself to take sides. For him, Tutor Weng had long been a moral compass, a personal god. Guang-hsu was frustrated that I refused to change my mind about investigating his mentor.

In order to prove Tutor Weng's innocence, Guang-hsu decided to conduct his own investigation. To everyone's surprise, Tutor Weng was found guilty. The Confucius scholar and the late Prince Ch'un had not only misappropriated naval funds but also used my birthday to request great sums, which soon disappeared. After Guang-hsu obtained all the accounting books and other material evidence, he came to me to apologize. I told him that I was proud of his fairness.

I decided to announce that I would accept no gifts for my birthday. My action exposed Tutor Weng: people converged from all over the country, like fleas to a blood meal, trying to get their money back.

Emperor Guang-hsu confronted his mentor. 'You were my faith and my spiritual mighty pillar!' he said, and demanded an explanation. Tutor Weng admitted no wrongdoing. He continued his wise-man attitude and warned Guang-hsu about becoming crooked-minded for listening to 'an old lady.' In the end, the grand tutor was fired. He was given a week to pack up and leave. He would never enter the Forbidden City again.

Guang-hsu was embarrassed by the fact that he picked Tutor Weng to be the chief architect of the war against Japan. He shut himself in his room while Tutor Weng knelt outside, begging for a chance to explain. When this had no effect, the old man went on a hunger strike.

The Emperor finally opened the door and the two men spent an entire day reconciling. As in their classroom, Guang-hsu listened while Tutor Weng discussed the source of the failures. The conclusion was that Li Hung-chang should be the one to blame.

While I put up with Guang-hsu's sensitivity, I was annoyed by the tutor's ability to sway the thinking of the Emperor. In my eyes nothing would justify Weng's misconduct. And when Weng made Li Hung-chang the scapegoat, I lost all respect for him. I didn't intend to create enemies by openly taking Li's side, but I saw the necessity of speaking my mind to the Emperor.

In my silence to the court's demand for his prosecution, Li Hung-chang challenged the Emperor for the right to prosecute the Manchu princes who supplied the defective ammunition. Li also demanded the right to choose his own commissioners in the future.

At Tutor Weng's suggestion, Guang-hsu summoned Li Hung-chang for an official audit. The Manchu princes were invited to be witnesses.

Li came prepared. His detailed documentation not only advanced his case but also gained him great sympathy from the nation. Letters of support for him poured in from every provincial governor. The pressure mounted. Some began to criticize Guang-hsu himself.

The frustrated Emperor came to me for help. He was humiliated and ridiculed, and he sensed that he was losing the respect of his people. 'It is obvious that Li Hung-chang is the one who fits the role of ruler of China,' Guang-hsu told me.

The time came when I had to choose between Guang-hsu and Li Hung-chang. I had long sensed my fate, but it was in that moment that I saw the depth of the tragedy. My conscience told me that Li Hung-chang would be good for the people, that he alone could run China. But China was the Manchus' China – I had to go against my principles to save Guang-hsu.

After sleepless nights of weighing my options and gathering my courage, I did the unreasonable and unconscionable thing: I signed the edict denouncing Li Hung-chang. The man was stripped of all his honors. He was charged with mishandling naval funds and for losing the war.

I was ashamed of myself.

I thought I had done enough for Guang-hsu, but this was wishful thinking. Under the influence of his uncle Prince Ts'eng, his cousin Prince Ts'eng Junior and his brother Prince Ch'un Junior, the easily swayed Guang-hsu was persuaded that the punishment already endured by Li Hung-chang was insufficient, that he must be eliminated altogether.

When I was requested to give approval for Li's further prosecution, I could no longer contain my rage. My fierce expression must have scared the Emperor, for he started to stutter and got down on his knees.

The truth was that I was mad at myself. I had allowed Tutor Weng and Prince Ch'un to escape their responsibilities. Why would any clearheaded Chinese be willing to serve his Manchu master after seeing what happened to Li Hung-chang?

I pointed out to Guang-hsu that Li was too valuable to destroy without crippling the government. 'He can strike back by seizing power for himself! It would be as easy as flipping his hand. You will find me watching an opera in the Summer Palace when that happens!'

The air in the court was dense and threatening. Suddenly I realized that I was alone and that I could be repudiated by my own clan. All it would take would be to convince Guang-hsu. To protect myself, I negotiated. In exchange for retaining Li Hung-chang's offices, including the vice-royalty of Chihli and the leadership of the Northern Army and the Chinese navy, I suggested that the throne take away Li's prized double-eyed peacock feather and the yellow silk field marshal's riding jacket. 'It would cause Li extreme loss of face. However, anything more would be rash and unmerciful.'

When Prince Ts'eng accused me of missing the opportunity of a lifetime for the Manchus to bring Li to his knees, I withdrew in the middle of the audience.

I could hear the creek splashing behind the palace garden in the Forbidden City. I got up before dawn and sent my eunuch to summon Li Hung-chang.

Li arrived at sunrise wearing a simple blue cotton robe, which made him look like a different man.

'You have been packing?' I began, knowing that he was leaving Peking.

'Yes,' he replied. 'My carriage will depart in an hour.'

'Where will you go?' I asked. 'Chihli? Hunan? Or your hometown, Hefei?'

Unable to answer, Li dropped to his knees.

I reminded him that etiquette allowed us only a brief meeting and I had to speak my mind.

Li nodded, but insisted on remaining on the floor.

I let him and said, 'Please understand how awful I feel about what I have done to you. Though hardly a decent excuse, I had no choice.'

'I understand, Your Majesty.' Li's voice was calm and almost undisturbed. 'You did what any mother would do.'

My tears came and I broke down.

'If it helps the throne, I am honored,' Li said.

'Can you at least let me offer help for your long journey south?'

'There is no need,' he said. 'I have enough to support my family. My wife understands that if I were charged with treason and found guilty, my life would be forfeited. She only wants me to make sure that our children escape with their lives.'

'Has the matter been taken care of?' I wiped my face with a handkerchief.

'Yes, arrangements have been made.'

My eunuch came and announced softly, 'My lady, the Emperor is waiting.'

'Farewell.'

Li Hung-chang rose. He took a step back and got down on his knees and kowtowed.

Custom did not allow me to accompany him to the gate, but I decided to ignore it for once.

The door curtain was lifted and we went out to the courtyard. The eunuchs were still doing their morning cleaning. They rushed to get themselves out of sight. Those who crossed our path apologized.

The sky was beginning to brighten. The glazed wing roofs were bathed in golden light. Unlike the Summer Palace, where the air carried the scent of jasmine, Forbidden City mornings were cold and windy.

I heard the sound of my own footsteps, the wooden platform shoes hitting the stone walk. Li Hung-chang and I walked side by side. Behind us, sixteen eunuchs carried my room-sized ceremonial palanquin.

Two weeks later, Prince Kung, who was sixty-five, was called out of retirement. Emperor Guang-hsu issued the decree at my urging. Kung was reluctant at first. For ten years he had nursed grievances against those who had removed him from leadership, including his two half-brothers. I pleaded with him, saying that the death of Prince Ch'un should put the unpleasant past to rest. The twenty-four-year-old Emperor needed him.

Guang-hsu and I met with Prince Kung in his chrysanthemum garden, where the ground was covered with star-shaped purple flowers. Prince Kung picked up a leaf. He laid it flat on his palm and hit it with his other palm, creating a sound like a firecracker.

'The balance of power in Asia has been decisively altered since the Japanese took our fortified harbor at Weihaiwei.' Prince Kung's voice had softened over the years, but his passion, perspective and wit remained. 'Past misdeeds have bred present impotence. In the world's view, the war is essentially over and China has been defeated.'

'But our spirit hasn't!' Guang-hsu's face turned red and his chest swelled. 'I refuse to call it a defeat. Our admirals, officers and soldiers committed suicide to show the world that China is not surrendering!'

Prince Kung smiled bitterly. 'Our admirals committed suicide to redeem themselves and save their families from death and the confiscation of their estates. You stripped their titles and ranks but allowed them to remain in the field. You told them that they would be beheaded if they lost a battle. Their deaths were not their choice but yours!'

'Your uncle is right,' I said. 'I am sure the Emperor has also realized that our nation's patriotism hasn't stopped Japan from occupying the Liaotung Peninsula. We understand that Japan is aiming at Port Arthur's sister fortress and taking over all of Korea.'

Guang-hsu fell back into his chair. As if having difficulty breathing, he inhaled deeply.

Kung continued to pick up leaves and slap them, making annoying sounds with his palms.

I was glad that Prince Kung addressed the issue of the suicides, for I had argued with Guang-hsu many times over his death orders. I had desperately tried to convince him that devotion couldn't be forced. There would be no loyalty if mercy and kindness were not first assured. But I had to end the conversation because Guang-hsu could not comprehend this – he had been raised to take devotion and loyalty for granted. The first thing he had learned about mankind was his tutor's display of sincerity and dedication. I gave in when Guang-hsu complained that I was interfering with his autonomy.

'Mother, are you all right?' Guang-hsu said gently. I had told him that I had been feeling tired and weak.

Then he said, 'I have thrown out the petitions demanding Li Hung-chang's punishment.'

I knew by doing this my son meant to please me. But I didn't want to talk about it. Especially not in front of Prince Kung. So I changed the subject. 'Have we tried any other option on the Japan front?'

'We have tried through various intermediaries, including the American diplomats,' Prince Kung replied. 'We tried to reach an accommodation with Japan, but Tokyo has been refusing.'

'I don't see any point in wasting time negotiating,' Guang-hsu said. As if trying to hold in his emotions, he looked away. 'I don't negotiate with savages!' he said through clenched teeth.

'What do you want *me* to do, then?' Prince Kung was irritated.

'I need your help with defensive preparations,' the Emperor said.

'I am not sure I can help,' said Prince Kung. 'You are wrong to think that I can do better than Li Hung-chang.'

I turned to both of them. 'Should we not think about walking with both legs? Continuing to seek negotiations with Japan and at the same time preparing our defense?'

Guang-hsu followed Prince Kung's advice and offered to commission foreigners to do the defensive work. A German army engineer who in 1881 had supervised the fortification of Port Arthur was named the chief of China's armies. Guang-hsu hoped that under the leadership of a Western general, he would be able to turn around the situation with Japan.

Both Prince Ts'eng and Prince Ch'un Junior insisted that hiring a past enemy was itself an act of betrayal.

Guang-hsu bore the pressure until the last minute. Then he changed his mind and canceled the commission.

'Had it been done,' the disappointed Prince Kung complained later, 'China would have been safe and Japan would have eventually paid us an indemnity.'

I did not realize it then, but the moment the Emperor changed his mind, his uncle became disheartened. So disheartened that, over the days and weeks to come, Prince Kung would gradually withdraw. I suspected that his pride had been injured but that he would eventually get over it and continue his fight for the dynasty. But Prince Kung's heart retreated to his chrysanthemum garden and he would never come out again.

By the end of January 1895 Guang-hsu realized that he had no other option but to negotiate with Japan. To his further humiliation, Japan refused to discuss the treaty with anyone except the disgraced Li Hung-chang.

On February 13, Guang-hsu relieved Li of his duties as viceroy of Chihli and instructed him to lead the Chinese diplomatic effort. Once again, I was to receive Li Hung-chang in the name of the Emperor.

Li did not want to come to Peking. He begged to be excused from his duty. Believing that the Emperor and the Ironhats would sooner or later make him a scapegoat, he had no confidence that he would survive. He pointed out that things had changed. We had lost our bargaining chip. There was no way to bring Japan to the negotiating table.

'Any man who represents China and signs the treaty will have to sign away parts of China,' Li predicted. 'It will be a thankless task, and the nation will blame him no matter what the reason for the outcome.'

I pleaded with him to think it over, and sent him a personal invitation to have dinner with me.

Li responded, saying in his message that he was not fit for the honor and his advanced age and ill health made travel difficult.

'I wish that I weren't the Empress of China,' I wrote back to Li. 'The Japanese are on their way to Peking, and I can't bear to even begin to imagine how they will violate the Imperial ancestral grounds.'

Perhaps it was my urgent tone, perhaps it was his sense of noblesse oblige – whatever the reason – Li Hung-chang honored me with his presence, and he was quickly appointed as China's chief negotiator. He arrived at Shimonoseki, Japan, on March 19, 1895. About a month later, the negotiations took a startling turn: while leaving one of the sessions with Prime Minister Ito Hirobumi, Li was shot in the face by a Japanese extremist.

'I was almost glad the incident took place,' Li replied when I wrote asking after his condition. 'The bullet grazed my left cheek. It gained me what I could never get at the negotiating table – the world's sympathy.'

The shooting resulted in an international outcry for Japan to moderate its demands on China.

I felt that I had sent Li to die and he survived only by pure luck.

Also in his message Li Hung-chang prepared Emperor Guang-hsu for the most difficult decision: to agree to the negotiated terms, including the cession to Japan in perpetuity of the island of Taiwan, the Pescadores and the Liaotung Peninsula; the opening of seven Chinese ports to Japanese trade; the payment of two hundred million taels, with permission for Japan to occupy Weihaiwei Harbor until this indemnity was cleared; and recognition of the 'full and complete autonomy and independence of Korea,' which meant relinquishing it to Japan.

Guang-hsu sat on the Dragon Throne and wept. When Li Hung-chang returned to Peking for consultations, he could not get a word out of the Emperor.

It was then that I told Li what I had been thinking: 'Give up what China must in the form of money, but not land.'

He raised his eyes. 'Yes, Your Majesty.'

I told him that once we had sanctioned foreign occupation inland, as we had allowed to happen with the Russians in our Ili region, China would forever be lost.

Li understood perfectly and negotiated accordingly.

The image of Li Hung-chang in the audience hall with his forehead touching the ground remained in my mind after he was gone. I sat frozen. The sound of a big clock in the hallway grated on my nerves.

'Korea and Taiwan are gone,' Guang-hsu muttered to himself over and over.

He didn't know, of course, that within months we would also lose Nepal, Burma and Indochina.

Another rape. And then another.

Japan had no intention of stopping. Its agents now had spread deep into Manchuria.

The dragon carvings on the palace columns again went unpainted this year. The old paint had started to peel and the golden color turned a parched brown. The Board of the Interior had long run out of money. The danger was not only the visible dry rot, it was the invisible termites.

One morning Chief Eunuch Li Lien-ying ventured to make a formal plea to the throne: 'Please, Your Majesty, do something to save the Forbidden City, for it is built with nothing but wood.'

'Burn it down!' was Guang-hsu's response.

The audiences went on. In Li Hung-chang's tele-grammed updates the Japanese demanded the right to build factories in the treaty ports. 'Accept these terms or there will be war,' Japan threatened.

Guang-hsu and I understood that if we granted Japan's demands, the same demands would be made by all the other foreign powers.

'The latest concessions also brought up the issue of mineral rights,' Li's telegram continued, 'and there is little we can do to resist . . .'

The sun's rays came through the windows of my bedroom, throwing shade like rustling leaves onto the floor and furniture. A large black spider hung on its thread by a carved panel. It swung back and forth in the gentle breeze.

This was the first black spider I had seen inside the Forbidden City.

I heard the sound of someone dragging his feet. Then Guang-hsu appeared in the doorframe. His posture was that of an old man with his back hunched.

'Any news?' I asked.

'We lost our last division of Moslem cavalry.' Guang-hsu entered my room and sat down on a chair. 'I am forced to disband tens of thousands of soldiers because I have to pay the foreign indemnities. "Or war," they say. "Or war"!'

'You haven't been eating,' I said. 'Let's have breakfast.'

'The Japanese have been building roads connecting Manchuria to Tokyo.' He stared at me, his big black eyes unblinking. 'My downfall will come along with the fall of the Russian tsar.'

'Guang-hsu, enough.'

'The Meiji Emperor will soon be unchallenged in East Asia.'

'Guang-hsu, eat first, please . . .'

'Mother, how can I eat? Japan has filled my stomach!'

26

THE IMPERIAL KITCHENS tried to find reasons not to cancel my birthday banquets. The same attitude was shared by the court, which saw my retirement as an opportunity for everyone to make money. Li Hung-chang was forced to negotiate additional loans to save the day.

I concluded that the only way out of my birthday trap would be to address the nation in a public letter:

The auspicious occasion of my sixtieth birthday was to have been a joyful event, and I understand that officials and many citizens have subscribed funds wherewith to raise triumphal arches – twenty-five percent of your yearly income, I was told – to honor me by decorating the Imperial Waterway along its entire length from Peking to my home . . . I was not disposed to be unduly obstinate and to insist on refusing these honors, but I feel that I owe you, above everything else, my true feelings. Since the beginning of the last summer our tributary states have been taken, our fleets destroyed, and we have been forced into hostilities causing great despair. How could I have the heart to delight my senses? Therefore, I decree that the public ceremonies and all preparations be abandoned forthwith.

I sent my draft directly to the printer without going through a grand councilor. I was afraid that my words would be violated, just as had my wish to cancel my birthday banquets.

I would have also liked to share with the nation my regret that our neglect of Li's advice had only stiffened the penalties China had to pay. I could not begin to express my anger that Li Hung-chang, at the age of seventy-two, returned home from Japan only to be called a traitor. People in the streets spat at his palanquin as it passed.

As a way to show support for Li, I persuaded the court to send him to St. Petersburg not long after the coronation of Tsar Nicholas II.

Li requested that an empty coffin accompany him on the trip – he wanted to be prepared. He asked me to inscribe his name on the lid, which I did.

As a result of Li Hung-chang's visit, a secret agreement between Russia and China was negotiated and then signed. Each country agreed to defend the other against aggression from Japan. The price we paid was to accept a clause allowing Russia to extend its Trans-Siberian Railway across Manchuria to Vladivostok. We would also allow the Russians to use the railway to transport troops and war materiel through Chinese territory.

It was the best Li Hung-chang could achieve under the circumstances. He and I had a gut feeling that Russia could not be trusted. As it turned out, once we gave the Russians the right to harbor their fleet in our ice-free

Port Arthur, they refused to leave, even after Japan was expelled.

Around this time, as Guang-hsu and I were working out the practicalities of a land-leasing program to generate payments for our foreign loans, his wife, my niece Lan, arrived unexpectedly.

The moment Guang-hsu saw Lan entering, he excused himself and left the room.

Lan was dressed in a robe embroidered with patterns of roses. Matching ornaments of tiny roses made of ribbon were in her hair. The high collar of her robe forced her chin up and out, making her discomfort palpable. It seemed that she had quit caking her cheeks with white powder; her heartache was visible in her expression. The corners of her mouth drew downward. Tears fell before she could speak.

Witnessing their troubled marriage was worse than living with the deaths of my husband and son. The deaths of Hsien Feng and Tung Chih cured nothing, but they set the stage for healing. Memory was selective and altered itself over time. I no longer remembered the hard feelings. In my dreams my son loved me, and Hsien Feng was always adoring.

With Guang-hsu and Lan, misery was like mold growing in a wet season: it started in the corner of an eave and slowly took over the entire palace.

'I came from the bedside of my mother-in-law.' Lan was speaking, of course, about my sister. 'Rong is doing poorly.'

My sister had been bedridden and had refused my visits. Rong had insisted that I was the cause of her illness, so I had sent Lan in my place.

'I know you are not here to talk about my sister,' I said to Lan. 'All I can tell you is that Guang-hsu is under great pressure.'

Lan shook her head, setting the ornaments in her hair fluttering. 'He needs to spend time with me.'

'I can't force him, Lan.'

'Yes, you can, Aunt, if you truly care about me.'

I felt guilty and promised her that I would try again. I moved Lan and her household to a compound right behind Guang-hsu's, using the termite problem as a pretext. My thinking was that the couple could visit each other through a connected archway door. But the very next day, Guang-hsu blocked the passage with furniture. When Lan had the furniture removed, Guang-hsu issued an order for the doorway to be permanently sealed with bricks.

In the meantime, I could see that Guang-hsu was falling in love with his Pearl Concubine, who had just turned nineteen and was a stunning beauty. Her curiosity and intelligence reminded me of my own youth. I was fond of her because she inspired Guang-hsu to live up to the nation's expectations.

I felt sorry for Lan when she tried to compete with Pearl. Lan carried too much of my brother's blood. She had ambition but not the will to realize it. When she threatened to commit suicide, Guang-hsu only became more disgusted with her.

I called Kuei Hsiang for help, but he said, 'You are the matchmaker, sister Orchid. You have to fix it.'

I arranged a tea party for just the three of us. When Lan insisted that Guang-hsu taste the peach cake she had made for him, he became fretful and got up to leave. I touched his elbow and said, 'Let's take a walk in the garden.' I fell in behind them, hoping that they would start a conversation. But Guang-hsu kept his distance, as if his wife carried a disease. Lan held on to her pride and kept silent.

*　　*　　*

'You have to make a choice, Lan,' I said after Guang-hsu had left to attend a court function. 'You were aware that things might not go as you wished. I did warn you.'

'Yes, you did.' My niece wiped her face with a handkerchief. 'I believed that my love would change him.'

'Well, he hasn't changed. You must accept that.'

'What am I going to do?'

'Get busy with your duties as Empress. Conduct ceremonies and pay homage to the ancestors. You can also do what I do: learn about the world and try to be helpful.'

'Will that lead me to the affection of Guang-hsu?'

'I don't know,' I replied. 'But you should never deprive yourself of the possibility.'

Lan began her apprenticeship with me. First, I assigned her to read a recent report on the death of Queen Min of Korea.

' "Led by informers, the Japanese agents forced their way into the palace of the Queen." ' Lan gasped, covering her mouth with her handkerchief.

'Keep going, Lan,' I instructed.

' "After . . . after murdering two of her ladies in waiting, they cornered Queen Min. The minister of the royal household came to her rescue, but the intruders lopped off both his hands with a sword . . ." ' Lan was horrified. 'What . . . what about her bodyguards? Where were they?'

'They must have been killed or trapped or bought off,' I replied. 'Go on and finish, Lan.'

' "Queen Min was stabbed repeatedly and was carried outside . . ." ' Lan went on reading, but her voice was no longer audible. She turned toward me with her head leaning to one side, like a puppet with a broken string.

'What happened?' I asked.

'The Japanese set a pile of firewood doused with kerosene outside her courtyard.'

'And then?'

'They threw her on top of it and lit the torch.' Lan's lips trembled.

I took the report back from her and placed it on my desk.

Lan sat silently, as if frozen. After a while she rose and walked out like a ghost.

Lan never again threatened suicide, although she continued to complain about her husband. She believed that she didn't have to learn the court's business, but that did not stop her fantasies of being worshiped by the nation. She never shared the bed of the Emperor or made friends with Pearl. She pursued longevity, cosseted herself and spent time with Pearl's sister, Lustrous Concubine, who was the opposite of Pearl. Lustrous had little interest in much of anything. She loved food and could sit around daintily nibbling all day.

On June 18, 1896, Rong died. It was after she accused her doctors of poisoning her. Her mental illness became known to the court, so my decision of years before to bar her from visiting Guang-hsu was now understood. The unfortunate thing was that the Emperor was now considered the son of an insane woman, and the Clan Council used this excuse to start thinking about his replacement.

I was sick of the infighting among the Manchu princes, the brothers and cousins who seemed to share nothing but greed and hatred. When I tried to explain the great affection between Emperor Hsien Feng and Prince Kung, the young Ironhats grew bored. In splendid court robes this generation of royal Manchus fought like a pack of wolves over residences, sinecures and annual stipends.

I lost my temper at a family gathering during my sister's funeral. It had to do with the fact that I didn't get a chance to say goodbye to Rong – her revenge. And the grousing among Prince Ch'un Junior and his Ironhat gang over their inheritances hit my nerves and I exploded.

'Your mother's death means that you will no longer be shielded.' I spoke in a cold voice. 'The next time you offend the throne, I will not hesitate to order your removal, and if you defy me, your execution.'

Ch'un knew that I meant what I said – after all, I had executed Su Shun, the former grand councilor, and his powerful gang.

My harsh words put a stop to the bickering, and I was left alone.

Laying my cheek against Rong's coffin, I remembered the two walnuts she placed in my palm the day I departed home for the Forbidden City. I regretted that I hadn't tried harder to care for her. She had succumbed to her illness, but there had been moments of lucidity and affection. I wondered if she knew of the marital troubles of Guang-hsu and Lan. I would never know her feelings. How I missed talking with her when we were girls! I wished I could talk to Kuei Hsiang, commiserate together, but he was not interested. To my brother, Rong's death was a relief.

Lan and Guang-hsu looked like a harmonious couple at Rong's funeral. After bowing toward the coffin together, they tossed golden grain toward the sky. It made me think that I should not give up hope.

Throughout our recent troubles, Yung Lu had continued working alongside Li Hung-chang, strengthening the army. During this time we seldom met; he was determined not to breathe life into any rumors about us that might compromise his efforts on the throne's behalf. I had to be satisfied with reports of his whereabouts from Li.

But one morning Yung Lu came to me to request permission to leave his current position as commander in chief of the army to head up the nation's navy. I granted his wish, knowing that he must have thought through the decision, but I warned him that many would regard his transfer as a demotion.

'I never live by others' principles' was his response.

'The navy has been having great difficulty since Li Hung-chang's departure abroad,' I reminded him.

'That's exactly why I want the job.'

'Li had said to me, "It takes a man of Yung Lu's stature to influence the navy." Did he suggest your move?'

'Yes, he did.'

I tried not to think that Yung Lu's new duties would take him even more often away from Peking.

'Who will be your replacement?' I asked.

'Yuan Shih-kai. He will report to me directly.' I was well aware of Yuan's qualifications, of course. As a young general he had fought the Japanese and succeeded in keeping peace in Korea for ten years.

'Then you will be working two jobs.'

'Yes, I will.' He smiled. 'So are you.'

'I won't feel safe with you gone.'

'I'll be in Tientsin.'

'That's hundreds of miles away.'

'Compared to Sinkiang, it is no distance.'

We sat quietly sipping tea. I looked at him, his eyes, nose, mouth and hands.

27

GUANG-HSU ASKED me to move with him to Ying-t'ai, the Ocean Terrace Pavilion, which stood on an island in the South Sea lake next to the Summer Palace. The seclusion, he said, would help him concentrate.

Ying-t'ai was a paradise that had long been unoccupied. Its elegant buildings, which were in need of repair, were linked to the mainland by a narrow causeway and a drawbridge. The pavilion had marble terraces dropping straight into the water, with canals spanned by pretty bridges between them.

In the summer the surrounding lakes were covered by flotillas of green lotus. By August large pink flowers would shoot up from the green mats. The views were astonishing. When the restoration work started, I was asked to rename the living quarters. I chose the names Hall of Cultivating Elegance, Chamber of Quiet Rest, Study of Reflection on Remote Matters and Chamber of Singleness of Heart.

I was beginning to realize that there could be dignity without friends. I found myself becoming more attracted to Buddhism. Its promise of peace was appealing, and it did not discriminate against women, as did Confucianism. The

Buddhist pantheon included women, prominent among them the goddess of mercy, Kuan-yin, with whom I felt a special affinity. The truth was that I had nowhere else to turn.

I believed in mercy, but I was losing faith in the people around me. For example, I had thought that my fairness toward house eunuchs would assure their honesty and gain their loyalty, but with a piercing look straight in the eyes I would catch a liar.

I had asked my eunuch Chow Tee to send a honey-nut cake to Li Lien-ying, who was away on vacation for the first time in twenty-nine years. When Chow Tee reported Li Lien-ying's thanks to me, I asked, 'Did you deliver the cake yourself?'

'I did, of course. I ran, so Chief Li could have the cake while it was still hot.'

'It's raining outside, isn't it?' I asked.

'Yes.'

'How is it that your clothes are completely dry?'

In the end, the liar suffered ten strokes of a bamboo stick.

Trying to calm myself, I looked at the blooming camellia outside my window. The trees were loaded with fat buds. It was hard to believe that Li Lien-ying had turned fifty. He was thirteen when An-te-hai first brought him to me.

I was now sixty-one and had become suspicious of others and increasingly questioned my own judgment. I repeatedly warned that I would tolerate no liars, but lying had always been a part of the life of the Forbidden City. Since our war with Japan, I had never received a single report of a military loss. The only news the court sent was of victory, for which I foolishly awarded promotions and bonuses.

On impulse, I would pick a moment to test my eunuchs and ladies in waiting. I felt sick at heart, yet I couldn't act differently. I had to be unpredictable and domineering. I made it a rule to be swift with the rod. This had become my way to survive mentally.

I tried to let go of small matters. For example, I did not pursue his punishment when Li Lien-ying poked a hole ('to let out the air') in all of my champagne bottles – Li Hung-chang's gifts from France. The eunuch believed that the popping sound would harm me.

Throughout 1896 I had worked daily with Emperor Guang-hsu and was pleased with his progress. He desperately tried to catch up on the court's business but faced tremendous obstacles, and getting things organized was our first step. I rose early and walked the stone bridges to get my mind ready for the day. I watched the lotus from their early budding to their final blooming. I caught the first flower, which opened on a summer dawn.

I felt at odds with the tranquility of the setting. As I watched my eunuchs plunging waist-deep in the mire to extract lotus roots for my breakfast, my mind struggled with whether or not I should press the Emperor to approve Li Hung-chang's recent proposal to secure additional loans. We were behind in our current payments, and the foreign banks were threatening. It was clear to us that the foreign powers were after our territories and were looking for any pretext to invade.

When the stir-fried lotus roots were served, Guang-hsu had no appetite. I sat beside him but had no words to comfort him. By now I had learned that Guang-hsu most often craved to be left alone. I had been worrying about his health, but I dared not utter a question or even encourage him to pick up his chopsticks.

After finishing my meal, I quickly rinsed my mouth and went into the office to prepare for the morning audiences.

Guang-hsu would follow in a few minutes. I would wait for the eunuchs to finish dressing him and we would get into our palanquins.

Withdrawing from audiences in the afternoon, Guang-hsu and I would continue to discuss the day's issues. Often we had to summon ministers and officials for detailed information. When Guang-hsu saw me begin to yawn, he would beg me to stop and relax. I would ask him for a cigarette, and he would light it for me. I would smoke and continue to work until dark.

'China has given no offense, has done no wrong, does not wish to fight, and is willing to make sacrifices,' Robert Hart's article read. 'She is a big "sick" man, convalescing slowly from the sickening effects of centuries, and is being jumped on when down by this agile, healthy, well-armed Jap – will no one pull him off?'

Guang-hsu and I hoped that Hart's remarks would help China gain sympathy and support from the rest of the world. Unfortunately, things went in the opposite direction. Our defeat by Japan only encouraged the Western powers to take further advantage of us. 'The worm has reduced the stout fabric of China to handfuls of dust' – the remnants were there for anybody to take.

We had lost Korea, and our new navy lay in ruins. After slavishly emulating Chinese civilization for centuries, the Japanese had nothing but supercilious scorn for the true fountainhead of Eastern wisdom. The world seemed to have forgotten that as recently as 1871, Japan had paid tribute to China as a vassal state.

Like everyone else, Guang-hsu suspected that Li Hung-chang had cut private deals with the foreigners for his own benefit. 'Li could have done better with the treaties,' he insisted. Guang-hsu's only evidence was that Li Hung-chang entrusted his son-in-law with the military supplies of the army.

'That's because Li's experience with your uncles, brothers and cousins was so terrible,' I told him. 'Li has committed no corruption – it is the way of China to rely on personal connections. Focus on what you have gained. Li has succeeded in securing the funding to rebuild the navy.'

'I can't forgive him for squandering the opportunity for an early defense!' Guang-hsu's voice pierced through the hallway. 'He sold us down the river!'

Guang-hsu couldn't live with the fact that we had been forced to sign the Shimonoseki Treaty, the most humiliating ever signed by an emperor in Chinese history.

'Japan provided opportunities for him to make money. Am I not right that Li Hung-chang is the wealthiest man in China?'

'I will not kick the family dog,' I said quietly. 'I'd rather fight the bully neighbor. Li didn't want to take part in the negotiations in the first place. He was sent,' I reminded Guang-hsu, 'by you and me. The Japanese rejected the representative you had sent before him. Li was the only man whose credentials the Japanese considered adequate.'

'Exactly!' Guang-hsu said. 'They picked him because he was a friend. Japan knew Li would cut them a good deal.'

'For heaven's sake, Guang-hsu, the bullet just missed Li's eye! If it hadn't been for his near assassination, Japan would have pushed for its original demands, and we would have lost all of Manchuria plus three hundred million taels!'

'It is not I alone who accuses Li.' Guang-hsu showed me a document. 'The court censor has been investigating. Listen.' He read, ' "Li Hung-chang was heavily invested in Japanese businesses, and he did not wish to lose his dividends through protracted war. He seems to have been afraid that the large sums of money from his numerous speculations, which he had deposited in Japan, might be lost; hence his objections to the war." '

'If you can't tell that attacking Li Hung-chang is itself an action against the throne, there is no way that I can or should work with you.' I was upset.

'Mother.' Guang-hsu got down on his knees. 'I only share with you what I know. You rely on Li so much. What if he is not who you think he is?'

'If only we had a choice, Guang-hsu.' I sighed. 'We need him. If Li hadn't played on international jealousies, Japan would not have withdrawn from the Liaotung Peninsula.'

'But Japan charged us another thirty million taels in compensation and indemnities,' Guang-hsu said bitterly.

'We were the defeated nation, my son. It was not all up to Li Hung-chang.'

Guang-hsu sat quietly biting his lips.

I begged him not to take Li for granted. 'Only we can balance Li Hung-chang's graft against what he is able to bring us.'

When I asked how the reception with the foreign delegation went, Guang-hsu replied flatly, 'Not well.' He sat down and stretched his neck. 'I am sure the foreigners were equally disappointed. They spent so much time and energy trying to secure the audience, only to find out how dull I was.'

I remembered my husband Hsien Feng's comments when foreigners requested an audience with him. He felt that he would only be giving them an opportunity to spit in his face.

'I couldn't stand the sight of them,' Guang-hsu said. 'I tried to tell myself, I am meeting with individuals, not the countries that bullied me.'

'You received all the delegates?' I asked.

Guang-hsu nodded. 'Russia, France, England and Germany acted like dogs. They tried to make me commit to borrowing more money. What could I do? I told them China couldn't afford it anymore. I told them that all my revenues go to pay the Japanese indemnity.'

The foreign bankers were savage dealmakers, I remembered Li Hung-chang once told me. 'What happened in the end?'

'In the end? I borrowed from all of them, pledging my customs revenue and transit and salt taxes as security.'

The pain in his voice was unbearable. I felt helpless and tremendously sad.

'I am unprepared for what's coming.' My son sighed again. 'The Russians continue to transport troops and supplies by our railway across Manchuria to the sea.'

'We granted them the right only in times of war, not in times of peace.' I could hear the weariness in my own voice.

Guang-hsu shook his head. 'The Russians are determined to keep their Trans-Siberian running in times of peace as well, Mother.'

Stepping out on the terrace for fresh air, I held my son's shoulders. 'Let's hope Li's scheme of using one barbarian to control another will work.'

Guang-hsu was not sure. 'Japan is approaching Peking,' he said, 'and we have lost our sea defense completely.'

I stood in the wind and tried to get through the moment.

For my son, each day brought another decision, another defeat, another humiliation. He had been living in a manure pit. Tung Chih had been lucky: death had helped him to reach peace.

Darkness filled the room after Li Lien-ying retreated. I lay against soft pillows and recalled that once Li Hung-chang had advised me to deposit gold and silver in banks outside China.

'In case Japan . . .' I remembered that he was afraid to say more, but I got the idea: I might be forced to flee China. The image of Queen Min burned alive was never far from my thoughts.

Li Hung-chang must have assumed that I was a wealthy woman. He had no idea how penniless I was. I was too embarrassed to let anyone know that I had sold my favorite opera troupe. I owned practically nothing but my seven honorary Imperial titles. Li hadn't insisted on having me consult the English bank managers in Hong Kong and Shanghai. But when he left my palace, he was no longer confused – he understood more than ever where I stood in terms of China's survival.

Guang-hsu and I had expected that the Western powers would cease their aggression after the deals were executed, but in May of 1897 Germany found another excuse to attack us. The incident began when Chinese bandits robbed a village in Shantung near the port of Kiaochow, a German settlement. Houses were burned and the inhabitants were murdered, along with two Roman Catholic German missionaries.

Before our government had a chance to investigate, a German squadron proceeded to Kiaochow and seized the port. China was threatened with the severest repression unless it instantly agreed to pay compensation in gold and prosecute the bandits.

The Kaiser made sure that his protest was heard by the world: 'I am fully determined to abandon henceforth the overcautious policy which had been regarded by the Chinese as weakness, and to show the Chinese, with full power and, if necessary, with brutal ruthlessness, that the German Emperor cannot be made sport of and that it is bad to have him as an enemy.'

Four days later, my son came to me with the news that the Chinese garrison of Kiaochow had been routed. After its capture, Guang-hsu was forced to lease the port and the land around it, in a fifty-kilometer radius, from Germany. The ninety-nine-year lease came with exclusive mining and railway rights in the area.

Guang-hsu had trembled as he listened to Li Hung-chang describe what would happen if he refused to sign.

In the next few months, Li would bring more bad news: Russian warships sailed into fortified Port Arthur, as they were allowed to by the treaty of 1896, and announced that they had come to stay for good. By March of 1898, Port Arthur and the nearby merchant port of Talienwan were likewise leased to Russia, for twenty-five years, with all mining and railway rights for sixty miles around.

Joining the fray, the British prime minister claimed that 'the balance of power in the Gulf of Pechili has now been upset.' England demanded that Weihaiwei, which was on the same spur as Kiaochow, controlled by the Germans, 'be handed over to the British as soon as the Japanese indemnity had been paid and the town had been evacuated.' The British also granted themselves an increase in the area of Kowloon, on the mainland opposite Hong Kong.

Not wanting to be left behind, France demanded a similar ninety-nine-year lease on the port of Kwangcho-wan, south of Hong Kong.

When the court pleaded for the Emperor to take control of the situation, Guang-hsu handed each minister a copy of what he had received from Li Hung-chang. It was an announcement made by the united Western powers regarding the 'spheres of influence' in China. Germany and Russia had agreed that the entire Yangtze basin from Szechuan to the delta at Kiangsu was British. Britain agreed that southern Canton and southern Yunnan were French. A belt from Kausu through Shensi, Shansi, Hunan and Shantung was German. Manchuria and Chihli were Russian. The freedom-loving United States secured equal rights and opportunities for all nations in the leased areas and termed their attitude 'the Open-Door Policy.'

28

I HAD NO IDEA that I would be meeting with Prince Kung
for the last time. It was a gloomy overcast day in May
1898 when I received his invitation. Although he had been
ill, he was a man of robust health and spirits, and everyone
expected him to recover. When I arrived at his bedside, I
was taken aback by his condition and knew instantly that
his life was coming to an end.

'I hope you don't mind that the dying fish keeps making
bubbles,' Prince Kung said in a weak voice.

I asked if he would like me to bring the Emperor.

Prince Kung shook his head and closed his eyes to gather
energy.

I looked around. There were cups, bowls, spittoons and
basins arranged around the bed. The smell of herbal
medicine in the room was unpleasant.

Prince Kung tried to sit up, but he no longer had the
strength. 'Sixth brother,' I said, helping him up, 'you
shouldn't have hidden your condition.'

'It's Heaven's will, sister-in-law,' Prince Kung gasped. 'I
am glad I caught you in time.'

He raised his right hand and stuck up two trembling
fingers.

I drew closer.

'First, I am sorry for Tung Chih's death.' Remorse filled Prince Kung's voice. 'I know how you suffered . . . I apologize. My son Tsai-chen deserved his end.'

'Stop it, sixth brother.' Tears came to my eyes.

'I never forgave Tsai-chen, and he knew it,' Prince Kung said.

But it was himself he wouldn't forgive. I never had the heart to ask how Prince Kung got through the days after his son died.

'Pity the hearts of parents,' I said, passing him a towel.

'I owed much to Hsien Feng.' Prince Kung wiped his face with the towel. 'I failed in my duty. I let Tung Chih down, and now I have to quit on Guang-hsu.'

'You didn't owe Hsien Feng anything. He wrote you out of his will. If there was any duty regarding how to raise and influence Tung Chih, Hsien Feng left the power to Su Shun and his gang.'

Prince Kung had to agree with what I said, although he had chosen to believe that it was Su Shun, and not his brother, who manipulated the Imperial will.

Exhausted, he closed his eyes again as if going to sleep. Looking at the prince's sallow face, I remembered the days when he was strong, handsome and full of zest. His dreams for China were great, and so was his talent. Once I had even fantasized that I had married him instead of Emperor Hsien Feng.

I suppose I had always believed that Kung would have made a better emperor. He should have been given the throne – and would have been but for the wiles of Hsien Feng's grand tutor, who counseled his student to pretend compassion toward the animals of the autumn hunt. Prince Kung outcompeted all his brothers that day, but his father was moved by the younger son's heart. It was a misfortune for the country that the crown went to Hsien Feng. And misfortune bred misfortune.

I wondered whether Prince Kung resented living in the shadow of Hsien Feng, knowing that he had been betrayed.

'If you have a question, you'd better ask before it is too late,' Prince Kung said when he opened his eyes again.

The thought of losing him was unbearable. 'I don't think you want to know the question I have,' I said. 'I don't think it is even decent for me to ask.'

'Orchid, we have been each other's best friend and worst curse.' Prince Kung smiled. 'What more can come between us?'

So I asked if he resented his father's unfairness and his brother's theft of the kingdom.

'If I had any resentment, my own guilt took away the sting,' he replied. 'Do you remember September of 1861?'

'The month Hsien Feng died?'

'Yes. Remember the deal we made? It was a good deal, wasn't it?'

Back then, when we were in our twenties, we didn't know that we were making history. Prince Kung found out that he had been written out of Hsien Feng's will. He was left helpless for Su Shun to slaughter. And I faced the possibility of being buried alive, to accompany my husband on his journey to the next life.

'Su Shun had both of us in a corner,' I said.

'Was it you or I who first came up with the idea of lending each other the legitimacy?' he asked.

'I can't recall. I only remember that we had no option but to help each other.'

'It was you who drafted my appointment as Su Shun's replacement,' Prince Kung said.

'Did I?'

'Yes. It was audacious – and unthinkable.'

'You deserved the title,' I said softly. 'It should have been Heaven's will in the first place.'

'I am guilty because it wasn't what my father and my brother Hsien Feng intended.'

'The dynasty wouldn't be where it is without you,' I insisted.

'In that case, I'd like to thank you for the opportunity, Orchid.'

'You are a good partner, although you can be difficult.'

'Can you forgive me for Tung Chih's death?'

'You loved him, Kung, and that is what I will remember.'

The second thing Prince Kung wanted was my promise to continue to honor Robert Hart, a man he had worked with closely over the years.

'He is the most precious connection China will ever have. Our future place in the world depends on his help.' Kung was sure that the court would not follow his instructions once he died. 'I am afraid that they will drive Robert Hart away.'

'I will see that Li Hung-chang follows your path,' I promised.

'I couldn't get the court to grant Hart a private audience,' Prince Kung said. 'Will you receive him?'

'Does his rank allow me?'

'His rank is high enough, but he is not Chinese,' Kung said bitterly. 'The ministers are jealous of him because I relied on him for so much. He is resented not because he is English, but because he can't be bought.'

Prince Kung and I both wished that we had more men of Robert Hart's character.

'I heard that he was honored in England by the Queen. Is that true?' I asked.

Prince Kung nodded. 'The Queen made him a knight, but she cares far more about Hart's achievement in opening China for England than his rank.'

'I will never take Robert Hart for granted,' I promised.

'Hart loves China. He has been tolerant and has put up with the court's disrespect. I fear that his patience will soon run out and he will quit. China is absolutely dependent on Hart's leadership. We would lose a third of our customs revenue, and . . . our dynasty . . .'

I did not know how to carry on Prince Kung's work. I had no way to communicate with Robert Hart, nor was I confident of convincing the court of his vital importance.

'I can't do it without you, sixth brother.' I wept.

Kung's doctor hovered nearby and told me that I'd better leave.

The prince looked relieved when he waved goodbye to me.

I returned the next day and was told that Prince Kung had been drifting in and out of consciousness. A few days later he went into a coma.

On May 22, he died.

I helped to arrange a simple funeral for Prince Kung, as he had requested. The throne personally notified Robert Hart of his friend's passing.

It was hard for me to let go of Prince Kung. The day after his burial, I dreamed of his return. He was with Hsien Feng. Both men looked to be twenty again. Prince Kung wore purple, and my husband was dressed in his white satin robe.

'To live is to experience dying and is worse than death,' my husband said in his usual depressed tone.

'True,' Prince Kung said, 'but "living death" can also be interpreted as "spiritual wealth."'

254

I followed them in my nightgown as they talked to each other. I understood the words, but not their meanings.

'The understanding of suffering enables the sufferer to walk on the path of immortality,' my husband went on. 'Immortality means the ability to bear the unbearable.'

Prince Kung agreed. 'Only after experiencing death can one understand the pleasure of living.'

Still in the realm of dreams, I interrupted them. 'But there is no pleasure in my living. To live means only to die over and over. The pain has become impossible to bear. It is like a continuous punishment, a lingering death.'

'Dying over and over gives you the rapture of being alive,' my husband said.

Before I could argue, both men faded. In their place I saw a very old woman squatting on her heels in the corner of a large, dark room. It was myself. I was in servant's clothes and I looked sick. My body had shrunk to the size of a child. My skin was deeply wrinkled and my hair gray and white.

29

'Reform has been on my mind,' Emperor Guang-hsu confessed. 'It is the only way to save China.' Over breakfast in the Forbidden City he told me he had found a 'like-mind,' a man whom he much admired. 'But the court has rejected my meeting with him.'

This was the first time I heard the name Kang Yu-wei, a scholar and self-proclaimed reformer from Canton. I found out that the reason for the court's rejection was that Kang Yu-wei had neither a government position nor any rank. In fact, he had failed the national civil service examination three times.

'Kang Yu-wei is an extraordinary talent, a political genius!' Guang-hsu insisted.

I asked how the Emperor had learned about this man.

'Pearl introduced his writings to me.'

'I hope Pearl is aware that she could be punished for smuggling books,' I said.

'She is, Mother. But she was right to bring me his books, for I have learned a way to set China on the right path.'

Pearl's daring reminded me of my own when I was her age. I also remembered how I was hated by the entire court, especially Grand Councilor Su Shun, who had set his mind on destroying me.

'Pearl believes that I have the power to protect her.'

'Do you, Guang-hsu?'

My son got up from his chair and went to sit in another. His foot nervously tapped the floor. 'I guess I wouldn't be here if I did.'

'You are willing to protect her, aren't you?' I asked.

'Yes . . .' He seemed to hesitate.

'I want to make sure you mean what you say, so I know where I stand.'

'I love Pearl.'

'Does that mean you are willing to give up your throne for love?'

Guang-hsu looked at me. 'You are trying to scare me, Mother.'

'One thing I can see clearly. You may be forced to sign Pearl's death sentence if she is found to be involved in the Emperor's business. It doesn't matter if the invitation was from you. You know the rules.'

'I am sorry for encouraging Pearl,' Guang-hsu said. 'But she deserves nothing but praise. She is brilliant and brave.'

'I shall judge Pearl myself,' I said.

'I am prepared to go ahead with or without the court's support,' the Emperor said to me a few days later. His usually pale skin was flushed. 'I have studied the reform models of Russia's Peter the Great and Japan's Hideyoshi. Both helped me clarify what I am setting out to do. Reform will make China strong and prosperous in ten years. Within twenty years China will be powerful enough to recover her lost territories and avenge her humiliations.'

'Is this Kang Yu-wei's prediction?' I asked.

Guang-hsu straightened his posture and nodded. 'Pearl has met with Kang Yu-wei on my behalf at Tutor Weng's.'

'Are you sure Kang Yu-wei didn't approach Pearl first?'

'In fact, he approached Tutor Weng first. He asked him to pass a message to me.'

'I assume he was refused.'

'Yes, but Kang persisted. Pearl saw him at Tutor Weng's door, passing out pamphlets to anyone who was interested.'

My son showed me a few of them. They were self-published and poorly made, but the titles caught my eye: *Study of the Reforms in Japan, Confucius as a Reformer* and *Essays on China's Reconstruction*.

'After I finished reading Kang Yu-wei,' Guang-hsu said, 'I ordered copies to be sent to the key viceroys and governors.'

'You believe that Kang Yu-wei has a cure for China?'

'Absolutely.' Guang-hsu was excited. 'His writings are revolutionary. They speak my mind. No wonder the court and the Ironhats consider him dangerous.'

I told Guang-hsu that the court had informed me of the scholar's background. 'Do you know about Kang's failure to pass the civil service exams?'

'The court misjudges him!'

'Tell me, what is it about Kang Yu-wei that impresses you?'

'His insistence that drastic steps must be taken if reform is to succeed.'

'Don't you think Li Hung-chang and Yung Lu are already making great progress?' I asked.

'They are not effective enough. The old ways must be abandoned completely.'

If I were a portrait painter, I would have painted my son at that moment. He stood by the window as sunlight played on his shoulders. His eyes glowed, and he motioned with his hands to make a point.

'According to Kang Yu-wei, Japan was also a tradition-bound nation,' the Emperor continued. 'It was able to transform itself almost overnight from a feudal society to an industrial state.'

'But when Japan began its reforms, it was not under attack,' I pointed out, 'nor did it carry tremendous domestic and international debts. Let me finish, Guang-hsu. People in Japan were ready to follow their Emperor when he called.'

'What makes you think that my people won't follow me?'

'Guang-hsu, your own court is against you.'

The Emperor screwed up his eyes. 'The first thing on my reform agenda will be to get rid of that roadblock.'

I felt a chill but tried not to show it.

'My edicts will bypass the Clan Council and the court.' Guang-hsu sounded determined. 'Kang Yu-wei believes I should speak directly to my people.'

'The court will fight you, and there will be chaos.'

'With your support, Mother, I shall fight back and win.'

I didn't want to discourage him, although I believed that abandoning the court was a dangerous idea.

'Think again, son. The defeat by Japan has frightened our nation. Stability is everything.'

'But reform can no longer wait, Mother.' The gentleness in my son's voice was gone.

'I want you to be aware of the political realities.'

'I am, Mother.'

'There has been insurrection in the countryside. The radicals in Canton have been gaining political momentum. The latest spy report shows that the movement calling for a Chinese republic is being funded by the Japanese.'

Guang-hsu grew impatient. 'Nobody will stop me from moving forward. Nobody.'

The standing clock in the corner struck twice. Li Lien-ying came in to remind me that lunch had already been reheated.

'May I tell the court that I have your permission to meet with Kang Yu-wei?' Guang-hsu asked.

'I'll see if I can get the court to loosen its grip.'

'You have the power to dictate your will.'

'It is better to make the granting of permission the court's decision.'

He walked toward the door and then walked back, visibly upset. 'Fear has caused China its sickness, its weakness, and soon its death!'

'Guang-hsu, may I reveal a bit of my struggle? Your uncles and senior councilors have been coming to me.'

'What do they want?'

'They want you out.' I opened a stack of documents I had been reviewing. 'Listen to this. "The Emperor has acted impetuously and is not to be trusted without a guiding hand." "Guang-hsu has not demonstrated the capability to arrive at decisions by consensus. It is necessary to remove him from the throne. We suggest that P'u-chun, Prince Ts'eng's grandson, succeed him."'

'How dare they!' Guang-hsu was enraged. 'I shall prosecute them for conspiracy!'

'Not if the entire court signed the petition.' I pushed the documents aside.

Guang-hsu continued to protest, but his tone changed. He lowered his voice, seemed to pull himself back, and eventually he stopped talking, leaned against the window and folded his arms in front of his chest. He stared outside for a while and then turned toward me. 'I need your support, Mother.'

'Use me well, my son. When the court talks about putting the power back in my hands, it means *their* hands. My role has been a ceremonial one. The only time I become important is when I am needed as a figurehead. It is to lend legitimacy to the princes, grandees and high mandarins – the people who possess true power.'

'But Mother . . .'

'I have ignored Li Hung-chang and Yung Lu, who have expressed their own doubts about you. To be honest, I have doubts myself. You have never proved yourself.'

'But I am trying to do the right thing.'

'That, my son, I do not doubt one bit.'

When Guang-hsu begged me for the third time for a chance to meet with Kang Yu-wei, he was in tears. The redness in his eyes showed that he hadn't been sleeping well. 'As you know, Mother, I'm a "eunuch." It is unlikely I will produce an heir, so successful reform will be my only legacy.'

I was struck by his honesty and desperation. But I had to ask: 'Do you mean you can't even make love to Pearl?'

Guang-hsu's voice was filled with sadness and shame when he murmured, 'No, Mother, I can't. I will be despised by the nation because all believe that Heaven rewards sons only to those who behave virtuously.'

'My child, I forbid you to speak like this. You are only twenty-six years old. You'll keep trying –'

'Mother, doctors have told me that it's over.'

'It doesn't mean that you are finished.'

He wept, and I opened my arms and embraced him. 'You have to help me to help you, Guang-hsu.'

'Let me meet with Kang Yu-wei, Mother. It is the only way!'

At my request, an interview of Kang Yu-wei was arranged. The interviewers I chose were Li Hung-chang, Yung Lu, Tutor Weng and Chang Yin-huan, the former ambassador to England and the United States. I wanted an evaluation of the Emperor's 'like-mind.'

Kang Yu-wei was summoned to the Board of Foreign Affairs on the last day of January. The interview went on for four hours. I had assumed it would be intimidating for a provincial Cantonese, but the transcript showed that the man's audacity was inborn. Kang demonstrated his ability as a dynamic speaker and was aggressive in pressing his views. I now understood why Pearl and Guang-hsu were captivated by him. A palace lad like Guang-hsu had never before met someone so brash, a man who apparently had nothing to lose.

According to Li Hung-chang, Kang Yu-wei had a moon face and was in his late thirties. Li's evaluation read that the interviewee 'posed himself in a theatrical fashion' and that he 'spent the whole time lecturing on subjects of reform and the advantages of a constitutional monarchy as if he were a teacher in his town's elementary classroom.'

I had to credit the forbearance of the four powerful men who had to listen to Kang.

Li Hung-chang told Kang that his ideas were nothing original and that he was exploiting the work of others, which Kang denied. When Li asked Kang Yu-wei for his thoughts on generating revenue to repay foreign loans and to fund the national defense, Kang became abstract and vague. When Li pressed, Kang responded that the treaties 'were signed unfairly, and therefore deserved to be dishonored.' When asked how he would deal with a Japanese invasion, Kang Yu-wei gave a sage's dramatic laugh. 'You can't make it my job to wipe your ass!'

In conclusion, Li Hung-chang found the man offensive and believed that he was an opportunist, a zealot and probably mentally ill.

Tutor Weng, in his report, for the most part agreed with Li Hung-chang, despite having initially claimed credit for the discovery of 'a true political genius.' Kang Yu-wei's arrogance offended the founding father of China's premier academic institutions. Tutor Weng took offense when Kang criticized the Ministry of Education and called the Imperial academies 'dead ducks floating on a stagnant pond.'

'He is resentful because of his own failures,' Tutor Weng remarked in his evaluation. 'I was the chief judge when he took the national examination, although I never personally graded his paper. Kang had enough tries, and he proved himself a loser each time. He didn't oppose the system until the system booted him in the gut.

'According to Kang's own description of himself,' Tutor Weng continued, 'he was "destined to be a great sage like Confucius." This is rude and unacceptable. I conclude that Kang Yu-wei is a man who craves the limelight and whose main goals are notoriety and celebrity.'

Ambassador Chang Yin-huan expressed less disgust in his comments, but he didn't offer a positive evaluation either. It was his job, after all, to bring interesting people together. If the mingling produced results, he would gladly take the credit.

Yung Lu, who had returned from Tientsin especially for the interview, handed me a blank piece of paper as an evaluation. I imagined him losing interest the instant Kang began evading Li Hung-chang's questions.

I trusted Li Hung-chang, Yung Lu, Tutor Weng and Ambassador Chang; however, I felt that they, like me, belonged to the old society and were inescapably conservative in outlook. We weren't happy with the customs, but we were used to them. Emperor Guang-hsu's reform plan would naturally create difficulties and even suffering for the likes of us. My son had reason to remind me to expect the pain that goes along with the birth of a new system.

I had great hope in Guang-hsu, if not yet great faith. By choosing to stand by him, I believed I would be offering China a chance to survive.

30

I HAVE NEVER been so inspired!' The Emperor handed me a transcript of his long discussion with Kang Yu-wei. 'He and I went to work almost immediately on my plans. Mother, please don't object, but I granted him the privilege of contacting me directly. The censors and guards cannot be allowed to stand in my way!'

Before I had a chance to respond, Guang-hsu handed me a list of high-ranking ministers he had just fired. The first was his mentor of more than fourteen years, the sixty-eight-year-old Tutor Weng, the head of the Grand Council, the Board of Revenue, the Board of Foreign Affairs and the Hanlin Academy.

My son and Kang Yu-wei didn't seem to care that without Tutor Weng's approval they would have never met in the first place.

The grand tutor had been a father figure to my son. He had been his closest confidant throughout his adolescence, and since then they had weathered many storms together. Guang-hsu had even sided with Weng in his conflict with Li Hung-chang over the prosecution of the war with Japan, when the evidence so clearly weighed against him. Not until now, however, did Guang-hsu admit to me that Weng was responsible for having aggravated his nervous condition ever since he was a child. I had always wondered whether Guang-hsu's sense of self-doubt was the result of his tutor's constant correction.

I asked the Emperor the reasons he would give for firing Weng.

'His mismanagement of revenues and his faulty judgment in the war with Japan,' Guang-hsu replied. 'More than anything, I want to put a stop to his interfering with my decisions.'

The proud old Confucian bureaucrat would be heartbroken. It was near his birthday, and the disgrace would shatter him. I sent Tutor Weng a silk fan as a gift that might suggest this was simply a cooling-off period.

I wasn't entirely unhappy about his dismissal. Weng had been the Emperor's money man, and I was glad he was made to bear some responsibility. I had been accused of pocketing funds intended for the navy while Tutor Weng was praised for his virtues, and his firing would help to exonerate me. It was true that he had never embezzled a penny, but the people he hired, most of them his former students and close friends, stole from the treasury shamelessly.

Tutor Weng begged for a private audience, and I refused. Li Lien-ying told me that the old man was on his knees outside my gate all day. I let the tutor know that I had to respect the Emperor's decision – 'I am not in a position to help' – and that I would invite him for dinner after he calmed down. I would tell him that it was time to leave his student alone. I would quote his own famous line: 'Tea, opera and poetry should not be missed – longevity depends on one's mental cultivation.'

*   *   *

I sat down to review the transcript of Guang-hsu's conversation with Kang Yu-wei. In my opinion, Kang's perspective was not much different from Li Hung-chang's. I didn't want to conclude that it was the young Emperor's willing ear that made Kang Yu-wei seem larger than life, but the transcript failed to show otherwise:

KANG YU-WEI: China is like a ruined palace, with every door broken and every window gone. It's useless to repair the doorsills and window trim and patch the walls. The palace has been hit by hurricanes, and more are coming. The only way to save the structure is to tear it down completely and build a new one.

GUANG-HSU: It's all controlled by the conservatives.

KANG YU-WEI: But Your Majesty is committed to reform.

GUANG-HSU: Yes, yes I am!

KANG YU-WEI: The buffoons at court are too incompetent to carry out Your Majesty's plans – assuming they agree to follow you.

GUANG-HSU: You make perfect sense!

KANG YU-WEI: The throne should learn from the Western establishment. The first thing to do is create a system of law.

This went on for page after page. I wondered what made my son think of Kang Yu-wei as an original mind. Prince Kung had long preached the idea of civil law. Li Hung-chang had introduced a system of laws not only in the northern states, where he had been viceroy, but also in the south. These laws met with great resistance, but their implementation had been going forward. The treaties we had signed with the Western powers were based on the understanding of such laws.

When Li Hung-chang traveled to the Western countries, his purpose was to 'check out the real tigers' – get firsthand information on how their governments worked. So it seemed to me that what Kang Yu-wei preached to the Emperor was already being accomplished by Li. Another example was education reform. Li Hung-chang supported the funding of Western-style colleges. With Robert Hart's help, we hired foreign missionary scholars to head our schools in the capital. At Li's suggestion, I encouraged the Manchus to send their sons and daughters to study abroad. Li believed that it would make his work easier if our own elite understood what he was trying to achieve. For me, if Manchus were to maintain their position as rulers, wider knowledge and perspective were as important as power itself.

Li Hung-chang made sense when he said, 'China's hope will arrive when her citizens feel proud to have their children take up such professions as engineering. We need railroads, mines and factories.' China had been transforming itself, but slowly and painstakingly. Young people were enthusiastic about seeing the world, even if they could not yet afford to go abroad. Before Li was shot in Japan, the royal families had made arrangements for their sons to go and live abroad. Afterward, some families changed their minds, fearing for their children's safety. Li himself continued to travel overseas, in part to show that such fears were unfounded, but no one followed his lead.

Kang Yu-wei emphasized the importance of establishing schools in the countryside. But for years the government had been offering tax credits to provincial governors and earmarking funds to help set up schools. Our efforts had to contend with superstitious peasants who protested when rundown temples were converted into classrooms. One group of angry peasants set fire to school buildings and the home of the governor of Jiangsu province.

Kang Yu-wei challenged the texts traditionally used in Chinese schools. He refused to see that in the states where Li Hung-chang governed, industrial techniques were already being taught in schools. Talented Chinese writers learned to become translators and journalists. In the newspapers Li controlled – the *Canton Daily* and the *Shanghai Daily*, among others – China's political concerns were addressed and foreign ideas introduced.

I kept reading Kang's conversation with the Emperor in the hope of finding something surprising and valuable.

Kang Yu-wei, I came to realize, was not suggesting reform but a revolution. He asked the Emperor to set up an overarching 'Bureau of Institutions,' which Kang would head. 'It will handle reforms in all fields of China.' When the Emperor hesitated, Kang tried to convince him that 'determination conquers all.'

Guang-hsu was uneasy and emboldened at the same time. In Kang Yu-wei my son felt an absolute force, which he had long desired for himself. A force that would stop at nothing, acknowledge no boundary. A force that could transform a weak man into a powerful one.

I began to understand why Guang-hsu thought of Kang Yu-wei as his 'like-mind.' I didn't know Kang personally, but I had raised Guang-hsu. I was responsible for cultivating his ambition. I was aware that my boy had been tortured by self-doubt, which had stayed with him like a lingering disease.

As a boy, Guang-hsu took up clock repair. Soon his room filled up with clocks. Gears and springs and escape wheels and pendulums were strewn all over his room, and the eunuchs complained that they couldn't clean the place. But taking clocks apart and putting them together again improved his concentration and problem-solving skills. Doing something he could succeed at reassured him. But his doubts always returned.

Kang Yu-wei's criticism of the 'eight-legged essay' was fair, if unoriginal. The essay was a formal composition in eight parts, required of every student who took the civil service examination. A good score was a must for anyone who applied for a government position. The few brilliant minds who did well on the essay were fluent in the arcane works of ancient Chinese literature and usually too bookish to function in daily life. Nevertheless, their high scores would earn them governorships.

Li Hung-chang had long concluded that the shortcomings of our educational system lay behind our sense of backwardness in the world. The court had already added subjects to the Imperial examination, such as math, science, Western medicine and world geography. The conservatives believed that to study the enemies' culture was itself an act of betrayal and an insult to our ancestors. In any case, the majority of the country supported the education reforms.

I spoke before a large audience in support of Guang-hsu's decree to abolish the eight-legged essay. 'My son Tung Chih was not able to make good use of himself as Emperor,' I began, 'and this made me question his education. He spent fifteen years with China's top minds, but he had no idea where our enemies come from, what they are capable of or how to deal with them. The grand tutors are the chief judges of the national examination, and all they know is to recite ancient poems. It is time for them to lose their jobs.'

When Guang-hsu's decree became effective, thousands of students protested. 'It is not fair to test us on what we haven't been taught,' their petition read.

I understood their frustration, especially that of the senior students who had invested their lives in mastering the eight-legged essay. It was harder for families whose hopes had rested on their sons' eventually passing and securing a government position.

As Guang-hsu pushed forward his reform, several senior students hanged themselves in front of the Confucius Temple, not far from the Forbidden City. The Emperor was accused of causing the despair that led to the tragedy. I comforted the families with honorific titles and taels. In the meantime, the throne continued to encourage the younger generation to embrace nontraditional subjects. What we did not expect was that when the government finally made learning possible and free to all, the schools ended up shutting down because of a lack of students.

Reformer Kang Yu-wei sent the throne sixty-three transcripts in three months. Although overwhelmed, I reviewed every one the Emperor sent on to me.

'Most of your high ministers are hidebound conservatives,' one read. 'If Your Majesty wishes to rely on them for reform, it will be like climbing a tree to catch fish.'

Kang suggested that lower-ranking officials (like himself) be promoted to the reform bureau, bypassing the 'cranky old boys.'

I didn't allow the alarm in the back of my head to ring until I read the following:

KANG YU-WEI: Speed is where Your Majesty should concentrate. It took the Western powers three hundred years to succeed with modernization, and it took Japan thirty years. China is a bigger nation and is capable of generating more manpower. I predict that in three years we shall turn ourselves into a superpower.

GUANG-HSU: It won't be that easy, will it?

KANG YU-WEI: With my strategies and Your Majesty's determination, of course it will be.

I thought about a remark Li Hung-chang had made about Kang Yu-wei's being a zealot and recalled a story Yung Lu had related. It concerned a brief encounter he'd had with Kang outside the audience hall, where both were waiting to be received by the throne. When Yung Lu asked Kang about his plans for dealing with the conservatives, Kang replied, 'All it takes is to behead a couple of first-ranking officers' – which of course included Yung Lu himself.

Though it was easy to be skeptical of Kang, I tried to stay neutral. I reminded myself that I might be blinded by my own limitations. China had a deserved reputation for being self-righteous and inflexible – opposed to change of any kind. I knew we had to change, but was unsure of the way. I tried to hold my tongue.

The throne was caught in the middle when the court broke into two factions: the reformers versus the conservatives. Kang Yu-wei's friends claimed that they represented the Emperor and had the support of the public, while the Manchu Ironhats, led by Prince Ts'eng, his son Prince Ts'eng Junior and the Emperor's brother Prince Ch'un Junior, called their counterparts 'bogus experts in reform and Western matters.' The conservatives labeled Kang Yu-wei 'the Wild Fox' and 'the Bigmouth.'

The Ironhats played right into Kang's hands. Overnight, their attacks raised the failed Cantonese scholar from relative obscurity to national renown – 'the throne's leading advisor on reform.'

The moderates at court were in a bind. The reforms Yung Lu and Li Hung-chang had set in motion were swept aside by Kang's more radical plans, and now they themselves were being pushed to choose sides. Making matters worse, Kang Yu-wei boasted to foreign journalists that he knew the Emperor intimately.

On September 5, 1898, Guang-hsu issued a new decree stating that he had 'ceased to be concerned with pruning branches' – Kang Yu-wei's language – and was 'looking to rip out the rotten roots.'

A few days later the Emperor dismissed the Imperial councilors along with the governors of Canton, Yunnan and Hupeh provinces. My palace gate was blocked because the governors and their families had come to Peking seeking my support. They begged for me to control the Emperor.

My office was filled with memorandums sent by Guang-hsu and his opponents. I concentrated on learning about my son's new friends. Touched by their patriotism, I was concerned about their political naiveté. Kang Yu-wei's radical views seemed to have changed my son's way of thinking. Guang-hsu now believed that he could achieve reform overnight if he pushed hard enough.

As the leaves took on autumn colors, it became more difficult to restrain myself – I was sorely tempted to interfere with my son.

In the midst of the turmoil, Li Hung-chang returned from a trip to Europe. He requested a private audience and I was pleased to receive him. Bringing me a German telescope and a cake from Spain, Li described his trip as an eye-opening experience. He even looked different; he'd left his beard untrimmed. Replying to his suggestion that I should travel myself, I could only lament that the court had already rejected the idea; Guang-hsu had worried that I might also be shot. The court believed that I might be taken hostage and that the price of my release would be China's sovereignty.

I assumed Li Hung-chang had let his beard grow fuller to hide the scars of his wound. I asked if his jaw still bothered him, and he assured me that it was no longer painful. I asked him to show me how to use the telescope. He pointed out the eyepiece and how to focus and told me that at night I could see distant planets and stars.

'The Emperor would love this,' I marveled.

'I did try to bring one to His Majesty,' Li said, 'but I was denied entrance.'

'Why?' I asked.

'His Majesty dismissed me on September 7.' Li Hung-chang spoke matter-of-factly. 'I am jobless and titleless.'

'Dismissed you?' I could hardly believe what I heard.

'Yes.'

'But . . . my son didn't inform me.'

'He will soon, I am sure.'

'What . . . what are you going to do?' I didn't know what else to say. I felt terrible.

'With your permission, I would like to leave Peking. I want to move to Canton.'

'Is that why you came, Li Hung-chang?' I asked. 'To inform me?'

'Yes, I come to bid farewell, Your Majesty. My close associate S. S. Huan is prepared to serve you in all matters. However, it would be best to keep him away from royal politics.'

I asked Li Hung-chang who would replace him on the diplomatic front. Li replied, 'Prince I-kuang has been the court's choice as far as I understand.'

I felt desolated.

Li nodded slightly and smiled. He looked frail and resigned to his fate.

We sat staring at the exotic cake in front of us.

After watching my friend disappear down a long corridor, I sat in my room for the rest of the afternoon.

Just before dusk I heard loud noises at my front gate. Li Lien-ying entered with a message from Yung Lu, who had joined the crowd outside begging me to stop the Emperor.

'Kang Yu-wei has talked His Majesty into issuing death warrants for the officers who refused their dismissals,' Yung Lu's message read. 'I have been ordered to arrest Li Hung-chang, who the reformers believe has been the major roadblock. I am sure it won't be long before I receive the order for my own execution.'

Should I open the gate? Things seemed to be falling apart. How could the dynasty survive without Li Hung-chang and Yung Lu?

'The newly dismissed ministers and officers have come to kneel in front of the palace gate.' Li Lien-ying looked overwhelmed.

I went out and crossed the courtyard and looked through the gate. Casting long shadows in the dying sunlight, the crowd was on its knees.

'Open it,' I said to Li Lien-ying.

Two of my eunuchs pushed the gate open.

The crowd turned silent the moment I appeared on the terrace.

I was expected to speak, and I had to bite my tongue in order to swallow the words.

I remembered my promise to Guang-hsu. My son was only exercising his rights as Emperor, I told myself. He deserved complete independence.

The crowd stayed on its knees. It hurt me to see that people were filled with hope in me.

I turned around and told Li Lien-ying to shut the gate.

Behind me the crowd stirred, rising to its feet and muttering louder and louder.

Later I would learn that Yung Lu had other reasons to join the dismissed officials. While working on building the navy, he kept an eye on foreign governments to make sure they were not connected with subversive elements in China. However, intelligence showed that British and American missionaries and English adventurers with military backgrounds were secretly agitating in favor of a constitutional monarchy. Although Yung Lu's true purpose was to avoid being forced to crack down on reform, which by then had turned into a country-wide movement, he was especially alarmed by the high level of subversive activity going on at the Japanese legation. The suspected agents were members of the Genyosha Society, ultra-nationalists who were responsible for Queen Min's assassination in Korea.

Prince Ts'eng, his son and Prince Ch'un Junior were convinced that Kang Yu-wei was supported by the foreign powers as a cover for an armed coup.

Yung Lu said in a message to me, 'The Emperor's trust in Kang Yu-wei has made my work impossible.'

'I have no option but to support the throne,' I wrote back to Yung Lu. 'It is up to you to block any uprising.'

31

EARLY ONE MORNING Yung Lu appeared unannounced at my palace. 'Ito Hirobumi is on his way to Peking.' Ito was the architect of Japan's Meiji Restoration and had served as prime minister during our recent war. He had played a leading role in the murder of Queen Min.

'Is . . . Ito not afraid?' I asked. 'Guang-hsu could order his beheading for what Japan has done to China.'

Yung Lu paused a moment and then replied, 'Your Majesty, Ito comes as the Emperor's guest.'

'My son invited him?'

'Ito claims that he has retired from politics and is now a private citizen.'

'Does Li Hung-chang know about this?'

'Yes. In fact, he sent me. While Li feels that it is no longer his role to offer the throne advice, he didn't want you to get the news from the Ironhats.'

'His enemies accuse him of being self-serving, but our friend has always embodied what is most kind and wise in the Chinese character.'

Yung Lu agreed. 'Li refuses to offer the Ironhats an opportunity to jeopardize the Emperor's reform plans.'

*   *   *

According to my son, Ito's visit was initiated by Kang Yu-wei and arranged by his disciple, a twenty-three-year-old scholar-adventurer named Tan Shih-tung. I remembered Tan had written an extraordinary analytical essay on Japan, and knew his father, who was the governor of Hupeh.

Like his master Kang Yu-wei, Tan had also failed the national civil service examination. He was quoted as having called the government post his father once offered him 'a beggar's livelihood.' Together with Kang Yu-wei, Tan became known for publishing letters condemning the Imperial examination system. He was second in command in the Emperor's new council.

In my view, Tan's belief in Ito as China's savior was naive and dangerous. I did not doubt Ito's ability to manipulate the Emperor, so it would be pointless for me to try to persuade my son to dismiss Ito.

'You'd be a fool to invite yourself,' Yung Lu offered as we discussed Guang-hsu's meeting with the Japanese. 'They would just shut up and look for another opportunity to meet privately.'

Over the next few days Yung Lu and I sought Li Hung-chang's advice.

'The Japanese intelligentsia have already become part of the fiber of our society, as they had done in Korea,' Li warned in a letter. 'Ito's move will further Japan's penetration.'

I begged Li Hung-chang to travel north to help. 'You must personally receive Ito so he knows that my son is not alone.'

Li did not respond to this plea, so I officially summoned him. I felt I needed his advice in person. There was no telling what might happen, especially as my son had not said a word to me about his plans.

After Yung Lu left at the end of each day, my frustration would overwhelm me. Li Hung-chang still hadn't responded, and I was worn out by the mere mention of Ito's name. I understood my son's fascination with the man. But if they met, Ito would quickly discover all the shortcomings of the Emperor of China.

I feared that my son would hastily move to replace China's feudal power blocs with Japanese sympathizers. In fact, he had already begun doing so. The pro-Japan scholar Tan's appointment as emissary between Ito and Guang-hsu was but a prelude. The Emperor fancied China as a power broker among modern industrial nations – but Japan would be calling the shots. And my son would be none the wiser.

On September 11, 1898, Yung Lu welcomed Ito Hirobumi to China. The former prime minister was received in Tientsin. A few days later, on his arrival in Peking by train, Li Hung-chang met with him.

Yung Lu had few words to describe the guest. It was as if he wished to forget the experience as soon as possible. 'I have received five messages from the throne asking me to bring Ito to the Forbidden City,' Yung Lu said. Although he told me he was uncomfortable throughout the reception, he did his best to show hospitality.

'Ito must have sensed that our welcome was not heartfelt,' Yung Lu remarked. 'I don't know how he managed to maintain his poise and offer his gratitude.'

It was from Li Hung-chang that I learned more details. 'Ito carries himself in the style of a samurai,' Li said. In his opinion, Ito was a genius. Li envied him his service to the Japanese Emperor and his success in reforming his country. Li would never forget the humiliation he had suffered before Ito at the negotiating table. 'Ito was shameless, virtueless and ruthless. He was also the hero of his country.'

I remembered the nights when Li negotiated the Shimonoseki Treaty. I counted every tael of war compensation paid, every hectare of land we were forced to part with. Li Hung-chang's telegrams came like a snow squall in January. My eunuch wore out his shoes shuttling messages between Li Hung-chang and me.

It had been like talking to the Great Wall when I tried to make Guang-hsu appreciate Li's negotiating efforts. 'You should at least acknowledge that Li Hung-chang has been bearing the blame that should have been ours.'

'Li Hung-chang deserves nothing but our loathing,' Guang-hsu had responded.

Under the influence of Kang Yu-wei, my son ignored the telegrams Li sent concerning Ito's visit.

I was upset and said to my son, 'You don't get tired because Li is the one carrying the heavy load.'

'Well, I don't need him. I fired him long ago. You are the one who invited him back.'

'I invited him because Russia and Japan won't talk peace with anybody else!'

'Mother, don't you find it suspicious?'

'What?'

'Li's foreign connections?'

When I learned that my son had again dismissed Li Hung-chang, I refused to speak to him for days. Guang-hsu had his eunuchs bring me an offering of lotus-seed soup, but he was not apologizing.

I held on to Li's telegrams until Guang-hsu couldn't bear to hear the name of Li Hung-chang anymore. My son insisted that China would be better off without him.

*   *   *

Instead of acknowledging Li Hung-chang's devotion, my son believed that every negative development was the result of Li's manipulation.

I began to realize that Guang-hsu lived in his own fantasy world. Like his mentor Tutor Weng, whom he had just fired, he hated yet worshiped Japan. In the future I would blame myself for believing that my son was capable of good judgment.

Guang-hsu despised me for continuing to seek help from Li Hung-chang, and I despised myself for being incapable of ending the trouble.

In responding to the throne's 'Ito is no threat to China' edict, Li wrote in a memorandum: 'In the world's eyes, Ito gives the impression that he is a supporter of Chinese culture. He might be a moderate, he might have opposed Japan's true political bosses like the militarist Yamagata Aritomo and other godfathers of the Genyosha, but he nevertheless conducted the Sino-Japanese War. China has fallen into a deep well because of its self-indulgence and ignorance, while Japan has proven capable of throwing heavy rocks.'

I wished that I could tell my son how much I hated Ito. I wanted to yell, 'Go and talk to the Emperor of Japan man to man instead of blaming Li Hung-chang!'

I had reasons not to respond to foreign and domestic attacks on me. It was to make sure that my son would not be held responsible for his possible failure. I betrayed Li Hung-chang in that sense – by purposely ignoring his warnings, I made Li a scapegoat. On my part, it was a self-betrayal before anything else.

I wondered if Li regretted his devotion.

Forgiveness was a gift I could not afford but which I fortunately received from Li Hung-chang.

There was no other way to love my son.

*   *   *

Guang-hsu wanted to prove to me that he and Ito could be friends. I did not know that they had scheduled to meet privately before the official meeting on September 20, to which I was invited.

It was impossible for me to concentrate on anything else. My son's words rang danger in my ears. 'Mother, Ito only seeks to help me!'

I fought on the issue of trust, but my son's mind was made up.

I did not want to bring up Yung Lu's spy report, but I felt that I couldn't afford not to. 'Japan's intrigues have been set in motion by Yamagata,' I said to Guang-hsu. 'Yamagata is the leading promoter of Japanese expansion and lord protector of the Genyosha.'

'You have no proof that Ito is part of the Genyosha.' My son was more than annoyed. 'Yung Lu has fabricated this information to prevent me from meeting Ito!'

'But shouldn't we trust Yung Lu and Li Hung-chang more than Ito?' I pleaded.

'The only thing I can say is that Yung Lu has made himself an obstacle to reform. I should have dismissed him.'

I went to sit down, weakened by what I was hearing.

'I am firing Yung Lu, Mother,' Guang-hsu said in a flat voice.

I screamed, 'For heaven's sake, Yung Lu is the last Manchu general who would die for you!'

My son stormed out.

Two days later I sent an apology to Guang-hsu along with Li Hung-chang's newly arrived telegram. It read, 'The spy network set up by Genyosha agents has been operating under cover of a pharmaceutical syndicate with the trade name "Halls of Pleasurable Delights." To maintain their secrecy, the spies travel the countryside as salesmen. There is no evidence suggesting that the Japanese army, navy, diplomats and the representatives of Japan's trading houses, the zaibatsu, weren't behind Genyosha's assassinations, kidnappings and extortions.'

32

THE EMPEROR'S SECRET meetings with Ito provoked a backlash among the court's conservatives. Led by Prince Ts'eng, the Ironhats pressed me to replace Guang-hsu on the throne. At the same time, Ts'eng prepared his Moslem troops in the northwest to move toward Peking. I was caught in the middle, unable to decide and unable to get out.

When the minister of the royal cemetery requested my presence for an inspection, I used it as a pretext to escape the Forbidden City. Li Lien-ying hired a carpenter to make an adjustable seat for my horse carriage so I could ride in a reclining position. I bounced and dozed through the three-day journey covering 125 kilometers from Peking to Hupeh province.

By the time I arrived at the cemetery it was early morning. The sky was overcast and a fine mist fell over the blue rivers. White bridges, golden roofs, red walls and cypress trees formed breathtaking views.

The cemetery minister greeted me at the Grand Sacred Way. An elderly man who was hard of hearing, he apologized for the dirt and mud and said that Nuharoo's tomb was being repaired.

'Wild animals dug up the ground and damaged the drainage system,' the minister explained. 'A few of the tombs, including Empress Nuharoo's, flooded during the last storm.'

I thought about how Nuharoo would have hated the flood and asked, 'How soon will the repairs be completed?'

'I am embarrassed to say that I can't give you an exact date,' he replied. 'The work has been sporadic. Sometimes we have to stand idle for weeks while we appeal for more funds.'

I was led to my own tomb, which seemed well maintained.

'It flooded too, but I gave the repair work top priority.' The minister was not humble about claiming credit.

My tomb stood next to Nuharoo's like a twin sister. When Tung Chih ascended the throne in 1862, he ordered construction to begin on our tombs. It took thirteen years to complete the outer tomb and another five years to finish the interior.

Having reached the age of sixty-three, I had become familiar with the process of death. I continued to attend sacrificial ceremonies whenever I could. I honored the gods of all religions, not just Buddha. I believed in paying attention to the force of energy inside me. Not everyone would be lucky enough to achieve the Great Void, but I understood that the point was to try. I struggled to balance yin and yang, however difficult it seemed to be.

While the nation applauded Guang-hsu's dismissal of so-called corrupt officials, few of the throne's edicts had been executed, which meant no significant progress in reform had taken place. Guang-hsu expected to harvest his reforms by the end of the year, but the only thing that seemed to be coming was war with Japan.

'Young women in Japan are offering their virginity to soldiers willing to volunteer for service in China,' one Peking newspaper reported.

Guang-hsu kept his door closed and worked with his reformer friends in the Hall of Spiritual Nurturing until 'the wild geese flew across the dawn sky,' according to the eunuchs. The country was on the brink of chaos. The ministers and officers who were fired continued to kneel at my front gate while the Ironhats trained their Moslem troops.

I looked at myself in the mirror and a saying came to mind: 'The ship sinks when a female goes on board.' I had never believed it before. On the contrary, I had intended to offer myself as proof that it wasn't true. But the thought persisted: *Hsien Feng's ship sank! Tung Chih's ship sank! And now Guang-hsu's – all with you on board!*

When I recounted my recent trip to the royal cemetery, Guang-hsu showed little interest. It was time to begin construction on his own tomb, but I had been told that funds were unavailable. When I implored my son to find a way to fund the project, he replied, 'There were Manchu emperors who were not buried at the royal cemetery.'

'It was circumstance, not their choice.' I told Guang-hsu that it hurt me to think that he would be excluded from the family cemetery.

'If I raise any money, it will go toward reform,' Guang-hsu said.

Through the transparent curtain I observed Ito Hirobumi. I was sitting on the side of the Grand Hall, where I could see the guest but he couldn't see me.

Ito sat in front of my son dressed in a plain blue Japanese garment, which reflected his position as Li Hung-chang had described it, that of 'a private citizen in his leisure time.' Ito's hands rested on his knees. His back was straight and his chin was low.

My son, although dressed in the golden dragon robe of the Emperor, sat like a pupil, leaning forward, listening. An ensemble of strings and gongs softly played ancient music in the background. The gongs were meant to evoke distant peaceful times, but to my ear it sounded like explosives – Japanese cannons destroying our fleet. I fought to separate the humble man in front of me from the murderer of Queen Min. I tried to view Ito through my son's eyes.

The two men exchanged words about the weather and each other's health. My son asked whether Chinese food would suit his guest. Ito replied that there was no better cuisine in the world than Chinese cuisine.

I expected a conversation of political significance to follow, but it did not occur.

The guest began to talk about his favorite Chinese poets, and recited, 'While moonbeams danced on the crest of waves where the water touches the sky . . .'

My son smiled and took a sip of tea.

'In Japan,' Ito said, in a gentle voice, 'only the children of the privileged class are taught Chinese poetry, and only the nobility can read and write Mandarin.' His voice was full of admiration.

Guang-hsu nodded respectfully, slouching his shoulders and then sinking back into his chair.

When the clock struck four times, the minister of the interior appeared and pronounced that the Imperial reception was over.

I withdrew quietly before the two men rose.

*   *   *

The minister of national security, who worked directly for Yung Lu, sent me a memorandum. He asked for permission to issue Kang Yu-wei a Warning of Violation. Our spy had discovered that the reformer had gone to the Japanese embassy, where he supposedly met with Ito.

My son would be offended was the thought that came to mind. Guang-hsu would take such a warning as Yung Lu's as a personal attack on him.

I sent for Yung Lu and asked whether he was aware of the connection between the Board of National Security and Prince Ts'eng's Ironhats, whose goal was to replace my son on the throne.

Yung Lu said that he knew of the connection. He agreed with me that 'in trying to shoot the fly, we might end up shattering the vase instead.'

I asked what we should do.

'It must be your decision, Your Majesty.'

I protested and said that my priority was to avoid jeopardizing the Emperor's reform plan. 'My son should be the one to issue Kang a warning. I cannot talk him into doing that until you provide solid evidence that Kang's activities threaten the nation's security.'

'It is impossible to obtain the full facts at this stage,' Yung Lu said.

'Then I cannot grant your minister the permission.'

Quietly Yung Lu said that if he was not allowed to do his job, he would resign.

'You would not abandon me' was my reply.

We sat staring at each other for a long moment.

'You let Li Hung-chang go,' he said.

'You are not Li Hung-chang.'

'I can't work with your son. He doesn't respect me and he thinks he doesn't need me!'

'I need you!' My tears came.

Yung Lu sighed, shaking his head.

My son let me know that reformer Kang Yu-wei claimed that he was the friend of ambassadors all over the world.

'What about Li Hung-chang?' I asked my son. 'Li has actually met the "real tigers" and has negotiated with them for years.'

'Sure, Li negotiated, but for himself, not for China.'

'Li Hung-chang has been behind every major reform.' I tried to keep calm.

'But he won't call for complete political reform!' My son could no longer keep his voice down.

'Guang-hsu, calling for such radical change could mean your dethroning . . .'

The Emperor laughed. 'As it is, I am an emperor without an empire! I have nothing to lose.'

'Let me ask you this. Do you know why Japan stopped the Allies from setting fire to the Forbidden City back in 1861?'

Guang-hsu shook his head.

'Because the Japanese Emperor plans to live here one day.'

'Another clever story from Li Hung-chang and Yung Lu!'

'I have evidence, my son.'

'Mother, nothing I say will convince you that Ito is not a monster. All I ask for is your patience. Please judge me by results. My plans are yet to take effect.'

There was a resounding confidence in Guang-hsu's voice. I remembered the days when he feared the sound of thunder, when he trembled in my arms. What more could or should I ask of him?

33

THE REFORMER SPENT his nights in the Forbidden City and discussed the implementation of the reform plans with the throne' – the foreign newspapers printed Kang Yu-wei's lies day after day. Anyone familiar with Imperial law would know that a commoner could not stay overnight in the Forbidden City. Not until I read 'The solution to China's reform is the permanent removal of the Dowager Empress from power' did I understand what Kang Yu-wei was up to.

I did not want the world to think that Kang mattered to me, or that he had the power to manipulate my son. His lies would be exposed as soon as my son established himself and I could retire completely. The citizens of the world would see with their own eyes what I had been up to.

I did myself a favor and started to wear wigs. Thanks to Li Lien-ying, who was trained as a hairdresser, I was able to sleep for an extra half hour in the morning. His wigs were lavish, with beautiful ornaments, and comfortable to wear.

In June I decided to move back to the Summer Palace. Although I had been comfortable living with Guang-hsu at Ying-t'ai, our island pavilion nearby, I realized that he needed to be out from under my wing. He never expressed it, but I could tell that he disliked the fact that my eunuchs could see everyone who went in or out of his quarters. Guang-hsu worried about exposing his friends to the Ironhats, who meant them only harm. I agreed that the Emperor had reason to worry: my eunuchs could be bribed to betray anyone.

The court's conservatives were unhappy about my moving because they expected me to spy on the throne for them. I believed that my son knew my intentions and trusted me despite our ongoing disagreements. Letting Guang-hsu be on his own meant my total trust, which was the biggest help I could offer.

In the evenings, after I finished bathing, Li Lien-ying would light jasmine-scented candles. As I read Guang-hsu's latest updates, my eunuch sat at the foot of my bed with his bamboo basket of tools. There he would work on my new wigs. When my eyes got tired of reading, I watched him as he stitched jewels, pieces of carved jade and cut glass onto a wig. Unlike An-te-hai, who expressed himself by challenging his fate, Li Lien-ying found expression in wigmaking. The first few years after An-te-hai's murder, I was lonely and depressed and even suspected that Li Lien-ying had a role in his death. 'You were jealous of An-te-hai,' I once accused. 'Did you secretly curse him so you might be his replacement?' I told Li Lien-ying that he would never get what he wanted if I found out that he was involved in An-te-hai's murder.

My eunuch let the wigs speak for him. He never resented my stormy ways. It wasn't until I saw how his wigs saved my appearance that I began to truly trust him. After I turned sixty, it became harder for me to live up to the expectation that I look like the goddess Kuan-yin. Li Lien-ying served my needs in ways that made him the equal of An-te-hai.

When I asked him why he put up with me, he replied, 'A eunuch's greatest dream is to be missed by his lady after his death. It comforts me that you have not gotten over An-te-hai. It means that you would miss me too if I should die tomorrow.'

'I am afraid that I must go on living in order to display your beautiful wigs,' I teased. 'I am so poor that the wigs will probably be the only things I can leave you when I die.'

'There would be no better fortune, my lady.'

By the time the wisteria climbed over the trellis I still wasn't able to retire. Guang-hsu's inability to exert control over the court left him vulnerable. He had made an enemy of every senior member of the old court, and his new advisors had neither the political influence nor the military clout for effective action. No critical reforms had been made, and it seemed that Guang-hsu's whole program for change was petering out.

I would lose everything if Guang-hsu's reforms were to miscarry. I would be forced to replace him, and it would cost me my retirement – I would have to start all over again, choosing and raising another infant boy who would some-day rule over China.

What frustrated me equally was that the consequences of Li Hung-chang's dismissal began to show. The hoped-for industrialization of the country had now ground to a halt. Everything awaited Li Hung-chang, the only man with the international and domestic connections necessary to get things done.

Yung Lu continued his duty on the military front, but only because I intervened at the last minute to stop my son from firing him. Under the spell of the reformer, Guang-hsu was becoming even more radical in his actions. It grew more and more difficult for me to comprehend his logic.

The Emperor went on insisting that progress was being impeded by Yung Lu and Li Hung-chang. 'But most of all,' he said with angry tears in his eyes, 'it is because your shadow still sits behind the curtain!'

I quit explaining. I could not make Guang-hsu see why I had to stay engaged. I had given him permission to fire Li Hung-chang but had immediately begun to lay the ground-work for his return. It was only a matter of time before the Emperor would discover that he couldn't function without Li and would need to mend his relationship with him, as well as with Yung Lu. I would serve as the glue, so that neither party would risk the loss of face and reputation. As it turned out, no matter how much my son angered and humiliated them, the two men always came back.

'The failure of a thousand-mile dike starts with an ant colony.' So began a message from Li Hung-chang in the fall of 1898 that warned of a foreign conspiracy against me. The goal was to make Guang-hsu a puppet king.

I couldn't say I was surprised. I was aware that my son had been carried away by his vision of a new China, reinvigorated by his own hand. Yet I chose ignorance because I couldn't stand fighting him anymore. I wanted to please him so he would think of nothing but my love.

While I was admiring the lotus flowers swaying in the gentle breeze at Kun Ming Lake, reformer Kang Yu-wei secretly contacted General Yuan Shih-kai, Yung Lu's right-hand man in the military. I had no idea that Guang-hsu's permission for Kang's 'unlimited access to the Forbidden City' extended to my bedroom door.

A week after the scurrilous attack on me in the foreign press, I received a formal letter from Guang-hsu. Seeing the familiar seals and opening the envelope, I couldn't believe what I read: a request that the capital be moved to Shanghai.

I was not able to stay calm. I summoned my son and told him that he'd better give me one good reason for such an outrageous idea.

'The *feng shui* in Peking works against me' was all he could say.

I tried to block a loud 'no' from rolling out of my chest.

Guang-hsu stood by the door as if getting ready to escape.

I paced the room, then swung around to look at him. Sunlight hit his robe, making his accessories glitter. He was pale.

'Look me in the eyes, son.'

He couldn't. He stared at the floor.

'In history,' I said, 'only the Emperor of a fallen dynasty, such as the Soong, relocated the capital. And it didn't save the dynasty.'

'I have an audience waiting,' Guang-hsu said flatly. He no longer wanted to listen. 'I must go.'

'What are you going to do about the Tientsin military inspection? It has already been scheduled.' I chased him to the gate.

'I am not going.'

'Why? You can learn what Yung Lu and General Yuan Shih-kai are doing.'

Guang-hsu stopped. He pivoted his body at an odd angle, and his hands went to the wall. 'You are going, aren't you?' He looked at me nervously, blinking his eyes. 'Who else? Prince Ts'eng? Prince Ch'un Junior? Who else?'

'Guang-hsu, what's wrong with you? It was your idea.'

'How many people are going?'

'What's the matter?'

'I want to know!'

'Just you and I.'

'Why Tientsin? Why a military inspection? Is there something you want to do there?' His face was inches from mine. 'It's a setup, isn't it?'

As if suddenly gripped by fear, Guang-hsu's frame began to tremble. He held himself against the wall as if trying to conquer it. The moment took me back to his childhood, when he once stopped breathing while listening to a ghost story.

'Here is the reason I am going,' I said. 'First, I'd like to find out if the foreign loans we took have indeed been spent on our defenses. Second, I would like to honor our troops. I want the world, especially Japan, to know that China is on its way toward having a modern military.'

Guang-hsu remained tense, but he finally let himself breathe.

It took me ten days to get him to explain what had been on his mind. His advisors had told him that I had planned to use the military event to depose him. 'They are concerned about my safety.'

I laughed. 'If I were to dethrone you, it would be much easier to have it done inside the Forbidden City.'

Guang-hsu wiped the sweat from his face with both hands. 'I didn't want to take a chance.'

'As you know, there have been proposals regarding your replacement.'

'What do you think of the proposals, Mother?'

'What do I think? Are you still sitting on the Dragon Throne?'

Guang-hsu looked down but spoke clearly: 'The way you listen to the Ironhats made me worry that you were changing your mind about me.'

'Of course I listen. I have to in order to play fair. I must listen or pretend to listen to everybody. That's how I protect you.'

'Will Prince Ts'eng's idea become yours?'

'It depends. I will look foolish if it has to happen. I want the world to think that I knew what I was doing when I picked you to be the Emperor of China.'

'And moving the capital to Shanghai?'

'Who would be responsible for your safety in Shanghai? After all, it *is* closer to Japan. Queen Min's assassination and Li Hung-chang's being shot certainly were no accident.'

'It will not happen to me, Mother.'

'What would I do if it did? I only know what Japan would demand in exchange for your life. Ito would get to collect the architectural splendor of the Forbidden City.'

'Kang Yu-wei has assured me of my safety.'

'Moving the capital to Shanghai is a bad idea.'

'I have given Kang Yu-wei my word to do whatever it takes to achieve reform.'

'Let me meet with Kang Yu-wei myself. It's time.'

34

EITHER AFRAID THAT Kang Yu-wei would not get a fair
hearing from me or unsure about the reformer himself,
my son ordered him to move to Shanghai and run a local
newspaper. This Imperial edict Kang disobeyed. The reformer would later tell the world that the Emperor was
forced to send him away and that he, 'despite the danger,
remained in Peking in order to rescue the throne.'

In any event, I didn't pursue a meeting with Kang Yu-wei
because something more pressing demanded my attention.
An attack on foreign missionaries by inland peasants
quickly became an international incident. I guessed that
Prince Ts'eng's Ironhats were secretly encouraging the
peasants. Since I denounced neither the prince nor the
troublemaking peasants, the foreign papers soon labeled
me a 'suspected murderer.' In the meantime, the so-called
conflict between my son and me, which was created and
trumped up by Kang Yu-wei, led the masses to believe that
there was a 'Throne Party' and a 'Dowager Party.' I was
beginning to be described as a 'mastermind of evil.'

I was naive to think that the tension whipped up by the
incident could be defused without the use of force. I spoke
to my ministers about the power of superstition among

Chinese farmers, and that we must not joke about their belief that the rusty water that dripped from oxidized telegraph wires was 'the blood of outraged spirits.' I emphasized that only by our respect and understanding could we begin to educate the peasants.

I summoned Li Hung-chang to Peking again. The railroad he himself had championed and built delivered him almost in no time. On my behalf Li spoke before an audience of the court about how to influence the provincial *feng shui* experts. 'Only money will flip their tongues' was his conclusion. 'That is the only way we can continue to build railroads and raise telegraph poles throughout the country.'

I also encouraged Li to send word to foreign officials and missionaries. 'I want them to know that the killings might have been avoided if the foreigners had learned how to communicate with our people.'

On the last day of the audience, the minister of historical records gave a presentation on the history of Christian missionaries in China. 'The root of the problem is that these missionaries built their churches on the outskirts of villages, often on land already consecrated as a cemetery,' the minister explained. 'The foreigners did not mean to disturb the spirits or the locals, but ended up doing just that.

'Farmers had never seen churches in their lives,' the minister went on. 'They were awed by how tall they were. When the missionaries explained that the height enabled their prayers to reach God, the locals panicked. In their eyes, the long, sword-like shadow crossing the cemetery cast a spell, and the cursed spirits of their ancestors would come to haunt them.'

For half a century Chinese peasants had been demanding that the missionaries relocate their churches. The peasants believed that the enraged Chinese gods would surely wreak revenge and punishment. Whenever a severe drought or flood came, the peasants feared that unless the churches were removed and missionaries expelled, they would starve to death.

Prince Ts'eng had been in the north stirring up the peasants' fear and superstition. Every memorandum he sent back to Peking repeated the same message: 'The conduct of the Christian barbarians is irritating our gods and geniuses, hence the many scourges we are now suffering . . . The iron road and iron carriages are disturbing the terrestrial dragon and are destroying the earth's beneficial influences.'

I knew I couldn't afford to turn Prince Ts'eng into an enemy. He was my husband's only remaining brother. I was also aware that he had a growing number of rebels at his command and at any moment could attempt to overthrow Guang-hsu. My strategy was to keep peace and order so that Li Hung-chang and the court's moderates could buy some time in which to modernize the country.

'When farmers lose their land, they lose their soul,' I said to my son, trying to make him see how difficult it was for Li Hung-chang to keep the railways and telegraph wires running. 'If it hadn't been for Li's Northern Army, we wouldn't have been able to keep up with the local rebels' destruction.'

Only a few years after the building of the railroad, towns had sprouted around the stations. When these towns grew prosperous, the peasants were transformed from 'robbers' to 'guards': they would do anything to protect the tracks that brought them a better life. But the towns that hadn't benefited saw themselves as victims of modernization. The townspeople viewed Li Hung-chang as the foreigners' spokesman and his business efforts 'part of the spell the foreigners had cast upon China.'

As a result, violent gangs and secret societies formed and grew. Serious crime spread. The rebels not only destroyed the tracks and sabotaged the rolling stock but also raided churches and took missionaries as hostages. The situation became so dire that even Li Hung-chang could no longer contain it. Signs posted on city gates threatened to hang the 'rice Christians' – the locals who converted to obtain needed food.

I was in the middle of a dream. I was watching my mother getting dressed in the morning. Her bedroom faced Lake Wuhu and had a large window. Sunlight splashed on the woodcarvings and over the floral-patterned window panels. The small bamboo and golden trumpet trees in her room were green even in winter.

Mother stretched like a cat, her long, bare arms extended over her head. She ran her fingers through her silky black hair. Pulling on a peach-colored cotton shirt over her head, she smoothed it down. She took her time buttoning the shirt, and then she turned around and looked at me.

'My daughter had a good night's sleep, I can tell,' she said. 'You are the prettiest girl in Wuhu, Orchid.'

I laid my head on her pillow and buried my face in her sheets to smell her scent.

I had the same dream the following morning. It was when my mother's fingers softly touched my cheeks that I woke up.

There was a loud noise in the hallway. Something heavy fell to the floor. It was followed by a eunuch's ear-piercing cry.

I sat up, still in a fog. Then the image of the dead Queen Min flashed before my mind. I pulled open my curtains.

Yung Lu, in full uniform and with a sword in his hand, rushed toward me.

I thought I was still dreaming.

Before he could reach me, Li Lien-ying jumped him from behind. The eunuch's weight pulled Yung Lu down along with the bed curtains.

In one motion Yung Lu pinned Li Lien-ying to the ground like a bug.

'Assassins, my lady!' Li Lien-ying screamed.

I froze, unsure of what was happening.

Yung Lu ordered his men to search the entire palace. 'Every moving object, human and animal! Every tree and bush!'

My hands were shaking and I could not find my clothes. All my attendants were down on their knees on the floor. I reached for a sheet and wrapped myself in it.

Several of Yung Lu's men entered and told him that all was clear.

'Give me a moment to dress, will you?' I asked when I could finally speak.

Yung Lu pointed at a chair and said, 'Please, I need you to conduct a private audience, right here, right away.'

Dragging my sheet, I went to sit down. I felt like a big moth inside a broken cocoon.

On his knees Li Lien-ying collected my clothes. Holding his stomach with one hand, with the other he spread a coat over my bare shoulders.

'I'll let Yuan Shih-kai tell you what happened,' Yung Lu said, sheathing his sword.

'Yuan Shih-kai?' I thought the young general was in Tientsin, commanding the New Army and preparing for a royal inspection.

'Your Majesty, Yuan Shih-kai was sent by your son to collect your head.'

35

His majesty summoned me on September 14,' General Yuan Shih-kai began. He stood erect in full dress uniform, his head shaved, his neck muscles taut. His voice was clear but subdued. 'Emperor Guang-hsu asked about my record in Korea and my use of Western military tactics. I said that during my twelve years stationed in Korea, I had learned much but not enough. His Majesty wanted to know my troop strength in comparison to Yung Lu's. I answered that I had seven thousand and Yung Lu more than a hundred thousand.'

I glanced at Yung Lu, whose expression was grave. I turned back to Yuan Shih-kai and asked, 'What was the Emperor's response?'

'His Majesty asked if my men were better armed and trained.' Yuan Shih-kai paused.

'Keep going,' Yung Lu ordered.

'Yes, sir. On September 16, His Majesty summoned me again,' Yuan continued. 'I was honored with a promotion: vice minister of the Board of War and National Security. I was surprised, for I had done nothing to deserve it. I knew that His Majesty had been impatient about implementing his reform plans and that he had met strong opposition at the court. I had been approached by Prince Ts'eng and his Ironhat sons. They wanted to join forces with me and asked me to train their Moslem troops. I figured that His Majesty meant to prepare me to fight his opposition.'

'Yuan Shih-kai was summoned one more time,' Yung Lu said, trying to speed the general along.

'That's right,' Yuan Shih-kai went on. 'It was three days after our first meeting, the morning of September 17.'

I remembered that the seventeenth was the day when Guang-hsu and I had our biggest fight. I told my son that he would have to kill me before I would agree to do either of two things: one, surrender to Japan; and two, surrender my power at Kang Yu-wei's request. It seemed that our fighting had pushed Guang-hsu to the other side.

'His Majesty asked if I understood my power,' Yuan Shih-kai said. 'I said that I was a bit confused. His Majesty said, "Your new title means that you and Yung Lu are to operate independently." I begged him to explain further, and he said, "From now on, you take orders directly from me." At that point I was truly lost, because it had been my duty to take orders from no one but Yung Lu.'

Yung Lu cut in: 'Late the same night, Kang Yu-wei's right-hand man, Tan Shih-tung, visited Yuan Shih-kai. He claimed that he represented the "Throne Party."'

'That's right,' Yuan Shih-kai said. 'I knew Tan was the son of the governor of Hupeh. There was a reason he woke me at two o'clock in the morning. He told me that the Emperor was in great danger and that I must go and rescue him. I was ordered by the Emperor to return to Tientsin immediately. I was to call up my troops and return to Peking to suppress the enemy. Tan specifically said that the Emperor wanted me to eliminate two people . . .' Yuan tried to steady his quavering voice.

'Was I one of the two?' I asked.

Yuan Shih-kai looked at me. His face was solemn. 'Yes.'

'And the other?' I asked.

Yuan Shih-kai looked down, then turned to Yung Lu.

'I see.' I nodded.

Yung Lu stood expressionless, like a bronze statue.

'I . . .' Yuan Shih-kai made an effort to finish his sentence. '. . . was asked to collect both of your heads.' He fell to his knees and kowtowed, knocking his forehead on the ground.

'Rise, Yuan Shih-kai,' I said and felt my mouth stiffen.

'Tell Her Majesty how you asked Tan for proof of the authenticity of the edict.' Again Yung Lu tried to hurry him along.

'Yes, of course.' Yuan Shih-kai rose. 'I demanded that Tan show me the Emperor's signed edict. Tan said he couldn't. He said that the evidence had to be hidden. He said the situation was reaching a critical moment and Emperor Guang-hsu's life was in danger.'

'Did you believe him?' I asked.

'Believe or disbelieve, I couldn't risk it either way. But I did let Tan know that His Majesty and I had met that very morning, and His Majesty mentioned nothing of a coup. Tan became upset and said that "things had changed" and that "His Majesty's life hadn't been threatened until the afternoon." I asked for witnesses, and he gave me a list of names to contact. Among them were Secretary of the Supreme Court Yang, Chief Judge Lin, Chief General Liu and Kuang-jen, Kang Yu-wei's brother.'

'When did you learn that the Emperor wanted you to murder me?' I asked. I was losing all sense of the connections, the logic between events. A feeling of shock began to overtake me. I kept hearing the cries of the four-year-old

Guang-hsu, and my mind flashed back to the scene of the night when Yung Lu had brought him to the Forbidden City.

'Tan said that he wasn't able to produce the actual edict,' Yuan Shih-kai replied. 'Anyway, Tan told me that His Majesty had ordered "to put to death anyone who dared use his or her power and influence to block reform from moving forward." When I told Tan that I would not bite the hand that fed me, he said that all I had to do was provide an opportunity. He wanted me to take him inside the Summer Palace. These were Tan's words: "I will slash the Dowager Empress's throat myself." He opened his shirt to show me a foot-long knife he was carrying.'

'What did you think, Yuan Shih-kai?' I asked.

'I saw myself getting in trouble either way, assuming Tan was being truthful, which I seriously doubted. If I betrayed the Emperor, my punishment would be death, and if I betrayed Yung Lu and Your Majesty, it would be the same. So I weighed my decision while Tan talked. I wanted to make sure that he truly represented the throne. Tan kept saying, "Cut off the head of the anti-reform monster and the body will wither and die."'

'Have some water, Yuan.' Yung Lu offered his cup.

The general drank the water and wiped his mouth with the back of his hand. 'Tan then showed me his map. It was meticulously detailed. It marked the entrances of the Summer Palace, in particular where Your Majesty's bed-room was. Several alternative plans had also been set in motion, according to Tan. Every exit of your palace would be blocked, including the underground storage tunnels. Tan's in-palace partners included one of your close attendants. I was amazed at the thoroughness. It must have been drawn up by an experienced military hand. I couldn't help but think of Queen Min's assassination. The plot bears the same signature.'

I felt cold and shaken inside.

Sweat dripped from Yuan Shih-kai's shaved head, making it shine like a melon in the rain.

Yung Lu paced the floor as he listened.

'Tan demanded an instant answer from me.' Yuan Shih-kai took a deep breath. 'When he saw that I wasn't going to give him one, he threatened me: "My knife will do whatever it takes to secure reform." At this point I knew my next move. I excused myself with a lie, promising that I'd be ready to act on October 5, the day the Imperial military inspection would take place in Tientsin. "All my troops will be assembled," I told Tan. It made sense to him, for he knew that the inspection would be attended by both Emperor Guang-hsu and Your Majesty. Tan was satisfied when he left.'

Yuan Shih-kai looked tired.

'You may sit down,' I said.

Yung Lu pulled over a chair.

I have no memory of the next two days. Yuan Shih-kai's voice kept repeating itself inside my head: 'I couldn't imagine that the throne would order his mother's execution, but Tan was certain about it.' I denied the possibility. With body and soul I tried to protect myself against a terrible assault. Every fiber of my being went to defend my son against Yuan Shih-kai's accusation.

According to Yung Lu, I had called Yuan Shih-kai a liar and had ordered his beheading on the spot. Yung Lu described how Yuan was terrified and begged for his life. Yung Lu believed that my mind 'went under,' that I was in a state of shock, so he did not carry out my order.

A few hours after Yuan Shih-kai's report, Yung Lu assembled the Grand Council, the key Manchu princes and nobles, and the high officials of the boards, including the ministers the Emperor had previously fired and others who had begged me to reinstate them.

I was asked to resume command of the empire.

I sat through the audience. The court took my silence as an assent to their request.

Under cover of night, together with Yuan Shih-kai, Yung Lu moved his forces up from Tientsin and replaced the palace guards. The Forbidden City and the Summer Palace were tightly secured. Before dawn, Tan's partners inside the palace were secretly arrested. Trusted eunuchs were then sent to Ying-t'ai to spy on Guang-hsu and his attendants.

When I woke that morning it felt as if I were surfacing from a deep well. I dressed, fed myself and went to sit on the Dragon Throne in the Hall of Spiritual Nurturing.

The court's eyes were on me, some curious, some sympathetic, some unreadable. The testimony of individual ministers confirmed what I had been told by Yuan Shih-kai. There was no doubt that a coup had been set in motion.

'Emperor Guang-hsu needs to be dealt with,' Yung Lu proposed.

I gave my approval.

'Go to Ying-t'ai and break the news to Emperor Guang-hsu,' I instructed Yung Lu. 'If my son knew of the plot, tell him I don't want to see his face again.'

On his knees, Guang-hsu begged permission to end his life. He was in his pajamas. He hadn't even finished brushing his teeth. His lips were white with toothpaste.

At the sight of him I had to turn my head away and take a breath. Finally I got up and returned to my bedroom and shut the door. Days went by and I fell ill. My stomach was burning. My tongue developed ulcers and it was painful to swallow.

'Your Majesty's internal being has caught fire.' Doctor Sun Pao-tien insisted that I stay in bed. 'Drink only lotus-seed soup to cool off.'

I was running a fever and had no wish to recover.

Empress Lan arrived, her eyes and cheeks red and swollen. She reported that Guang-hsu had attempted suicide.

Although I could barely sit up, I delivered myself to my son. I wanted him to tell me why.

'I might have been impatient, angry. And yes, I wanted to fire Yung Lu and remove your influence,' Guang-hsu said, 'but I have never considered taking your life.' He fumbled inside his robe and produced a sheaf of papers. 'This is my edict to have Kang Yu-wei and his associates arrested and beheaded.'

'How do you explain their actions?' I asked.

'I don't know how my reform project turned into assassination plans. Kang proposes one thing and carries out another. I am guilty and deserve to die because I trusted him.'

Guang-hsu was more desperate than angry. I wished that he would defend himself and declare his innocence. Although I would never find out the truth, I needed to believe that he was set up. Deep in my heart I knew my child had been taken advantage of.

The bright light in Guang-hsu's eyes disappeared. The Emperor spent days on his knees beseeching me to grant him death. 'So the country can move on,' he said and wept. 'So you can move on. Kang Yu-wei didn't invite himself to the Forbidden City, I did.'

He was broken, his eyes sunken and his back hunched. 'I am sick of myself and sick of living. Have mercy and pity, Mother.'

Before I got a chance to let out my own rage, I was forced to confront Guang-hsu's distress. He refused food and water. Blood was found in his spittoon.

'His Majesty wants to punish himself so badly,' Doctor Sun Pao-tien said. 'He is willing himself to die. I have seen it in patients before. Once the decision is made, there is no stopping them.'

The order to arrest Kang Yu-wei and his associates, signed by Emperor Guang-hsu, stirred the nation. The Ironhats and the court's conservatives took their seats in the Hall of Punishment, where the trial was to begin. They were ready to flex their muscles and teach a brutal lesson.

'The moderates will be hurt once the trial opens,' Yung Lu said. 'Their names, once exposed, will be linked to the reformers. The Ironhats are out for blood.'

Both Yung Lu and I feared armed confrontation. We received intelligence about plans for a riot, instigated by the Ironhats. It would be led by General Tung's Moslem troops. Tung took his orders from Prince Ts'eng – no friend of the throne.

'Where are General Tung's troops now?' I asked.

'They are camped on the southern outskirts of Peking. If a confrontation occurs, the troops will gallop through the streets of Peking. I am concerned about the British and American legations.'

'I can imagine General Tung inviting himself into the Forbidden City. Prince Ts'eng can't wait for the chance to intimidate me. He will force me to dethrone Guang-hsu.'

'That is the picture I see too,' Yung Lu said.

'A painful tourniquet must be applied to avoid a fatal hemorrhage,' I said to Yung Lu. 'Present me a list of the must-be-executed and I'll see that the Emperor signs it. I hope it will help stop the popular displeasure that fuels the riot.'

Future historians would unanimously damn me as a 'villain of immense power, dedicated to evil' when referring to Emperor Guang-hsu's attempted reform, which would be called the Hundred Days, counting from the date of his first edict to the last.

On September 28, 1898, only one day into the trial, the proceedings were halted when news came of Kang Yu-wei's escape – he had been rescued by British and Japanese military agents operating behind the scenes. Fearing that there would be more 'international rescues,' Guang-hsu issued an edict ordering the beheading of six of the prisoners, including Kang Yu-wei's brother Kuang-jen. They became known as the Six Martyrs of the Hundred Days.

All I could say in defense of my son was that the sacrifice was made to avoid a much greater tragedy. The beheadings served as a clear statement of where Emperor Guang-hsu stood, and proved that he was no longer a threat to me. As a result, Prince Ts'eng's notoriously independent General Tung withdrew his Moslem forces eighty miles east of Peking, which meant that the possibility of disturbances, or even killings, at the British and American legations was removed.

The execution of the six spared the moderates, which prevented polarizing confrontations that could have easily escalated into civil war. And the deaths made the advocates of revenge cautious. It allowed the moderates to make a comeback, so that they could achieve what the Ironhats were afraid of – opening up the existing political system.

I was sitting in my courtyard staring at the pistachio trees when the beheadings of the six young men took place. The leaves were bright yellow and had started falling. I was told the six went bravely. None of them spoke of regrets. Two of them had turned themselves in. Tan Shih-tung, the son of Hupeh's governor, had been given a chance to escape, but refused.

Yung Lu's men would have eventually captured Kang Yu-wei if he hadn't been aided in his escape by John Otway Percy Bland, the Shanghai correspondent of the London *Times*. The British consul general wired instructions to the consulates up and down the China coast to be on the lookout for Kang while Yung Lu's manhunt was on.

On September 27, in company with the warship *Esk*, British agents escorted a steamer with Kang Yu-wei on board into Hong Kong harbor. Meanwhile, the British consulate in Canton made arrangements for Kang's mother, his wife, his concubines, his daughters and his brother's family to flee. In Hong Kong, Kang was picked up by Miyazaki Torazo, the powerful Japanese sponsor of the Genyosha, and sailed directly to Tokyo.

The executions made Tan, the governor's son, immortal. The people's sympathy was with the underdogs. The Dowager Empress hates her adopted son, therefore she beheaded his friends – so went public opinion. A poem Tan recited before his death became so famous that it was taught in elementary schools for many years:

I am willing to shed my blood
If thereby my country may be saved.
But for everyone who perishes today
A thousand will rise up to carry on my task.

36

'CHINESE EMPEROR KILLED. May Have Been Tortured – Some Think He Was Poisoned by Conspirators.' This came from the *New York Times*. It was Kang Yu-wei's version of reality. I had 'murdered Emperor Guang-hsu by poison and strangulation.' My son 'was subjected to frightful torture, a red-hot iron being thrust through his bowels.'

Kang Yu-wei 'informed me,' J.O.P. Bland wrote in the London *Times,* 'that he left Peking in compliance with a secret message from the Emperor warning him of his danger. He further stated that the recent events were entirely due to the action of the Manchu party, headed by the Dowager Empress and Viceroy Yung Lu . . . Kang Yu-wei urges that England has an opportunity to intervene and restore the Emperor to the throne . . . Unless protection is afforded to the victims of the coup, it will be impossible henceforward for any native official to support British interests.'

I had told Li Hung-chang to stop sending me the newspapers, but he pretended to be deaf. I couldn't blame him for trying to educate the Emperor. Li made sure two copies arrived at the same time, one for me and the other for His Majesty. I tried to stay calm, but whatever I read made me miserable. It was painful to remember that Guang-hsu had called Kang Yu-wei a genius, his 'best friend' and his 'like-mind.'

Kang went on a worldwide tour. The newspapers quoted a speech he gave at a conference held in England: 'Since the Emperor began to display an interest in affairs of state, the Dowager Empress has been scheming his deposition. She used to play cards with him, and gave him intoxicating drinks in order to prevent him from attending to state affairs. For the greater part of the last two years, the Emperor has been relegated to the role of figurehead against his own wishes.'

Both my son and I were poisoned by our own remorse. It didn't matter how I tried to justify the situation; what remained was the undeniable fact that Guang-hsu had allowed a plot for my murder to be hatched.

Kang Yu-wei continued his traveling campaign: 'You all know that the Dowager Empress is not educated, that she is very conservative . . . that she has been very reluctant to give the Emperor any real power in managing the affairs of the empire. In the year 1887 it was decided to set aside thirty million taels for the creation of China's navy . . . The Dowager Empress appropriated the balance of the money for the repair of [the Summer Palace].' Such slander went on and on.

My son sat idle in his chair for hours on end. I no longer wished that he would come to me or beg me to talk with him. I lost the courage to face him. A distance settled between us. It was frightening. The more Guang-hsu read the newspapers, the deeper he withdrew. When asked to resume his audiences, he refused. He could no longer look me in the eye, and I could no longer tell him that I loved him despite everything that had happened.

Yesterday I found him sobbing after reading Kang Yu-wei's newest calumny: 'There is a sham eunuch in the palace who has practically more power than any of the ministers. Li Lien-ying is the sham eunuch's name . . . All the viceroys have secured their official positions through bribing this man, who is immensely wealthy.'

If I ever were to forgive my son, what happened next made it impossible. I was given no chance to defend myself, while Kang Yu-wei was free to harm me by calling himself the spokesman of the Chinese Emperor and me a 'murderous thief' and 'the scourge of the people.'

The world's reputable publishers printed Kang's malicious accusations detailing my life. They were then translated into Chinese and circulated among my people as the discovered truth. In teahouses and at drinking parties stories of how I had poisoned Nuharoo and murdered Tung Chih and Alute spread like a disease.

The underground publication of Kang Yu-wei's version of the Hundred Days reform became a sensation. In it Kang wrote: 'In combination with one or two traitorous statesmen, the Dowager Empress has secluded our Emperor and is secretly plotting to usurp his throne, falsely alleging that she is counseling in government . . . All the scholars of my country are enraged that this meddling palace concubine should seclude [the Emperor] . . . She has appropriated the proceeds of the government's Good Faith Bonds to build more palaces to give rein to her libidinous desires. She has no feelings for the degradation of the state and the misery of the people.'

My son shut himself inside his Ying-t'ai office. Outside the door lay piles of newspapers he had finished reading.

317

Among them were reports of Kang Yu-wei's life in Japanese exile and his glad-handing Cantonese rebel leader Sun Yat-sen, whom the Genyosha had hired to be a front man for my assassination. In the name of the Emperor of China, Kang asked the Japanese Emperor to 'take action to remove the Dowager Empress Tzu Hsi.'

Over the next eight years, even as my son issued repeated edicts condemning his former mentor, Kang Yu-wei would continue to plot my murder.

Now I begged Guang-hsu to open the door. I said I had lost Tung Chih and I could not go on living if I had to lose him.

Guang-hsu told me he was ashamed and would never forgive himself for what he had done. He said that he could see in my eyes that I no longer had any love for him.

Yet I could not tell him that my love for him hadn't been affected. 'I am not myself because I am hurting,' I confessed. I dared not speak further – I felt the anger beneath my skin. To give voice to that anger would only cause more harm. I was on the lookout to keep the damage to myself and those around me to a minimum.

Guang-hsu asked what I wanted from 'a worthless skin-bag' like him.

I said that I was willing to work to mend our relationship. I let him know that his refusal to pick himself up hurt me more than anything. Yet I could feel myself giving up too. I knew that I had failed with this boy I had adopted and raised since the age of four. I had also failed to keep my promise to my sister Rong. 'After Tung Chih's death, I invested my hope in you,' I said to Guang-hsu. Not only had I lost hope, but also the courage to try again.

Some part of me would never believe that Guang-hsu meant to murder me. But he had made a grievous error, and it was too big even for me to fix.

Guang-hsu begged to be dethroned and said that all he wanted was to retreat from the public eye and never be seen again.

It was the saddest moment of my life. I refused to accept such defeat. Turning cold and hard, I said to him, 'No, I will not grant you the right to quit.'

'Why?' he cried.

'Because it will only prove to the world that what Kang has said about me is true.'

'Aren't my seals on his arrest warrant proof enough?'

Suddenly I wondered what my son would regret more, the loss of my affection or Kang Yu-wei's incompetence in having me killed.

Yung Lu abandoned the manhunt for Liang Chi-chao – Kang Yu-wei's right-hand man and disciple – because 'the subject had made a successful escape to Japan.'

Liang Chi-chao was a journalist and translator who had worked as a Chinese secretary for the Welsh Baptist and political activist Timothy Richard, whose goal was to subvert the Manchu regime. Liang was known for his powerful writing and was called by the court 'the poison pen.'

When the edict ordering Liang Chi-chao's arrest and beheading was issued, he was still in Peking. Yung Lu's men secured the city gates, and Liang sought refuge at the Japanese legation. It must have been a sweet surprise for the fugitive to find out that Ito Hirobumi happened to be a guest there.

'Liang was disguised as a Japanese and sent off to Tientsin,' Yung Lu reported. 'His escort was an infamous agent of the Genyosha.'

My son looked like a blind man, gazing blankly into the middle distance as he listened to Yung Lu.

'Under the protection of the Japanese consul, Liang Chi-chao reached the anchorage at Taku and boarded the gunboat *Oshima*,' Yung Lu continued. 'Since we had been watching his movements closely, we caught up with the *Oshima* on the open sea. My men demanded the fugitive's surrender, but the Japanese captain refused to hand him over. He claimed that we had violated international law. It was impossible to carry out a search, although we knew Liang was hiding in one of the cabins.'

My son turned away when Yung Lu placed a copy of Japan's *Kobe Chronicle* in front of him. The paper claimed that on October 22 the *Oshima* was bringing to Japan 'a very valuable present.'

Japan had reason to celebrate. In exile Kang Yu-wei and Liang Chi-chao were reunited. As the houseguest of Japan's foreign minister, Shigenobu Okuma, for five months, Kang was well fed and his braided hair, according to one report, had a 'healthy, glossy shine.' Over the next several years the two men worked together tirelessly. They succeeded in cobbling together a portrait of me as an evil tyrant, confirming everyone's worst suppositions and prejudices.

Kang and Liang achieved the international recognition they craved. The West regarded them as the heroes of China's reform movement. The 'moon-faced' Kang Yu-wei was described as 'the sage of modern China.' His interviews and articles were made into books that sold thousands of copies in many lands. Readers far from China had their first authoritative glimpse of who I was.

But more than my pride was at stake. Kang and Liang's salacious attacks provided opportunities for those who wished war on China. Since 'the true leaders of China are begging the country to be saved,' what more excuse did anyone need to oust a 'corrupt,' 'besotted,' 'reptilian' female dictator?

Western audiences that gathered to hear Kang Yu-wei wanted so much to see China transformed into a Christian utopia that they were susceptible to Kang's lies. From Li Hung-chang I learned that Japan had provided funds for Kang Yu-wei to make a separate tour of the United States, where he was lauded by critics and scholars as 'the man who would have brought China American-style democracy.'

'Heaven gave us this saint to save China,' Kang would open his speeches praising my son. 'Although His Majesty has been imprisoned and dethroned, luckily he is still with us. Heaven has not yet abandoned China!'

Collecting more than $300,000 from overseas Chinese merchants who wanted to guarantee the goodwill of any new regime, and with the assistance of Japan's Genyosha secret agents who operated from inland China, Kang Yu-wei began to prepare an armed uprising.

The duet of Kang Yu-wei and Liang Chi-chao was picked up by the *New York Times*, the *Chicago Tribune* and the London *Times*. 'All Dowager Empress Tzu Hsi knows is a life of pleasure-seeking, and all Yung Lu knows is a lust for power. Has the Empress ever spared a thought for the good of her country? A tortoise cannot grow hair, a rabbit cannot sprout horns, a cockerel cannot lay eggs, and a withered tree cannot produce blossoms, because it is not in her nature to do so – we cannot expect what doesn't exist in her heart!'

37

On top of the reform disaster, 1898 also turned out to be a long and bitter year of flood and famine. First the harvest failed in Shantung and surrounding provinces, then the Yellow River engulfed hundreds of villages in a savage flood. Thousands became homeless, making it impossible to sow the next year's crops. Worse, locusts descended to devour the meager remains. The squatters, the out-of-work, the discontented and the dispossessed longed for a reason, a cause, a scapegoat.

I was kept busy trying to put out the fires. The Ironhats had proposed hanging Pearl Concubine as a means of making the Emperor bear responsibility. Pearl was found guilty of violating numerous palace rules. I rejected the trumped-up charges, offering no explanation.

The anti-foreign riots continued. An English missionary was murdered in the southwest province of Kweichow, and a French priest was tortured and killed in Hupeh. In the provinces where foreigners lived in close quarters with Chinese, grievances fomented unrest, particularly in German-controlled Kiaochow, the birthplace of Confucius. Locals resented Christianity. In the British- and Russian-controlled areas of Weihaiwei and Liaotung violence broke out when the foreigners decided that they, as leaseholders, were entitled to benefit from Chinese taxes.

In the name of protecting me, Prince Ts'eng and his sons called for the Emperor's abdication. Ts'eng's faction was backed by the Manchu Clan Council and General Tung's Moslem army. Though hard for me to continue to support Guang-hsu, I knew the dynasty would fall with Prince Ts'eng in power. All of the industries and international connections Li Hung-chang had built, including our diplomatic relationships with Western countries, would end. A civil war would give the foreign powers a perfect excuse to intervene.

Stability would require Guang-hsu's continuation as Emperor. I granted an alternative plan presented by the conservatives which said I was to resume the regency. Guang-hsu signed his name but wanted nothing more to do with it.

'The affairs of the nation are at present in a difficult position,' the edict read, 'and everything awaits reform. I, the Emperor, am working day and night with all my powers. But despite my careful toil, I constantly fear being overwhelmed by the press of work. Moved by a deep regard for the welfare of the nation, I have repeatedly implored Her Majesty to be graciously pleased to advise me in government, and have received her assent. This is an assurance of prosperity to the whole nation, its officials and its people.'

It was a humiliation for both Guang-hsu and me. It spoke of the Emperor's incompetence as well as my poor judgment in putting him on the throne in the first place.

Shortly after the edict was issued, Guang-hsu fell ill. I had to rush through my audiences in order to be with him. Soon my son was bedridden. All Doctor Sun Pao-tien's efforts failed, his herbal medicines exhausted. The rumor that the Emperor was dying, or had already died, spread. It seemed to prove Kang Yu-wei's earlier assertion that the poison I was said to have been giving Guang-hsu was now 'showing its deadly effect.'

I-kuang, our minister of foreign affairs, received numerous inquiries regarding the throne's 'disappearance.' I-kuang was no Prince Kung. All he could say to me was 'Invasions have been discussed among the legations.'

My son knew that he must show himself in the court, but he could barely get out of bed.

'If you insist that His Majesty attend, he could easily pass out in the middle of an audience,' Sun Pao-tien warned.

Yung Lu agreed. 'His Majesty's appearance would do more harm than good.'

After witnessing a fit of vomiting that left my son wrung out and sobbing, I put out an urgent call to all the provinces for able physicians. No Chinese doctors dared to come forward. Surprisingly, I received a collective request from the foreign legations. From the letter's wording, the legations seemed to give credence to Kang Yu-wei's version of events: 'Only a thorough medical examination of His Majesty will clear the air of the corrosive rumors and restore British and international confidence in the regime.' The letter offered the assistance of Western doctors.

But the court and Guang-hsu himself declined the offer. To the court, the throne's health was a matter of national pride and his current condition a secret. As for Guang-hsu, he had suffered enough humiliation as Emperor and didn't want to suffer more as a man. He knew his own condition, and didn't want the world to find out why he was childless.

I was reluctant to subject my son and China to further embarrassment, but as a mother I was committed to try everything to save my son's life. A Western doctor might be Guang-hsu's last hope for regaining his health. I might not have been a worldly woman, but I wasn't stupid. I believed that 'in a tiny piece of spotted skin one could visualize an entire leopard.' My French hair dyes, English clocks and German telescope spoke of the people who created them. The industrial marvels of the West – telegraph, railroad, military armaments – spoke even louder.

I asked delicately if Guang-hsu was willing to reveal the complete truth, meaning mention of his sexual dysfunction. My son gave a positive reply. I was relieved and went to share the good news with my daughters-in-law. We became hopeful, and together we went to the Palace Temple to pray.

In the last week of October, a French physician, Doctor Detheve, was escorted to the Forbidden City and into the Emperor's bedroom. I was present throughout the medical interview. The doctor suspected a kidney ailment and concluded that Guang-hsu suffered a number of secondary symptoms brought on by that illness.

'At first glance,' Doctor Detheve's evaluation read, 'His Majesty's state is generally feeble, terribly thin, depressed attitude, pale complexion. The appetite is good, but the digestion is slow . . . Vomiting is very frequent. Listening to the lungs with a stethoscope, which His Majesty gladly allowed, did not reveal indications of good health. Circulatory problems are numerous. Pulse feeble and fast, head aching, feelings of heat on the chest, ringing in the ears, dizziness, and stumbling that gives the impression that he is missing a leg. To these symptoms add the overall sensation of cold in the legs and knees, fingers feeling dead, cramps in the calves, itching, slight deafness, failing eyesight, pain in the kidneys. But above all there are the troubles with the urinary apparatus . . . His Majesty urinates often, but only a little at a time. In twenty-four hours the amount is less than normal.'

Guang-hsu and I were left with a favorable impression of the doctor and looked forward to his treatment. What we didn't expect was that his evaluation would find its way to the public. We had no way of knowing whether it was intentional or not. Nevertheless, the evaluation became the inspiration of gossips in China, Europe and the United States. It was the last blow to Guang-hsu's self-image. From the grinning expressions of the court during audiences I could tell that our ministers had read a translation of Doctor Detheve's opinion.

Chinese provincial newspapers and magazines spread the gossip as news: 'His Majesty habitually had his ejaculations at night, followed by voluptuous sensation. Doctor Detheve's evaluation concluded, "These nocturnal emissions have been followed by the lessening of the faculty to achieve voluntary erections during the day." It was Detheve's opinion that the Emperor's illness made sexual intercourse impossible. The Emperor could not make love to his Empress or his concubines. And without sex, His Majesty would remain childless, which means that there will be no heir to the throne.' Such reports made the Ironhats demand Guang-hsu's replacement.

I witnessed the sacrifice of my son's dignity. Although the French doctor's examination demonstrated that

Guang-hsu was alive and that therefore I could not be his murderer, I was devastated.

Although Guang-hsu continued to suffer – high fever, little appetite, his throat and tongue swollen and raw – for the sake of appearances he offered to sit with me during audiences.

For the radical reformers, the image of the two of us sitting side by side served as proof of my being a tyrant. The newspapers published their observations, describing how the victimized Emperor must have felt about his living hell. In a popular version, Guang-hsu was seen 'drawing huge pictures of a mighty dragon, his own emblem, and tearing them up in despair.'

The Ironhats, on the other hand, found justification in orthodox Chinese thought: Guang-hsu had virtually plotted matricide, and there was no crime in the Confucian canon more heinous than a dereliction of filial piety, especially in an emperor, the moral exemplar of his people.

I was supposed to brandish before Guang-hsu the proper moral righteousness. But I could not ignore his pain. My son was brave enough to face the men he had ordered to resign before the attempted coup. Every day now he sat on a carpet made of a thousand needles. He might continue to have the court's loyalty, but would he have its members' respect?

Given my son's delicate health, I was moved to accept the Ironhats' proposal of considering his replacement. I acted sincerely throughout the debates and in the end pronounced P'u-chun, Prince Ts'eng Junior's adolescent son, my grandnephew, the new heir. However, I insisted that P'u-chun undergo a character evaluation, a test I was sure the spoiled boy would fail. As I predicted, he did fail, miserably, and he was removed from consideration.

Guang-hsu's throne was secure, for the time being at least, but he appeared bored and would slip away from audiences the first chance he got. Afterward, I would find him playing with his clocks. He wouldn't open the door, nor would he talk to me. His sad eyes showed emptiness, and he told me that his mind 'wanders like a homeless ghost.' The only thing he didn't tire of saying was 'I wish I were dead.'

I summoned my daughters-in-law. 'We must try to help,' I said.

'You should leave His Majesty alone,' Pearl Concubine was quick to respond.

I asked why I should do so, to which Pearl replied, 'Maybe Your Majesty should consider going back to your retirement. The throne is a grown man. He knows how to run his empire.'

I asked Pearl if she remembered that it was she who introduced Kang Yu-wei to my son.

The girl was furious. 'The reform failed because Guang-hsu was never left alone to run his business. He has been under investigation, imprisoned in his own quarters, separated from me. I am sorry . . . this is – I can't think of any other way to put it – a conspiracy against Emperor Guang-hsu.'

I didn't know what to make of this wild outburst. Was she really trying to provoke me?

When Pearl asked to attend Guang-hsu, I refused. 'Not in your state of mind. My son can take no more harm.'

'You are afraid I will tell him the truth.'

'I don't think you know what the truth is.' I told Pearl that unless she cooperated with me and acknowledged her past wrongdoings, she would not be allowed to see Guang-hsu again.

'His Majesty will ask for me,' Pearl protested. 'I will not be a prisoner!'

38

T HE SHOUTING GREW louder in the streets of Peking: 'Uphold the great Ch'ing Dynasty!' 'Exterminate the barbarians!' The Ironhats used these outcries to force me to take their side. Until reformer Kang Yu-wei's murderous intentions were exposed, I hadn't the chance to ask myself: Who are my real friends?

Kang's repeated calls for international intervention disappointed and disillusioned my son. By the time Kang's seventh hit man was arrested for making an attempt on my life, my son vowed to get even with the 'wily fox.'

Not one nation responded to Guang-hsu's demand for Kang Yu-wei's arrest. Britain, Russia and Japan refused to offer any information of his whereabouts. Instead, foreign newspapers continued to print Kang's lies that 'the Emperor of China is being imprisoned and tortured.'

Japan also began to apply military pressure by calling for my 'forever disappearance.' Guang-hsu was believed to have been 'drugged, dragged and tied to his dragon seat' to attend audiences with me. In the world's eyes he had been given a 'poisonous breakfast' with 'mold as a topping.' What the Emperor of China desperately needed, it was said, was an invasion by the Western powers.

The situation drove my son deeper into melancholy. He resumed his solitude and refused contact of any kind, including the affection of his beloved Pearl Concubine.

No words could describe my feelings as I watched my son deteriorate. Every morning before we ascended the throne, I would ask him about his night and brief him about the issues before the court. Once in a while Guang-hsu would answer my questions politely, but it was as if his voice came from a great distance. Usually he would simply utter 'fine.'

From his eunuchs I learned that he had stopped taking the medicine the Western doctors had prescribed. He ordered his bedroom to be draped with black velvet curtains to seal out the sunlight. He stopped reading newspapers and spent his time tinkering with his clocks. He grew so thin that he looked like a fifteen-year-old. Sitting on the throne, he would drift off to sleep.

When I consulted my astrologer, he requested permission to speak freely.

'Your son's interest in clocks is significant,' he told me. '"Clock," in Mandarin, is pronounced the same as "zone." It has the same sound and tone as the character *zhong*, meaning "ending."'

'Do you mean his life . . . ending?' I asked.

'There is nothing you can do to help, Your Majesty. It is Heaven's will.'

I wished that I could tell the astrologer that I had been fighting Heaven's will all my life. My standing alone was proof of my struggle. I had survived what was meant to be my death many times, and I was determined to fight for my son. It was hope that I lived for. When my husband died, Tung Chih became my hope. When Tung Chih died, hope became Guang-hsu.

*   *   *

My hairdo and wigs had never bothered me before, but they did now. I complained to Li Lien-ying that his designs were boring and that the bejeweled ornaments were too heavy. Certain colors that were favorites before irritated me. Washing and dyeing my hair became a burden. Li Lien-ying replaced all his hairdressing tools. Using lightweight wires and clips to pin jewelry onto my fan-shaped hair board, he gave me new height, creating what he called a 'three-story umbrella.'

This effort to project me as larger than life appeared to succeed – the court seemed humbled by my new look – yet the agony came from within myself. My listlessness grew along with my son's decline. My eyes filled with tears in the middle of a conversation as I remembered the days when Guang-hsu was a loving and courageous child.

I refused to accept the court's conclusion that the Emperor had pushed the country backward. 'If Guang-hsu had rocked the ship of state,' I reminded the audience, 'the ship had long been rudderless, adrift on a chaotic sea and at the mercy of any wind of change.'

No one thought about the possibility that Guang-hsu might be suffering a nervous collapse. Given his mother's sad history (Rong's life had been, if anything, more tormented), I should have been the first to understand. But I didn't, or my mind willed me not to. Guang-hsu's focus on the world had shifted downward and settled between his legs – when others stared at him, he grew agitated.

Sitting absent-mindedly, he seemed to hear the audience without following its discussions. The moment he got up from his chair, he would suffer an imagined attack. Maybe he didn't imagine it – in any case, it was real to him and left him shaken. He would excuse himself, sometimes in the middle of an important subject, and would not return.

Perhaps my astrologer was correct in believing that the Emperor 'had already chosen disappearance and death.' Only I, however, was cruel enough to force him to continue to show his face.

In looking back on the Hundred Days, I concluded that my son's attraction to Kang Yu-wei had to do with the allure of a foreign myth. The scholar peddled his fantasy of the West, and Guang-hsu had no idea what he was buying into. Li Hung-chang was right when he said that it wasn't foreign troops that defeated China, but our own negligence and inability to see the truth amid a sea of lies.

The throne's planned inspection of the navy had been canceled because of the failed reforms. Everyone had been convinced of the rumor that the inspection would mark the day of Guang-hsu's dethroning. Our intelligence showed that the foreign powers were prepared to intervene.

With Li Hung-chang's encouragement, I took a train to meet privately with the governors of key provinces, north and south. I stopped in Tientsin and visited the Great Machine Show, organized by Li Hung-chang's partner, S. S. Huan. I was most impressed by a machine that pulled individual threads out of silk cocoons, a task that had been done painstakingly by hand for centuries. The 'flushing ceramic bowl' made me want to install them inside the Forbidden City.

I couldn't believe the written description that said the toilet had been invented by a British prince for his mother. True or not, the story was telling: apparently the royal children of Great Britain were given a practical education. Tung Chih and Guang-hsu were taught the finest Chinese classics, yet both had led ineffectual lives.

My fear increased as I admired all the other foreign inventions. How could China expect to survive when its enemies were so scientifically minded and relentless in their pursuit of progress?

'The way to win a war is to know your enemy so well that you can predict his next move,' Sun Tzu wrote in *The Art of War*. I could hardly predict my own next move, but realized that it would be wise to learn from my enemies. I decided that on my sixty-fourth birthday I would invite a number of foreign ambassadors to Peking. I wanted them to see the 'murderess' with their own eyes.

Li Hung-chang was excited by the prospect. 'Once it is known by the citizens of China that the Dowager Empress is herself willing to see and entertain foreigners, their own antipathy toward outsiders will be allayed.'

As expected, the Manchu Clan Council protested. I wasn't supposed to be seen at all, let alone talk with the barbarians. It was no use arguing that the Queen of England had not only been seen by the world, her face was stamped on every coin.

After long negotiations, I was given the approval to host an all-female party, with the condition that Emperor Guang-hsu join me so that I would be accompanied by an Imperial male. The party was presented as an opportunity to satisfy my fashion curiosity. My guests included the wives of the ministers of Great Britain, Russia, Germany, France, Holland, the United States and Japan.

According to the foreign affairs minister I-kuang, the foreign ministers had insisted that their ladies be received 'with every mark of respect.' It took six weeks to settle on everything from the style of palanquins to the choice of interpreters. 'The foreigners are standing firm on all es-

334

sential points,' I-kuang reported. 'I was afraid that I might have to cancel the invitations, but the ladies' curiosity finally proved stronger than their husbands' opposition.'

On December 13, 1898, the foreign ladies in all their finery were escorted to the Winter Palace, one of the 'sea palaces' next to the Forbidden City. I sat on a dais behind a long, narrow table decorated with fruit and flowers. My golden costume was heavy and my hair board piled dangerously high. My eyes were having a feast.

Aside from the wife of the Japanese ambassador, whose kimono and obi closely resembled our Tang Dynasty costumes, the ladies were dressed like magnificent festival lanterns. They curtsied and bowed to me. As I uttered 'rise' to each of them, I was fascinated by the color of their eyes, their hair and curvaceous bodies. They were presented to me as a group, but they demonstrated complete individuality.

I-kuang introduced the wife of the British minister, Lady MacDonald. She led the procession and was a tall, graceful woman in her forties. She wore a beautiful light blue satin dress with a large purplish ribbon tied behind her waist. She had a head full of golden curls, which was complemented by a large oval hat displaying ornaments. Lady Conger was the wife of the American minister. She was a Christian Scientist and was dressed in black fabric from head to toe.

I told I-kuang to speed up his introductions and cut short the interpreter's ceremonial greetings. 'Escort the guests to the banquet hall and have them start eating,' I said. I was confident in presenting our cuisine, for I remembered something Li Hung-chang had said, that 'there is nothing to eat in the West.'

I already regretted that I had promised the court not to speak or ask questions. After the meal, when the ladies were brought back so I could present them gifts, I took each by the hand and placed a gold ring in her palm. I let my smile tell them that I wanted us to be friends. I was grateful that they came to see this 'calculating woman with a heart of ice.'

I was fully aware that I was being observed like an animal in a zoo. I expected a certain arrogance from them. Instead, the ladies showed nothing but warmth. I was overwhelmed by a feeling that if I treated them as my foreign sisters, maybe a conversation would follow. I wanted to ask Lady MacDonald about her life in London, and Lady Conger what it was like to be a Christian Scientist and a mother. Was she happy with the way her children were being raised?

Unfortunately, observing and listening were the only things I was allowed to do. My eyes traveled from the ornaments dangling from the ladies' hats to the beads sewed onto their shoes. I stared at the ladies, and they stared back. My eunuchs turned away their heads when my guests moved with protruded torsos, chests and exposed shoulders. My ladies in waiting, on the other hand, stared wide-eyed. The foreigners' elegance, intelligent speech and respectful responses gave new meaning to the word 'barbaric.'

When Lady MacDonald delivered a short well-wishing speech, I knew from her sweet voice that this woman had never starved a day in her life. I envied her bright, almost childlike smile.

Guang-hsu hardly raised his eyes during the party. The foreign ladies stared at him in fascination. Though extremely uncomfortable, he kept his promise to stay until the end. He had initially refused to attend, for he knew that these ladies had learned of his medical condition from their husbands. I had promised to end the reception as soon as I could.

I didn't expect any real understanding to come out of the party, but to my great surprise, it did. Later these women, especially Lady MacDonald, gave favorable impressions of me, against the world's opinion. The editor of the London *Times* published a criticism of the party, calling the ladies' presence there 'disgusting, offensive and farcical.' In response, Lady MacDonald wrote:

> I should say the Dowager Empress was a woman of some strength of character, certainly genial and kindly . . . This is the opinion of all the ladies who accompanied me. I was fortunate in having as my interpreter the Chinese secretary of our legation, a gentleman of over twenty years' experience of China and the Chinese. Previous to our visit, his opinion of the Dowager Empress was what I may call the generally accepted one. My husband had requested him to take careful note of all that passed, especially with a view of endeavoring to arrive at some estimate of her true character. On his return he reported that all his previously conceived notions had been upset by what he had seen and heard.

39

By the spring of 1899, the name of the roaming bands of youths was on everyone's lips: Fists of Righteous Harmony, I Ho Ch'uan – in short, the Boxers – had turned into a nationwide anti-foreigner movement. Although the I Ho Ch'uan was a peasant movement with strong Buddhist roots and Taoist underpinnings, it drew its adherents from all walks of life. With its professed belief in supernatural powers, it was, in Yung Lu's words, 'the poor man's road to immortality.'

Governors across the country had been waiting for my instructions on how to deal with the Boxers. Support or suppress them was the choice I had to make. The Boxers were reported to have spread over eighteen provinces and were beginning to be seen in the streets of Peking. The youths wore red turbans and dyed their outfits red, with matching wrist and ankle bands.

The youths claimed to employ a unique style of combat. Trained in the martial arts, they believed they were incarnations of the gods. One governor wrote in an urgent memorandum, 'The Boxers have been rallying around Christian churches in my province. They have been threatening to kill with sword, ax, staff, fighting iron, halberd and a myriad of other weapons.'

In my eyes it was another Taiping rebellion in the making. The difference was that this time the ringleaders were the Manchu Ironhats, which made arrests difficult.

On a clear morning in March, Prince Ts'eng Junior requested an immediate audience. He entered the hall and announced that he had joined the Boxers. Waving his fists, he swore loyalty to me. Lining up behind him were his brothers and cousins, including Prince Ch'un Junior.

I looked at Prince Ts'eng's face, which was marked with smallpox scars. His ferret-like eyes gave the impression of brutish ferocity. Ts'eng kept looking at his handsome and dashing cousin Ch'un, who had the look of his Bannerman ancestors. Although Prince Ch'un had grown into a personable character, his foul mouth revealed his flaws. Both princes were passionate sloganeers. Ch'un could move himself to tears when describing how he would sacrifice his life 'to restore the Manchus' supremacy.'

'What do you want from me?' I asked my nephews.

'To accept us as Boxers and support us,' said Prince Ts'eng.

'To allow the Boxers to be paid like government troops!' said Prince Ch'un.

As if out of nowhere, men wearing Boxer uniforms streamed into my courtyard.

'Why come to me when you have already exchanged your resplendent Manchu military uniforms for beggars' rags?' I asked.

'Forgive us, Your Majesty.' Prince Ch'un got down on his knees. 'We came because we heard that the Forbidden City was under attack and you were in grave danger.'

'Out!' I said to him. 'Our military is not for hooligans and beggars!'

'You can't thrust aside a Heaven-sent force of champions, Your Majesty!' Prince Ts'eng challenged. 'The masters of the Boxers are men with supernatural powers. When the spirits are with them, they are invisible and are immune to poison, spears, even bullets.'

'Let me inform you that General Yuan recently lined some Boxers up before a firing squad and had them all shot dead.'

'If they died, they were not real Boxers,' Ts'eng insisted. 'Or they only seemed to die – their spirits will return.'

After dismissing the make-believe Boxers, I went to Ying-t'ai. The Emperor sat in the corner of his room like a shadow. The air around him reeked of bitter herbal medicines. Although he was fully dressed and shaved, he was spiritless.

'I am afraid that if we don't support the movement,' I said, 'it could turn against our rule and bring it down.'

Guang-hsu made no response.

'Don't you care?'

'I am tired, Mother.'

I got back in my palanquin, angrier and sadder than ever.

The winter of 1899 was the coldest in my life. Nothing could keep me warm. My astrologer said that my body had run out of its 'fire.' 'Cold fingertips indicate bad blood circulation, reflecting problems of the heart,' the doctors said.

I began to dream more frequently of the dead. First to show themselves were my parents. My father would appear in the same drab brown outfit with a disapproving expression. My mother would keep talking about Rong. 'You need to take care of your sister, Orchid,' she would repeat again and again.

Nuharoo entered my nights with Hsien Feng by her side. The diamonds in her hair board grew larger in each succeeding dream. She held a bunch of pink peonies in her hand. Sunshine highlighted her shoulders like an aura. She looked content. Hsien Feng would smile, although he remained silent.

Tung Chih's visit was never predictable. He usually appeared just before dawn. Often I wouldn't recognize him, not only because he had grown, but also because he had a different character. On a recent night he came as a Boxer wearing a red turban. After he identified himself, he described how he was shot by Yuan Shih-kai. He showed me the gaping hole in his chest. I was terrified and woke instantly.

There were more reports of locals blaming foreigners for their hardship. Massive unemployment of bargemen on the Grand Canal was brought about by the introduction of steamships and railways. Several bad growing seasons in a row convinced the peasants that the spirits were angry. The governors pleaded for the throne to 'ask the barbarians to take away their missionaries and their opium.'

There was little I could do. Yung Lu didn't have to remind me of the consequences of murdering missionaries. A German naval squadron had used the violent incidents involving their nationals to seize forts guarding the city of Tsingtao. Kiaochow was occupied, turning the bay into a German naval base.

I tried to gather information on the missionaries and their converts, only to be told bizarre stories: some said the missionaries used drugs to woo converts, made medicine from fetuses, and opened orphanages only to collect infants for their cannibalistic orgies.

In more logical and believable accounts, I found the missionaries' and their governments' behavior disturbing. Catholic churches seemed willing to go to any lengths to increase their conversions, taking in derelicts and criminals. Village ne'er-do-wells facing lawsuits had themselves baptized in order to gain a legal advantage – by treaty agreement, Christians were given Imperial protection.

The mess left by the failed reform movement became a breeding ground for violence and riots. More trouble-makers showed up on the political scene, among them Sun Yat-sen, whose idea of a Chinese republic attracted the nation's young. Working with the Japanese, Sun Yat-sen plotted assassination and destruction, especially of the government's financial establishments.

I often conducted audiences alone these days. Guang-hsu's ill health left him so tired that he couldn't be counted on to be more than half awake. I didn't want the provincial governors, who sometimes waited a lifetime to meet with the Emperor, to be disappointed.

I wanted the world to believe that the Guang-hsu regime was still powerful. I carried on so that China could continue to honor the treaties and rights granted to foreigners. In the meantime, I tried to gain understanding for the Boxers. My edict to all governors read: 'The result of the failure to distinguish between good and evil is that men's minds are filled with fear and doubt. This proves not that the people are inherently lawless, but that our leaders have failed.'

I removed the governor of Shantung province after two German missionaries were killed there. I replaced him with the no-nonsense Yuan Shih-kai. I didn't order the former governor's prosecution – I knew such a move would enrage the citizenry and make myself more vulnerable. Instead, I had him transferred to another province, away from any heated response by the Germans. My investigation revealed that the main reason the former Shantung governor came under the intense pressure of the German government was not the death of its missionaries but the rights to China's resources.

Another governor also reported trouble. He had tried to strike a balance by cajoling the Boxers into remaining a defensive and not an aggressive force. But before long the Boxer hooligans were setting fire to the railways and Christian churches and occupying government buildings. 'Persuasion can no longer disperse the rebels,' the governor cried, asking for permission to suppress them. 'Our commanders, if hesitant and tolerant, will certainly lead us into unnecessary calamities.'

In Shantung, the new governor, Yuan Shih-kai, took matters into his own hands. He ignored my admonition that 'the people must be persuaded to disperse, not crushed by brute force,' and he hounded the Boxers out of his province.

'These Boxers,' Yuan wrote afterward in his telegram to the throne, 'are gathering people to roam the streets. They cannot be said to be defending themselves and their families. They are setting fire to houses, kidnapping people and resisting government troops; they are freely engaging in criminal activities; they are plundering and killing the common people. They cannot be said to be merely anti-Christian.'

Because of the political disruptions, governments in villages along the Yellow River neglected the ever-present problem of flood control. In the summer of 1899 a disaster of great magnitude took place. Thousands of square miles in the north of China were inundated, crops were destroyed, and famine followed. Next came a period of drought, resulting in a million farming families becoming homeless. The recruitment of Boxers soared. 'Until all the foreigners have been exterminated, the rain will never visit us,' the frustrated poor believed.

Under pressure from the Ironhats, the court began to lean toward supporting the Boxers. After being driven out of Shantung by Yuan Shih-kai, the Boxers traveled north, crossing Chihli province and then on to Peking itself. Joined along the way by thousands of peasants who believed they were invulnerable, the Boxers became an unstoppable force in Chinese society. 'Protect the Manchu Dynasty and destroy the foreigners!' men shouted as they encircled the foreign legations.

Yung Lu and I were helplessly undecided about whether or not to suppress the Boxers. The rest of the court, however, had made up their minds to join them.

Yung Lu told me that he had no faith in the Boxers' true ability to win battles against foreign invaders. Yet I couldn't get him to challenge the court. I asked him to submit a memorandum, and I would explain to the court why the Boxers must be stopped. He agreed.

When I received Yung Lu's draft, I thought about how strange our relationship had become. He was my most loyal and trusted official, and I depended on him constantly. We had come a long way from the days when we were young and poised on the brink of passion. I could, and did, relive those moments at my most private times. Now we had grown old, and the roles that brought us together were both comfortable and absolute. The feelings were still there, but they had mellowed and become deeper and lived side by side with the fact that now, in the midst of China's turmoil, our lives and survival depended on each other.

The day I read Yung Lu's draft to the audience, Princes Ts'eng and Ch'un accused me of losing momentum in the war against the barbarians. With the Boxers already massed in Peking's legation district, the princes had come to obtain the throne's permission to move in for the kill.

I started by saying that it was indeed gratifying for the throne to see our people display courage, to witness their enthusiasm for settling old scores against the foreigners. Then I asked the youths to bear in mind the consequences of their actions and to temper their fury before reality was swept away.

I told them what Yung Lu had told me: 'As a fighting force the Boxers are absolutely useless, but their claims to supernatural arts and magic might help to demoralize the enemy. It would be quite wrong, not to say fatal, however, for us to attach any real belief to their ridiculous claims, or to regard them as of any real use in action.'

My speech had the desired effect. Several of the conservatives ended up voting to cancel any immediate action against the legations. Nevertheless, the Boxer movement continued to ferment, and I knew that before long I would run out of options.

Requests for instructions on handling the situation continued to come in from all over the country. Yung Lu and Li Hung-chang devised a strategy. The throne would focus on discouraging the Boxers in southern China, where foreign nations had the most commercial enterprises and where we were vulnerable to intervention. The edict read, 'The main goal is to prevent the throne's decree from becoming an excuse for the banding together of disorderly characters.'

Once again the edict sounded ambiguous. It didn't condemn outright, but granted a degree of autonomy so that Li Hung-chang and other southern governors could carry on business as usual with foreign countries and suppress the Boxers, when necessary, with their provincial armies.

'The throne would like to remind the citizenry that the nation has been forced to pay compensation for the murders of foreigners. In the case of Shantung alone, on top of the governor's dismissal and the disbursement of six thousand taels of silver for bereaved families, Germany gained exclusive rights to our northeastern railways and coal mines and the license to build a naval station in Kiaochow. We lost both Kiaochow and Tsingtao; Germany gained them as leased concessions for ninety-nine years.'

40

G UANG-HSU DID NOT raise his eyes from the clock he was fixing when I told him that ten thousand Boxers had taken control of the rail lines in the city of Chochou, fifty miles southwest of Peking. 'They attacked and burned down stations and bridges along with telegraph lines. The local authorities were repeatedly beaten for "offering foreign devils the supply line."'

'What else is new?' Guang-hsu muttered.

'Guang-hsu, the foreign legations have sent letters threatening military action if we don't suppress the Boxers, but if we do, the Boxers will topple the throne.' I stopped, furious at Guang-hsu's apathy. For him, the world was enclosed in an old French porcelain mantel clock, clouds and cherubs painted on its surface.

Noticing my emotion, Guang-hsu looked up from the clock.

'For heaven's sake,' I yelled, 'say something!'

'Forgive me, Mother . . .'

'Please don't ask my forgiveness. Fight me or fight with me, Guang-hsu. Just do something!'

My son buried his face in his hands.

*   *   *

In early June 1900, the streets of Peking became the Boxers' parade ground. Crowds grew thick where 'magic' was performed. The Boxers dashed forward and back, waving swords and spears. The weapons shone ominously in the sun.

East of the capital, near Tientsin, Yung Lu's forces tried to keep the Boxers from cutting the rail link between the foreign ships off Taku and the legations in the city. Yung Lu thwarted them, but his capture of the Boxers made him extremely unpopular. Prince Ts'eng Junior told his friends that he had put Yung Lu on his death list.

On June 8, Boxers set fire to the grandstand of the Peking racecourse, a popular gathering place for foreigners. Overnight the 'China crisis' had caught the world's attention. George Morrison of the London *Times* wrote, 'It is now inevitable that we should have to fight.'

The next day Prince Ts'eng, with several Boxer leaders in tow, burst into the Summer Palace. Ts'eng's red turban was sweat-soaked and his skin was the color of a yam. I was told that he had been building up his muscles by pounding a sledgehammer under the hot sun. He smelled of liquor and his ferret eyes sparkled.

Before I had a chance to question him about the burning of the racetrack, Prince Ts'eng ordered all my eunuchs into the courtyard. He and a Boxer leader named Master Red Sword proceeded to examine their heads. He wanted to see whether any of them had a cross there. 'This cross is not visible to an ordinary eye,' he said to Li Lien-ying. 'Only a certain few can identify a Christian this way.'

Minutes later, Prince Ts'eng came to my chamber with Master Red Sword. Ts'eng told me that Master Red Sword had discovered that two of my eunuchs were Christians. He asked for permission to execute them.

I could not believe this was happening. I sat unmoved as Master Red Sword performed his kowtows. I could tell the man was thrilled and nervous at the same time – an ordinary Chinese peasant could only dream of seeing my face.

'What else have you promised this man?' I said to Prince Ts'eng. 'Are you going to make him the minister of the Board of National Defense?'

Not knowing what to say, Prince Ts'eng rubbed his nose and scratched his head.

'Has this master had any schooling?' I asked.

'I know how to read a calendar, Your Majesty,' the Boxer volunteered.

'So you must know what year it is.'

'Yes, I do.' The Boxer was pleased with his own quick tongue. 'It is the twenty-fifth year, Your Majesty.'

'The twenty-fifth year of what?'

'Of . . . of the Guang-hsu era.'

'Did you hear him, Prince Ts'eng? What era again, Master Red Sword?'

'The Guang-hsu –'

'Louder!'

'The Guang-hsu! Era! Your Majesty!'

I turned to Prince Ts'eng. 'Have I made my point clear to you? Guang-hsu is still the sitting Emperor.'

I told the confused Boxer to remove himself.

Prince Ts'eng looked offended. 'Your Majesty, you don't have to support the Boxers, but I need money to bring you victory.'

'Shut up' almost rolled off of my tongue. I had to inhale a mouthful of air to calm down. 'When I was asked to fund the Taku forts, I was told that it would keep away the foreigners for good. And when I was asked to fund a new navy, I was told the same. Tell me, Ts'eng Junior, how your bamboo spears will defeat the foreigners' guns and cannons?'

'Your Majesty, it will be fifty thousand Boxers against a few hundred foreign bureaucrats. I will select a moonless night and flood the legations with my men. We will be so near that their cannons will be useless.'

'And how will you deal with the foreign rescue forces that will come by sea?'

'We'll take hostages! Legations provide the perfect base for negotiations. The hostages will be our bargaining chip. I'll just have to make sure my men don't behead their captives.' Ts'eng laughed as if he had already won.

Prince Ts'eng insisted that he be given an opportunity to demonstrate his magic and that the Emperor be present. So the following day in my spacious courtyard, before Guang-hsu and me, the Boxers performed. Their martial arts skills were magnificent. They chopped hard stone with their bare hands. In an intense fight of one against ten, Master Red Sword went hand to hand against swordsmen, besting them all. He was then attacked with spears and bullets and scorched by fire, yet he walked away unwounded. His opponents, on the other hand, were all on the ground, stunned and bloodied. Disbelieving my eyes, I tried to figure out his tricks. From beginning to end, Master Red Sword seemed in a drunken trance, which Prince Ts'eng explained was called 'spiritual engagement with the god of war.'

I was impressed, though not convinced. I praised the Boxers for their patriotic passion. A strange feeling came over me when I turned to Guang-hsu and saw his none-of-my-business expression. I thought about Prince Ts'eng: *Terrible as he is, at least he is willing to fight.*

I had failed both my sons, and both my sons had failed China. Every time the Western papers accused Ts'eng of being 'pure evil' while honoring Guang-hsu as the 'wise Emperor,' my old scar would tear open. I envisioned how Guang-hsu would be 'rescued' by the foreign powers and turned into a puppet king. I began to hear my voice turn soft when speaking to characters like Prince Ts'eng.

The next morning, after Prince Ts'eng left, my eunuch appeared dressed in a Boxer's ragged red uniform. When Li Lien-ying presented me with a uniform of my own – a gift from Prince Ts'eng – I slapped his face.

Around noon Guang-hsu and I heard a strange noise like the sound of distant waves. I couldn't locate its source: it was not squirrels clambering in the trees, not wind blowing through the leaves, not the creek running beneath the rocks. I became alarmed and called for Li Lien-ying, but there was no answer. I looked for him around the grounds. Finally my eunuch returned, out of breath. He pointed behind him with his finger and mouthed the word 'Boxers.'

Before I could figure out what was going on, Prince Ts'eng was in front of me.

'How dare you surround my palace with your bloody bunch of killers!' I said.

He performed a sloppy kowtow. 'Everyone wants to personally hear your edict.' Ts'eng acted as if the Emperor were not in the room.

'Who says I am going to issue an edict?'

'It must be done without delay, Your Majesty.' Prince Ts'eng's hands went to tighten his belt. 'The Boxers won't leave until they hear your edict.'

I noticed that Li Lien-ying was now pointing toward the ceiling. When I looked up, I didn't see anything unusual. I looked back down and saw a ladder being carried past my window. A few moments later came the sound of footsteps on my roof.

'The Boxers are getting ready to fire on the legations, Your Majesty,' announced Prince Ts'eng.

'Go and stop them,' I ordered.

'But . . . Your Majesty!'

'Emperor Guang-hsu would like to order Prince Ts'eng Junior to remove the Boxers immediately.' I turned to Guang-hsu, who was staring off into space.

Guang-hsu turned and said, 'Prince Ts'eng Junior is ordered to remove the Boxers immediately.'

Ts'eng's eyebrows twisted into a ginger root and his breath was thick. He went to grab Guang-hsu's shoulders and hissed, 'The attack will take place at dawn, and that *is* your edict!'

41

THE MIGHTY MANCHU had fallen so low that no one dared to defend the throne, and the throne was afraid to ask.

Prince Ts'eng Junior was not shy about speaking his mind. He believed that his young son should become the next Emperor. I could see him appointing the boy himself. What couldn't a man do when he had tens of thousands of Boxers and Moslem troops at his disposal? Ts'eng entirely dropped his pretense of being loyal to me, for he now controlled the palaces' security guards and the Board of Punishment.

Whispering had been going on behind my curtains. Eunuchs made secret trips outside the Forbidden City. They had been gathering information on how to escape. The ladies in waiting and the servants were preparing for the worst: they kept red Boxer clothes under their beds.

Prince Ts'eng had demanded that I order Yung Lu to remove his troops so that he could 'move forward without worrying about being shot in the back.'

I warned Ts'eng that an attack on the foreign legations would mean the end of the dynasty, to which he replied,

'We will die if we fight and we will die if we don't. The foreign powers won't stop until the melon of China is sliced and eaten!'

I had ordered a telegram sent to Li Hung-chang, but during its transmission, the lines were cut. From then on, Peking was isolated from the outside world.

'I am sorry, Mother,' Guang-hsu said when I told him that we had lost control of Prince Ts'eng's Boxers and General Tung's Moslem troops.

Guang-hsu and I sat side by side in the empty audience hall. It was a bright morning in early summer. We stared at the teacups in front of us. I lost track of how many times the eunuchs had come to refill our cups with hot water. I had no idea what to expect of the situation. I only knew that it was getting worse. I felt like a convict in the lonely moments before her execution.

By ten o'clock Prince Ts'eng's message came. The Boxers had moved forward with their knives, bamboo spears, antique swords and muskets. The 'outer ring,' General Tung's twelve thousand 'Moslem Braves,' had entered the capital. They encountered an allied relief force and had been trying to take the 'middle ring' position.

According to Yung Lu, the 'inner ring' comprised Prince Ts'eng's 'Manchu Tigers,' a former Bannerman troop with tiger skins thrown over their shoulders and tigers' heads mounted on their shields.

'Prince Ts'eng's strategy is another Ironhat fantasy,' Yung Lu said. His army had been keeping an eye on General Tung's Moslem troops. Yung Lu's best Chinese commander, General Nieh, was sent to scatter the Boxers.

On June 11, Prince Ts'eng announced his first victory: the capture and killing of a Japanese embassy chancellor, Akira Sugiyama.

I received the news in the afternoon. Sugiyama had been on China's most-wanted list. He was responsible for Kang Yu-wei's and Liang Chi-chao's escape to Japan. Sugiyama had left his legation in Peking to greet the Allies' relief force at the railway station. Before he arrived he was set upon by General Tung's Moslem soldiers, who dragged him from his cart and hacked him to pieces.

The murder escalated the crisis. Although in the throne's name I issued an official apology to Japan and Sugiyama's family, the foreign newspapers believed that I had ordered the murder.

The London *Times* correspondent George Morrison confirmed that the murderer 'was the favorite bodyguard of the Dowager Empress.' A few days later, the *Times* published a follow-up article by Morrison that contained this fanciful fabrication: 'While the crisis was impending, the Dowager Empress was giving a series of theatrical entertainments in the Summer Palace.'

With the help of Li Lien-ying I climbed to the top of the Hill of Prosperity. While looking down over a sea of rooftops, I heard gunshots from the direction of the foreign legations. The legations occupied an area between the wall of the Forbidden City and the wall of inner Peking, a neighborhood of small houses and streets, canals and gardens. I was told that the foreigners in the legations had been building barricades. The exposed outer perimeter and all gates, crossroads and bridges were sandbagged.

Meanwhile, Yung Lu withdrew his divisions from the coast and attempted to insert them between the Boxers and the legations. He let the Boxers know that he wasn't against them, but he issued an order that anyone who violated the legations would be summarily executed.

As Yung Lu withdrew his forces, he worried about the weakened coastal defenses, especially the Taku forts. 'I wish I knew how many foreign troops are headed this way,' he said to me later. 'I fear what they may do in the name of rescuing the diplomats.'

My eunuchs worried about my safety. Since the Boxers had entered Peking, Li Lien-ying had climbed the Hill of Prosperity every day. It was there that he witnessed both the eastern and the southern cathedrals go up in flames. My eunuchs also informed me that the Americans would fire a volley from their roof every fifteen minutes on the off chance of hitting anyone who might be coming down the road. Nearly a hundred Boxers had already been killed. According to the Western press, legation residents had been shooting at any Chinese who wore 'even a scrap of red.'

The Allies' ultimatum was delivered by the British fleet's Admiral Seymour through our governor of Chihli. It read that the Allies were to 'occupy provisionally, by consent or by force, the Taku forts by 2 a.m. on the 17 June.'

What the governor hid from me, out of fear of his removal, was that his defensive line had already collapsed. Only a few days before, he had falsely reported that the Boxers in his province had 'beaten the foreign warships back toward the sea.' By the time I read the ultimatum, two British warships were gliding silently toward the forts under cover of darkness. The Taku forts would be captured in a matter of days.

With Guang-hsu at my side I summoned an emergency audience. I drafted a decree in response to the ultimatum: 'The foreigners have called upon us to deliver up the Taku forts into their keeping, otherwise they will be taken by force. These threats are an example of the Western powers' aggressive disposition in all matters relating to intercourse with China. It is better to do our utmost and enter into the struggle than to seek self-preservation involving eternal disgrace. With tears we announce in our ancestral shrines the outbreak of war.'

Memories of the 1860 Opium War filled me with grief while I read the draft for the court's approval. Painful images flooded back: of past exile, of the death of my husband, of the unfair treaties he was forced to sign, of the destruction of my home Yuan Ming Yuan.

Seeing that I was unable to go on, Guang-hsu took over. 'Ever since the foundation of the dynasty, foreigners coming to China have been kindly treated.' My son's voice was weak but clear. 'But for the past thirty years they have taken advantage of our forbearance to encroach on our territory, trample on the Chinese people and absorb the wealth of the empire. Every concession made only serves to increase their insolence. They oppress our peaceful subjects and insult the gods and sages, inciting fierce indignation among our people. Hence the burning of chapels and the slaughter of converts by the patriotic troops.'

The Emperor stopped. He turned to me and gave back the draft. His eyes filled with sorrow.

I continued. 'The throne has made every effort to avoid war. We have issued edicts enjoining protection of legations and pity toward converts. We declared Boxers and converts to be equally the children of the state. It is the Western powers who forced us into this war.'

The minister of foreign affairs, I-kuang, was sent to give the legations' residents twenty-four-hour notice to leave Peking, under the protection of Yung Lu's troops. The foreign affairs office in Tientsin and Sir Robert Hart's Chinese customs service were ordered to receive the residents and make arrangements to escort them to safety.

But the legations refused to abandon their rightful places in China. The *Times*'s George Morrison told legation residents, 'If you leave Peking tomorrow, the death of every man, woman and child in this huge unprotected convoy will be on your heads. Your names will go down in history and be known forever as the wickedest, weakest and most pusillanimous cowards who have ever lived!'

On June 20, a German minister, Baron von Ketteler, was murdered.

Klemens August von Ketteler was a man of strong views and had a flaming temper, according to those who knew him. Only a few days before his death, he beat a ten-year-old Chinese boy with his lead-weighted walking stick until he was unconscious. The beating took place outside the German legation in full view of witnesses. Ketteler had suspected that the boy was a Boxer. After the beating, the boy was dragged into the legation. By the time the boy's family was informed and went to retrieve him, the boy was dead. The incident infuriated thousands of Chinese, who soon gathered outside the legation looking for revenge.

I never understood why Ketteler chose to set off in his palanquin at that particular moment, knowing the danger. He and his interpreter were heading toward the Board of Foreign Affairs. Ketteler had told his house staff that he had waited long enough for China's response to the ultimatum and intended to check on the progress himself.

A crowd of Boxers spotted Ketteler while he jolted toward the Foreign Affairs building. Within moments Ketteler was shot dead at point-blank range. His interpreter was wounded in both legs but was able to drag himself back to the German legation.

The murder of the German minister marked the beginning of what future historians would call the Siege of the Legations. Amid the mounting violence, the various legations united, and daily their guards fired their rifles, indiscriminately killing innumerable Chinese. Four times the legations' security guards attacked the East Gate of the Forbidden City, but were repulsed by General Tung's troops. Armed legation residents occupied the perimeter walls, which made it harder for Yung Lu's forces to maintain a defensive stance and carry out his mission – to prevent the Boxers from succeeding with the siege.

It was midnight when I woke to the burning of the Imperial front gate. The fire had been set by the Boxers as a result of a confrontation with Yung Lu's troops, which had been blocking the three 'ring' assaults on the legations.

Next, the vast triple-tiered gateway to central Peking blazed in the darkness, engulfing in its flames the richest quarter of Peking. The Boxers had meant to burn only the shops that sold foreign goods, but in that dust-dry season, everything had been consumed.

I ordered the palace kitchen to make mounds of dumplings, for I had a procession of ministers, officials and generals tramping in and out at all hours. Dining etiquette was abandoned. Most of the men hadn't sat down for a meal in days. There was no place for plates – my table was covered with maps, messages, drafts and telegrams.

Now the foreign press, too, went on the attack. The world had begun calling the siege 'the Peking Massacre.' The papers howled, 'The Dowager Empress wanted the barbarians dead. All of them.' So-called anonymous sources had me 'directing the murderers' myself.

'We have been out of touch with the world's reactions since the telegraph wires came down. The repairs are taking too long,' I-kuang complained.

Understanding that the accusations would provide ample excuse to declare war on China, I became extremely nervous. I kept looking at Yung Lu, who sat across from I-kuang.

'How is Emperor Guang-hsu?' I-kuang asked. 'He's been absent from the audiences.'

'Guang-hsu hasn't been feeling well,' I replied.

'Are his wives with him?'

I found the question odd, but decided to answer anyway. 'Empress Lan and the concubines visit His Majesty daily, although my son prefers to be alone.'

I-kuang gave me a quizzical look.

'Is there something wrong?' I asked.

'No, but the foreigners have been inquiring after the throne's health. Apparently my answers are no longer satisfactory to them. They suspect that His Majesty has been tortured and left to die.' I-kuang paused, then added, 'The rumor has appeared in papers around the world.'

'Go and see with your own eyes!' I became enraged. 'Pay His Majesty a visit at Ying-t'ai!'

'The foreign journalists have requested face-to-face interviews . . .'

'We will not allow foreign journalists inside the Forbidden City,' Yung Lu put in. 'They will pick the bones out of an egg no matter what we do.'

'It's getting personal,' I-kuang said, handing me a copy of the London *Daily Mail*.

'The legations stood together as the sun rose fully,' one 'eyewitness' told a reporter. 'The little remaining band, all

Europeans, met death stubbornly, and finally, overcome by overwhelming odds, every one of the Europeans remaining was put to the sword in the most atrocious manner.'

Later, the London *Times* would publish a special report on a memorial service held at St. Paul's Cathedral for the British legation's 'victims.' Pages of death notices would be printed. Sir Claude MacDonald – the husband of Lady MacDonald – Sir Robert Hart and the *Times*'s own devoted correspondent George Morrison all lived to read their own obituaries.

On June 23, General Tung's troops surrounded the three-acre compound of the British legation. His Moslem force tried to break through the north wall, where stood China's elite Hanlin Academy. When all other efforts failed, Tung ordered his soldiers to toss lighted firebrands into the academy, intending to smoke the foreigners out. A strong wind whipped up the flames, which consumed the oldest library in the world.

Yung Lu watched the Boxers hurl themselves futilely against the legation barricades. No one was aware that Yung Lu, at the age of sixty-five, had fallen ill. He had been hiding his condition from me, and I was too preoccupied to notice. I treated him as if he were made of iron. I did not know that he had only three more years to live.

Convinced that a massacre at the legations would bring retribution from the Western powers, Yung Lu refused General Tung's demand for more powerful weapons. Yung Lu controlled the only battery of heavy artillery.

I wondered how Western journalists and their 'eyewitnesses' could miss the fact that since the siege began, fewer assaults were made from those sectors held by Yung Lu's troops. It was a known fact that not long before, China had purchased advanced weapons through its diplomatic connections – Robert Hart among others. If those weapons had been used against the legations, their so-called defense, which involved around a hundred men, would have been reduced to rubble within hours.

On behalf of the Emperor of China, I-kuang held a conference to declare a cease-fire. To the throne's shame, it meant nothing to the legations or the Boxers. The fighting continued.

General Tung and his Moslem troops changed their strategy: they moved to cut off the legations' supply line. From the Chinese servants who had run away from the legations, we learned that all were short of water and food. The shortage grew critical as the fighting intensified. And besides the wounded, the legations had their share of sick women and children.

Yung Lu asked for permission to send the legations supplies of water, medicine, food, and other supplies. It was difficult to give my assent, for I knew I would be committing an act of betrayal. The number of casualties among the Boxers and our own troops far exceeded that of the foreigners. Revenge had been the only thought on my people's minds.

'Do what is necessary,' I said to Yung Lu. 'I don't want to know the details. In the meantime, I want my people to hear the sound of your cannons firing at the legations.'

Yung Lu understood. By late evening his cannon fire lit up the sky like New Year's fireworks. The shells flew over the roofs and exploded in the back gardens of the legations. While the citizens of Peking cheered my action, Yung Lu's relief squad pushed their cartloads of supplies through the no man's land and into the legation compounds.

Yet my gesture of good faith didn't work. Our requests for the foreigners to vacate the legations were repeatedly ignored.

The foreigners knew that help had arrived – an international relief force had broken through China's last line of defense at the Taku forts.

My messengers described the colossal dust clouds wafting up around the mouth of the Taku River. The latest news was that the governor of Chihli had committed suicide. (To add to my stunned surprise, on August 11 his replacement also committed suicide.)

I lit several candles and sat down before them, my mind clogged with dead thoughts.

'I have retreated from Ma'to to Chanchiawan,' the governor's last report read. 'I have seen tens of thousands of troops jamming all the roads. The Boxers fled. As they passed the villages and towns, they plundered, so much so that there was nothing for the armies under my command to purchase, with the result that men and horses were hungry and exhausted. From youth to old age I have experienced many wars, but never saw things like these . . . I am doing my best to collect the fleeing troops and I shall fight to my last breath . . .'

In a memorandum Yung Lu included a desperate message from Li Hung-chang. It suggested that I send a telegram to the English Queen to 'petition that as two old women we should understand each other's difficulties.' He also suggested that I send a plea to Tsar Nicholas of Russia and the Emperor of Japan 'for help in settling the crisis peacefully.'

I had to give myself credit for having the nerve to follow Li's advice. I outlined the necessity for each country to remain on good terms with China. To Britain the reason was trade; to Japan it was the 'Eastern alliance against the West'; to Russia it was 'the ancient border dependency and friendship of the two countries.'

What a fool I made of myself.

42

A T DAWN ON AUGUST 14, 1900, the cat-like cries I heard
turned out to be the sound of bullets flying. Fourteen
thousand troops, including British, French, Japanese, Russian, German, Italian, Dutch, Austrian, Hungarian, Belgian
and American, had invaded. They arrived in Peking by the
Tientsin train. General Nieh, who had been sent by Yung
Lu to guard the railway from the Boxers, was killed by the
Allies.

I was dressing my hair when the cat cries came. I
wondered how there could be so many cats. Then something hit the tip of my wing-shaped roof and broken
ornaments crashed into my yard. Moments later a bullet
flew through my window. It hit the floor, bounced and
rolled. I went to examine it.

Li Lien-ying rushed in, visibly shaken. 'The foreign
soldiers have entered, my lady!'

How is this possible? I thought. *Li Hung-chang has
supposedly begun negotiations with the Western powers.*

It wasn't until my son came with his wife and concubines
that I realized it was the Opium War all over again.

After I had dressed, I went to see Guang-hsu. He looked
frightened. With frantic haste he pulled the pearls off his

robe and threw away his red-tasseled hat. Although he had changed from his golden robe into a blue one, the embroidered dragon symbols would make him recognizable. I asked Li Lien-ying to quickly find the Emperor a servant's clothes. Lan, Pearl and Lustrous helped their husband into a long, plain gray coat.

The sound of bullets over our heads grew louder. I opened my drawers, wardrobes and closets trying to decide what to take and what to leave. I picked out dresses and coats, only to be told by Li Lien-ying that my travel cases were full. It was difficult to part with the carved wooden maiden-case left to me by my mother and Tung Chih's calligraphy practice book.

Holding my jewelry box, Li Lien-ying directed the work of the eunuchs, who packed whatever they could into carts.

I took off my jewelry and my jade nail protectors and ordered Li Lien-ying to cut off my long nails.

When I ordered him to cut my knee-length hair, he wept along with my daughters-in-law.

After my shortened hair was tied in a bun, he helped me into a peasant's dark blue tunic. I put on a pair of worn shoes.

Following my example, Lan and Lustrous removed their jewelry, cut their hair and changed into servants' clothes, but Pearl refused. She turned to Guang-hsu and whispered in his ear. My son shook his head and remained silent. Pearl pressed. He shook his head again. Pearl was upset.

'Why don't you talk to the Emperor after we get out of the city?' I said to Pearl.

As if she didn't hear me, Pearl continued to press Guang-hsu for a response.

Guang-hsu hesitated. He glanced around, avoiding my eyes.

366

A messenger sent by Yung Lu advised us to depart immediately. As I walked toward the gate, Pearl pulled Guang-hsu aside. They began to walk back to the Forbidden City.

Li Lien-ying rushed in. 'The carriages we ordered are blocked by the Allies! What are we going to do, my lady?'

'We will have to walk,' I replied.

'The throne is not leaving.' Pearl Concubine threw herself on the ground in front of me. With my son standing silently behind her, Pearl let me know then and there that she and Guang-hsu were saying goodbye. Pearl, in a vermilion satin robe with a matching scarf around her neck, was stunningly beautiful, like an autumn maple tree. When she raised her chin, I saw determination in her eyes.

Li Lien-ying begged me to hurry. 'Men are dying trying to defend your exit route, my lady. Bullets are flying and there have been fires and explosions outside the city.'

'You may stay, but my son must come,' I said to Pearl.

'His Majesty the Emperor will stay,' the girl challenged.

Li Lien-ying got between Pearl and me. 'Lady Pearl, we either leave now or never! Yung Lu's men are ready to escort the throne!'

'Pearl, this is not the time,' I said, raising my voice.

'But the throne has made up his mind,' Pearl insisted.

'Get your concubine moving,' I told Guang-hsu.

Loud enough for everyone to hear, Pearl yelled, 'Fleeing is humiliating and it will imperil the empire!'

'Control yourself, Pearl,' I said.

'Emperor Guang-hsu has the right to defend the honor of the dynasty!'

'The Emperor can talk for himself!' I replied angrily.

'His Majesty is too frightened of his mother to speak his mind.'

I asked Pearl to stop embarrassing herself. 'I understand that the pressure is almost too much to bear. I promise to listen once we get out of the city and reach safer ground.'

'No!' Pearl shouted. 'Emperor Guang-hsu and I would like to request our release.'

'Pearl Concubine! What are you –'

Before I could finish, a shell exploded in the middle of the courtyard. The earth shook. Both wings of my palace roof collapsed.

Amid clouds of dust, eunuchs and ladies in waiting screamed and ran to hide.

Pearl and I stood face to face in the center of the courtyard, engulfed in dust. Guang-hsu stood a few yards away, distraught and steeped in guilt. I realized what Pearl was up to: she believed that the Western powers had come to rescue Guang-hsu. To Pearl, my departure meant Guang-hsu's restoration to power.

Under any other circumstances, I would have considered Pearl's request. I might even have admired her daring. But at this moment all I could see was Pearl's lack of perspective and consideration for my own and my son's safety.

In a way I felt sorry for Pearl, for she trusted in a strength of character Guang-hsu didn't possess. She saw who he might become instead of who he was.

'Take her with us,' I instructed Li Lien-ying.

Several eunuchs began to tie Pearl up. She struggled, calling Guang-hsu for help.

He just looked on in despair.

'Guang-hsu,' Pearl yelled, 'you are the ruler of China, not your mother! The Western powers have promised to treat you with respect. Stand up for yourself!'

Li Lien-ying emptied a cart and the eunuchs hoisted Pearl into it like a sack of rice.

I ordered my son to get into his palanquin, and he obeyed.

Again we began to leave.

Smoke filled the air. The kitchen woks and lids clanged loudly as the bearers walked quickly toward the gate.

The eunuchs pushed the carts while the ladies in waiting walked alongside, carrying my belongings in baskets and cotton bags.

We didn't get far. Before we reached my own gate, Pearl broke free of the cart and ran toward Guang-hsu's palanquin. She pulled down his curtain and hit her head on the side of his palanquin, knocking down one of the bearers.

I stopped my palanquin and yelled her name. I made it clear that she was not going to stay behind.

The girl kissed Guang-hsu's feet, and then in a sudden motion she sprang back toward the Forbidden City.

Li Lien-ying took off after her.

'Leave her alone!' I called.

'My lady, Pearl is running toward the East Gate, where the foreign troops are.'

'Let her,' I said.

'She could be raped by the foreign soldiers!'

'It is her choice.'

'My lady, Lady Pearl might also mean to jump into the well.'

Against all reason, I ordered our palanquins to turn around. We went after Pearl, back into the city, heading toward the well. We were not fast enough. In front of my eyes, Pearl leapt. But the well opening was too small. Pearl struggled, using her own weight to pull herself down.

'Guang-hsu!' I screamed.

Hiding inside his palanquin, my son made no response. He didn't know what was going on, or didn't want to know.

Using a knife, Li Lien-ying cut loose the longest bamboo stick of my palanquin. With the help of the other eunuchs, the stick was lowered down the well.

Li Lien-ying threw in a rope.

But Pearl was determined to have her way.

Li Lien-ying cursed and threatened. Eunuchs lit fireballs and threw them into the well, trying to smoke the girl out.

'Leave her to her wishes!' Emperor Guang-hsu cried out from his palanquin.

With Pearl's suicide on everyone's mind, we began our seven-hundred-mile journey northwestward and along the Great Wall. We pushed our carts and walked. Guang-hsu sobbed and refused my comfort.

I wondered what would have happened if I had allowed Pearl to have her way. It wouldn't do, I concluded. Once the powers succeeded in 'rescuing' Guang-hsu and taking him hostage, we would lose ground in any negotiation. I would be forced to give up everything in exchange for my life, or my son would be forced to order my execution.

'I wouldn't survive either way,' Guang-hsu would tell me later.

Nonetheless, my thoughts returned to Pearl as I played out what I might have said to her. She and I had shared the same fantasy, that my son and her husband had within him the power to transform himself. I had labored on that transformation since the day I adopted him. I credited myself for exposing Guang-hsu to Western ideas, and his fascination with Western culture had been my pride. But it hadn't been enough, I would have said.

I would have also let Pearl know that there are truths a mother knows about her child that she can never share with anyone else. The fact that I had been proud of Guang-hsu didn't mean that I didn't know his limitations. I had challenged his potential with all my might. Submitting myself entirely to his call for reform was a personal decision I had made. I had thrown the dice, prepared to lose everything, and I had.

Believing that my son could outmaneuver a man like Ito Hirobumi had been my weakness. Allowing Guang-hsu to appoint Kang Yu-wei as his chief minister was also a mistake on my part. I had known that Kang was not the man he pretended to be, but I'd said yes to please my son.

I had been devastated by my son's suffering. He couldn't accept his own failure, which I considered more mine than his. If I had been murdered on my own son's order, I would have considered it my fate, for I knew how much he loved me.

The most important thing I might have said to Pearl, however, was that my son, her husband, had been up against forces beyond his control: the weight of tradition, the blindness and selfishness of power, history itself. China's great wealth and the glories of its civilization had made it complacent and unfamiliar with change. Resource-poor Japan had been forced to expand, move forward, modernize; the Japanese Emperor had merely led the way for a willing people. China had been surpassed and needed to change, but no Emperor alone could move a nation that was only just wakening to the need for change. No *man* alone – attempts at such change had already claimed the lives of so many: my husband, my son, Prince Kung, others, and I feared that number would soon include another son.

For the next few weeks we traveled day and night. If we were lucky enough to reach a town by evening, I would get to sleep on a bed. Most days we settled on camping in the fields and forests, where insects crawled all over me.

Although Li Lien-ying made sure that I was covered from head to toe, I was bitten on the neck and face. One bite became so swollen that I looked as if I had an egg growing from my chin.

I had summoned Li Hung-chang to begin negotiating with the foreigners, but was told that he hadn't yet left Canton.

There were two reasons Li Hung-chang had been dragging his feet, Yung Lu believed. 'First, he considers the negotiation an impossible task. Second, he doesn't want to work with I-kuang.'

I understood his reluctance. I had selected I-kuang because the Manchu Clan Council had insisted on having one of their own to 'lead' Li.

'I-kuang is ineffective and corrupt,' Yung Lu said. 'When I questioned him, he complained about Li's overbearing ways and blamed others for "forcing gifts" on him.'

Yung Lu and I were frustrated because all we could do was discuss our misfortune. I told him that Queen Min had visited me in a dream. It began with her rising from a pyre two stories high. 'Then she sat by my bed in her burned clothing. She told me how to survive the flames. She didn't seem to realize that she was half flesh and half skeleton. I couldn't understand a word she said because she had no lips.'

Yung Lu promised that he would stay near.

Days later, Yung Lu found out the real reason Li Hung-chang had been slow in coming. 'The Allies have a list of the people they believe are responsible for the destruction of the legations. They are demanding arrests and punishment before negotiations begin.'

'Did Li Hung-chang know about the list?' I asked.

'Yes. In fact he has it, but is afraid to present it to you himself. Here is a copy.'

I put on my glasses to read it. Though hardly unexpected, I was still shocked: my name was first on the list.

Yung Lu believed that Li Hung-chang was also reluctant to come to the aid of Guang-hsu yet again. The Emperor had repeatedly been the cause of Li's forced departures, which had resulted in great political and financial losses for Li. His rivals and enemies, mostly the Manchu princes, had gradually taken over his major industrial holdings, including the China Merchants Steam Navigation Company, the Imperial Telegraph Administration and the Kaiping mines.

After ignoring several of my summonses, which promised to restore his original post and business properties, Li moved to Shanghai for several weeks, claiming age and illness for slowing him down. Yung Lu hurried him along by saying that an edict of punishment had been drafted listing the names the foreigners had requested.

After many more summonses demanding his presence, Li Hung-chang arrived in Tientsin on September 19. 'Until the publication of the edict, there is little I can do,' his message to Yung Lu read.

Strangely, at this point the prospect of my own death didn't sound so threatening to me. The idea presented itself more as a negotiation point.

'Do you think Li Hung-chang really expects me to turn myself over to the Allies?' I asked Yung Lu.

'Of course not. What would Li be without you?'

'What does he want, then?'

'He is using this moment to make sure that you don't give in to his enemies, especially to Prince Ts'eng Junior and General Tung.'

*   *   *

373

Strong northern winds blew through the grasslands, making our palanquins look like little boats floating on green waves. The Boxers had ruined the planting season, and we couldn't get any help because the farmers had fled.

We kept pushing north and inland, pursued by the foreigners. We had been trudging on rutted dirt roads for over a month. My mirror broke and I could only guess how I looked. Guang-hsu was covered with dust and he no longer bothered to wash his face. His skin was sallow and dry. Our hair smelled rank and our scalps itched. My clothes were infested with lice and other bugs. One morning I opened my vest and saw hundreds of sesame-seed-sized eggs in the lining. The tiny eggs seemed glued to the vest, so Li Lien-ying burned it. I no longer cared how my hair looked. I soaked my head in salt water and vinegar, but the lice returned. When I got up in the morning I would see them fall onto my straw mat. We had been sleeping where we could, one night in an abandoned temple, another in a roofless hut on brick beds.

Guang-hsu was disgusted when he saw Li Lien-ying combing the flaky lice eggs out of my hair. The Emperor shaved his head and wore a wig during our makeshift audiences. It was hard for us to keep our composure when receiving ministers – the urge to scratch was overwhelming. I had to smile. I saw the absurdity in all this; Guang-hsu did not.

The rainy season brought its storms. Our palanquins leaked and Guang-hsu and I soon became soaking wet. The journey recalled my first exile, to Jehol with Emperor Hsien Feng. I did not want to think of the future.

On September 25, the throne's first edict of punishment would be published. I already suffered from remorse. Prince Ts'eng and General Tung had both come to let me know that they understood the reasons for what I must do. I was to turn them over to the Allies, a condition for releasing me from responsibility.

'I cannot order their beheadings,' I said to Yung Lu. 'Prince Ts'eng is a blood relation, and General Tung's troops are all that is protecting my court-on-legs.' I sighed. 'What happened to Queen Min will sooner or later happen to me.'

'Li Hung-chang is getting what he wanted and will find a way to save you,' Yung Lu said.

One morning, my eunuch found a duck egg in the cupboard of an abandoned house. Guang-hsu and I were thrilled. Li Lien-ying boiled the egg, and Guang-hsu and I cracked the shell carefully and ate the egg bit by bit, scraping the shell clean.

We had been short of food and had been surviving on small portions of millet porridge. It made us hungrier. With the egg we celebrated Li Hung-chang's long-awaited arrival in Peking; he had been in Tientsin for three weeks. I made sure he knew about all the vermin I had encountered.

Finally the negotiations opened. Our friend Robert Hart served as a go-between. Li Hung-chang made significant progress by convincing the foreign powers that 'there is more than one way to slice a melon,' and that deposing me and my government would not only prevent the foreigners from extracting the most benefits from China, but would also foment unrest, leading to more uprisings.

The foreign powers wanted to partition China, but Li made them recognize that China was simply too vast, its population too large and homogeneous for partition to work, and that attempting to install a republican government would be fraught with too many unknowns.

Guang-hsu was appreciative of Li Hung-chang's effort. When he began to call Li by his former title of Viceroy of Chihli, I wept, because nothing was more comforting than Guang-hsu's merciful gesture toward one of the 'old boys.' After all, the Western powers and their military forces were on our soil, and he could have called on them to help him declare his independence.

43

A s my husband's court had done forty years before, we were heading toward the safety of the Manchu homeland. After being on the run for more than six months, we arrived at the ancient capital of Sian. The initial plan had been to cross the Great Wall, but we were forced to alter the route when Russia invaded from the north and began their annexation of Manchuria. We turned southwest, where we hoped a range of mountains would shield us.

I have few memories of the landscape we passed through or of the beauty of the ancient capital. I was consumed by small but annoying troubles. The palanquins were not made for long-distance travel. Mine started breaking down almost from the beginning. Besides fixing the leaky roof, Li Lien-ying had to make other repairs constantly. The moment he heard a squeak, he knew where the problem lay. Since he had no tools or spare supplies, he had to make do with whatever he could find along the roadside – a piece of bamboo, a length of frayed rope, a rock to hammer a new piece in place.

When my palanquin eventually fell apart, the bearers carried me in a sedan chair. That didn't last either: I had to walk until the chair was fixed. And our shoes wore out faster than we could replace them. Of course there was nowhere to buy new ones. By the end of the journey most of us were walking barefoot. We got blisters on our feet, which sometimes led to infections – a few of the bearers died as a result.

Guang-hsu and I took turns riding a pitiful-looking donkey. There were days when Li Lien-ying could find nothing to feed the animal, and it kept collapsing.

Drinking water became another problem. After a five-hundred-mile journey, we reached the provincial capital of Taiyuan. The wells in the nearby villages had been poisoned by the Boxers, who had made sure to 'leave the barbarians nothing but a wasteland.'

The Emperor and I developed fever blisters, and we had run out of medicines. It was silly to hear the doctors advise a balanced diet when we could barely find food. We got used to not having tables or chairs; we ate while squatting on our heels and were no longer bothered by lice.

When fall set in, the air became frigid at night. Both Guang-hsu and I had caught the hundred-day cough and lost our voices. We were always fed something, but many went without. The Emperor helped to bury some of his most favored eunuchs. For the first time my son developed a sense of compassion for those beneath him. The rough travel had shocked and educated him. Although he had been in poor physical condition, his mental state improved. He took notes on what he saw on the road and kept busy writing in a journal.

Li Lien-ying became frantic because we had run out of food and water. It was the Shantung governor, Yuan Shih-kai, who came just in time with desperately needed supplies. My son spoke to the man whom he had been calling a traitor since his reform failed. Although he would never forgive Yuan Shih-kai for betraying him, Guang-hsu expressed gratitude. We ate delicious lotus-seed soup and chicken-scallion pancakes until we were so full we had to lie on our backs just to breathe.

On October 1, we left Taiyuan for Tung-kuan. Turning due west for the final seventy miles, we marched through Shanhsi province to arrive at Sian, the Moslem state still controlled by General Tung's loyalists. While the court believed that we could hold out indefinitely, the Emperor and I became suspicious of the Imperial Guards – men who recognized no authority but General Tung's.

My jade comb was missing. Li Lien-ying, who carried the comb, believed that it had been stolen while he slept. He cursed and vowed to catch the thief. I told him I wouldn't mind borrowing another's comb, but Li Lien-ying refused: 'I don't want you to end up picking someone else's lice eggs.'

When we reached Tung-kuan I received a telegram from Li Hung-chang reporting that the negotiations had come to a halt. 'The Allies demand we show evidence of punishment,' Li wrote.

I was expected to hand over General Tung and Prince Ts'eng. I had never felt so manipulated. No matter how I justified it, I would be betraying my own people.

It wasn't until the arrival of Yung Lu that General Tung complied with the throne's instructions to reduce his troop strength by five thousand. He withdrew to the distance the Allies had requested, outside of Peking, which meant our further vulnerability.

Li Hung-chang sent me a transcript of his day's negotiations as a reply to my complaints regarding the foreigners' demands:

ALLIES: Do not such people as Prince Ts'eng and his Ironhats deserve death?

LI: They did not accomplish their purpose.

ALLIES: Sixty people were killed and one hundred sixty wounded in the legations.

LI: The number of deaths of Ironhats, Boxers and civilians of China were in the thousands.

ALLIES: What would you think if the Prince of Wales and cousins of the Queen had headed an attack on the Chinese minister in London?

LI: The Ironhats were foolish people.

Under pressure from Li Hung-chang, on November 13 I issued an edict announcing punishments. Prince Ts'eng Junior and his brothers were to be imprisoned for life at Mukden, near Manchuria. His cousins were to be either placed under house arrest or degraded in rank and would lose all of their privileges. The punishment of the former governor of Shantung was waived because he had died. Other governors who had failed to protect the foreign missionaries were to be banished for life, exiled to the remote frontier in Turkistan and condemned to hard labor. Master Red Sword and two other ringleaders, who were distant royal relatives, were to be executed.

The Allies considered the punishments inadequate. They called what had happened 'unprecedented in human history, crimes against the laws of nations, against the laws of humanity, and against civilization.'

I had no other choice but to issue another decree assigning stiffer sentences. I failed to please the Allies again, for my words were believed to be worthless – and I would surely find a way to help the criminals evade punishment.

In order to prove myself, I invited the foreign press to witness a public execution, to be held at the vegetable market on Greengrocer Street in central Peking.

The locals suffered tremendous humiliation when the tall, high-nosed, blond-haired foreigners showed up with their flashing cameras.

'It is impossible to know what large fee was paid to the executioner,' George Morrison of the *Times* wrote of the event. 'Two mats were laid down. There was a great crowd, a multitude of correspondents, and photographs by the score were taken. Rarely has an execution been seen by so many nationalities . . . One slice in each case was sufficient.'

The journalists cheered when the heads rolled.

I was deeply ashamed.

At the Allies' request, I ordered the execution of ten additional Boxer ringleaders. Except for the two beheadings carried out in public, the rest I granted an honorable suicide.

Family members came begging for the lives of their loved ones. 'Your Majesty supported the Boxers,' they cried, gathering outside my palace. Their petitions were written in blood.

I hid behind my gate, peering out like a coward. I sent Li Lien-ying to offer the wives and children a few taels for the winter. It was impossible to forgive myself.

Li Hung-chang argued back and forth with the Allies over the life of General Tung. They yielded only after an understanding was reached that the general could be useful in ensuring stability in northwestern China. Tung was deprived of his rank, but he would be allowed to remain the warlord of Kansu if he departed the capital immediately and permanently.

Yung Lu carved out a portion of his army expenses and delivered the taels to General Tung. It would keep him from calling for a rebellion.

Emperor Guang-hsu and I received the Twelve Articles, as they were called, from the allied nations regarding the final terms. Members of the Clan Council and the court telegraphed Li Hung-chang requesting substantial changes. Li replied that he could do no more. 'The attitude of the foreign powers is stern, and the contents are not open to discussion,' he said. 'The Allies have been threatening to break off negotiations and move their troops forward.'

In the spring of 1901, the Emperor and I gave permission for Li Hung-chang to accept the terms. There were no words to describe my shame and pain. At the same time, I learned that Li had been gravely ill, so ill that he had to be helped by servants to the negotiating table. Li did not reveal until then what would have upset me the most: that the Allies had originally required that I step down as the head of the government and restore the rule of Emperor Guang-hsu; that all of China's revenues be collected by foreign ministers; and that Chinese military affairs be overseen by foreigners.

'What I have achieved is hardly any bargain,' Li's memorandum read. 'The reason I pushed the signing was because I'm afraid that my time is running out. It would be regrettable if I died before completing the mission that Your Majesty had entrusted me with.'

On September 7, 1901, after bringing China to its knees, the Allies signed the peace agreement. I would suffer eternal torment, for China was forced to apologize to Germany and

Japan, which meant enormous indemnities and surrendering natural resources. China was ordered to destroy its own defensive facilities and had to accept a permanent foreign military presence in Peking.

44

O N THE MORNING of October 6, the Allies began to withdraw from Peking and I was able to depart Sian for home. Our procession would travel seven hundred miles on the return journey. After nearly a year of exile, every effort was made to regain face. There would be no sleeping rough this time. Guang-hsu and I each rode in our own covered carriages decorated with flags and banners. We were surrounded by cavalrymen in brilliant silk. Provincial governors were notified of our passing and made sure that every inch of road was cleared of stones. In a ceremony to chase away bad spirits, eunuchs walked ahead and swept the roads and sprinkled yellow chalk to invite favorable spirits. Wherever we stopped for a rest or for the night, banquets were held. The court toasted its luck in surviving the deadly ordeal.

Yet I couldn't help but feel bitter.

China had been given a good kicking, and the burden of huge debts would keep us on our knees indefinitely. But according to Li Hung-chang, it wasn't the mercy of the Western powers that had mitigated their demands. What stayed their hand was the idea that China would someday be a vast economic market. Their business sense told them not to plant the seed of hatred in the hearts of the Chinese people – their future customers – or to destroy China's ability to buy foreign goods. My government was merely a useful tool, especially when the foreign powers considered the likelihood that Guang-hsu would be restored as a puppet emperor.

Guang-hsu had never said that he wanted to step down, but his actions spoke of his wishes. He was a prisoner inside his own palanquin. My sense was that he felt so trapped he didn't bother to look for a way out.

I tried talking to him about starting the process of changing our government into a republic. I began with 'As you can see, our efforts have made little difference.'

Guang-hsu's response was 'It's all up to you, Mother.'

'But I'd like to know what you think,' I insisted.

'I don't know what I think,' he said. 'The biggest thing I've learned by being the Emperor of China is that I don't know anything.'

It's easy to play dead – I had to force the words back down my throat.

'Becoming a republic will make you more powerful than you are now.' I took a breath and went on. 'The empire of Japan thrived, and so can China.'

My son gave me a tired look and sighed.

Going back and forth from the capital, Yung Lu was eager to discuss the candidate who would run the proposed parliament.

'I am not considering others when Li Hung-chang and you are holding up the sky,' I said to him. 'Isn't your new title Prime Minister of China?'

'Yes, for the moment. But I'd like to remind Your Majesty that Li Hung-chang and I are in our seventies and in ill health.'

'All three of us are in that boat, I'm afraid.'

We smiled at each other, and I asked whom he had in mind.

'Yuan Shih-kai,' Yung Lu said. 'Li Hung-chang and I have gone over the choices and it boils down to him.'

Of course I was familiar with Yuan Shih-kai, who had recently come to my aid on our retreat into exile. He had built his name in the southwest during the Sino-French War. After returning from Indochina, he was appointed by Li to take over the Northern Army as its youngest commander in chief. Yuan was known for his no-nonsense training style. A few years later, when Yung Lu combined his forces with the Northern Army and created the New Army, Yuan was appointed as its commander in chief.

Yuan Shih-kai had proved his loyalty by saving my life during the chaos of the Hundred Days reform. He was promoted to the post of senior governor and oversaw key provinces while keeping his military role. Working closely with Li Hung-chang and Yung Lu, Yuan had learned from the masters.

A recent event had also made Yuan Shih-kai a household name in China. According to the terms of the treaty agreement, China was not allowed a military presence in the greater Peking area. Humiliation aside, the stipulation made those who supposedly held the reins of power feel at once vulnerable and vaguely ridiculous.

Yuan studied the treaty and international law and came up with the idea of establishing a Chinese police force. 'There is nothing in the agreement that says China can't have its own law enforcement,' he stated in his proposal.

Within weeks of my granting permission, Yuan Shih-kai dressed his army as policemen – they looked like British bobbies. In their smart uniforms his men patrolled the coasts and marched around the legations in Peking. The mean-spirited foreign journalists couldn't say a word about it.

Because of Yuan Shih-kai, I could now sleep.

When the homecoming procession arrived at a town near Tientsin, I boarded a train, still a novelty for me. The locomotive pulled twenty-one shining carriages, which had been presented to the nation by Yuan Shih-kai. 'Moving rooms,' Li Lien-ying called them. My carriage had silk-draped walls, soft-cushioned sofas and a built-in porcelain basin with hot and cold water taps. The car even had its own toilet.

Although Guang-hsu did not give his opinion regarding Yuan Shih-kai's leadership of the parliament, he understood that we were not choosing him because he was a personal friend. Yuan's passion for China's prosperity was what mattered. Already we had been relying on him to execute our edicts.

I witnessed my son's struggle with himself – logic battling his feelings. Often Guang-hsu's dark moods would return. 'I'd rather die than support that traitor,' he would say. He would break dishes and kick his chair.

'It is a matter of making use of a talent,' I said to him. 'You can replace him if you find a better person.'

When I learned that Yung Lu had fainted on his way to join us in Tientsin, I sent a message wishing him renewed health and requesting that he come as soon as he was able. The moment Yung Lu entered my private car, accompanied by his doctor, he smiled and said, 'I got kicked out by the god of death!' He tried to sound as if he had never been sick. 'Maybe it was because I hadn't eaten and Hell wouldn't accept a hungry ghost.'

'Don't you dare abandon me.' I could not hold back my tears.

'Well, I wasn't notified when my body decided to quit.'

'How are you feeling?'

'I am fine. But my chest whistles like a wind harp.'

'It's your lungs.'

He nodded. 'In any case, it makes the issue of my replacement urgent. You need both Li Hung-chang's and my help to persuade the court to accept Yuan Shih-kai.'

'But Guang-hsu hates him.'

Yung Lu sighed. 'Yes, I know.'

'And Li Hung-chang hasn't sent in Yuan's confirmation,' I said. 'Has he any reservations?'

'Li is concerned about Yuan's loyalty after I'm gone. He believes that Yuan Shih-kai is not likely to serve a lesser mind.'

'Guang-hsu? How dare he!'

'Well, perhaps not a lesser mind but a less-driven mind. The Emperor doesn't inspire, and he doesn't care.'

I could not disagree. 'It's my misfortune.' I sighed. 'But he is my son.'

'How can Guang-hsu expect Yuan's loyalty?' Yung Lu asked. 'Yuan Shih-kai has our vote because of what he can do for China. But once you are gone, Yuan could stop considering China your son's China.'

'Is this Li Hung-chang's fear as well?'

Yung Lu nodded.

'What should I do?'

'It's up to Guang-hsu to let Yuan Shih-kai know who the Emperor is.'

The moment my train pulled into Peking's Paoting Station I was given the news that Li Hung-chang had died.

The band that greeted the train was in the middle of playing a gay tune when the messenger fell at my feet. I had to make the man repeat what he had said three times. My mind went blank as I struggled to hold my composure.

'Li Hung-chang is not dead!' I kept saying. 'He can't die!'

Li Lien-ying held my arms to keep me from collapsing. The Manchu Dynasty as I knew it had ended.

'Yuan Shih-kai is here to see Her Majesty,' someone announced.

Yuan appeared in front of me in a white mourning gown. He confirmed the news. 'The viceroy had been sick,' he said in a confident tone. 'He forced himself to go on until the negotiations were completed.'

'Why wasn't I informed earlier that his condition was critical?' I asked.

'The viceroy didn't want you to know. He said you would stop him from working if you were told.'

Sitting on my makeshift throne, I asked if the Emperor had been notified and if Li Hung-chang had left any requests for me. Yuan Shih-kai replied that the viceroy had made several arrangements before his death, including that S. S. Huan take over the funding of the military.

I had no memory of when Yuan Shih-kai left. Yung Lu came in and said that he was delivering his friend Li Hung-chang's last wishes. It was his final confirmation of Yuan Shih-kai as his successor.

It seemed that besides me, only the Western powers had realized that Li Hung-chang had been the true boss of China. Li had been the one who protected and provided for the Manchu Dynasty, and his loyalty had sustained me.

I didn't have to use my imagination to know that the arduous negotiations had killed Li Hung-chang. He had fought for inches and pennies for China. It was too easy to accuse him of being a traitor. He had endured degradation and humiliation. The transcripts of the daily negotiations demonstrated his courage. Perhaps only future generations would recognize and appreciate his true value. Li Hung-chang went into the negotiations knowing that he had nothing to bargain with and that suffering would be part of any deal.

'My country is being raped' was his first response after being presented with drafts of the treaties drawn up by the foreign powers. 'When a sheep is cornered by a pack of wolves, will the wolves allow the sheep to negotiate? Will the sheep help decide how she should be eaten?'

Li Hung-chang was a master of business, and his skillful bargaining had saved his country but cost him his life. 'Carving up China means creating a nation of new Boxers,' he pointed out to the foreigners when they threatened to abandon negotiations. 'Calling on Her Majesty to step down makes for a bad business deal because everyone in China will tell you that it is the Dowager Empress, not the Emperor, who will see your loans paid.'

Li volunteered for the role of scapegoat so that the Emperor and I could save face.

I was sure that Li had regrets. He had given me so much, yet all I offered in return was disappointment after disappointment. It was amazing that he didn't overthrow Guang-hsu's regime. He would not have needed an army. He knew my vulnerability all along. His integrity and humanity humbled me. He was the best gift Heaven ever bestowed on the Ch'ing Dynasty.

45

THE WELCOMING BANNERS on the Forbidden City walls hid the damage done by the foreign artillery. When my palanquin approached my palace I saw that many statues and ornaments had been shattered or stolen. The Sea Palace, where all my valuable possessions had been hidden, was raided. The offices at Ying-t'ai had been burned. The fingers of my white-jade Buddha were broken. The Allies' commander in chief, the German field marshal Count Waldersee, was said to have slept in my bed with the notorious Chinese courtesan named Golden Flower.

Not wanting to be reminded of the shame, I moved to the modest Palace of Serenity, in the northeast corner of the Forbidden City. Its remote location and unkempt appearance made it the only spot the foreigners had not violated.

Three days after the court's return, Guang-hsu and I resumed audiences and received foreign envoys. We tried to put smiles on our faces. Sometimes our emotions slipped and unexpected words would tumble out. As a result, translators kept getting fired. One foreign minister later described my facial expression as 'in between crying and smiling' – a kind of twisted grimace that he suspected was the result of a stroke. He also detected 'a swelling around Her Majesty's eyes.' He was right – I frequently wept at night. Others noticed that I rocked my chin and appeared to have trouble sitting still. They were right too: I was still trying to rid myself of lice.

I forced myself to apologize. With great effort I managed to wish happiness and health to the foreign representatives and dismiss them with a gracious nod.

When Li Hung-chang's name was mentioned at such audiences, which was often, I could not control my tears.

Li Lien-ying kept a close watch over me. He would call for a recess and take me to the back of the hall, where I would fall on my knees and sob. He kept a water basin and a makeup kit behind the curtains. I tried not to rub my eyes so that the swelling would go down.

The daughter of Yung Lu was going to be married, and he asked for my blessing. The groom was Prince Ch'un Junior – my sister's youngest son and Emperor Guang-hsu's brother. I had had my reservations about Ch'un until I'd recently met him again. He had just returned from a trip to Germany to apologize on behalf of the Emperor for the death of Baron von Ketteler. Prince Ch'un was a changed man. He was no longer so over-bearing, and he listened more. For the first time, he credited Li Hung-chang and acknowledged and honored Li's diplomatic accomplishments. I offered my blessing not only because Yung Lu had accepted him as a son-in-law, but also because Prince Ch'un was the only hope left in the dynasty's bloodline.

I attended the wedding and found Yung Lu and his wife, Willow, to be happy, although Yung Lu's cough had worsened. None of us could have predicted that he would soon gain a grandson who would become the last Emperor of China.

Instead of having a traditional opera troupe, the guests were entertained with a silent moving picture show of a horserace. The idea came from Yuan Shih-kai, of course, who had borrowed the film from a diplomat friend at one of the legations. It was a grand experience for me. At first I thought what we saw were the images of ghosts. I kept turning my head back and forth between the screen and the film projector.

Yuan Shih-kai took this occasion to ask for my help. He said, 'Your Majesty, my police force is having difficulty disciplining the royal princes.'

I gave Yuan permission to enforce the law, and I asked him if he in turn could help me take care of a recent scandal.

'Elderly students who are against my abolishing the old civil service exam system have been protesting outside my palace,' I said. 'They demand that I withdraw my support of Western-style schools. Yesterday, three seventy-year-old students hanged themselves.'

Yuan Shih-kai understood his mission. Within a week, his police cleared out the protesters.

When Yung Lu became too ill to attend audiences, Yuan Shih-kai took his place. I was not used to having someone else sit in Yung Lu's spot, and it was difficult not to let it affect me. The court without Li Hung-chang and Yung Lu didn't feel like my court. Perhaps I sensed that I would soon lose Yung Lu. I became desperate to hear his voice, but he couldn't come to me, and etiquette forbade me from visiting him at his home. It was kind of Willow to keep me informed of her husband's condition, but I was not satisfied.

I was never unhappier to have to attend the audiences, but the situation was delicate and demanded my presence. Yuan Shih-kai was a Han Chinese in a Manchu court. He was competent, clever and charming, but still, Emperor Guang-hsu refused to even look in his direction when addressing him. Prince Ch'un didn't get along with Yuan either. The smallest disagreement would turn into a fight. Neither side would back down unless I intervened.

On a freezing February morning in 1902, Robert Hart came for a private audience. I had wanted to meet with this man for many years. I got up before dawn and Li Lien-ying helped me to dress.

Looking at myself in the mirror, I thought about what to say to the Englishman. We would have been bankrupted if he had not so capably run the customs service, which provided one third of China's annual revenue. 'Neither Li Hung-chang nor Yung Lu could manage it,' I explained to Li Lien-ying, 'because half of Hart's job is to collect taxes from foreign merchants.'

'Robert Hart has been China's good friend,' the eunuch said. 'I can tell that my lady is excited about finally seeing what he looks like.'

'Make me look as good as you can, please.'

'How about a phoenix hairdo, my lady? It will take a bit longer, and the weight of the jewelry might make your neck sore, but it will be worth it.'

'That would be nice. I don't have anything else to award Sir Robert. My appearance will speak of my gratitude. I wish I were younger and prettier.'

'You look splendid, my lady. The only thing you need to complete your image is the long nails.'

'They haven't grown back since we escaped Peking.'

'I have an idea, my lady. Why don't you put on your golden nail cases?'

At eight o'clock Sir Robert Hart was led into the audience hall. He sat down ten feet from me. He was sixty-seven years old. My first impression was that he looked more like a Chinese than an Englishman. He wasn't ceiling-tall or as monstrously framed as I had imagined. He was a medium-sized man, dressed in a gold-laced purple Chinese court robe. He performed a perfect kowtow. He wished me health and longevity in flawless Mandarin, although I noticed that he had a southerner's accent.

I would have liked to ask him so many questions, but I did not know where to begin. Since there were other officials and ministers present, I could not simply speak my mind; I had to be careful what I said to a foreigner. I began with the royal formula and asked about his journey – the time of his departure, how long it took for him to reach Peking. I asked if his trip was a smooth one and if the weather had been fair. I also asked if he had been well fed and if he had slept soundly.

Our twenty minutes was nearly over and I felt that I barely knew my friend. He told me that he had a residence in Peking, but he was hardly home because his work required constant travel.

After tea, I asked him to move three feet closer – both to honor my guest and so I could make out the details of his face.

The man had gentle but penetrating eyes. I found it humorous because he appeared eager to get a good look at me as well. Our eyes met and we both smiled and were a little embarrassed. I said that I could not thank him enough for what he had done for the throne. I told him that he had first been recommended by Prince Kung, then by Li Hung-chang.

'I admire your dedication,' I said. 'You have been working for China for forty-one years, haven't you?'

Sir Robert was moved that I remembered his years of service.

'You have a Ningpo accent.' I smiled. 'Have you ever lived in southern China? I am from Wuhu, in Anhwei province, which is not far from Ningpo.'

'Your Majesty is very perceptive. I landed in Ningpo when I first came to China. I was twenty-five years old and was a student translator. I haven't been able to rid myself of my backward ways.'

'I love your accent, Sir Robert,' I said. 'Don't you ever correct it.'

'One always tries to escape one's past, but one never can,' he said.

Then our time was up.

On April 11, 1903, I was shattered by the news: Yung Lu had died. Guang-hsu and I were preparing a motion for a parliamentary government when word came. I felt that my insides were collapsing and had to ask my son to finish reviewing the documents. Li Lien-ying escorted me to a side room where I could have a moment to myself. I became dizzy and fainted. Li Lien-ying called for a doctor. Guang-hsu was scared. He came to my palace and stayed with me through the night.

In a way, Yung Lu had been preparing me for his death for months. He had worked tirelessly with the reluctant Emperor, trying to smooth over his relationship with Yuan Shih-kai. Both conservatives and radicals were using terror as a means to get their way. It was hard to control the situation without Li Hung-chang.

Doctors attended Yung Lu during our meetings in the Forbidden City. In order to introduce Guang-hsu and me to the men he trusted, Yung Lu came to audiences every day, and the last few days he arrived on a stretcher. No matter how ill he was, he always wore his official robe with the starched white collar.

Together we received S. S. Huan, the 'money man' Li Hung-chang had recommended and whose relationship with Yuan Shih-kai had recently grown sensitive. Huan proposed that Yuan's responsibilities be expanded to include those of the commissioner of trade, suggesting there was disharmony between the two. Yung Lu and I had understood Huan's fear of Yuan Shih-kai, whose police were rumored to be responsible for the disappearance of a number of his powerful rivals.

In his sickbed, Yung Lu had talked with both Yuan Shih-kai and S. S. Huan. The two men promised to embrace harmony and let go of their differences.

Two days later, Willow notified me of her husband's collapse. Ignoring etiquette, I went to Yung Lu's residence in a palanquin to see him for the last time.

He was weak and thin, his skin paler than the cotton sheet beneath him. His body lay straight and flat, with both hands by his thighs. He had had a stroke and could no longer speak. His eyes were wide and his pupils were dilated.

Willow thanked me for coming and then excused herself. I sat by Yung Lu and tried to keep my composure.

He was in his eternal robe. Beneath his ceremonial hat, his hair was oiled and colored lacquer-black.

I reached out and touched his face. It was hard not to cry, and I forced myself to smile. 'You are about to go on a hunting trip, and I will join you. I will prepare the bows and you will do the shooting. I'd like you to bring me a wild duck, a rabbit and a deer. Maybe not a deer but a wild pig. I will build a fire and roast it. We will have sweet yam wine and we will talk . . .'

His eyes became moist.

'But we will not talk about the Boxers or legations, of course. Only our good times together. We will talk about our friends Prince Kung and Li Hung-chang. I will tell you how much I missed you when you went to Sinkiang. You owe me a good seven years. You already know this, but I am going to tell you anyway: I am a happy woman when I am with you.'

Tears slowly fell from the corners of his eyes.

46

M Y ASTROLOGER SUGGESTED that I dress like the Kuan-yin Buddha to invite good spirits. Li Lien-ying told me I looked so weary that his labors over my hair and makeup no longer helped. Devastated by Yung Lu's passing, I asked myself: Why bother to go on? If Li Hung-chang's death had shaken me, Yung Lu's swept my legs out from under me. I no longer wanted to get out of the bed each morning. I felt dead inside.

On my seventieth birthday the royal photographer was sent to take a picture of me. I had no desire to be seen, but the court convinced me that there should be a record of how I looked. European kings and queens posed throughout their lives, and even on their deathbeds, I was told. In any case, I finally agreed; perhaps I was attracted by the idea that this would be my final image.

When the costumes and props arrived, Li Lien-ying was conveniently assigned to stand in as the Buddha's servant boy. A couple of my ladies in waiting were asked to take the role of fairies.

The photographing took several afternoons. After I left an audience, I would pose on a boat by Kun Ming Lake or in my receiving room, which was transformed into an opera stage. Against a backdrop of mountains, rivers and forests, I concentrated on looking my part while my mind dealt with the troubles at court. I had conducted both Li Hung-chang's and Yung Lu's funerals and was burdened by the guilt that I had worked both men to death. Li Lien-ying stood next to me holding a lotus flower. When the photographer told him to relax, the eunuch broke down and sobbed. When I asked why, he replied, 'The parliament has called for the abolition of the eunuch system. What do I tell the parents whose boys have just been castrated?'

The photographer asked if I wanted to look behind his camera. I wished that the upside-down ghostly image I saw there might bring me closer to the world where Li Hung-chang and Yung Lu had gone.

A few weeks later the finished pictures were presented to me. I was shocked by my own likeness. There was no trace of the beautiful Orchid in them. My eyes had shrunk and my skin sagged. The lines on both sides of my mouth were hard, as in a crude woodcarving.

'You must go on,' the astrologer encouraged. 'A picture of Your Majesty sitting on a boat floating among acres of lotus symbolizes your leading the people as they rise above the water of suffering.'

Yesterday, five members of the new parliament whom I had granted permission to study governments abroad were killed by explosives. The news shocked the nation. The murders were plotted by Sun Yat-sen, who had been living in Japan and spreading his message that the Manchu government would fall by violence.

I spoke at the memorial service for the five men. 'Sun Yat-sen means to stop me. He does not want China to establish a parliament. I am here to tell him that I am more motivated than ever before.'

Afterward, my son asked me about the intentions behind my words.

'It is time for me to step down,' I said. 'You should run for the presidency of China.'

'But Mother.' Guang-hsu became nervous. 'I have survived by staying in your shadow.'

'You are thirty-five years old – a grown man, Guang-hsu!'

The Emperor went down on his knees. 'Mother, please. I . . . don't have faith in myself.'

'You must, my son.' The words pushed themselves out through my clenched teeth.

'Yuan Shih-kai has been shot,' Guang-hsu announced, entering my room.

'Shot? Is he dead?'

'No, fortunately. But his wound is critical.'

'When and where did this take place?'

'Yesterday, at the parliament.'

'Everyone knew Yuan Shih-kai represented me.' I sighed. 'I am the real target of this.'

My son agreed. 'Without Yuan Shih-kai I would be an emperor without a country. The fact that I hate him makes it worse. It is why you can't step down, Mother. Yuan doesn't work for me, he works for you.'

The day Yuan Shih-kai got out of the hospital, I joined him for a military inspection. We stood side by side, to show my support and to compensate Yuan for the injustice done him. He had been shot by a jealous prince, a cousin of the Emperor, which meant that a rigorous prosecution was unlikely to happen.

The morning was windy at the military field outside Peking. I could hear flags fluttering as I stepped out of my palanquin. Li Lien-ying had secured my hair board so tightly that my scalp hurt.

The soldiers stood in formation, saluted and shouted, 'Long live Your Majesty!'

Yuan Shih-kai's movements were stiff and he moved with difficulty. We were led to a giant tent where a make-shift throne was set up for me. My son had declined to attend because he did not want to be seen with Yuan.

I watched the soldiers march and was reminded of Yung Lu and his Bannermen. The memory of the morning when I met with him on the training ground came back. Tears blurred my vision. Yuan Shih-kai begged to know why I was weeping. I replied that sand had gotten into my eyes.

I stood by him until the inspection was over. The soldiers stood at attention to listen to my speech. I began by asking Yuan whether he was bothered that some in our nation hated him. Before he could answer, I turned to the crowd and said, 'There are only two people who are truly committed to reform. I am one, and Yuan Shih-kai is the other. As you can see, both of us have been putting our lives on the line.'

'Long live Your Majesty!' the soldiers cheered. 'Hail to our commander in chief, Yuan Shih-kai!'

It was time to depart. I decided to try something I had never done before – I offered my hand for Yuan to shake.

He was so startled he could not make himself take my hand.

I had learned about shaking hands from Li Hung-chang, who had learned it during his trips to foreign countries. 'Amazing the first time I did it,' I remembered him saying.

I meant my handshake to be the talk of the nation; I meant to shock the Ironhat conservatives; and I meant to send the message that everything was possible.

'Take it,' I said to Yuan Shih-kai. My right hand was in the air right under his stunned face.

The commander in chief threw himself at my feet and knocked his forehead on the ground. 'I am too small a man to accept this honor, Your Majesty.'

'I am trying to lend you legitimacy while I am still alive,' I whispered. 'I am honoring you for what you have done for me, and also for what you will do for my son.'

My dreams were consumed with the dead.

'It wasn't easy to find my way back to you, my lady,' An-te-hai complained in one dream. He was as handsome as before, except his transparently white cheeks were tinted with rouge, which gave off a hint of the underworld.

'What brings you here?' I asked.

'I have questions about the decorations for your palace,' An-te-hai said. 'The eunuchs are planting oleander. I had to yell at them: "How can you put in these cheap plants for my lady?" I asked for peonies and orchids.'

Tung Chih was always in the midst of a rebellious prank when he entered my dreams. Once he was riding the dragon wall of the Forbidden City. He broke the dragon's beard and hit his eunuchs with the dragon's scales. 'Try to catch me!' he shouted.

I held a fashion parade in the back of the Summer Palace and invited all the concubines, regardless of rank. I displayed gowns and robes and dresses that I had collected since I was eighteen. Most of my winter clothes had a theme of plum flowers, and my spring outfits featured peonies. My summer dresses favored lotus flower motifs, and my fall frocks had chrysanthemums on them. When I told the concubines that each of them could pick out one thing as a souvenir, the ladies charged the clothing like tomb robbers.

I let Lien-ying keep my fur coats. 'This will be your pension,' I said to him. The opposite of An-te-hai, Li Lien-ying lived modestly. Most of his savings went to buy virtues: instead of collecting wives and concubines for show, he gave away money to families whose boys were castrated but were not picked to enter the Forbidden City. Li Lien-ying was known to refuse most bribes. Once in a while he would take a small bribe just so he would not make enemies. He would then find a way to pass it on in the form of a gift. In this way, he avoided being in anyone's debt.

Li said that he would become a monk after I died. I didn't know that he had already joined a monastery near the tomb where I would soon rest for eternity. I only knew that he had been sending contributions there.

My health had started to decline. For months the doctors' efforts to stop my persistent diarrhea had failed. I began to lose weight. I felt dizzy constantly and developed double vision. Small movements would leave me short of breath. I had to quit my lifelong habit of walking after meals. I missed watching the sunset and strolling down the long paths of the Forbidden City. Li Lien-ying ground all my food to make it easier for my system to digest, but my body no longer cooperated. I soon became as thin as a coat hanger.

Watching my body abandoning itself was a terrifying experience. Yet there was nothing I could do. I continued to follow the doctors' advice and took the bitterest herbs, but each morning I felt worse than the day before.

My body had begun to consume itself, and I knew my time had come. Before the eyes of the court I tried to mask my condition. Makeup helped. So did cotton batting worn under my clothes. Only Li Lien-ying knew that I was a bag of bones and that my stools lacked all formation. I began coughing up blood.

I tried to prepare my son, but stopped short of revealing my true condition. 'Your survival depends on your domination,' I said to him.

'Mother, I feel unwell and unsure.' Guang-hsu looked at me sad-eyed.

The dynasty has exhausted its essence was the thought that came to my mind.

My astrologer suggested that I invite an opera troupe to perform happy songs. 'It will help drive out the mean spirits,' he said.

A letter of farewell from Robert Hart reached me. He was returning home to England for good. He would depart on November 7, 1908.

I could hardly bear the thought that I was losing another good friend. Though I was in no condition to receive guests, I summoned him.

Dressed in his official Mandarin robe, he bowed solemnly.

'Look at us,' I said. 'We are both white-haired.' I did not have the energy even to tell him to sit down, so I gestured toward the chair.

He understood and took the seat.

'Forgive me for not being able to attend your farewell ceremony,' I said. 'I haven't been well, and death is waiting for me.'

'Also for me.' He smiled. 'However, it is the good memories that count.'

'I could not agree more, Sir Robert.'

'I come to thank you for offering me so much over the years.'

'I can only take credit for my effort to meet you this time. Once again the court was against it.'

'I know how hard it is to make exceptions. Foreigners have a bad reputation in China. Deservedly so.'

'You are seventy-two years old, aren't you, Sir Robert?'

'Yes, I am, Your Majesty.'

'And you have been living in China for . . .'

'Forty-seven years.'

'What can I say? You should be proud.'

'I am indeed.'

'I trust that you have made arrangements for someone to take over your duties.'

'There is nothing to worry about, Your Majesty. The customs service is a well-oiled machine. It will run itself.'

It surprised me that he never mentioned the honors he received from the Queen of England, nor did he talk about his English wife, from whom he had been separated for more than thirty-two years. He did mention his Chinese concubine of ten years and the three children they had. Her death. His regrets. He mentioned her suffering. 'She was the sensible one,' he said, and wished that he had done more to protect her.

I told him of my troubles with both of my sons – something I had never shared with anyone else. We sighed over the fact that loving our children was not enough to help them survive.

When I asked Sir Robert to tell me about his best time in China, he answered that it was working under Prince Kung and Li Hung-chang. 'Both were courageous and brilliant men,' he said, 'and both were helplessly stubborn in their own unique ways.'

Last we mentioned Yung Lu. From the way Sir Robert looked at me, I knew he understood everything.

'You must have heard the rumors,' I said.

'How could I not? The rumors and the fabrications of the Western journalists and some of the truth.'

'What did you think?'

'What did I think? I didn't know what to think, to be honest. You were quite a couple. I mean, you worked together well.'

'I loved him.' Shocked by my own confession, I stared at him.

He didn't seem to be surprised. 'I am happy for my friend's soul, then. I had long sensed that he had feelings for you.'

'We did the best we could. Which was less than what it should have been. It was very hard.'

'I had great admiration for Yung Lu. Although we were friends, I didn't get to know him well until the legation mess. He saved us by firing his shells over the rooftops. Afterward, he delivered five watermelons to me. I was certain it was you who had sent him.'

I smiled.

'Just out of curiosity,' Robert Hart said, 'how did you get the court to agree?'

'Yung Lu and I never discussed sending the watermelons.'

'I see. Yung Lu was good at guessing your mind.'

'He was.'

'You must miss him.'

' "The silkworm labors, until death its fine thread severs." ' I recited the first line of a thousand-year-old poem.

Sir Robert finished the verse: ' "The candle's tears are dried when it itself consumes." '

'You are an extraordinary foreigner, Robert Hart.'

'I am disappointed that Your Majesty doesn't consider me Chinese. I consider myself one.'

This gave me great pleasure.

'I do not want you to go,' I said when it was time to part. 'But I understand that a leaf must fall by the roots of its tree. Remember that you have a home and family here in China. I will miss you and will always be waiting for your return.'

We both became tearful. He got down on his knees and placed his forehead on the ground for a long time.

I wanted to say 'until next time,' but it was clear that there would be no next time.

'I wish to see you off, Sir Robert, but I am too weak to get up from my chair. By the time you reach England, you might hear the news of my passing.'

'Your Majesty . . .'

'I want you to be happy for the freedom my spirit will finally enjoy.'

'Yes, Your Majesty.'

47

M Y DEATH WAS written all over their faces when the doctors begged for punishment for failing to cure me. I sent them home so that I could have time to make the necessary arrangements.

The depressing thing about dying is its dreariness. People around you no longer tease or joke, and they keep their voices low and walk on tiptoe. Everyone waits for the end, and yet the days stretch on.

Li Lien-ying was the only one who refused to give up. He made my healing his religion and guarded me from anything he believed would disturb me. He withheld news of Guang-hsu's condition, and I had no idea that my son's health had taken a critical turn for the worse. I planned to visit Ying-t'ai to see him as soon as I could get out of bed.

On November 14, 1908, I woke to the sound of loud crying. I thought my time must have come because my eyelids felt so heavy. The right side of my body felt hot, and the left side cold. With my blurred vision I saw a roomful of eunuchs on their knees.

'The Dragon has ascended to Heaven!' It was Li Lien-ying's voice.

'I am not dead yet,' I uttered.

'It is your son, my lady. Emperor Guang-hsu has just passed away!'

I was carried to Guang-hsu's room. The sight of my son brought back the memory of the day Tung Chih died. I looked up and said, 'Heaven's mercy! Guang-hsu is only thirty-eight years old.'

His corpse was still warm. His face was as gray as when he was alive.

This must be how drowning felt. The water was warm. My lungs felt sealed. My spirit welcomed the eternal darkness.

'Come back, Your Majesty,' Li Lien-ying wailed. 'Come back, my lady!'

Then I remembered my duty – the heir I hadn't named.

I willed myself to summon the Grand Council.

I don't know how long they had to wait before me. When I opened my eyes again I saw Yuan Shih-kai standing on my left and Prince Ch'un Junior on my right. The room was filled with people.

'The heir, Your Majesty?' everyone asked at the same time.

'Puyi' was all I said.

I named Prince Ch'un Junior's son, the three-year-old Puyi – Yung Lu's grandson and my grandnephew – as the new Emperor of China. The royal bloodline was becoming thin.

I could not move my arms or legs, could hear only my own labored breathing. My body had been loaded with medicine. I felt no pain. My thoughts had slowed down but hadn't stopped.

My eunuchs helped me onto the throne for one last audience. Since I could no longer sit up straight, the carpenters extended the arms of my chair with long wooden sticks. Li Lien-ying rested my arms on the sticks and draped me with golden fabric.

I thought of Emperor Hsien Feng's last day when he was settled into the same pose. Making the dying look larger than life was meant to suggest power, and I had personally witnessed its effect. Still, it felt ridiculous. My husband must have felt the same absurdity. However, I understood that if I wanted my will to be executed, this was a necessity.

I was also doing this for the sake of those who had faith in me, especially the lower-ranking governors and officials who counted their calendars first 'in the year of Emperor Tung Chih' and then 'in the year of Emperor Guang-hsu.' I owed them a final impression.

The grand secretary drew near in order to hear me.

Li Lien-ying stared at the ornaments on my hair board. Worried about their weight, he had rigged up several strings to hold everything in place. It seemed to be working, but there was still a danger that my body might collapse.

Eunuchs stood behind the throne, concealed from sight. Li Lien-ying had told them how to hold the ropes that held the Dragon Throne and myself in place.

I was amazed by my mind's clearness. But it was the delivery I needed to get through.

'It is my wish to die,' I began. 'I hope you will understand that no mother wants to outlive her children. I have achieved nothing in my life except to keep China in one piece. Looking back on my memories of the past fifty years, I perceive calamities from within and aggression from without that came upon us in relentless succession.' With great difficulty I was able to take a breath and project my voice. 'The new Emperor is a little child, just reaching the age when instruction is of the highest importance . . .'

I felt ashamed to continue, because I had spoken the same words when Tung Chih became Emperor, and then again with Guang-hsu. 'I regret that I won't be here to guide Puyi, but this might not be his misfortune . . . I hope all of you will try to do a better job than I achieved in shaping the throne's character.'

Memories of Tung Chih and Guang-hsu flooded my mind. I could hear Nuharoo yelling for me to quit disciplining Tung Chih. Then came Guang-hsu's bright eyes as he spoke passionately about reform: 'Ito is my friend, Mother!'

'It is my earnest prayer,' I pushed myself to continue, 'that Emperor Puyi diligently pursue his studies and that he may hereafter add fresh luster to the glorious achievements of his ancestors.'

What I said next shocked not only the court but also the nation. I declared that empresses and concubines should be forbidden from ever holding supreme power. It was the only way to protect the young Emperor from the likes of Nuharoo, Alute and Pearl. I would not have made this decision if my niece Lan hadn't voiced her disappointment after learning that she was not going to be the acting regent for Puyi. She let me know that she was determined to seek her proper position.

My strength began to disappear. My neck was yielding to the weight of my hair board. As hard as I tried, I could no longer utter a sound.

'What do you see, my lady?' Li Lien-ying asked.

I saw the carved dragons on the ceiling. I remembered I had dreamed of these dragons before I entered the Forbidden City. Now I had seen them, all 13,844 of them.

'What is . . .' I remembered my astrologer's warnings about bad-luck dates on which to die.

'What is the date today?' Li Lien-ying guessed.

I meant to nod but couldn't.

'November 15, 1908, my lady. It is a good-luck day.'

Strange thoughts began to surge inside my head: *I was wrong to stay. Did I know the steps? Words do not stop a flood.*

'My lady?' I heard Lien-ying's voice and then, in an instant, I could not hear –

'It is the end of my world but not others', Orchid.' I could see my father speaking on his deathbed.

I blinked my eyes and took a good look at Li Lien-ying. I felt sad about abandoning him.

A thick white fog enfolded me. In the middle of the fog was a soft egg yolk like a red sun. The yolk began to sway like a Chinese lantern in a gentle breeze. I heard ancient music and recognized the sound. It was from An-te-hai's white pigeons. I remembered him tying whistles and bells on the birds' legs. I saw them now. Hundreds of thousands of white pigeons flew in circles above my palace. The tune was 'Wuhu, My Lovely Hometown.'

POSTSCRIPT

O RCHID – Lady Yehonala, Empress Tzu Hsi – died at the age of seventy-three.

China began to fall apart after her funeral. The country entered a dark time of warlords and lawlessness. While the Western powers carved up coastal China into colonial concessions, Japan penetrated into northern China, establishing what would be called the Kingdom of Manchuria.

In 1911, Sun Yat-sen landed in Shanghai. He succeeded in stirring up a military uprising and declared himself the first provisional president of China's new republic.

On February 12, 1912, Emperor Puyi abdicated power to Yuan Shih-kai, who declared himself president of the republic, taking over from Sun Yat-sen, and then immediately founded his own dynasty. Yuan Shih-kai soon died of a stroke, and he was ridiculed as 'the eighty-three-day Emperor.'

In 1919, a warlord named Chiang Kai-shek declared himself a disciple of Sun Yat-sen. After Sun's death in 1925, Chiang Kai-shek became the new president of the republic. He relied on American financial and military support and promised to build a democratic China.

In 1921, backed by Soviet Communists, Mao Tse-tung, a student rebel and guerrilla soldier from Hunan province, founded, with twelve followers, the Communist Party of China.

In 1924, Japan made Puyi the puppet emperor of Manchuria and pushed him to 'take back Imperial China.'

In 1937, Japan invaded China.

Reformer Kang Yu-wei continued to live in Japan. He broke with his disciple Liang Chi-chao, who first joined Sun Yat-sen, then Yuan Shih-kai. He finally quit both and became a private citizen.

Li Lien-ying left the Forbidden City after the Dowager Empress's funeral. He went to live in the monastery near his beloved lady's tomb until his death.

A NOTE ON THE AUTHOR

Anchee Min was born in Shanghai in 1957. At seventeen she was sent to a labour collective, where a talent scout for Madame Mao's Shanghai Film Studio recruited her to work as a movie actress. She moved to the United States in 1984. Her memoir, *Red Azalea,* was an international bestseller with rights sold in twenty countries. Her other novels, *Becoming Madame Mao, Katherine, Wild Ginger* and *Empress Orchid* were published to wonderful reviews and impressive foreign sales.

BLOOMSBURY

Also available by Anchee Min

Empress Orchid

Love is survival, seduction is power, and treachery a way of life . . .

'I loved *Empress Orchid* . . . a riveting read' Judy Finnegan

To rescue her family from poverty and avoid marrying her slope-shouldered cousin, seventeen-year-old Orchid competes to be one of the Emperor's wives. When she is chosen as a lower-ranking concubine she enters the erotically charged and ritualised Forbidden City. But beneath its immaculate façade lie whispers of murders and ghosts, and the thousands of concubines will stoop to any lengths to bear the Emperor's son. Orchid trains herself in the art of pleasuring a man, bribes her way into the royal bed, and seduces the monarch, drawing the attention of dangerous foes. Little does she know that China will collapse around her, and that she will be its last Empress.

'*Empress Orchid* delivers a fictional peek into the intrigues of the Forbidden City . . . strong on both sexual chicanery and violent conspiracy . . . a fascinating account' *Guardian*

ISBN: 9 780 7475 6833 9 / Paperback / 7.99

Order your copy:

By phone: 01256 302 699
By email: direct@macmillan.co.uk
Delivery is usually 3–5 working days. Postage and packaging will be charged.
Online: www.bloomsbury.com/bookshop
Free postage and packaging for orders over £15.

Prices and availability subject to change without notice.

Visit Bloomsbury.com for more about Anchee Min including a downloadable reading guide for *Empress Orchid*